In the end, I pitied him.

The man who lived free of all convention, though he turned out to be as trapped as everyone else. More so, in fact. In the end, I ended up being the one to free *him*.

The greatest thing I ever did. My biggest regret.

By Craig DiLouie

My Ex, the Antichrist
How to Make a Horror Movie and Survive
Episode Thirteen
The Children of Red Peak
Our War
One of Us
Suffer the Children
Tooth and Nail
Strike
The Alchemists
The Great Planet Robbery

The Infection Series
Crash Dive Series
Armor Series
The Aviator Series

My Ex, The Antichrist

CRAIG DiLOUIE

This book is a work of fiction. Names, characters, places, and incidents are the product of the author's imagination or are used fictitiously. Any resemblance to actual events, locales, or persons, living or dead, is coincidental.

Copyright © 2025 by Craig DiLouie

Excerpt from *How to Make a Horror Movie and Survive* copyright © 2024 by Craig DiLouie

Cover design by Lisa Marie Pompilio
Cover images by Shutterstock
Cover copyright © 2025 by Hachette Book Group, Inc.
Author photograph by Jodi O

Hachette Book Group supports the right to free expression and the value of copyright. The purpose of copyright is to encourage writers and artists to produce the creative works that enrich our culture.

The scanning, uploading, and distribution of this book without permission is a theft of the author's intellectual property. If you would like permission to use material from the book (other than for review purposes), please contact permissions@hbgusa.com. Thank you for your support of the author's rights.

Run For It
Hachette Book Group
1290 Avenue of the Americas
New York, NY 10104
hachettebookgroup.com

First Edition: July 2025

Run For It is an imprint of Orbit, a division of Hachette Book Group.
The Run For It name and logo are registered trademarks of Hachette Book Group, Inc.

The publisher is not responsible for websites (or their content) that are not owned by the publisher.

The Hachette Speakers Bureau provides a wide range of authors for speaking events. To find out more, go to hachettespeakersbureau.com or email HachetteSpeakers@hbgusa.com.

Run For It books may be purchased in bulk for business, educational, or promotional use. For information, please contact your local bookseller or the Hachette Book Group Special Markets Department at special.markets@hbgusa.com.

Print book interior designed by Bart Dawson

Library of Congress Cataloging-in-Publication Data
Names: DiLouie, Craig, 1967– author.
Title: My ex, the antichrist / Craig DiLouie.
Description: First edition. | New York, NY : Run For It, 2025.
Identifiers: LCCN 2024044925 | ISBN 9780316578189 (trade paperback) | ISBN 9780316578196 (ebook)
Subjects: LCGFT: Horror fiction. | Novels.
Classification: LCC PS3604.I463 M94 2025 | DDC 813/.6—dc23/eng/20241001
LC record available at https://lccn.loc.gov/2024044925

ISBNs: 9780316578189 (trade paperback), 9780316578196 (ebook)

Printed in the United States of America

LSC-C

Printing 1, 2025

To every song that saved my life

AUTHOR'S NOTE

*I*t's a familiar story: the starry rise and tragic fall of a rock band.
This is not that story.
This is one you haven't heard—a tale of prophecy, a breakup, and the apocalypse.
At the center of it all: the Shivers.
From 2000 to 2010, the band rode the pop-punk wave to mainstream success. Earworm hooks, high-energy sound, and catchy sing-along choruses earned the band a huge fan base among America's twenty million teens. During its red-hot career, the band released ten albums, six landing on the Billboard top 10.
It all came to an end when singer / lead guitarist Lily Lawless walked into a police station and confessed to murder.
All that feels like a long time ago now. When you hear the music of your carefree youth playing as Muzak in big-box stores, you know you're getting old. As if in compensation, music has an almost magical way of resurrecting the past.
Hearing one of the Shivers' songs, suddenly I'm twenty again, driving fast down a country road on a summer night. A buzzed pal straddles the passenger-door window frame and shouts along with the radio: "We're not satisfied!"
I also remember driving up from central New Jersey over two weekends to attend the Armageddon Battle of the Bands in '99. The epic showdown between the Shivers and Universal Priest, the bloody riot that claimed the lives of nine people. In the nightmarish stampede of howling bodies, my foot got crushed. Even today, sometimes, it hurts like hell.

Author's Note

Lily's confession proved lurid but included few details. A vague motive. No body and no murder weapon.

What drove her to do it? What made her confess ten years later, at the height of stardom?

So many questions, but what I really wanted to know was what actually happened that last night at Armageddon.

On an impulse, I reached out to say I was a writer interested in hearing her story. To my complete surprise, Lily agreed to be interviewed. The rest of the band followed her lead, and suddenly I had the opportunity of a lifetime in my hands.

At last, the Shivers seemed ready to break their long silence.

I'd expected to put together a true-crime book that scratched an old itch. After numerous interviews over the course of 2022 and 2023, I got something else.

You guessed it. Prophecy. Death. Apocalypse. And yes, a breakup.

If even half of it is true, we'd all better start praying.

Either way, this is their story, and they're sticking to it.

And what rough beast, its hour come round at last,
Slouches towards Bethlehem to be born?

—William Butler Yeats,
"The Second Coming"

In the year 1999…
Will come a great King of Terror

—Nostradamus

If you understand God, it is not God.

—Saint Augustine

I take a bad situation, gonna make it right
In the shadows of darkness I stand in the light

—Rancid, "Fall Back Down,"
Indestructible (2003)

My Ex, The Antichrist

IMPERFECT CONTRITION

THE *BASKET CASE* CONCERT TOUR
OCTOBER 2010

Lillian Lawlor—Lily Lawless *to her fans during the Shivers years—was born in Bethlehem, Pennsylvania, on the first day of spring in 1980. After founding the Shivers in 1999, she led the group to become one of America's loudest and punchiest rock bands, dominating the pop-punk scene for a blistering decade.*

In 2010, the party came to a crashing halt.

LILY LAWLESS (*singer / lead guitarist, the Shivers*): I should warn you, this story has some religion in it.

No, I'm not religious. It's not that I'm atheist or agnostic or anything. Far from it. When it comes to God's existence, I'm actually a true believer. In fact, I'm one of the very few people on the planet who knows with absolute certainty that a supreme being is out there pulling strings and keeping score.

I know this because I dated the Devil.

What I did back in 1999, I paid for the only way I knew how. In my old religion, it's called imperfect contrition. It's when you're sorry for sinning but not because you fear God. Otherwise, I can't say where I stand with the big man upstairs after I messed with his grand plan. Being all-knowing, I'm pretty sure he knows what I think of him after everything that happened and what's still to come.

I see you not reacting. You've got a great poker face. I can't tell what you're thinking, but I can guess.

Hey, you asked for it. The secrets we kept for twenty years.

The truth is rarely pretty. Sometimes it can be quite ugly. Every now and then, it sounds completely crazy.

If you want to keep going with me on this, you're going to get both.

LUCAS KELLY (*manager, the Shivers*): Lily Lawless knew how to put the teen experience into song and light up an audience. Inspire fifty thousand people to hop and scream her lyrics back at her at a concert.

With her carefree punk image, you'd never guess she was one of the hardest-working, most professional women in rock and roll.

I've seen artists rise and fall. The ones who let the fame go to their heads. The ones who fall off their crutches of drugs and booze and face-plant. The ones whose creativity goes to rot and wind up playing way past their expiration date.

Lily proved a different animal. She lived for rock. She didn't make it a lifestyle. She didn't confuse the real thing with the fantasy.

She never quit.

Every album better than the last, the albums releasing like clockwork, the music resonating on enduring themes of teenage longing, angst, and a desire to never grow up. At least one song in constant rotation at the top alt radio stations. The endless touring, cities and countries and continents.

One thing I've learned: Someone goes at that speed for that long after reaching the top, it isn't about the chase anymore. They're usually running from something.

She ran straight into a wall.

LILY: The night I lost my shit, I was limbering up before our concert at the Bell Centre in Montreal, though back then it was called the Molson Centre. One of the last shows on an eight-month, thirty-city concert tour promoting *Basket Case*.

The warm-up routine: You stretch and flex your fingers. You do some taps and rolls. You run through scales and arpeggios. Then you get on stage and play the song that you've played a thousand times before, on body memory.

Only, I couldn't find my collar.

You might recall that at my shows, I'd wear a party dress or a long tee or my old school uniform but always a spiky leather collar. Over the years, that crappy little collar became a signature look, though it was more than that. It hid something I wanted hidden. I couldn't perform without it.

I stormed around the green room, ransacking it. The band stared at me in wide-eyed silence as empty beer cans and bong water splashed across the floor. Some girls from Chick Whiz, who were opening for us, laughed and smoked in the hall. I started yelling at them, and that's when my voice crapped out.

Every part of me suddenly hurt. My back out of whack from shouldering my Gibson for too long. My throat scratchy and hoarse. My fingers rubbed to calloused marble by the strings. My brain turned to mush. My body shaking.

The next thing I knew, I broke down crying. An all-out panic attack.

All those years, I'd never missed a chance to perform. Years that now seemed to avalanche on top of me. A decade-long blur of nonstop planes and hotels and buses and dressing rooms and stadiums packed with screaming teens.

I wanted to tear my skin off.

Lucas helped me find my collar, which I'd somehow managed to hide from myself. A rock doc showed up and shot my ass full of vitamin B_{12}. Then he made me say *Ahhhh* while he injected cortisone directly into my inflamed vocal cords so I could sing. My heart raced at the edge of seizure.

Mascara streaked down my face like black tears as I took the stage. The fans loved the look. It became a hashtag. They thought it was part of the act.

LUCAS KELLY: Lily played that show with a ferocity I hadn't seen in years. I had no idea it would be her last.

"I think I need a break," she told me after it was over. "Can I take a break?"

The Lily I knew didn't take breaks. And she never asked my permission to do anything. This was new. But having witnessed her pre-show freakout, I understood.

I asked her what she meant by a "break," and she told me she didn't know. I asked if she could finish the tour, and she said she didn't know that either.

I had a business to run. Lily was a golden goose. Canceling Cincinnati and Chicago would cost us money and set the venues and fans to rampaging.

You get clients that think they can do better than you. You get clients that wind up hooked on whatever drug keeps them up or helps them come down, sometimes both. You get clients that hate each other's guts over creative differences and want you right in the middle of that shit, picking sides.

But some clients, you like them. You start to think they're your friends. Then they are. I could tell what happened before the show wasn't a stumble but a crash. Lily had reached a breaking point. She needed this.

I told her to go for it. Go take her break and rest up. I'd handle the details. I said, "Lady, take all the time you need."

She'd have to be the one to break it to the band, though.

LILY: I braced myself to tell Ramona, Malcolm, and Eric that I was ending the tour to take a breather. I expected them to throw bottles or at least smash a guitar, you know, the kind of mayhem you expect pissed-off rockers to do.

We had rules, see. Don't talk about Drake, that was one. Protect each other. Always make the music our way.

And most important: Never, ever give up.

Now here I was, breaking the big one.

They didn't say much at all. At first, they just stared in disbelief, which was somehow worse than their throwing a fit. They sagged. Tears glistened on faces that suddenly struck me as looking older than they were.

Eric said, "Okay, Lil. We'll take a break."

Malcolm said, "Good."

They didn't look pissed. They were actually relieved.

"Thank God," said Ramona. She walked straight out the door.

I said, "I didn't know. Shit. I'm sorry."

All this time, I thought they'd shared my passion for the music. And if not, they'd kept going because they had their own crosses to bear. Right then, I wondered if they were still at it after all these years because of me.

Malcolm said, "Now we're even." Confirming it.

LUCAS KELLY: Lily said she wanted to go home to Bethlehem. I thought, Okay, that's cool. I thought, This could be a good thing.

All along, I imagined she'd been running away from home. I'd sensed some bad blood there. I thought maybe she'd finally have a showdown with her demons, work out some shit, and storm back into the studio after a few months.

It wasn't until later I learned that what she'd been running from wasn't the kind of thing you could ever escape.

LILY: The prodigal child goes home to learn not much has changed, both the good and the bad. Sometimes you know all this, but you go anyway. You need to go home. You just do. So you go, and then you remember why you split.

Mom and Dad wanted a big family, but they couldn't make a child. Then I came along, their miracle baby. Growing up, I received all the attention, which had been good until I reached an age where it became stifling.

Like my band, they had rules too, and a lot more of them. The big kind: how I should behave, what I wore, who I could have as friends. While I lived with them, they had my whole life locked down and planned out.

I hadn't been back in a decade, the kind of time where you blink and go, Wow, has it really been that long? To my surprise, I found my old room almost exactly as I'd left it, a little museum of my angsty and yearning teen years. Mom had always prayed I'd come home and kept the proverbial candle burning in the window.

I reached under my mattress and smiled at the still-familiar feel of my old stash of music magazines, *Spin* and *Pulse!* and *Rolling Stone*. I slid them out and relived my teen yearnings gazing at my guitar heroes, snarling Joan Jett and dreamy Kristin Hersh and all the other rock goddesses.

Safe and warm under my parents' thick wings, I slept an entire day. Dinner was Irish comfort food: shepherd's pie. Everything here was the same. Stable, predictable, reliable. I needed this. A hard reset.

The only problem was, *everything* remained the same, including Dad telling me how to live. Over dinner, he said the rock-star thing had been fun, but maybe it was time to start living a real life.

Go back to school and finish my accounting degree. Find a stable job and marry a nice man and have children. Making it sound like I might just be ready to stop fooling around and finally grow up.

Mom said, "Grandchildren would be nice." Another candle in the window.

Okay, Dad wasn't *entirely* wrong.

The long blur of my twenties was almost behind me. To put it bluntly, I'd grown a bit long in the tooth to be a rock star.

My generation had traded their skateboards for laptops and cash registers. For ten years, I'd lived the life of a rocker, but it didn't feel all that free anymore. Half of it was image, the rest answering to an endless parade of managers, agents, video directors, engineers, and suits.

Everyone looking out for me, though no one did, not really. That was *my* job.

At some point, I'd have to question if there was life after rock. Whether I should interpret my hitting the wall as some kind of omen that I needed a big change.

Yeah, fine. I just didn't want to hear it from *him*.

The father who never let me date, take risks, have fun, even choose my own career—which is, that's right, how I ended up pursuing an accounting degree. My teen years divided between oppressive days at a Catholic school for girls and suffocating nights at home.

I remembered how I'd announce that I was going upstairs to do homework but instead practice my guitar until my fingers bled like stigmata and I'd finally mastered a Clapton riff. How I lied after my guitar was discovered by claiming it was for a school project. How I'd tell my parents I was going to the library and instead skip over to the skate park to watch the cute skater boys fly around.

The prodigal child returns and falls right back into old patterns. Hearing Dad tell me what to do made me want to do the exact opposite, but I hadn't come home for this. I'd come to reset and think and plan, not simply react.

I said, "I think I'll go check out the old library."

Dad knew I was avoiding. He said, "That's what you do, Lillian."

As for me, I was getting angry again. I had to get out of here.

He said, "You don't finish. You run away."

Before we ended up in a repeat of the blowout my leaving home ten years earlier had caused, I did just that. I bolted.

DANNY RODRIGUEZ (*A&R representative, Echo Harbor Records*): Lily Lawless still ranks as the most stubborn woman I ever met. And the easiest artist I ever managed. She made me nervous.

Artists and Repertoire, that's what A&R stands for. To America's musicians, I was the devil at the crossroads selling you a crack at fame and fortune in return for every ounce of creative juice you've got.

That was the fun part of the job, scouting and signing and then coaching a band into a professional team that packs the right sound and style and swagger. A lot of it, though, is babysitting.

You blow smoke up asses to inspire confidence. You provide. You are cheerleader, priest, psychiatrist, sometimes legal aid. Whatever a band needs to keep the party rocking. Anything to keep it confident, playing hard, and bringing in the bucks today, right now, always right now, before the party ends.

And boy, did the Shivers need hand-holding. The keyboardist and his megalomania, the drummer a bona fide kleptomaniac, the bassist falling into bouts of depression and compulsive eating. Compared to them, juggling the odd coke fiend and assault charge seemed simple.

As if to balance it all out, Lily didn't want anything at all from me aside from making sure Echo Harbor kept its basic promises.

You'd think that'd be cool, right? You'd say, well, that's less work for you, one less problem to worry about. Just keep your promises and you're fine.

It kept me up nights.

Lily Lawless was the frontwoman. She *was* the Shivers. Long before, word had come down from on high to keep her happy. If Lily didn't like how things were going, see, she might sign with another label.

Music is a people business, and it's based on trust. Sometimes you have to put in the extra effort to convince an artist she needs you.

The harder I tried, though, the more contrary she got.

I'd tell her how well the last album did in terms of sales and that the Shivers should maybe stick to the same groove to be safe. She'd completely mix things up for the next record by adding some ska in the vein of Operation Ivy and a cover of a goddamn k.d. lang cowboy punk song. I'd tell her Phoenix had never been a great market, and she'd insist it be the very first stop on the tour.

Seriously! I'd call Lily, she'd hear me out, and then she'd do her own thing. She made me crazy because she didn't make sense.

Every day was opposite day, dealing with her.

LILY: The prodigal child returns to her past to discover who she is now. Sometimes you leave for so long that home is no longer really home for you but instead just a collection of feelings and memories. The old places look the same but different, though they never really change.

Unlike many of the kids who listened to our music, I didn't grow up in suburbia or some dying small town. I was raised in blue-collar Bethlehem, one of three sprawling cities dominating the Lehigh Valley on the state's eastern side.

Named for Jesus's Judean birthplace, it got nicknamed "Christmas City USA" during the Great Depression. Bethlehem Steel operated here, supplying materials to build everything from warships during World War II to New York City skyscrapers, before the company shuttered the plant in '95 and everything changed.

I now explored and reclaimed the old neighborhood from memory. The tobacco shop a few blocks down had folded, replaced by a boutique clothing store. The record shop I used to frequent still stood next to it, however. I'd bought my first vinyl there with babysitting money, *Dookie* by Green Day.

The shop's window appeared bright and yellow and welcoming in the chilly night. A handful of kids riffled the CDs and records, seeking their separate paths to salvation or simply a little musical self-medication. The scene made me smile.

Then I spotted my snarling face on a poster in the window. Exactly what I'd come home to escape from. I kept on walking.

At Johnny Ray's Music a few doors down, I admired the guitars and gear in the window display. I'd bought my first axe here, a secondhand Fender acoustic with the original hard-shell case.

I didn't go inside this old haunt either. The walking was doing me good, a journey that offered its own destination. For once, I headed nowhere, even if it was all familiar. As always when a tour ended, the world seemed to keep rushing around me. But the ground under my feet had started to feel a little more solid, which struck me as progress.

And I thought, Screw having a real life.

I had one more good album in me. Dozens of performances in communion with an audience. All those beautiful moments of raw power on stage, letting it all hang out under blinding white light, bouncing and thrashing, hair dripping sweat.

Perhaps more than one album.

Shit, maybe I'd never quit my dream. Maybe I'd live forever free and young. I'd be like Ozzy Osbourne and the Who, signing off in a blazing farewell tour only to come roaring back for another encore a few years later.

Maybe I hadn't come home to escape so much as remember why I kept going.

DANNY RODRIGUEZ: When I heard what she'd done after going home to Pennsylvania and that the band was falling apart, the executives yanked me into the home office for a grilling. What did I know. Who did I call. Did I do enough. Why won't she let us give her legal help. Did I realize what this disaster would cost the company. Did I understand this might just kill the gold record goose.

It was a nightmare.

LILY: I found myself rolling by Holy Ghost Church. One part of my childhood from which I expected zero change, and it did not disappoint. The lights blazed inside, illuminating tall arched stained-glass windows depicting familiar scenes of ministry and suffering.

I hadn't been here in over ten years. Hadn't set foot in any church, actually. My relationship with God is complicated. My relationship with religion is toxic. My last visit to a church had exploded in surreal horror. The last time I'd been face-to-face with a member of the clergy, he'd tried to kill me.

Then I heard the music.

An angelic alto, singing to an organ melody. Choir practice. I'm a born sucker for music. Rock, grunge, country, whatever. Even choral hymns. It doesn't matter where the light comes from. If it's bright, it's bright, and I'm a born moth.

Despite the growing knot in my gut, I figured I'd go inside for a peek.

The smells and brooding atmosphere triggered long-buried feelings of dread, boredom, tension, and a little spark of wonder. This too felt like a homecoming. You know what they say. Once a Catholic, always a Catholic.

First Communion and a whole lot of Sunday mornings spent internalizing even the odd errant thought as deeply wrong and requiring penance. Endless incantations to ask for forgiveness for being born with sin.

I pushed all that aside to receive the music, the most profound and direct form of worship I've ever known. Sound that provoked God's attention. Sound that to me was God itself.

And what music. The boy could sing.

It reminded me of a part of life that I'd lost. Communing with something bigger than myself. That beautiful sensation of connecting to everything and catching a tiny glimpse of what it must feel like to be God. Surrendering to it. If God is love and joy, then singing with love and joy makes you divine. Worshipping from the heart, not the head.

It reminded me of Drake.

EXCERPT FROM "A LILY AMONG THORNS: THE SHIVERS' FRONTWOMAN TALKS PUNK AND POP FOR THE MILLENNIAL GENERATION," *INSTRUMENTAL*, 9/2006

Alicia Parker (writer): You were one of the first women to break into the pop-punk scene. What was that like?

Lily Lawless: The labels wanted to see more girls coming to the shows and buying records. They were into it. The male bands we played alongside were fairly welcoming, you know, aside from the usual juvenile stuff. Some of the female musicians were honestly tougher to be around, as a feeling of tokenization created intense competition of who'd get to be that one girl doing pop-punk.

Alicia Parker: Some say you trailblazed for artists like Avril Lavigne. *Bustle* recently labeled her the reigning queen of pop-punk. How does that make you feel, given what you achieved?

Lily Lawless: I love Avril's music. Otherwise, I'm working too hard to pay attention to who says what.

Alicia Parker: Some punkinistas would say you aren't punk rock at all. They say the Shivers sold out. It's an old rift as punk continued to go mainstream, vexing bands like Green Day—

Lily Lawless: We play a genre of punk music, but I never claimed to be a spokesperson or role model for the punk scene. I'm a musician who plays music and then wants that music to be heard by the largest audience possible. I've always been that girl. Everyone is invited to the party, not just the cool kids.

Alicia Parker: They also say the Shivers strayed too far from its roots.

Lily Lawless: Real punk isn't purity tests and just "Don't tread on me." It's a call for change with the understanding that the more certain things change, the more they stay the same. It's a call to keep trying. Our music is us struggling to evolve.

Alicia Parker: And evolve you did. In its early days, the Shivers had a different sound. How would you describe it?

Lily Lawless: Ramona—our drummer—used to call it demon

disco. Our first songs were about telling people to be free. After that, we decided to free ourselves.

Alicia Parker: Drake Morgan was the lead guitarist then. Back in '99, before he formed Universal Priest. I've heard some wild stories, urban legends.

Lily Lawless: If you know that, then you know we don't talk about him.

Alicia Parker: From what you're saying, it sounds like Drake controlled—

Lily Lawless: No comment.

Alicia Parker: Let's shift gears then. By all accounts, Drake was your lover. Ever since, you haven't had a serious—

Lily Lawless: This interview's over. Is that punk rock enough for you?

LILY: Led by a young priest in a black cassock, the choir practiced in the chancel. They sang the chorus, and then the boy swung back into his lilting solo. Singing about the Lamb of God, whose obedient sacrifice results in victory over death.

My mind flashed to Julian bolting out of Our Lady of Victory with a rocket launcher on his shoulder, with all hell at his heels. Before I could get sucked down that particular memory hole, I focused on the boy.

He was as beautiful as his singing. Nine or ten years old, face shining with innocence and youth. The light from a stained-glass crucifixion formed a halo behind longish hair angelically winged from prior wearing of a baseball cap.

The choir started another hymn. And the boy sang:

O Jesus, Thou the beauty art
Of angel worlds above;
Thy Name is music to the heart,
Enchanting it with love—

The boy froze. The choir faltered.

He now stared at me, his face a mask of fear. He actually looked terrified.

Slowly, everyone turned to give me a stink-eye stare.

The prodigal child returns, and what is lost is found. The criminal returns to the scene of the crime hoping to undo what she's done. Hoping to make things right.

I went back outside.

And walked straight to the police station, where I confessed to a terrible crime that had happened in 1999 but even now feels like only yesterday.

See, in all those years of music and roaming, I'd learned something. A truth that trumps what you desire and what you dream.

Just because you choose to live free doesn't mean you get to live free of responsibility.

LAWLESS PROPHET

NOVEMBER 1998–JANUARY 1999

The year 1999 saw President Bill Clinton acquitted in the Senate, the Dow Jones topping 10,000 for the first time, and the Columbine High School massacre.

Shakespeare in Love won Best Picture at the Oscars. The music downloading service Napster went online. Woodstock '99 ended in disaster.

Europe and Asia witnessed a total solar eclipse. Everywhere, people worried about the Y2K bug threatening a global collapse of computer systems that might crash civilization.

In Bethlehem, Pennsylvania, a first-year Lehigh University accounting student named Lily Lawlor dropped out to start the Shivers with Drake Morgan. Concerning Drake, no official records exist, suggesting he lived under an assumed name.

LILY: When I first met Drake, he said, "Follow me and live free."

It wasn't until way later that I realized this was an oxymoron.

Drake. My man Drake. Mandrake.

Our silly private joke.

Eat a little mandrake, and it can work as a strong sedative, narcotic, and hallucinogen. Eat a lot, and it can kill you.

That was my Drake, intoxicating and dangerous.

My devil in black jeans.

With him, it was always complicated. A man of endless contradictions.

He was my first love. My first serious betrayal. He opened my eyes. He tricked me into seeing the wrong things. He took me out of my cage only to put me in a far different but just as real kind.

In the end, I pitied him. The man who lived free of all convention, though he turned out to be as trapped as everyone else. More so, in fact. In the end, I ended up being the one to free *him*.

The greatest thing I ever did. My biggest regret.

Freedom isn't free. Drake taught me that a long time ago.

DR. EDWIN WOODWARD (*professor of religion studies, Lehigh University*): The Antichrist is a fascinating biblical concept. It's one of my favorite subjects because it is so open to interpretation. A few relevant passages can be found in 1 John, 2 Thessalonians, and Revelation.

Some regard the Antichrist as purely symbolic, representing rejection or opposition to Christ. Others believe it is various political leaders, with notable examples being Emperor Nero, Pope Innocent III, and Adolf Hitler. Still others see the Antichrist as a future leader who will beguile and take over the world, ushering in the end times.

A handful of references in the Bible produced a vast amount of lore. Like the Devil himself, the Antichrist is a blank slate onto which we project our fears.

LILY: It feels strange after all these years to break my one big rule and talk about Drake. I'm not quite sure where to begin. I suppose I should start over and tell you how we met. That was in the fall of 1998, my first semester at Lehigh. I paced outside the university library, waiting for it to open. Face buried in a textbook, learning about how to put together a balance sheet.

Oh, how I hated my accounting classes. If it were up to me, I would have been studying and making music, but my father had latched onto accounting as a safe career, something reliable that would provide.

Dad was a union man who'd worked at the steel mills until they closed down. The factories and mills now rusted across the valley. Growing up in the Rust Belt, you become an expert on three things: the resilience of community, the fragility of individuals, and the importance of self-reliance.

A voice said, "Have you ever asked what you expect of yourself?"

I looked up and saw him.

God, he was gorgeous. Tall and skinny, shaggy blond hair, and a shy smile.

Frowning, I said, "Of course."

The moment the words left my mouth, I knew I'd lied, which revealed a truth about myself I'd been denying. The truth being that up until that point, my life was run by what other people expected of me.

A single sentence can break your entire world, right? Drake seemed to know the right words for any given person. He'd utter them like a spell and step back while they seeded you and grew into change.

My second glance took in details, and I noticed he had heterochromatic eyes. His left a joyful blue, his right a smoldering copper.

Both pulled me right in.

At my old Catholic high school, the cool girls acted out, talked back to the nuns, smoked behind the gym, and played Spin the Bottle. They hung out with loud smiling boys who showed off and always wanted more. I'd never participated in any of their games. Not because I disapproved but because I couldn't afford the temptation.

The rebellious cool they worked so hard to project, Drake embodied in the fullest sense. No neediness. Nothing performative about it.

He told me a dream had informed him he was destined to meet me.

For some girls, this might sound like a red flag, but I was young and super naive and believed in serendipity. If I couldn't live dangerously, I'd been praying a little danger would come flirting my way.

I skipped the library and the study group I had in an hour. We talked all day until I had to go home. I told him everything I wanted but couldn't have.

Breathless, I said, "I want to be in a rock band that saves the world."

My innermost desire. Saying it aloud, it suddenly seemed possible, not caring how corny it sounded.

At the end, I asked him what *he* wanted.

He said, "I want you, Lilith."

No one had ever called me that. All my life, everyone had always called me Lillian or more commonly Lily. Lilith sounded mythic and a little dangerous itself. As if he recognized I had an alter ego whose time had come.

Either way, he already had me.

DR. WOODWARD: The concept of the Antichrist, some type of powerful adversary, is not exclusive to Christian belief.

In Islam, some believe Al-Masih ad-Dajjal will appear in the end times to spread corruption and lies until defeated by the true Messiah, the returning Jesus.

In Buddhism, we have Māra, who will oppose the future Buddha Maitreya.

And in certain Jewish mystical traditions, Armilus becomes an anti-Messiah who will conquer the world and persecute Jewish believers until defeated by the true Messiah.

LILY: Drake told me he'd been born at the maternity center at St. Luke's University Hospital in Bethlehem. He never knew his father.

His mother suffered bouts of untreated depression, false memory syndrome, and possibly paranoid schizophrenia. Drake cared for her until his seventeenth birthday, when she finally relented to answer his never-ending question about where he'd come from.

She told the story of his conception. How as a teen she'd danced at an impromptu party by a lake, young and beautiful and entitled. How she'd been seduced and assaulted in the dark by a giant black swan. With obsessive detail, she described the violent, burning thrash of its massive wings, timed to the discordant rhythm of her impregnation.

After hearing this, he left his childhood home and never looked back.

That poor woman. You might wonder whether, with such an upbringing, Drake wound up with low self-esteem, anxiety, depression. Maybe problems with resentment and aggression. *Something.*

But you'd be dead wrong. I've never known someone so enviably fearless and confident, even if it masked an inner fragility, a burning desire to be loved utterly. A vulnerability he showed me and no one else.

In the end, I was the one who wound up with the issues. A constant hunger for his approval. A burning desire to possess something I already had. When he looked at me, I shivered. When he touched me, I thought I was melting.

DR. WOODWARD: Regarding the Antichrist as a future apocalyptic figure, there is enough lore to generally characterize him.

Basically, the idea is his life will imitate the Messiah's in many ways, only to manifest as its corrupt mirror image. This has been an enduring belief since the Middle Ages. Satan as parody or God's ape, mirroring the divine but subverting and corrupting it at every turn.

He will be born in the East. Charismatic but deceptive, he will teach false doctrines. He will perform miracles and gain earthly power. He will use that power to proclaim himself to be above God, persecute Christianity, and ultimately start a global war that brings ruin to the earth.

He will also bear the mark of the Beast, which is the number 666. In biblical numerology, six denotes imperfection as it falls short of seven, considered divine.

The Antichrist will reign over chaos until God defeats Satan and permanently establishes his final kingdom.

LILY: Drake never gave me a phone number or made plans. Each time we parted, I'd worry he might disappear for good, as if I invented him. Then he'd reappear on campus, and we'd walk together, talking for hours. One night, we stopped in front of a run-down apartment building, and he said, "This is me."

And I thought, This is the moment the nuns warned me about. I was about to have my first real sexual experience or get murdered or both.

A thrill fluttered in my chest. Deep down, I didn't think Drake would hurt me.

Instead he showed me his guitar.

After numerous visits to Johnny Ray's Music, I knew my guitars and recognized his as a Fender Stratocaster. Black and white, chipped and scarred, and adorned with the kind of random stickers one found on skateboards.

Drake sat on his ratty couch and jacked into a practice amp.

The cold little basement apartment with its bare walls and random secondhand furniture was awful, but that only made it more exciting to me. Where others might see poverty, I saw bohemia, a reality where experience was the primary currency.

Then he played, and that's when my heart leaped from curiosity to love.

The song started slow, bending the bluesy notes before a smooth slide into a vibrato sustain, the amp dialed for just the right amount of reverb and depth.

Man, he was good.

The song picked up tempo, building to a climax with double stops and aggressive harmonics, and a vision struck me.

Resting in darkness, a crumpled Lovecraftian thing woke to the song and slowly flared to blinding radiance. Three vast pairs of wings unfurled to expose a beautiful face whose imperious gaze flash-burned me to a cinder.

As I gasped, the vision changed. Pealing like a trumpet in battle, Drake's guitar solo reached its climax. Naked winged giants spilled out of the blazing sun. Swords and shields and crested helmets. They tumbled toward the earth, their screams sounding in a single crystal note.

Then I was back in Drake's grungy apartment, blown away and speechless.

I finally managed to ask him how long he'd been working on it.

He offered up another one of his shy smiles and said, "I heard it in a dream last night."

DR. WOODWARD: What would the Antichrist's life look like before he becomes the Antichrist? Jesus didn't start his ministry until the age of thirty. Before then, scripture suggests he worked a trade as a carpenter. He lived in Nazareth, a village of no importance.

I would imagine the Antichrist might similarly come from such humble beginnings. In which case, he might attain power by becoming a celebrity in entertainment, business, or religion. Or maybe his origin would be the corrupt counterpart to Christ's, and he will be born into one of the world's richest families.

Either way, it begs the question whether he would even know his identity as the Antichrist until the appropriate time. Just as it's uncertain whether Jesus knew his destiny as the Messiah before John baptized him and Satan tempted him.

I've always wondered what Jesus the man thought the first moment he understood himself to be the Messiah. What was it like? Imagine the responsibility he must have felt, believing he carried the fate of the world on his shoulders, a load heavier than any cross.

Now imagine you're the Antichrist waking up on a typical day and having your own divine epiphany, only this one is a nightmare. That you are an enemy of the universe's supreme being. That you will reign over the earth for a short time only to destroy it and in the end be yourself destroyed.

I wonder if he'll regard this as quite a shock, or if he'll discover simple relief in finally discovering that his unique nature has a purpose.

LILY: A single sentence can break your world. In my case, it was Drake's song.

Music always shook me from the roots on up.

I had a normal if straitlaced childhood. Catholic school. The nuns warned me about the world's evils, while Mom and Dad kept me safe from them. They told me what I could wear, who I could hang out with, what they expected in terms of grades and behavior. They defined what a good girl was and molded me into it. Even when they weren't there, I acted as if they were watching.

I felt God judging me all the time.

Music transformed me. I think for every teen, there comes a day when you figure out there's really good music out there, and your life changes. During a sleepover, a friend put a record on her turntable and I heard David Bowie's "Life on Mars?" for the first time. I tilted my head, and the world disappeared until it was over. For a short time, I existed outside time and space, and from that moment forward, music lived in my bones.

And then it was one big explosion. The hooks for Madonna's "Express Yourself," George Michael's "Freedom," and Green Day's "Welcome to Paradise" lived rent-free in my head for months at a time. A song popped into my brain, and it elevated a quick walk to the corner store into a personal odyssey, my own private music video. I lived in and through music, sometimes an entire life in a song.

When I reached my teens, it wasn't enough to love the music; I started to crush on the musicians. I wanted everything they were selling, all the good, the bad, and the ugly. I craved excitement, unpredictability, danger, horror, growth. Music sucked all these feelings into form like a kind of exorcism.

When Drake played his song for me, it was like lightning shot straight from my organs to my brain. And I realized a few things.

I didn't want to be an accountant anymore. I never did. I wanted to create music with this beautiful genius and conquer the world, starting with me.

DR. WOODWARD: The point I'm making is that at any given time, the Antichrist might be walking the earth, and it might be anyone. It's not like he—or she—is going to be born with horns and hooves.

From descriptions written down for us by medieval saints, you'd think he was Bigfoot or aliens, showing a wide variety of physical traits so strange that it's difficult to parse the literal from the symbolic. Reddish gold hair, hands reaching his feet, fifteen feet tall, large head perched on a thin neck, eyes like stars.

I'd say if the Antichrist looked anything like these descriptions, he'd be easy to spot. Some even depict him with ANTICHRIST spelled out on his forehead!

If Lucifer is as skilled at deception as he is often credited, I doubt the Antichrist would look like a monster, though the scholars may have been describing his true aspect rather than his worldly appearance. If Christ is the lamb, then the Antichrist will be a wolf dressed up like one.

Like the Angel of Light himself, he'd very likely be quite good-looking, which would enhance his natural charisma. Otherwise, he'll be some guy who puts his pants on one leg at a time and brushes his teeth before he goes to bed.

If we assume he begins his ministry at thirty as Christ did, then anyone under that age living today could be the Antichrist but not know it yet. Just a stranger sitting next to us on a bus, as Joan Osborne's song goes.

LILY: It didn't take me long before I started skipping classes on the regular to hang out with Drake. I don't know if you want to hear about everything we did, but I can tell you that it was always fun, crazy, and surprising, and that I had plenty of lost time from my teen years to make up. We partied on rooftops, learned wisdom from trees while doing acid on South Mountain, took part in a pillow-fight flash mob at the Plaza, and broke into empty vacation homes during a treasure hunt. I went to my first live rock show, the Benders playing the Funhouse in Allentown.

And every night, like Cinderella, I had to leave the party early.

If you can't tell yet from all the gushing, yeah, I fell for Drake pretty hard. I can't point to anything he did that was particularly romantic. He didn't believe in grand demonstrations of affection or even in saying the simple words *I love you*. I wouldn't call him selfish, but he was definitely self-centered.

But the *idea* of him. It filled with me with a mad hunger. The thing is, Drake was everything I lacked, the manifestation of all the things I felt and believed about rock and roll. I craved his confidence, his willingness to try any drink once. The way he lived without fear or shame and entirely on his own terms. His innate and singular genius with a guitar.

In his halo, I glowed, seeing myself as the freer version of myself I'd always dreamed of being.

Every night, he'd say, "Don't go this time. Stay with me."

Not on Saturday nights, though. Sunday mornings were for church.

"Say hi to the old bastard for me," he'd tell me instead.

DR. WOODWARD: Until he ever reveals himself, America's apocalyptic imagination will continue to play the game of Name the Antichrist. In this country, there are millions who regard the world as a cosmic battleground between good and evil, in which every mundane decision is a contest between invisible angels and demons.

If you win, God loves you. If you lose, God is testing you. If you screw up, the Devil made you do it. Cultural change is interpreted as American decline, and this decay is regarded as the direct result of satanic forces. The Antichrist is always here, and the world is always about to end.

A frightening way to live, though I imagine it's strangely comforting. If all evil is Satan's fault, then one never truly has any real moral responsibility.

LILY: Drake believed wholeheartedly in the existence of God, but of course he had subversive views on the matter. He considered the Christian God a cruel, narcissistic absentee dad who said, *Love me or suffer for eternity*. It amazed him that anyone not only worshipped

God but actually conjured up any sort of genuine affection. In his view, humans had two choices. They could be a slave to rules or live a free, authentic life, in effect becoming gods themselves.

Raised in Catholicism's myriad bureaucratic doctrines and having incanted a million Hail Marys, I'd never heard anyone talk like this before.

A student of ancient religious beliefs, Drake hoped to harness cosmic forces and reach the true God, the being known in Gnosticism as the Unknown Father. On one of my visits to his apartment, he produced a baggie filled with magic mushrooms. He took out a knife and pricked his thumb, which bled into the bag.

"Take and eat," he said—reverently, like we were exchanging vows. "This is my body and blood, given to you of my own accord."

Gross, but I had decided to become a student of experience. I ate, completely ignorant of how profound an effect this one decision would have on my life.

The psilocybin kicked in, altering my perception. Colors appeared intense. Colors I'd never seen before, reds and yellows I could taste. My hand seemed like someone else's, too small, a child's hand, leaving a trail of shimmering light.

Then I looked at Drake, and I felt connected to him, his blood metabolizing inside me, germinating in my own blood. He blazed with light, but this turned out to be the reflection of a gleaming silver door that appeared, framed in black thorns and engraved with a head with two beautiful faces.

Wow, I thought, I am full-on hallucinating.

He said, "The Gate of Babylon. One of Huxley's doors of perception."

His voice too loud, practically booming. Drake slithered off the bed and went to the door. He asked if I was coming.

Surprised he could see it too, I said, "Maybe next time."

I wasn't afraid. I wanted to go, I really did. But I needed to hear music. I needed to play music. Because an entirely different door had materialized inside me, bursting open to admit a flood of songs.

At first, they blipped in flashes of sound as if someone cranked the FM dial on a car radio. Blink-182's Mark Hoppus saying this is growing up, the Descendents' Milo Aukerman chasing non-existent dreams, David Bowie pining about life on Mars. My whole brain lighting up, left side for lyrics, right side for melodies, pouncing on these musical fragments like a cat chasing its dinner.

Drake went through his own door, which vanished.

"Oh shit," I said. He was actually gone.

Then the first crystal-clear melody blazed across my psychic ether. One of those life-changing songs, only I'd never heard this one before. Another followed, and then another. I believed I'd dialed into God's radio station, where songs wait in purity and innocence to be born.

And I understood. These were *my* songs. All the songs I would create in my lifetime. I needed to write them down because if I didn't, they might be lost and then I'd have to wait years to find them again.

Ablaze with music, I got straight to work.

I didn't see Drake again for three days. He never told me where he went.

CHARLOTTE SKINNER (*executive director of public affairs, United States Conference of Catholic Bishops*): The Catechism of the Catholic Church includes a statement of belief that prior to Christ's second coming, the church must pass through a final trial in which all believers' faith will be tested. The Antichrist will appear as a pseudo-Messiah exalting man over God, promising earthly salvation that comes at the expense of spiritual salvation.

With this deception, the secret power of lawlessness will exert itself and hold sway. The twentieth century witnessed several such movements, including Nazism and communism.

Under the Antichrist's persecution, the church itself will emulate Christ's journey through death and resurrection. While she will be destroyed, she will ultimately triumph because the Lord will return to destroy all evil.

Otherwise, the church does not maintain a detailed doctrine about the Antichrist. This allows a great deal of diversity in theological opinion regarding the Bible's eschatological themes and, of course, clues to the Antichrist's identity.

On that score, there is little mystery. We will know him when he comes.

LILY: I filled my school notebooks with lyrics and cassette tapes with humming and singing. My head swirled with chords and riffs and melodies.

Simple, dumb songs about wanting a different life, falling in love, going crazy for its own sake. Teen angst music. Reach for the stars and howl at the moon stuff. Snappy ear candy, up-tempo and happy, even if the lyrics often ached with longing.

Back from wherever he went, Drake sat cross-legged on the couch wearing his most attentive expression and asked me to play him one. This had me nervous, as I'd made them just for me. It'd be like reading aloud from my diary.

But I did it. Parked on that ratty couch, I thrashed out a song on my Fender. A tune about a young woman saving up her money to go to Hollywood, where she'd be a star, thinking everything would be better if she were on TV. A whole new life waiting.

The song ended with her watching instead of being on TV, forever living in her dream. It described the desire to escape and the roots that pin us to a certain patch of ground.

When I finished, he said, "I love it, but she doesn't get what she wants."

I told him that's what made the song relatable. Because people often don't.

Drake said, "She should. Teaching people how will be our ministry."

I didn't understand.

He reached under his bed and pulled out a guitar like a rabbit from a hat. A brand-spanking-new cherry-red Epiphone SG Special P-90 electric. Mahogany body. Skinny neck for fast-necking. Totally sexy looking.

Drake said, "Merry Christmas, Lilith."

Looping the strap over one shoulder, I let the axe hang low at my waist. I stood in front of his mirror and gaped at myself holding this beautiful instrument. I looked like a rock star. I swore I'd never let go of it. I wanted to play it and hear its iconic sound forever.

Drake said, "I had another dream."

He suffered lucid nightmares that left him pale and trembling. He'd dream about a black sea. A great horned beast rising from the depths to blot out the dying sun, the sky cracking like smoky glass, the beast spraying its rotten breath from scores of nostrils like a symphony of water flutes. A tidal wave of blood.

His nightmares always came with an epiphany. Something he was supposed to do, like meet me or get a certain tattoo. He'd been waiting for another sign.

Drake said the words that changed my life: "We're going to start a band."

I ran screaming around the apartment. I screamed my head off. I kissed him for all I was worth. That night, we made love for the first time in candlelight, and he seemed to glow like fire, our bed surrounded by a howling orgy of winged men and women.

My last orgasm just about killed me, and I lay there smiling and gasping and thinking: So that's what all the fuss is about.

Seeing me so happy, Drake gently placed two fingers against my forehead like a benediction and said, "There's a whole universe in there."

CHARLOTTE SKINNER: Speaking solely for myself, yes, I suppose it is easy to imagine an Antichrist who bawls at the end of rom-coms and adores children and dogs and always stands on the right side of social causes. I'm sure there were Nazis in the Third Reich who wrote beautiful poetry.

This is the banality of evil. For the Antichrist to hold such sway in the material world during the end times, he will almost certainly be charismatic and even lovable, which allows him to pull off his great deception.

It's also entirely possible he'll retain enough of his humanity to be a reluctant agent of the apocalypse. Maybe he doesn't want to be what he is; he just *is* what he is. Maybe he'll have his own Garden of Gethsemane moment, where he agonizes over what he must do and begs the Lord not to assign him his burden.

It doesn't matter. The Antichrist has a role to play in God's plan. In the end, he will obey God and his own nature.

Some like to cast Lucifer as a misunderstood monster, but he is not. We understand him perfectly.

LILY: When anything is possible, one gets hooked on finding out what comes next. It was time for me to go all the way. Cut the cord. Burn my ships behind me. Pick whatever metaphor you want. The time had come to move out.

I pretty much lived at Drake's apartment already, only I didn't sleep there. This would be the final leap. I would wind up moving in without ceremony, but first I had to evacuate my parents' house in what felt like a full-scale war.

Mom and Dad had already figured out I'd been lying to them all this time about how I was spending my days, and that I'd earned an incomplete in all my courses. When they found out I intended to live in sin with a slacker and start a rock band, Mom melted down while Dad's anger volcanoed into all-out rage.

Mom went full maudlin, wailing about how she'd failed as a mother, practically rending her garments. Dad shook the house yelling every hurtful thing he could think of, how I was a good-for-nothing whore hell-bent on ruining her life.

By the end, it was unclear whether I was leaving on my own or being thrown out. I lugged my suitcases into Drake's apartment and collapsed crying on the bed.

Angry at my folks, he said, "You're not them. And they don't get to be you."

I pointed out they'd created me. They'd given me life. They'd raised me. If nothing else, I owed them for that. I didn't want to hurt them.

He said, "You don't owe them anything."

He said, "This is when you grow up and live on your terms, Lilith."

I said, "That's why I'm here."

To live my life with him. To start a band.

Still, I carried a ton of guilt around with me like a reinvention of original sin. I didn't share this fact with Drake. He believed in God but not in regret.

I threw myself into the music. As the days rolled by, we'd play for hours at a stretch, coming up with complex melodies as if inventing a private language. Every day, I'd ask if we were ready to actually, you know, start building the band, and Drake told me he was waiting for another sign.

Then it arrived. After he told me about his dream, I said, "Draw it for me."

We often painted our dreams on the walls of our apartment. Colorful depictions of me as a babysitter juggling a dozen laughing babies, ballroom dancing, making a margarita for David Bowie. Drake's grim, gray visions of the Great Beast.

This time, his nightmare took a different turn. Drake produced a brush and painted a figure holding a guitar on a stage, one fist raised in triumph. Below the stage, his manic strokes manifested a sea of fleeing, howling faces, each looking like a variation on the distressed subject of Edvard Munch's *The Scream*.

Drake said, "Surround him with golden light. Light reclaimed from Heaven."

I did, trying to replicate as best as I could the light I sometimes saw during our lovemaking, applying shades of yellow until the guitarist seemed to come alive. All I had on was a pair of denim overalls, and soon my bare arms glowed too.

After we finished, we appraised the disturbing image. I wondered why the figure stood alone. Where was the rest of the band?

I said, "Jesus, Drake. I hope that's not an omen."

He said, "It's Armageddon."

Drake thumbed some of the black paint drying on the wall and etched a cross on my forehead, like a blessing or a baptism.

He said, "It's time to start calling the band together."

I rubbed my hands together fiendishly and tittered like a movie villain. Finally!

He told me *Lilith* would make a great stage name, but I considered his pet name our secret. A gift from him that I refused to share.

I told him that henceforth, I would be known as Lily Lawless.

I was already finding it embarrassing, but Drake applauded. He said it sounded perfect. Grudgingly, I thought so too, even if

I had to admit the moniker was more aspirational than accurate. From here on, I vowed, I would be ungovernable. Large and in charge of my own life for the first time.

"Now you should name our baby," he said.

He was right. Our band didn't have a name yet.

I remembered all my guitar heroes and how every song felt like a promise of a new experience, thrilling and dangerous.

And so I named the band *the Shivers*.

DISCIPULAR GENESIS

FEBRUARY 1999

In the winter of 1999, Drake and Lily discovered three musicians seemingly by random chance but in a way that appears purposeful.

To each, Drake said, "Follow me."

RAMONA PEREZ (*drummer, the Shivers*): Back in '99, I listened to Rage Against the Machine, Korn, Marilyn Manson. If you told me that in a year I'd be swinging sticks in a bubblegum pop–punk band, I'd have laughed in your face.

Though the Shivers didn't start out doing that kind of music. Not while Drake played with us. The pop-punk thing came later, after he left.

When he was our frontman, we played what I called Demon Disco. Radiohead meets Pink Floyd with some shoe-gazing. Drake specialized in tunneling riffs that weren't so much musical earworms as literal parasites that bored into your brain and started munching. Between songs on stage, he'd commit the cardinal sin of allowing dead air, and you could hear a pin drop.

Whatever he turned out to be, you have to admit he had star power. Even if his playing drove people mad. Even though people died.

The man could goddamn perform.

ERIC BORKOWSKI (*bassist, the Shivers*): The millennial generation. We're the first American crop not to do better in life than our parents.

If you believe the media, this is all our fault. Cell phones or avocado toast or something. An addiction to overpriced coffee. We'd rather have a participation trophy and a handout than a job.

We don't spend money we don't have on oversize houses we can't afford. We're all lazy and entitled, blah, blah, blah.

If I hadn't met Drake and Lily, I'd have ended up another sad statistic. More roadkill on America's long path to decline. No matter what, I owe them for that.

MALCOLM WILLIAMS (*keyboardist, the Shivers*): One of the first things Drake ever said to me was, "Follow me and do what you love."

He'd say shit like that, and you'd believe it.

They tell you success in the music industry is all about timing. The right place at the right time. It's true. Hell, it's true in any industry. In '99, the dot-com boom was starting to peak, and I had a music website and a few domain names. I sold them all for a ridiculous amount of money and bought a house with it in West Bethlehem. I wasn't even out of college yet.

The only problem with reaching that kind of success at a young age is you have an immediate desire to do it again. You start to think you're some kind of genius when really, you put in some hard work and got lucky, that's all.

Timing.

A chance meeting in a bar. That's how I ended up with a musical career.

RAMONA: A few years before I met Lily and Drake, I ran away from home because…Um. Yeah. A story for another day. Anyway, I wasn't searching yet but escaping. I headed east from Harrisburg to try my luck in New York and made it as far as Bethlehem. There I found Comrade Jenny and her anarchist commune, they found me, and I lived with them for a while.

They'd started out with the grandiose name of People's House, but everyone just called it the Squat. They'd occupied the old steel plant on the Lehigh River. Picture people living among giant blast furnaces, looming smokestacks, and rusting, graffiti-coated buildings. If the working class couldn't seize the means of production, we'd claim the castoffs. Communism in the cracks, along with a constant risk of flu and tetanus.

In the urban commons, it was all, "From each according to their ability, to each according to their need." I had nothing, but I didn't need anything. I was safe.

Some pitched in by staging protests against globalization and Big Oil or making art out of creative destruction. Me, I busked for food. That's how I started drumming.

ERIC: For thirty years, my dad worked at Western Electric in Allentown. When its parent company reorganized, he got let go and ended up working a string of jobs that eventually chained him to the night shift at a 7-Eleven.

During a robbery, a kid half his age stuck a .38 in his face, and he died on the spot from a heart attack.

I'd finished a two-year business degree from Northampton but couldn't score a job, which kept me at home. After Dad died, I gave up for a while.

Ma told me Burger King was hiring food prep workers.

I thought about Dad getting squeezed until his heart exploded. I pictured the same life waiting for me, working my ass off for shareholder value while getting knocked around like a pinball. All the years ahead of me like a crushing weight.

The world makes the man. Why fight it? Why play along at all?

Ma said Home Depot was hiring cashiers.

I embraced my inner generational stereotype. I played countless hours of *Silent Hill* and *Medal of Honor* on my PlayStation. I fooled around with my bass guitar and got baked on weed when I could bum some.

Still living in the same room I'd grown up in, the same house, sick of looking at it but unable to leave, a prisoner of my failed ambitions.

Then Joey Grasso, this guy I knew from high school, called me up to tell me he was starting a wedding band. Did I want to get in on the ground floor of this stupendous opportunity, he asked me.

I said, "Sure, whatever."

I needed to do something. It might as well be that.

MALCOLM: I am at least cool enough to admit that I never was actually cool.

I'd shown up at university romanticizing *Animal House* parties, easy hookups, friends who'd eat a bullet for you, and late-night philosophy sessions. That stuff always seemed to happen to other people, though. Any overtures I made to connect got treated as an invitation to share an ongoing train wreck of personal drama.

In short, I found people annoying and learned that solitude produced the best results.

After nearly four years of this, I itched to graduate but still lacked a clear plan of what I wanted to do with my life. As my last semester kicked into gear, I started taking long walks in an effort to corral my scattered ambition.

Near Lehigh University, there was this bar with a terrific vibe and a weak carding policy called the Rascal. As a result, college kids in army surplus jackets would fill it up every night. One afternoon, I went in.

In the daylight, the bar turned into a different animal, a refuge for the type of hermit who wants to be alone while sharing space with other people. They sat with the brims of their caps pulled down low over their eyes, experts on meditating on domestic beer and lost chances and otherwise minding their business.

It's also a very white, very blue-collar, much older joint during the day, and so I got a bit of the stink-eye the first time I wandered in wearing a long coat over my usual uniform of a buttoned oxford and cardigan. The second time, they simply accepted me as part of the crew. As for me, I felt a weird kinship with them.

Anyway, I'd come for a different kind of meditation. The bar kept an old grand piano in a corner, a holdover from a bygone era when the joint had been classy and hired lounge acts. Eighty-eight keys, ivories producing full notes and black sharps and flats, melody and harmony, any genre you want, solo or in a group. Among musical instruments, the piano stands complete, needing nothing.

I played Beethoven's "Moonlight Sonata" and Mozart's "Rondo Alla Turca." The townies ignored me, but I wasn't playing for them. I had one foot in university and the other in the real world. Playing brought it all into focus, present and future, straight to the edge of some epiphany, though the actual eureka remained elusive. A deal I just couldn't close.

I'd find myself going there a couple times a week to play and think, hoping the answer would come. It's how I met Drake and Lily. Again, a matter of timing.

Pure chance, you might call it. Looking at it another way, it was always going to happen, and so it did. Since then, I've learned a lot about predestination.

Some things, I've discovered, are simply meant to be. Possibly everything.

RAMONA: Here's your bucket drumming 101 lesson: Score a four-gallon plastic canister bucket from the dumpster behind a hardware store. Strip off the handles and wrap the bottom rim with duct tape. Steal some sticks or mallets. Then bang the shit out of the bucket. Now you're a bucket drummer.

Start with some basic kick-snare beats, the center of the bucket serving as the kick for a deep note and the rim providing the snare. Go to town until your brain learns how to play multiple rhythms at the same time.

I taught myself on a single bucket and then added two more, one plastic and one metal. Later on, I added other pieces, shit I'd find on my dumpster dives. Bongos, metal paint cans, pots, shards of sheet metal, a warped old baking sheet.

On a good day, I made forty bucks.

Over time, I continued to build out my kit. I'd slap down my throne and buckets and cast a circle of pieces around it Wiccan-style, cardinal points to represent air, fire, water, and earth. The day I met Drake and Lily, I was feeling air and earth, pivoting from tinkling staccato rhythms to booming percussion.

ERIC: Starting a wedding band turned out to be a bigger hassle than it sounded. Joey's dad fronted some cash for microphones, a high-quality PA, and lighting. Then we came up with a setlist, rehearsed it, cut a demo, and pushed the word out.

A lot of work, but we did it.

Iron & Ivories suffered the usual first-gig stumbles, but once we hit our groove, we did surprisingly well. We'd play five, six times a month, weddings and the odd pub gig. In the summer of '98, we scored eight bookings a month. After the band's cut, I earned enough to pay Ma a little rent and buy my own weed.

Meanwhile, Joey had started to get annoyed. He said I didn't bring enough energy to the stage. A function band survived by word of mouth, and people only talked you up if you got the crowd juiced and dancing.

The average American only gets married twice, Joey liked to say. We had to make it memorable. This wasn't a job but a career, and he wanted to see us all go straight to the top.

The top of what, he did not illuminate.

I don't know what he expected from *me*. I was half the rhythm section. I stood in the back near the drummer. I held the other instruments together. I pinned the groove. The solid, quiet, chill one, that's the bass player. The straight man.

Most nights, I stared at my big feet, though I rarely worked the few pedals I brought. I'd long ago given up even checking out the girls, as they all went for hunky Joey with his muscles, Italian curls, and blinding grin.

He said I acted like I didn't even want to be up there on stage. I didn't argue with him. Truth be told, I felt like a hamster wearing himself out on a wheel. Did he think I aspired to play "YMCA" to drunk bridesmaids the rest of my life?

I knew I had it in me to do something great, something that had meaning, only I didn't know what it could possibly be. The world doesn't exactly roll out the red carpet for that sort of thing.

MALCOLM: Then one day after my classes were over, I walked into the Rascal and noticed Drake and Lily right away. You couldn't *not* notice them. Like the world's easiest game of One of These Things Is Not Like the Other.

They sat on tall stools around one of the little tables, deep in private conversation and sharing intimate smiles that seemed to create a warped reality bubble around them. Young and striking, but more.

They were cool. That rarest and most intangible of currencies. The type who slum in nerdy glasses and ugly vintage clothes and somehow still come off like supermodels who have it all. The type who are perpetually broke but never poor.

To be honest, they annoyed me. Their presence somehow made fun of the rest of us. I suddenly noticed how shabby the place was, how sad it looked, how cool and bohemian it could be as long as they stayed. They struck me as the type who found themselves in college and would go on to describe these years as magical, while the rest of us lurched through disappointment.

Screw them, I thought. Who were they to judge me?

I received my usual pint at the bar and retreated to the piano. Cracking my knuckles, I settled in. My beer, as usual, went untouched. For the first time, I didn't know what to play. I felt nervous and didn't know why.

My fingers started to trill through Queen's "Bohemian Rhapsody," and I ran with it. After a while, I glanced at the couple and realized I'd been playing for them. Really playing. The next time I looked up, they were watching me.

Their attention felt strangely warm.

I realized I'd been in some way auditioning. Suddenly, I was one of them. Beautiful and effortlessly cool. A very small and exclusive club.

Magical. Some things, money can't buy.

RAMONA: Earth and air. Grounded but with my head in the clouds. My sticks, aluminum core with a plastic coating, felt right in my hands. Eyes shut, I pictured wind and snow-covered mountains as I thrashed my buckets, riding sound and momentum straight to euphoria. My drummer's high.

When I came out of it, I discovered I'd pivoted to fire, arms aching and sticks blurring in rapid taps that produced the rolling crackle of flames. My collection plate brimmed with money from the office lunch crowd, enough to feed the Squat ramen noodles for a day.

I'd lost track of time; the street was quiet.

I looked up and spotted the couple watching me. I instantly sized them up as a pretty boy who knew it and a hot chick who didn't.

The pretty boy smiled. Suddenly, my left hand didn't know what the right was doing, and I brought my jam home with an angry flat flam.

He was the most attractive man I'd ever seen, displaying a perfect tension of masculine and feminine that is so my type. His blond hair a tousled mop that somehow looked styled.

His poise, however, spoke of generosity on the verge of sudden violence. This unpredictable quality drew me even as it terrified me.

It all felt so familiar. The dark desire to receive a slap just to get it over with. The even darker desire to receive it because this time, I'd hit back, and once I started, I wouldn't stop until I was absolutely certain I'd never be slapped again.

As for the woman, she was beautiful. Smoky but fragile. And innocent in a way that inspired lust, either the sadistic or the masochistic kind. A lovely, lush Eve who'd only recently eaten the apple and learned how to be bad.

Now that I'd stopped playing, the frigid February air froze the sweat on my face, and I was suddenly very cold.

I said, "What the fuck are you looking at?"

Drake laughed and said, "I'm listening. What kind of music do you like?"

I gave him the only answer I've ever given. The answer is any sound that reminds me I have a soul, a pair of fists, or a clitoris.

He said, "We're starting a band. Follow me and make money."

Now I laughed. I'd never cared about money. The little I earned, I blew or donated to the Squat. My hair hung in dreadlocks halfway down to my ass, I didn't shave my armpits, my faded tank top was holier than Swiss cheese. My threadbare jacket barely kept me warm.

Did I look like the type who gave a shit about money? In my world, just thinking about signing with a record label made you a sellout.

Turns out, Drake knew me better than I knew myself.

MALCOLM: Drake asked me what kind of music I liked.

I've always loved classical music, but I didn't want to blow it. I wanted to hold on to this feeling of cool. I started to tell him about my music website, the thing I'd passed up the standard college experience to build and sell for gorgeous profit. He didn't care.

He said, "Follow me and do what you love."

What?

"Malcolm," he said to me, "we're starting a band."

I looked back at the piano and snorted a laugh. It all seemed so simple now. I'd parked on that bench for a week trying to discern my future while the whole time it literally sang under my fingers.

My problem hadn't been whether my dreams would come true. It had been deciding which would be worth the effort.

At that moment, I didn't even question if it was a good idea for a loner like me to join a group. Maybe I was ready to finally enjoy the kind of moment that only happened to other people. Maybe I wanted to be a cool kid for once.

Or maybe Drake was right. By playing music, I'd get to do something I truly loved.

I thought, Okay, okay. *Okay.*

A rock star? Sure, I could do that for a few years. I thought I was King Midas.

I had yet to learn that some things don't respond to basic touch. Caressing, prodding, even a sharp slap. Some things only make gold if you strangle them.

ERIC: The next thing I know, I'm at the Terrace Ballroom at the Hilton in Easton, performing to one anxious father and over a hundred wedding guests.

We ran through the usual favorites, from "Life Is a Highway" to "I Wanna Be Sedated." The crowd did the chicken dance, the macarena, the electric slide. We brought the house down with a 1980s medley playing off "Mony Mony," laying that cheese a foot thick. We played Lonestar's "Amazed" for the bridal dance.

The whole time, I stared at my feet. I think I *wanted* Joey to kick my ass out of the band. It was the only way to get off this wheel and find something else.

The set over, I ignored his scowl and headed to the bar for a cold beer. This guy walks over and says to me, "Do you think music can save the world?"

"I guess. Sure, why not." What else could I say?

He says, "Then why can't it save you?"

I drink my Corona and tell him I don't need saving. He says everyone does. It's all a matter of finding that one thing they need.

I ask him if he's speaking from personal experience. As if answering my question, he tells me he's starting a band. He has a message to deliver.

The message: "Everyone deserves it."

Deserves what?

"What they want," he says. "What they need."

I pat his shoulder and say, "That's awesome." Meaning I had to get back to the band to prep for the next set.

Then Drake says, "Follow me, Eric, and find your purpose."

I laughed all the way back to the stage. If the band thing didn't work out for this dude, he'd make a hell of a cult leader. It was right then I realized the guy's eyes seemed to change colors.

Joey got behind the microphone and turned to give us all a smile that ended in a warning glare for yours truly. Shape up or ship out, right.

As we launched into the first song, I thought about whether Drake's question worked the other way. If music can save a person, can't it then save the world? I mean, what a wonderful idea. A really beautiful thought.

Iron & Ivories played most covers with a high fidelity for the original in terms of timing, tone, even vocal inflection. Familiar favorites delivered with the energy of a live performance. For some songs, though, we put our own stamp on it. We played it our way, turning the familiar on its head to offer something new.

We started "Groove Is in the Heart," a hopping tune that bounces along from 1970s funk to rap to house with a 1990s groove. I played the pulsing bassline intro to kick off the rhythm. I always had fun playing this song, but this time I really went for it, boosting the signal and working the reverb and wah pedals.

And I kept thinking, He's right, that dude is right, the world *can* change, and I am the agent of its reconstruction.

Shape up or ship out. Man, I let it fly. I strummed right into the pocket and held it. Picturing each pluck and strum sending beautiful vibrations that shook the world, transforming it into a place that didn't crush hope. Vibes that inspired everyone to stop ripping each other off to reach the top and just enjoy life.

And when the dream ended, I found the band around me still half-heartedly jamming to hold it together, Joey fuming with a plastic grin stretched on his face.

The dance floor had cleared out except for a few patient bridesmaids. The rest of the wedding guests wore looks of wonder and not the good kind. A few wasted dudes laughed and howled encouragement for the wedding band bassist who couldn't take it anymore and had decided to cut loose with an epic solo.

The song came to an end. Someone slow-clapped in the silence. The groom laughed. The bride fumed.

Joey said, "Thank you. You're a beautiful audience."

At his table, Drake went on clapping.

RAMONA: *Make money*, Drake said. Man, I wanted to punch him.

Then I realized how hungry I was. In the lean months, I'd get so skinny my body would start to eat my boobs. I pictured living somewhere that didn't have mold in the corners, a place with heat and reliable electricity and a real drum kit and a never-ending supply of toilet paper. Somewhere I'd never go to bed freezing or have to dumpster dive for a meal or wake up to a cockroach dancing across my lips.

In that moment, my life at the Squat felt like just another punishment I'd made excuses for, not a real choice about how I wanted to live. Not a life of freedom but another prison.

"Money is theft," I said, like a final test.

Drake said, "Then let's go steal some. To each according to her need."

It wasn't money that he'd promised. He'd offered *security*. A chance to be truly safe, the kind of safety that didn't require sacrifice and around-the-clock vigilance and hiding.

For some people, self-discovery can be a real bitch.

Because oh, did I ever have need.

ERIC: The minute Joey Grasso informed me I was no longer a member of the prestigious Iron & Ivories band, I slunk back to my old habits of gaming, smoking weed, and tuning out Ma's nagging and attempts to overfeed me. I'd agreed to join the Shivers, but after a few days I honestly forgot all about it.

Then the phone rang. Ma said it was some guy asking for me.

It turned out to be Malcolm, who gave me an address for the first band meeting.

I hung up thinking, Wow, I'm in a rock band.

Ma gave me the stink-eye and said, "Another music group, huh?" She reminded me the local Roy Rogers was hiring a shift manager.

I said, "If this doesn't work out, I'll get any job you want, I swear to God."

Then I went back upstairs to practice, only to get stoned again.

Joining a band is an act of faith, but I didn't believe yet. Not deep in my heart.

I had no idea what was coming.

FIRST COMMUNION

MARCH 1999

In the first days of March 1999, all the members of the Shivers met for the first time in the basement of the town house Malcolm purchased in Bethlehem.

MALCOLM: It turns out I was the only member of the band who had a pot to piss in, so I did some fronting. I traded in my car for a 1993 Chevy van, bought some secondhand music gear, and spent days soundproofing as much of my basement as I could to turn it into a practice space.

Graduation was coming fast, opening up all sorts of possibilities. I'd decided to go all-in on this new venture without investing *too* much, you know, just in case. I wanted it to work but had no idea what I was getting into. Musicians are born wild cards, utterly unpredictable, and a band is only as strong as its weakest link.

I had a plan. Come up with some songs, practice them until perfect, and then perform at local venues before cutting an album. I figured I'd give it a year.

We all met for the first time in that basement. I felt like a kid again, opening presents on Christmas morning. I really hoped Drake had picked some star talent for the group.

Nothing about that night went the way I'd imagined.

As awkward as it was, though, given how far we'd wind up going, you might say it was a bit of a historic event.

RAMONA: I had no idea what to expect. Probably last on my list would be an IKEA-themed band space and a tall, skinny nerd offering me a Fresca. The basement looked like someone's mama had just cleaned it to welcome guests.

Then this big, doughy, Barney-Rubble-looking dude strutted in and looked around like he owned the place.

He whipped off these mirrored shades he had on—it was dark outside as it was night, mind you—and said, "I'm here for Shivers practice. I'm on bass."

I said, "Wrong house, dude. We're here to play D and D."

He dropped the act as he fumbled around a bit looking lost, and I thought, Okay, so that's the real you. Nice to meet you, Eric.

ERIC: I was working on my swagger. When you're in a rock band, you have to foster, you know, an attitude. You have zero clue if you're any good but you have to act like you are, hoping it might rub off just enough onto the real thing.

If I came across as a bit of a poser, hey, it was better than me skulking in to announce I'd just been kicked out of a wedding band and still lived with my mother. As they say, be the change you want to see.

RAMONA: My default attitude was more like letting you know if I thought you were going to mess with me, I'd put you on the floor first. It made things simple.

But man, that drum kit Malcolm picked up was gorgeous.

MALCOLM: The drummer looked homeless and half feral, and the bass player tried way too hard. That stomach-flipping Christmas-morning feeling faded fast.

And still, Drake and Lily hadn't showed. I was getting hella nervous.

LILY: Drake and I hauled our guitars all over West Bethlehem trying to find the house. He whistled a happy tune until I yelled at him that we were going to be late.

"We're meant to be there, so we'll get there," was all he'd say.

It was super cold that night. Safe in its case, the Epiphone grew heavier by the second. Without a word, Drake took it from me and carried it in his free hand.

"Maybe we're not meant to get there," I wondered. "Maybe it's a sign."

Getting lost certainly triggered all my rampant self-doubts. One by one, we'd recruited three musicians into the band. Precise people we were destined to meet. All of it supposedly prophesied by dreams and meant to be, but we couldn't even find the damn address.

Maybe I was stupid to hang on to this childish hope of becoming a rock star. I wondered if it was too late for me, if I really was an accountant at heart.

Drake halted in his tracks. I asked him what was wrong.

He smiled and said, "We're here."

Then he looked at me and said, "You don't have to if you don't want to."

Giving me an out. Damnit.

Whatever happened next, it was all on me.

I was scared. I was also learning that I could be very stubborn.

"Let's rock," I said, not caring how uncool I sounded.

ERIC: Malcolm looked at me like something he might have to return to the store. Ramona acted like she had a chip on her shoulder and itched to shiv someone with it. I ended up sitting on an orange sofa and pretended to tune my bass while the silence slid from awkward straight downhill to painful.

Then Drake and Lily finally showed up, and I thought, Oh, thank you, Jesus.

RAMONA: The gang was all here. Malcolm fussed like a mother hen, still offering everyone drinks. Lily gawked at us like we were already rock stars. Eric stared at her with his tongue hanging out. She hugged her electric guitar against her chest like she was afraid one of us might try to take it from her.

Drake smiled as if the whole thing struck him as hilarious, like a kid mixing chemicals just to see if they'd blow up the house. I noticed he had a tattoo of a barcode on one wrist and an upside-down cross on the other.

For real, I had no idea right then if his idea to build this band from scratch was bold genius or a really bad practical joke.

LILY: My eyes goggled as they tried to absorb everything at once. As if this weren't our first band meeting but a surprise birthday party thrown just for me.

God, I was nervous. I couldn't believe I was actually here and this was happening. I had no idea how to act. I barely said three words at first.

ERIC: They really were good-looking as a couple. Lily had these enormous bright eyes you couldn't look away from. I remember one of the first things I thought was, Well, at least we already look like a rock band.

MALCOLM: I learned everyone's backgrounds to find out what they brought to the table. A busking bucket drummer, a wedding band dropout, and a starry-eyed girl who wanted to be a rocker. Drake sure knew how to pick 'em.

A lot of musicians start young. School band, music school, garage bands. Not this crew. We were newbs.

On the other hand, no one joined to get laid or famous, the usual call célèbre. We weren't doing this to delay adulthood. We'd all joined out of some deep need. A mission to find ourselves in music. Starting where we were, with this kind of hunger, there was nowhere to go but up.

In short, I hoped Drake's madness had a method.

LILY: In February that year, we recruited three musicians into the band, which involved hanging out in a bar all day, cruising a park, and crashing a wedding. Do not ask me why Drake thought these particular people were important. How he even knew they existed to find. He laughed it off when I asked him, which meant he didn't really know either. More stuff that was simply meant to be. When you're young, it's so much easier to roll with the weird, so that's what I did.

As much as I would grow to love these people in time, right then, not a one would have been my first choice. I'd imagined riffling the pages of my music magazines and finding hardcore rockers to call up to curate an all-star band.

I can guess what they all said about me. That I probably presented an image of Bambi taking her first awkward steps. That would be fair. I mean, it's true.

But my own impressions of them weren't super hot either. My dreams of an all-star band might have been silly and naive, but I at least expected people who regarded music as what and who they were instead of just something they did. People who lived and breathed rock as an identity and a calling.

No classified ads, no friend-of-a-friend connections, no tearing phone numbers off bulletin boards in music stores. A dream told Drake to find them. One can't argue with dreams, but I didn't want to argue it so much as understand it.

I decided I didn't care. Whoever they were, they were my tribe now. I was in a real, live rock band. My own dream was happening as foretold.

MALCOLM: The thing is, I was under a ton of pressure. A whole lifetime of it, actually.

Dad worked as an electrician but had set a different bar for his three sons, of which I was the baby. He wanted us to go to college and have more options than he had. Back in the day, he'd been a jazz musician, but it was the electrician job that ended up paying the bills. With three growing boys to feed, he chose the day job.

Anyway, that was Dad's dream for us—to go farther in life than he'd gotten. Mom put it into practice, though, and with a vengeance.

Jackson, Thomas, and I called her Queenie behind her back. Everything I knew instinctively about how to manage a rock band, I learned from her. She called her parenting philosophy the *relentless pursuit of excellence*, a rosy term for perfectionism.

Jackson had become a successful architect in Allentown, Thomas an electrical engineer. At a family dinner the previous weekend, they took their turns telling my parents their recent successes, a ritual around our house while growing up.

Then my turn came. They wanted to know if I'd made any decisions about what I wanted to do with my life, now that I'd be graduating soon. They exchanged knowing smiles, expecting me to share that I already had job offers.

Taking a deep breath, I told them about the Shivers.

My dad said to me, "You want to be a *musician*?"

As if to say, *Didn't I warn you not to make my mistakes?*

"The Shivers," he muttered to himself. Making it sound like a rare disease. "You should be working on another website. That was good. You have a keen eye for business."

Queenie didn't say a word. She didn't have to. She gave me the *look*—a disapproving glance that sees right through you because you're lacking.

I mumbled a few words about doing what I love, but Dad had already moved on to asking Jackson about the office reno he was working on.

Keen eye? They had no idea. I'd show them exactly what I could do.

I just needed to make this band of misfits do it with me.

LILY: I didn't know what to do with myself, still overwhelmed by the exciting idea of it all but underwhelmed by the reality. Eric kept leering at me like he was on the verge of saying something as soon as someone mailed him a script. Ramona randomly paced around the place, coiled for sudden violence. Malcolm was talking to Drake about terms and conditions. The mind-blowing dialogue about the life-changing qualities of music I'd imagined did not appear to be forthcoming.

So I beelined to the practice area to check out all the equipment Malcolm had bought for the band. Microphones and stands, cables and amps, and drum throne and kit that he perfectly arranged on a rug as if he had strong views on feng shui for bands. I ignored most of it, finding my own ground.

Here was my amplifier along with a music stand for chord charts. A few pedals. A PA system with speakers and a mixer. Power strips and extension cords.

The equipment screamed to be used. It wanted someone to bring it to life.

I shot a longing look at Malcolm, who was now talking to Drake about writing a business plan while Drake chuckled along. I figured all this stuff was here for me too, and that I should tear a page from Drake's book and ask for forgiveness instead of permission.

Shrugging, I plugged in, adjusted the knobs, and started strumming. My axe responded with its strong tonal bite.

While I warmed up, everyone continued to eyeball each other, hope and doubt warring on their faces while Drake went on laughing at it all. Me, I didn't care about how or whether I fit in anymore. I'd come to make music.

RAMONA: The first official order of business for Malcolm was to show us a draft of a band contract he'd written up. This is something bands fall back on if they break up or someone important leaves. Who gets the band's name and the gear, who owns the songs, that kind of stuff.

I was like, Are you kidding?

Drake said to him, "You're logical, Mal. I dig that. Logistics are gonna be your domain. But let's see what we've got here before we get busy selling out."

ERIC: The party hadn't even started, and Malcolm was already trying to monetize it. Boo.

MALCOLM: I was trying really hard to like these people and not to think I'd made a big mistake and wasted my money because I wanted to be cool.

Drake lit a cigarette, and I walked off in a souring mood to get him something to use as an ashtray. I was like: I guess smoking is allowed in my house.

ERIC: I saw the drummer slip one of the spare brushes into her pocket, and I thought, Well, we're off to a real grand start here.

RAMONA: Comrade Jenny told me to bring back anything that wasn't nailed down. Drake caught me swiping a drum brush and winked.

LILY: From everything I've told you so far, you know I had a tendency back then to romanticize about a lot of things. I won't deny it. But even I could see the band wasn't remotely close to connecting.

RAMONA: As this was our first band meeting and Drake had been the one to pull us all together, we expected him to say a few inspiring words to start things off.

Instead the wallflower spoke up first.

LILY: I didn't say anything, actually. I started playing a riff I'd been noodling.

One thing I did not romanticize about was us all becoming fast besties. Before that could happen, we had to fuse around the music. The music came first. It was why we were here, ready to sacrifice our blood and sweat.

You listen to music to learn what kind of musician you'd love to be. Then you play to discover what kind of musician you are.

Regarding the second part, I was about to find out.

ERIC: When Lily started playing, Drake said, "Every song you will ever play is already in you. It's waiting for you to yank it out of the void."

I felt a sudden urge to get in on this song, playing bass with this beautiful girl who looked like she might burst into tears but was putting it out there.

LILY: Before that night, I'd never played for anyone except Drake.

ERIC: I came up with a walking bassline to harmonize on her melody. Everyone loves the bass's sound, even if bass players don't always get a ton of respect. It's the unsung hero of rock instruments. This was my chance to show what it could do when you take the leash off.

LILY: I reminded myself how bad I wanted this. My dream of becoming a professional musician. The one great gift Drake had given me, which was to convince me to stop living my parents' dream and start living my own.

Now I needed to let my guitar sing, and when I did, it was like hearing my own voice for the first time. When Eric joined in, I caught a blasting second wind.

RAMONA: Hell to the yeah, I thought. I'd been itching to smash those drums since I walked in there. I parked myself on the throne and started to lay down a beat that pushed the tempo.

LILY: My terror turned into thrill.

MALCOLM: Drake looked at me and said, "No songs tonight. No right or wrong. No failure, just feelings."

He didn't know me, how challenging this sounded. Or maybe he did.

I regarded a song as just another computer program. You press start, and it runs reliable and true with everything in its proper place. Inputs and outputs.

I looked at my bandmates and thought, Well, you have to start somewhere.

Closing my eyes behind the keyboard, I visualized the song that was coming together and where it could go. A hot mess, but I told myself: No failure. Before I could overthink it, I layered the beginnings of a countermelody.

Then Drake joined in with his Stratocaster, and wow.

RAMONA: I was like, Holy shit! What's happening?

ERIC: He cut loose with one mind-blowing, nerve-jangling lick after another.

LILY: For most of us making music, it's one part talent and nine parts hard work and endless practice. Then there's that maddening genius who's simply born to it.

That was Drake. A real monster on guitar. He played like David Gilmour—arresting note bends, confident sustains. In terms of attitude, his playing was pure Brian May, radiating power and grandiosity.

ERIC: You find yourself playing with a guy like that, it gives you an overwhelming desire to do one of two things. Sell your guitar and do something else with your life or step up and find your own mastery.

That night, I took my first step. But man, I had a long way to climb.

RAMONA: He pushed everyone to break out. We all fed off his energy and really went for it. I'd never played with people before, and I couldn't believe what I'd been missing all this time. How fun it was.

LILY: I played until my fingers turned raw and my hands started to cramp and I could feel the band flagging around me. We'd played for hours.

Damn, did it ever feel good! During that jam, I grew into my new guitar that up until that moment felt way too big for me.

And I thought, I'm home. This is my home.

MALCOLM: That first marathon jam session was a searing train wreck. Ramona's timing ran all over the map, Eric knew his business but sounded a little flat on the D string, and I still struggled with improvising.

The real problem was we played as five separate people, not yet as a band. Only natural, though, it being our first time.

When the jam ended, I thought, Okay, this might work. I could see we had the foundation. We just needed to put in the sweat and time to build on it.

And with Drake on lead guitar, we couldn't lose. The man appeared to be something of a musical genius. To put things bluntly, our band had a ringer.

RAMONA: The hardest part of drumming is training your brain to play multiple rhythms at the same time. I had that part down. I could shred when I needed to.

But this wasn't bucket drumming. I had to learn how to use my feet instead of my sticks for the kick. And I was playing with people who depended on me to hold the fort. I needed to master the basic discipline of keeping time by counting music.

That first jam, I learned how much I had to learn.

ERIC: So cool, making my own music instead of learning other artists' hits so I could imitate them. I actually started to glimpse what we could be together as the Shivers. How awesome it could be.

People are pinballs, bouncing around trying to find the right slot only to wind up stuck somewhere. Maybe I'd gotten lucky, chancing upon a job that didn't feel like counting down to a heart attack.

LILY: Drake once told me that every song ever played is still playing. That every song ever played joins the one great never-ending song.

I'd like to think that first chaotic jam is still out there in the universe. An echoing moment in time before Flanagan's, before the Hobo Underground, before Sunburst and Armageddon. Just five people expressing themselves in a struggle to fuse into something beautiful. So full of hope, and still so innocent, before it all went wrong.

DEMON DISCO

THE FLANAGAN'S SHOW
APRIL 23, 1999

*O*ver the next six weeks, the Shivers produced songs and practiced them. For Lily, this proved a happy time full of hope and promise. At last, the time came to take a chance on making all the hard work pay off. In April 1999, the Shivers played its first show at Flanagan's Irish Pub in nearby Allentown.

Every band believes or at least hopes it has a special something that makes it magical. The members of the Shivers were about to learn they had it.

The problem with magic is it can be good or bad.

MALCOLM: I recorded a demo tape with our two most polished songs, the ethereal "Freedom Isn't Free" and the razor-edged "Fucking for a Fight." I sent it out with a press kit and made some calls.

Everyone told me the music was great but not what they were looking for right now, which I learned was a standard rejection in this business. No one wanted to take a risk. They advised us to build up a following before calling back.

How the hell was I supposed to do that if I couldn't get us booked?

Then we got lucky, which is what success is. You work your ass off and put yourself out there over and over until luck goes your way. I arrived home from another tense dinner at my parents' house to find a message on my machine.

Flanagan's booked us for a Friday night.

ERIC: That was one weird night. Not the *weirdest* for us, mind you, but the first.

MALCOLM: No merch. No T-shirts, no CDs, and no master to hand out to industry types catching us on the fly. I looked at this as a beta test. Just another band practice, only this time with an audience. We had the world's permission to suck. I really hoped we didn't.

RAMONA: Malcolm warned us the space was small, and he hadn't been kidding.

MALCOLM: A smoky room in the rump of an Irish pub. Barely a stage, the audience almost in our faces. Minimal backline. The front of house consisted of a cranky bar manager working a soundboard and barking at us to turn everything down during sound check.

ERIC: I took one look at it and thought, We'll be lucky to get paid in beer.

MALCOLM: What did they expect for a first gig? Madison Square Garden?

LILY: Malcolm thought we were growing into a good band, but that didn't guarantee anything. Good bands are a dime a dozen. To succeed, you have to be special, and we'd never know that until we put it to the test. Flanagan's was that test. While Drake led the musical side, Malcolm handled the business side. I trusted his instincts. I just hoped he was right, that we were ready.

MALCOLM: The truth is I didn't know if we were ready to play even Flanagan's. We'd barely scraped together a decent set.

LILY: Our songs covered metaphysics and the human condition instead of the usual teen loneliness, alienation, and obsession with sex. Not exactly mass-appeal type of music. But hey, for a group that barely knew what it was doing—aside from Drake, of course—it was great. Like Radiohead and Muse had a baby that wanted to be a terrorist when it grew up. Real mad-scientist stuff.

I couldn't wait to see what impact it'd have once we let the monster loose.

RAMONA: I totally dug "Fucking for a Fight." It had a raw Nine Inch Nails flavor and so much reverb that you needed a long hot shower after listening to it. So many of our songs kept the drums on a leash, rim taps and the like to make the sound seethe and simmer, but this one cut me loose to bite some ears off.

MALCOLM: Of course Ramona loved that song. It had *fight* in the title.

RAMONA: To me, that song was about how some nights, you just have this feeling something is about to go down. A hot night you make a really big mistake that at the time strikes you as the world's best idea. You feel like you're in danger until you realize you're the one who's dangerous. The song captured that age when you have energy to burn and it doesn't matter what or who you burn it with.

The night we performed at Flanagan's felt just like that.

MALCOLM: A guy like Eric, it was like working with Play-Doh. Drake, like playing with fire. Ramona was more like woodworking, right down to the splinters.

RAMONA: Malcolm had made a lot of money doing coding. People aren't numbers.

LILY: When Malcolm called to tell us about the gig, I danced around the apartment until the anxiety kicked in. I ended up in our little bedroom rooting through my clothes. I tried on different outfits and posed with my guitar in front of the bedroom mirror. I prayed one of them screamed *rock star* enough that the audience wouldn't notice how scared I'd be.

Drake applauded every choice until he dug deep into my things and yanked out what he thought was the perfect outfit.

MALCOLM: Lily showed up at Flanagan's wearing a Catholic schoolgirl uniform in the tradition of youth mocking through emulation. Tartan skirt and button-down shirt and tie, knee-high socks, the works.

ERIC: It only made her look even cuter. Dudes in the audience shot curious glances at the band and then stared with their mouths hanging open. I was trying real hard not to stare myself.

LILY: I have no idea why I packed my old uniform in my mad rush out of my parents' house. It's like I knew it still had a purpose.

RAMONA [*laughs*]: Oh man. I loved having Lily around. All the guys would drool over her and leave me alone so I could play.

LILY: Day of Judgment, I kept thinking under those bright, hot lights.
Performing for an audience for the first time.
Yeah, I was terrified.

ERIC: We all liked Lily. She loved music. She lived for it. She worked really hard to be the best guitarist she could be. Besides all that, she was just easy to be around. On days when everyone grated against each other like sandpaper, she never lost her cool. With all eyes on Drake, we wouldn't know until later how much she held things together.

RAMONA: Eric was in love with her big time.

ERIC: I was not in love with Lily. Okay, maybe I was. A little.

RAMONA: He also had a big, fat crush on Drake.

ERIC: No comment.

RAMONA: To be fair, everyone was into Drake. He had such a big personality. It was like he was on every channel.

ERIC: Anyway, I was the only one who'd performed for a large crowd before, so I tried to help my bandmates know what to expect.

RAMONA: Eric acted like he'd played in the major leagues and was gonna show us how it was done. Dude, I *busked*. These jackoffs didn't scare me. As for our dear Eric, he actually showed up wearing a cheesy blue suit with a bow tie.

ERIC: I honestly don't know what I was thinking. I'd played so many weddings that it just felt natural to wear the suit. It was like putting on a uniform.

LILY: Drake sometimes talked about kenosis. In religion, it's the idea that Jesus emptied himself of worldly desires so he could become the Christ.

Of course, Drake had a subversive take. For him, kenosis was about asserting instead of surrendering. He said to reach your potential as a human being, you had to empty yourself of whatever held you back from achieving true free will. This included anything planted in you from outside. Your ego and upbringing. To be the Superman, you had to transcend both nurture and nature and rediscover your animal essence.

When we took our places on the stage, I experienced my own brand of kenosis. I felt emptied of *everything*. I hoped I'd remember how to play my guitar.

MALCOLM: Once I got behind my keyboard, I suddenly wanted to kill it. I wanted these people to fall in love with us. I wanted them to hear me. I'd gotten so hung up on the business side I'd forgotten I was doing this because I loved it.

LILY: The vibe in the room was receptive, but no one cheered or anything. I heard a lot of chatter while we got ready. We could have been playing to a restaurant or a lounge. We'd have to grab their attention and hold it tight.

ERIC: For the first time, I understood what Joey Grasso wanted every time we played a wedding. Tonight I was going to bring it. Though I have to admit, right then I wished real bad I'd given practice more of a major-league effort.

LILY: I shook like a leaf. The pub seemed to have its own crushing gravity. I wondered if the others felt as nervous as I did. They fussed over their instruments with grim looks on their faces, as if solving a math problem. It all screamed pro, but I knew they did it just to have something to do with their hands.

Not Drake, though. He didn't look scared at all.

He stood there wearing a black tee with a goofy smiley face and JUST SAY YEAH on it, the first thing he'd found on the floor of our apartment. He grinned in red-filtered glow until the crowd quieted and more and more eyes fell on him.

I'd always admired that about him, how fearless he lived, especially on stage.

RAMONA: Drake leaned into the mic and said, "Later in life, you'll remember this moment."

MALCOLM: No *Hello, Allentown!* He didn't even tell them our name. Jesus, God.

ERIC: The guy had balls. Ramona started laughing. It loosened us right up.

RAMONA: Yeah, fuck these guys, I thought. We're the Shivers. Take it or piss off.

MALCOLM: Drake kicked things off with "Prometheus." I'd put it at the head of the set because we all join in one by one. Each instrument cued up the next.

LILY: I stared over the audience's heads and started playing on autopilot.

Rhythm is the song's foundation. Eighty percent of guitar playing in a song is the rhythm guitarist. I held the songs together.

If I could keep my brain out of my body's way, I'd be fine. As long as I didn't look down, I couldn't fall.

Then I glanced over at Drake and saw how much fun he was having. Seeing him like that fed me energy.

Acting on their own, my feet moved and my hips swished in sync with the beat. My body knew exactly what to do, even if my brain was screaming.

MALCOLM: Drake always beamed a happy smile like it was everyone's birthday and he was here to sing them the special song. Otherwise he'd barely move except when he played his solos. Then he'd hunch over his guitar with a fierce look on his face, like he was murdering his instrument.

ERIC: The audience didn't clap or dance or anything. Our sound was too weird and sad. But they looked interested. Bodies stiffened to alertness. Eyes narrowed.

LILY: All I could think about was how magical the whole thing was.

The ear is one hell of a feat of engineering. It can discern a huge variety of sounds, isolate one to focus on, and then make a very good guess about what direction it's coming from and how far away it is.

Then you create music for it. Tempo, time, key. Melody, harmony, rhythm. Notes consisting of sound waves and vibrations. The inner ear filters it all into something the brain can understand. Electrical impulses firing up the auditory nerve, mainlining music right into the brain.

It's like a drug or, you guessed it, a spell. Sometimes it makes you happy. Other times, it makes you remember something and cry. Music plants the seeds of dreams, change, identity, protest, and love.

Yeah, it's magic. When you're performing, you're a bona fide witch.

MALCOLM: At the end of the first song, Drake didn't banter with the audience. He just let the dead air hang. Nobody applauded. It's like they were stunned.

RAMONA: I didn't know what to think. I had zero clue if they loved us or hated us. On the next song, I hammered the accents, making every stroke a cut.

ERIC: When Drake unleashed his first big solo, the crowd actually flinched as one, like a herd of deer hearing a gunshot.

LILY: Drake started wailing on his Stratocaster, and I ended up having one hell of a drug flashback. A brief lucid nightmare, which I'd later think was strange given I'd never suffered a bad trip during my experimenting.

The band morphed into grotesque images. Ramona screaming and thrashing her sticks as an angry thing tried to burst free of flesh and bone, Eric a sluggish golem made of dust, Malcolm jerking behind the keyboard while a swarm of winged monkeys scrambled over him. Drake a shining being of golden light. The audience fragments and puzzle pieces.

My hands splintered around my guitar strings, iron chains slithering from gaping wounds to wrap and weld around it.

Terrified, I flubbed a chord, and then the unsettling vision left me.

MALCOLM: If we hadn't already gotten used to the Shivers, I would have suggested Hell's Choir as a good name for us. Our songs sounded like symphonies Mozart might have composed if he went mad from syphilis.

Sure, Top 40 is bubblegum pop that all sounds the same, but it's Top 40 for a reason. People like it enough to listen and pay for it. Our music did not even come close to Top 40. But we were onto something.

That night, we held around eighty souls in the palms of our hands.

LILY: Ramona thrashed her skins. Eric walked the line. Malcolm layered on a dark orchestral flavor. Drake sang about people games, the way people play nice to get what they want. I held them together while absorbing them.

The power I felt. How do I even describe it?

Kenosis in action. An empty vessel filled with fire. Transcendental meditation. I was a goddess performing on that little stage, a perfect being, complete and needing nothing. My head in the zone, my music in the groove.

There's no high like it in the world.

At the same time, I felt something else, a different kind of power. The hot rush of seduction. The songs dragged the audience by the ear along a razor's edge separating pleasure and pain. With each chord, I gripped them in delicious tension at the edge of a vast release that was almost sexual, a single note away from death.

That night, Lily Lawless was born.

ERIC: Drake called our songs slider buzzsaws. Entirely accurate.

LILY: The crowd worshipped me. When we started "Freedom Isn't Free," they all fell into a solemn trance.

RAMONA: What Lily says she saw next, I mean, okay, but I didn't see it. The stage lights blasted right in my eyes, and I was too focused on keeping the songs on time. But after what happened later, I totally believe what she said.

LILY: This one guy near the stage. I couldn't take my eyes off him. During the last three songs, he didn't move a muscle. He just stood there glaring at Drake with this angry, scared, and determined look on his face.

As if Drake had just told him his family had been slaughtered. As if Drake had then handed over the address of the murderer. As if Drake had next told him where he could buy a gun real cheap, no questions asked.

When we closed with "Fucking for a Fight," he actually pissed himself. I saw his pant leg darken to his knee. He didn't even blink while he did it.

ERIC: At the end of the show, the crowd gasped, as if they just remembered how to breathe. Not a single clap. They all just stood there blinking.

On reflex, I called out, "Thank you. You're a great audience."

LILY: My ears rang. The power I felt only moments earlier bled away, replaced by a hot, restless energy. I turned to Drake and told him I wanted to find a place to dance with him all night and watch the sun rise.

ERIC: I stood there wearing this dumb grin, expecting people to come up and tell me what they thought of the music. They just filed out. Some of them were crying.

LILY: Then even the restless energy was gone, and I only felt empty and something else. Corrupt. Like I'd done something very wrong.

MALCOLM: I thought it went very well. It certainly wasn't the train wreck I'd predicted. I hadn't expected the zombie space-cadet glow reaction we got, but the point is we *connected*. For a full hour, we had their complete attention.

LILY: After we loaded out, Malcolm offered to take us to Denny's to celebrate and talk about how it went. I thought, Yes, we need to discuss this as a group.

MALCOLM: Band meeting time. We had a ways to go to sharpen our act. We still sounded like five musicians playing separately in singular determination not to be the one who screwed up. And we started to get cocky near the end and hit some clams.

Next time, we'd do better. I'd see to it.

LILY: We're sitting there facing each other across a table loaded with coffee and pancakes while chatting about how we rocked, and I was like, Are we going to talk about this? How we put a whole room full of people in a trance and made some poor dude whiz in his pants?

ERIC: I didn't know what to think. I mean, Drake seemed happy. Ramona looked pissed off, nothing new there. Lily was quiet. Malcolm as usual acted like he was our manager, but I had to admit his take on the night sounded legit.

LILY: Drake caught me scowling and said, "Music is language, emotion's shorthand. Mainlining truth and self-discovery. Tonight we talked to souls."

Which sounded terrific and all, but I thought it shouldn't feel so wrong. I still had this really nasty feeling, like I'd somehow sucker-punched those people.

RAMONA: Rock musicians hope and pray they'll get the crowd bouncing and howling, but that wasn't our kind of music. A trance proved just as awesome. The point is impact. I thought, Yeah, we nailed it.

MALCOLM: For a full hour, we held the lion by the tail. We were onto something. It blinded me to what would become obvious only way later for me, almost too late. How strange and unnatural it was. How wrong.

ERIC: Drake said, "Music is alchemy. Each song is a new recipe." I liked the sound of that, how we were wizards.

LILY: Drake lit a cigarette. He could take or leave them. I knew if I had one, I'd be hooked and there wouldn't be enough cigarettes in the world.

I really wanted one that night, though. The show had left a little black hole in me, and I wanted to stuff it with something.

ERIC: I don't think we stayed long. We barely ate anything. We were too strung out. Lily looked right on the edge. I wound up guzzling cups of coffee.

We went out into the night and listened to the traffic. Drake tilted his head to gaze at the skyglow above the city and said, "I wish I could see the stars tonight."

That's when I spotted the priest.

MALCOLM: The old man in the black cassock marched ranting across the parking lot.

RAMONA: I have a Spidey-sense for violence. I didn't see a priest. I saw trouble.

ERIC: For an old guy, he was stacked. A really big, tough-looking dude.

LILY: I could tell he was a bishop because his skullcap and sash were violet. He had a silver beard that ran like a silver waterfall down his chest. Then I noticed a strange curved knife flashing in his hand, long as a drumstick.

MALCOLM: I'm usually pretty good in a crisis—I mean, I keep my head—but I had nothing. I just stood there while that priest yelled something at Drake, who blanched.

The priest called on God to strengthen his hand as he surged toward us.

Then the truck came out of nowhere and smashed right into him with a heart-stopping *bang*.

RAMONA: I was getting set to maybe have to punch Father Nutter's clock when the truck plowed into him. It dragged his body maybe thirty yards before stopping. I'll never forget the sickening crunching and popping sounds it made. The long, wet trail glistening on the asphalt.

LILY: No one screamed. We just stood there. It was like I forgot how to breathe.

RAMONA: While we all stared in shock, the driver opened the door and had a major freakout before rushing past us into the Denny's to call 911.

Then Eric said, "Man, I hope that old guy didn't catch our show."

ERIC: Did I really say that? I probably did. When I'm upset, sometimes I just blurt out the first dumb thing that pops into my head.

MALCOLM: Drake said, "It was like he knew me."

LILY: Drake appeared downright rattled. Not only because he'd watched a man get run over by a truck, but because he felt like the man recognized him. As if the bishop had seen something in Drake that Drake didn't see in the mirror.

Right then, he looked like the sad, terrified little boy he must have been while he was growing up.

RAMONA: *Abomination.* That's what the priest yelled at Drake.

LILY: At the edge of tears, Drake said, "The beast in my dreams hasn't lied to me yet."

Then he looked at me and said, "You should go dancing."

I was like, What?

Drake said I'd mentioned I wanted to go dancing, so I should go do that.

I told him I wasn't going anywhere.

He said, "Go. Now." Like a warning.

Even after what had just happened, everyone tuned into the sudden weird tension. I thought he was testing me. He didn't seem to want to be alone.

I said, "I want to be with you."

Drake whispered, "Armageddon is coming."

Then he started walking toward the van.

ERIC: That was our first show. We hypnotized a crowd of people, ate some pancakes, and watched a priest die by vehicular manslaughter. Then to top it off, Drake got all weird on Lily.

This was about to be a normal night out for us.

BAND PRACTICE

MAY 1999

After Flanagan's, the members of the Shivers believed they were not just good but special. It proved transformational. The big question was what came next.

"AN ACT TO FOLLOW"
BY VINCE AMATO,
THE *VALLEY SCENE*,
APRIL 25, 1999

What caught my ear this weekend: Bethlehem-based the Shivers, a five-piece dystopian alt-rock band, playing Friday night at Flanagan's Irish Pub.

The single set was an art-rock tour de force marked by menacing riffs and spare lyrics themed around people obeying their desires. Each song maintains a tension between experimental and compositional techniques, showing influences of groups like Radiohead. It started out pretentious and pondering, but the melodies subtly hooked me and kicked me into a lucid dream followed by a harsh wake-up.

On stage, the main events are frontman Drake Morgan, whose lead guitar artistry, vocals, and onstage presence are frankly reminiscent of the late Jimi Hendrix and Jim Morrison, and eye-popping rhythm guitarist Lily Lawless, who laid down her dark melodies while decked out in a Catholic school uniform.

The gig was an arresting if punishing listen, each song audibly lumbering through multiple melodic acts toward a volumetric, discordant, and strangely hopeful climax.

Check them out if you're looking for something dark and different.

ERIC: Malcolm read that article aloud to us at practice, and I thought, Oh, wow. He's talking about *us*. We exist. We're a real band.

It's funny how sometimes you aren't really aware you're alive until someone else notices you.

RAMONA: "Pretentious and pondering." Kiss my ass, Vincent.

ERIC: "Check them out if you're looking for something dark and different." I mean, whoa.

MALCOLM: I read the review maybe twenty times. It was a great write-up. I made copies for the press kit and re-sent it and the demo tape.

We'd passed the test and needed another gig.

Too late now to get into Musikfest and the new NEARfest music festivals, but I still had hope we'd get billed for Sunburst, a small but well-attended outdoor music festival coming in July. Then I remembered Drake saying something about Armageddon after our Flanagan's show, reminding me that it was indeed coming.

December, in fact. The annual Armageddon Battle of the Bands, a big deal. With plenty of time to prepare, I sent in an application.

I also called Flanagan's thinking maybe they'd want us back, but they weren't interested. Apparently, we'd scared the hell out of the night manager.

CHARLIE BURKE (*manager, Flanagan's Irish Pub*): We hosted the Shivers' first-ever performance and launched them to fame. We're very proud of that. But no, we never had them back. It was a very bad night for us. As soon as the band left, beer sales tanked, though everybody acted wasted anyway. I had to break up a record number of fights. People whipped off their shirts and danced on tables. One did a whole strip show. People were getting each other off in the bathroom stalls. Somebody finger-painted the word SHIVER in menstrual blood on the mirror in the ladies'. I eventually had to call the cops and shut the place down early.

RAMONA: The manager told you *what*? That is nuts. I mean, when we left, the place felt like a funeral. I was all set to stick around and get shit-faced, but it was dead in there, so I took Malcolm up on his offer of midnight pancakes.

ERIC: Of course the world's wildest party started after I left and I missed it. It's the story of my life.

RAMONA: Don't get me wrong, though. I believe you. Seeing as what happened later, I'd say the place getting trashed by lunatics was pretty on brand for us.

LILY: I read about the accident in the paper. That poor man. Henry Lewis, a Canadian bishop. The driver didn't see him in his black vestments until it was almost too late, and then he panicked and stomped the gas instead of the brake.

I wondered what the bishop was doing so far from home. Why he'd traveled fifteen hundred miles to scream at Drake in a Denny's parking lot in the middle of the night with a knife in his hand.

The police said it was a medieval eucharistic knife used to prepare bread to celebrate the Mass. They planned to return this antique to the church.

CHARLOTTE SKINNER: Bishop Lewis was a venerated servant of the church. He earned his master of divinity at St. Peter's

Seminary in London, Ontario, and went on to gain a doctor of ministry degree.

After ordination to the priesthood, he taught sacred scripture at St. Peter's until returning to Canada. Following his ordination as a bishop, he took possession of the diocese of Saskatoon.

His untimely death was regrettable and a significant loss. It is not known why he was in Pennsylvania at that time. Any connection between his death and the tragic events that later occurred at Our Lady of Victory is gross speculation.

LILY: I read the newspaper article aloud to my bandmates before practice, but I had no takers on giving a crap. Everyone seemed focused on how big an impact we made on the crowd at Flanagan's and leveling up for the next gig. They'd all experienced the same performance high I had, and they wanted another taste.

As for Drake, he only winced and muttered, "He knew me."

Seeing how much the whole thing disturbed him, I dropped it.

MALCOLM: I didn't want any of us dwelling on the accident. It was bad luck.

Look, we'd debuted to a miracle review. We came out of the gate roaring. I wanted to keep that momentum going and win some traction. That meant we all needed to stay focused and polish our songs while I got us more gigs.

LILY: I went to the bathroom to be alone. There I prayed for Bishop Lewis's soul, that God would welcome him into Heaven. Then I prayed to Cecilia, patron saint of music and musicians, that she might intercede on the Shivers' behalf. I humbly asked her to help me make sure our music brought inspiration and joy.

MALCOLM: I felt like we'd invented a new musical form. This was lightning in a bottle. It was gonna be huge.

LILY: I just could not understand how our music had such a weird and powerful effect on people. It couldn't be the words, I thought.

"I'm fucking for a fight." A cool little hook and all, but come on. "No chains to hug me" and "Violence is a moniker for love" and "Why can't you be you?" They floated along the surface in our songs as feelings or points to ponder, like angry little koans with no right answer.

I asked Drake about it. He said, "The words don't say much, but the music itself is true. Our songs are like thought tattoos. A liminal STD."

If you say so, I thought. I mean, it had to be something. To me, music was magical, but it wasn't actual magic.

MALCOLM: Until then, practice, practice, practice.

RAMONA: I loved band practice. We'd get the annoying chitchat out of the way and warm up with a short jam. We'd share new ideas and sometimes yell at each other. Then we'd dive straight into it, developing new material while revisiting existing stuff to work through the tricky parts. The songs evolved to higher forms.

Kicking and screaming, I evolved too.

ERIC: The idea is you practice as a musician at home, and then you come together to practice as a band. You play until it looks effortless, which is where I learned swagger comes from, the real kind, not the fake-it-to-make-it kind.

What they call chops. You play enough, you start to gain style that shows not only in the music but also in how you walk and even how you brush your teeth.

LILY: Drake changed that night at Flanagan's. It started with the disappointed look he gave me when I refused to leave him. Like he didn't want me around.

I hated that look.

Two days later, he invited me to come with him to Easton, the easternmost of the Lehigh Valley's trinity of old industrial cities, to check out a new music shop. I couldn't resist. We hadn't gone on a real date since the show, and I hoped it would distract me from all the bad vibes.

You walk into a place like that, and it's instant gratification for a musician. You smell the wood, the metal, the new strings. You see guitars hanging on the walls, keyboards and drum kits, every other kind of instrument. Amplifiers sit stacked in rows, and books, audio gear, and accessories are on display. You hear musicians test-driving guitars with a little strumming, maybe a classic riff.

Music stores have always been one of my favorite places in the world. At the time, I rarely had enough money to buy anything, but boy did I ever love to look.

Drake saw me admiring a guitar pedal and hissed, "Take it."

I told him I couldn't do that.

He said, "Why?"

"Because it's wrong," I said.

He said, "Free will isn't tourism. It's living as a real person. As a god. Go for it."

Always the little voice in my head telling me a free spirit gave me a physical license to break the rules, only once again it sounded like Drake's and not mine. My gut, meanwhile, scolded me not to do it in my dad's voice, which settled it.

I said, "Okay." A little slip inside my messenger bag and I possessed it, along with a momentary thrill not unlike what I felt on stage playing at Flanagan's.

Drake said in a loud voice, "Hey, are you going to pay for that?"

I bolted straight out the door.

The next thing I knew, my sneakers pounded the sidewalk blocks away from the store. Arms pumping, lungs aching for oxygen, no longer propelled by any sense of thrill but instead a burning shame. Gasping for air, I finally stopped.

A hand landed on my shoulder, and I yelped.

It was Drake, laughing.

Pissed off, I yelled, "You dick! What the hell? That was humiliating."

He said, "Why?"

I told him I could have gotten caught doing something illegal.

He said, "So?"

Our song "Freedom Isn't Free" was about how you aren't truly free until it's tested. Until you test yourself to show you can walk the talk. Practice what you preach. Though in this case, Drake did the testing.

Inside the bag, the shoplifted stomp box felt heavy. I inspected it and thought about finding a way to return it. Whatever I'd gained wasn't worth everything I felt. What I'd actually paid for it.

He said, "Do you think God honestly cares if you took that pedal?"

In his view, all religion and even morality was the product of coercion. I only obeyed God because deep down, he scared me more than the Devil did.

"I just want to do unto others as I'd have them do to me," I said.

I pointed out the world worked better this way; it would be a moral truism whether God was there or not. The desire to be good is wired into us as much as selfishness. If we want to be tall, we should stand on others' shoulders, not on their faces.

He shook his head and said, "Why do you welcome shame as a friend?"

A long time ago, he told me, the first man and woman broke God's one rule and got themselves cast out of Eden. Ever since, humans lived with shame, even though they weren't cast out of paradise. No, they'd broken out of jail. In so doing, Adam and Eve sacrificed everything to give us free will. What Christianity labeled original sin, Drake regarded as a gift.

Why feel guilty about it?

I said, "If you love something, it's okay to put it first."

Drake said, "Then you really need to learn to love yourself."

RAMONA: Comrade Jenny told me the hotheads at the Squat had started talking behind my back. The amount of time and energy I gave the Shivers annoyed them. They said I was chasing a big record label contract and wanted to be a rock star.

She said, "They're calling you a sellout."

The worst insult you could give a punk and a hardcore class warrior. My first reaction was to punch some mouths that had been talking shit.

Comrade Jenny took me in when I was still running. She'd given me a home and a purpose. She was a tough old lady who'd fought the system her whole life. The Squat belonged to the people, but it ran on her anarchist philosophy.

In short, you could do anything you wanted as long as you didn't hurt anyone. Which meant I wouldn't be punching any loose lips.

I wanted to ask her if she thought I was selling out too, but I already knew I'd sinned. I'd swiped a few things from Malcolm's house that we could sell for the Squat, but they never left that basement. They ended up in a box. Every time I put something in it, I thought, This is mine, not yours.

MALCOLM: Things had a way of disappearing when Ramona was around.

ERIC: Once, I found a big box of stuff squirreled away near the drum kit. Missing gear and little items like a shoelace, a stale granola bar, a pair of sunglasses. It was weird. I knew it was Ramona's. I wanted to talk to her about it. I mean, most people don't just steal and hoard stuff for its own sake.

I never brought it up, though, because I didn't want to get murdered. Instead I'd dip into the box to get things when I needed them. A lost and found. Like, if I couldn't find my tuning peg, I knew where to look first.

RAMONA: All revolutions can be traced to one small act of rebellion. Not all revolutions work out the way you want them to.

To each according to her need, I thought. I gestured at the steel plant covered in rust and graffiti art and asked Comrade Jenny, "What if I need more than this?"

She said, "I see you wanting to give more to the movement. We could make music here. A record label for revolutionary music."

She was offering me a chance to do it my way. Get back to smashing the system with a sledgehammer. Be myself again.

It'd be angry music with zero production quality and hand-to-hand distribution, another lost cause. But it'd be my project. We're defined by our needs, and she thought that was what I needed.

The idea had its appeal. The Shivers had proven to be a whole lot of work for even more aggravation. Sometimes I'd look at Eric and want to punch him. He just had that kind of face. Malcolm I'd want to knock out for a whole lot of other reasons.

I'd take it out on my drums to good effect. It made me practice all the harder so I didn't have to hear Eric spew one of his theatrical sighs and Malcolm make his "helpful" suggestions while Drake laughed. Hell, I even started using a metronome so I could keep perfect time, all to avoid punching someone in the face.

MALCOLM: Speaking just for myself, I can say yes, my band drove me goddamn nuts. To call Drake challenging would be an award-winning understatement. The man seemed to walk around with a warning label that said, *Don't try this at home*, even though his mouth was always telling you to do just that.

I once came downstairs to find Drake strumming his guitar while Lily lay asleep on the floor, stark naked except for a primitive papier-mâché mask and headdress. Another nude couple snored on a couch, blood staining their mouths like clownish lipstick. Playing cards and shriveled mushrooms dotted the carpet.

At this point, I'd known Drake and Lily for like three weeks.

Drake said, "Oh, hey. We were playing strip poker, and it got out of hand."

When I launched my website, I'd done it all on my own. I enjoyed complete control. I answered only to myself. With the Shivers, I had to deal with this crap. Every single thing I wanted to do, I had to drag these toddlers with me.

He said, "This is my body."

He showed me a cut on his shoulder, which would scar into a question mark. Simultaneously, I regretted giving everyone a key to my basement while wondering if I had any Neosporin upstairs and if I should get it for him.

He said, "Pretty cool, huh?"

Then he started strumming again because he didn't care if I agreed it was cool.

RAMONA: Like Drake had months earlier, Comrade Jenny put me in one of those situations where a simple yes or no determines the rest of your life. In this case, a chance to build my own record label making revolutionary music.

I pictured it. Then I pictured going all the way with the Shivers. A miracle rise to the top. What that would actually mean.

Back then, a single record deal could buy you a house.

Then I thought about what it would cost, because nothing is free in this world. The music industry and its exploitation, the sellout bands cranking vanilla drivel like so many organ grinders and monkeys, the slow rationalization until you turned into a product, the fucking greed and egos—

Yeah, I was starting to want that.

Sellout? There were worse things one could be, like poor and helpless and alone. In Comrade Jenny's mind, I'd already strayed from the path. In my own mind as well. As Al Capone once said, If you're gonna steal, steal big.

Fucking for a fight, yes.

LILY: Drake suffered another one of his colossal nightmares. When I asked him about it the next morning, he said, "We'll play another show soon."

He believed his own dreams, however symbolic, contained real prophecy.

I was like, "That's a good thing, right?"

He only shook his head and said, "Things are about to get super weird."

I asked him what that meant.

"You wouldn't believe me if I told you," he said. "Even as a dream."

I said, "Paint it for me. What you saw."

He said, "Not here. The band needs to see this."

We walked over to Malcolm's house and went down into the band room. On one wall, Drake painted a giant black snake forming a question mark. While he worked, he said I could pitch in by surrounding the snake with firelight.

"But no fire," he said. "That's farther in the future. Just show the light, okay?"

I really went for it, shades of orange and yellow and gold. The snake appeared to dance on convection currents. I loved this about Drake, how a dream could become an act of creation.

He liked what I was painting. He said, "You got it. The light itself burns."

When the paint dried, I wrote out in capitals curving along the snake's back: THE SHIVERS.

Malcolm came stomping down the stairs wearing a black cap and gown.

I said, "Oh, did you graduate today?"

He ignored the question: "What in Christ's name are you doing to my wall?"

"This," I told him, "is our new band logo."

He said, "And this is me going to call a locksmith to change the lock."

With that, he stomped back upstairs while I yelled a congratulations after him. I started to feel a little bad for graffitiing his wall, but Drake laughed and reminded me that we were in a rock-and-roll band. If we couldn't make a mess every now and then, what was the point?

I looked at the painting we'd made. I could see his vision now. What did it mean? In dream symbolism, a snake can mean a lot of things. Creativity, sexual temptation, transformation. Also fear, callousness, and concealed threats.

He said, "It's a cross. A cross that's mine to bear. What it is, exactly, I'm not sure. But it's big. As big as the world. That I do know."

Later, I'd find out that Drake's cross belonged to all of us.

ERIC: We'd come up with this one song that really hit a nerve with me, called "You Can." It was about giving yourself permission to be who you are, even if you're something that society—or Ma, in my case, still nagging me about getting a real job—doesn't want you to be.

The song had this hook where Drake sang, "Why can't you be you?" And I thought, Yeah, why the hell not? Only I didn't know who I was, not really. And that was a sad thing but also a thrill, as it meant I could invent an ideal me, a true me. I could fake it and make it at the same time. Be the change I wanted to see.

During the first months of the Shivers, I found myself looking up to Drake as a role model. He made everything appear so damn easy. Being cool, making music, getting what you want through sheer force of personality, women thinking you're hot.

I mean, I would have murdered to be with a girl like Lily. Sometimes it was hard to even look at them, as they reminded me of so much I was missing.

MALCOLM: Drake had everything but acted like he didn't need anything.

ERIC: He once said to me, "Your bass has a soul. Are you in harmony with it? The souls of your bandmates, their instruments? Everything has a soul trying to get out and be heard."

I had no idea how to answer that. I thought: I'm still trying to get my own soul to come out and say hi.

Drake elevated everything we did to a higher level. Think what you want, but the dude was unique. Malcolm handled logistics, and we all loved Lily, but Drake was our leader.

He gave the Shivers its soul.

Another time, he told me, "We defined God. That makes us

God. You know how they say, *As above, so below*? Sometimes it's the other way around."

Reminding me again that if music can change a person, it can change the world. It was certainly starting to change me. The world, I thought, would fall in line.

RAMONA: Eric followed Drake around until he started imitating him. It was really annoying. He looked like a guy trying real hard to be something he wasn't.

MALCOLM: I think Drake liked the idea of being worshipped.

ERIC: I went into a diner one night after practice to grab some takeout, and there was Joey Grasso's high-wattage grin beaming at me from one of the booths. Jimmy Gibbs was there—I always liked him—along with the drummer and keyboardist. Wedged between them was this little guy with a pointed nose whom I assumed had replaced me on bass. They all looked flushed like they'd run a marathon, and I guessed they'd just performed.

Joey waved me over, and I asked them how they were doing.

He said, "Oh, you know, summer is always great for business. We're just enjoying our cake." Meaning they'd gotten paid.

The bassist snickered and said, "This is the guy?"

I said, "I joined a rock band."

I told them all about the Shivers, how the music's sound was like biting on tinfoil you couldn't stop eating, the review we'd gotten for our first show, how far we'd go. The whole time, I'm thinking about Drake and how he could make you feel in or out of the club with his attitude. Bragging without bragging.

I turned on the swagger full blast. I'd earned it. These guys played covers. They were technicians. Mechanics. I was an artist creating new music, inventing a whole new sound.

Joey said, "Never heard of you guys. But wow, you're in a band."

The bassist glanced over at him and said, "Yeah, I see what you mean now." Like they were having a whole other conversation I wasn't a part of. "Tinfoil."

Jimmy just gave me this sympathetic look. He said, "Good for you, man."

I left without my takeout. In some way, I'd been ambushed but couldn't understand what had happened. I'd thought after sharing my good news that I'd, you know, earn a little respect.

I ran the conversation in my head and imagined what I could have said different. The whole time, it'd been like they knew me better than I knew myself. I felt like nothing.

The next morning, Ma told me Walmart was hiring stock unloaders.

Nothing, I kept thinking. An empty vessel. That was me. A nobody.

Okay, I decided.

Like the song said: You can.

Since Dad died, the only thing that lit a fire under my ass was my PlayStation games. When I joined the Shivers, I only did it because I thought it sounded cool and it might make me cool too. I barely put in the time and effort to practice.

There was one thing I hadn't tried yet, which was to stop trying to be something and instead just *do* something. I dedicated myself to my bass, thinking it deserved its chance to be heard far more than a dumb nothing like me did.

Every day, all day, I practiced with the discipline of a Buddhist monk. I never worked so hard for so little and so much. I'd even play bass in my dreams, endless grinding repetition of notes and chords.

After a few days of this, I came home one night from band

practice sweaty and happy and fulfilled, as if I'd just played Madison Square Garden. The next morning, Ma didn't have the classifieds ready with job positions circled. Instead she asked me how practice went.

She saw a change in me and liked it. I'd found my purpose.

Drake was right. Music can change a man, and his world changes with him. I was living proof.

LILY: Drake's nightmares continued to plague him, more brutal and frequent. After a while, I started to dream along with him. Mine a recurring nightmare of a hideous, squat little gargoyle perched on his chest while he slept, whispering in his ear. I couldn't help him, breathless and paralyzed with fear.

These night terrors always shifted to my parents' house. My mother still bawling, my father still raging, only I wasn't actually there. I tried to tell them I was sorry and to please go on with their lives. I yelled over and over until I made myself hoarse, but they couldn't see or hear me.

At last, I decided I'd visit them and try to part ways on a better note.

Yes, they'd smothered me, but I understood how they'd had me late in life and saw me as their miracle baby, unique and precious. I knew they wanted to protect me even if I didn't need or want it anymore. I'd cut the umbilical cord, but there'd been no way of doing that without cutting them too.

I hadn't wanted to end the relationship. I simply needed to redefine it.

When I told Drake about it, he shook his head.

He said, "It's in their nature to control you. They'll never accept you if you walk any other path than the one they assigned you."

It made me angry, hearing this. I should have known what he'd say.

He added, "You can't both be happy. You have to choose. You or them."

After I shoplifted at the music store, Drake had kept up with his little tests. That's how I ended up going back into a bar to give some girl who'd mouthed off to me a black eye. How I ended up smoking after all. All to prove some stupid, stubborn point that I'd already done the worst thing I could imagine to free myself, which was break my mother's heart.

I should have refused to allow myself to be tested, but I didn't. I was a young woman still desperately in love. I hated disappointing him. I was in it so deep that I normalized behavior that should have set off fire alarms. This time, however, I finally stood up for myself. I needed him to understand it was important to me.

Drake said, "Go ahead, then. Talk to Mom and Dad, if that's what you want."

Only, I should do it right. He hated any injustice and believed it should be punished, not rewarded with empathy. No renegotiation needed. If I owed them the truth, then I should pay the bill in full.

Tell my father he was a controlling tyrant. Tell my mother she was a manipulative, passive enabler. Tell them both they would never see me again.

At the edge of tears, I glared at him until I found my voice.

I said, "Are you trying to drive me away? Because it seriously looks to me like you're trying to drive me away."

He said, "Where we're going, you can't have it both ways. Just like you can't have it both ways with your parents. You need to decide who you are and if you're in or out."

Drake changed after Flanagan's, but here's the thing.

I was changing too.

That power I felt playing on stage, I'd brought some of it

home with me. Joan Jett and the Great Kat felt less like idols to me now, more like spirit guides.

They told me the only test that counted was the one where I didn't fail myself.

MALCOLM: I'd been kicking myself that we still didn't have merch, have some CDs printed, or even put out a clipboard so people could sign up for a mailing list. When we played our next show, we'd go all-out. *If* we played a next show.

Drake told me not to worry about any of that stuff. He said we were going to be big. He said this like one might say the sun will come up tomorrow.

I didn't have his faith, but a part of me always loved hearing it, even after I found out his source of confidence was one of his prophetic dreams. I told him I hadn't gotten anywhere near scoring us another gig, even after the terrific *Valley Scene* review.

He said, "Try again, Doubting Mal."

Did I mention I was kicking myself I'd agreed to do this band thing at all? I'd just graduated, making all this starkly real to me. I could hear the clock ticking.

I made another Hail Mary round of calls. Imagine my shock as this time I scored not once but twice.

The Sunburst Music Festival was one, but that wasn't the big fish.

We'd also be playing the Hobo Underground. A slot in a triple-header the second weekend of June.

A huge step up for us, practically an evolutionary leap. Standing-room capacity of four hundred. Full backline. Quality gear. Great lighting. A ten-foot-square media screen behind the stage. A dedicated sound engineer.

After setting up the booking details, I hung up feeling weirdly unsettled, anxious, and thrilled. A strange feeling. Later I realized it was hope.

ERIC: The Hobo Underground! A huge deal. I mean, it was small by musical venue standards but a hell of a lot bigger deal than some pub. We all got super stoked at the news. It validated the hard work we were putting in. And Sunburst too, like icing on the big, fat cake.

RAMONA: It certainly simplified the decision I had to make.

MALCOLM: All hail the band manager.

LILY: Once you notice one small harsh truth, the big ones suddenly pop into focus. Drake hadn't changed after Flanagan's. I just saw some things more clearly, all the things I'd accepted as normal but weren't. The tests, the judgment, the way he controlled everything about our relationship, his inability to tell me he loved me. I got more and more pissed off about it.

One night, during practice, I stopped playing and said, "If I want to have a relationship with my parents, that's my choice."

The song came to a screeching halt. Awkward silence.

Eric said, "Good to know, Lil."

I glared at Drake, who shrugged, though my choice clearly rankled him.

He said, "Every ex-con misses prison a little."

No empathy, nothing. There's a line between living as a non-conformist and being a bit of a sociopath, and I'd lost my certainty where the man I loved stood.

Right then, I saw red, but I wasn't as angry at Drake as I was at myself. Even now, I was asking permission. Still acting like a child.

I said, "You hate my father, but you're just like him."

I hadn't freed myself at all. I'd simply traded.

Drake said nothing. What I'd said had struck him. Despair flickered across his face the way it had after the bishop called him an abomination.

Our first real fight, and I'd shattered him.

Ramona stood from her drum throne and looked at me and then at Drake as if deciding who to yell at.

She said, "Let's get out of here, Lily. You need a girls' night out."

She took me to the Squat where she lived.

The kids had a bonfire going and a rave in full swing. As upset as I was, it made a nice change of scene. Anarcho-punk graffiti covered the walls. People drank forties of malt liquor and danced around a bonfire while house music throbbed, a pounding four-on-the-floor beat that made me want to dance.

Ramona saw the look on my face and said, "Oh yeah, the Squat is Burning Man pretty much twenty-four seven."

Talk about freedom. I was ready for anything. For weeks, my life had revolved around Drake and the band. I also appreciated the chance to get to know Ramona better. She was a true punk. We each did a tab of E and started dancing. We ended up dancing most of the night.

Ramona started kissing me, and I thought, Okay, we're doing this.

RAMONA: Yes, I once kissed those lovely lips. Eat your heart out, boys.

I preferred men, but when it came to Drake or Lily, I preferred Lily. As attractive as Drake was, he never truly felt safe to me. Lily did. Kissing her was the easiest thing in the world.

So yeah, we were doing this.

The music stopped, and a voice boomed over the microphone: *Fee-fi-fo-fum! If you'd like to play, it's time to run!*

I told Lily, "It's basically Hide and Seek. If he catches you—it's against the rules to say what happens, but I can tell you it's pretty gross."

She said we might stay and keep dancing, then.

I said, "It's always more fun if you run."

Grabbing her hand, I took her to my favorite hiding spot. For a while, we stood gasping in the dark. Someone screamed in the distance. Tag, you're it. I put my hand on her breast and pulled her toward me.

It's the whole point of the game. It was the hookup hour.

LILY: I tried.

RAMONA: She wasn't into it. I told her not to sweat it. Music, chocolate, sex. It's all the same to the brain. But so, so different for the body and mind. You can't always just pull a trigger, and *bang.*

LILY: Even then, I was trying to be someone I wasn't. So many things ran through my mind, clamoring for recognition.

A little voice said I'd never be my true self until I'd freed myself from anyone trying to control me, even if it was under the guise of help.

A much louder voice worried that if I ever lost Drake, I'd go right back to the way I used to be. Small and insignificant, afraid and living the wrong life.

It all added up to a whole lot of anger. The honeymoon, it seemed, was over.

I might have traded Dad for Drake, but I still acted like a child, accepting the same dynamic. I needed to change. Performing at Flanagan's, I'd discovered my power. I only needed to use it. Learn to love yourself. Right.

I told Ramona, "If he wants to be with me, he's going to have to accept me the way I am and that I have rules." Saying it out loud made it real. "The relationship is going to have to be more equitable."

She said, "Uh-huh." Not buying it for a minute.

Her doubt triggered my stubbornness.

Later that night, I came home to hash things out and heard whispering in our bedroom. When I touched the doorknob, the whispering stopped.

"Lilith?" Sounding like a child crying out for his mother.

I went into the dark room. Drake lay alone on our bed. He'd been talking in his sleep. He raised the covers for me to climb in.

He said, "You were right. I'm sorry."

The bed was hot, but he shivered as I held his skinny, trembling body. Some kind of fever gripped him. Once again, I saw the terrified, uncertain little boy he must have been. That's who I believed he was, deep down. The part of him I could never stop loving.

I said, "I don't know why you're trying to drive me away."

Drake said, "It's coming, Lily. I can't stop it."

I had no idea what he was talking about.

He said, "If you stay with me, you'll be a part of it too. If you're a part of it, you have to be like me. If you can't handle it, it'll destroy you."

Drake was trying to protect me from something.

I told him, "Whatever's coming, we'll face it together."

Then I stroked his hair until he fell asleep again.

Once again, I thought I could have it both ways. That I could have him without losing myself entirely in the process. I didn't know yet who he really was.

INVOLUNTARY KENOSIS

THE HOBO UNDERGROUND SHOW
JUNE 12, 1999

On June 12, 1999, the Shivers played the Hobo Underground as part of a triple-header that included Hate Mail and Snuggle Skunk. It proved another pivotal moment that would change everything for the infant rock band.

MALCOLM: The Hobo Underground. Sheryl Crow and Sting once performed here, along with a whole lot of other artists.

In such august company, I felt fairly chuffed about my little band that could. Later, I'd realize how lucky we'd gotten. The gig at Flanagan's. Vince Amato showing up that very night and writing a review. My phone call to Hobo the same day a band dropped out of a triple-header offering equal billing.

The only downer was we'd be playing between Snuggle Skunk and Hate Mail. Shoe-gazer bands trying to be My Bloody Valentine. I didn't really see us in the same category, and I didn't like the idea of being typecast. But that's the problem with being somewhat original. They don't know where to put you, so they shoehorn you into the nearest slot.

LILY: That whole night turned out horrible. I hate talking about it, though it wasn't the worst of what we'd experience.

ERIC: An awesome thing to be playing the Hobo Underground, but I'd never been there. It wasn't until I walked into the box that my mind got blown.

I totally forgot to swagger, though right then I felt like a rock star.

LILY: The excitement walking into a place like that is hard to describe. Empty but full of potential, like a blank canvas, or a void hiding an act of creation. It's waiting for your sound to turn it into what you want it to be. It's still innocent.

We filled it with corruption.

MALCOLM: I wanted everything to go well and planned accordingly. I made lists of what to bring and what to leave home. Amp settings dialed, fresh batteries in the pedalboard. I even put together a respectable oh-shit box filled with emergency stuff like backup strings, tuning pegs, and aspirin.

We weren't pro yet, not by a long shot, but I saw no harm in acting like it.

RAMONA: Honestly, playing at such a big venue so soon scared me. I didn't like being scared. It made me want to hit first. Barring that, run until I'd reached sanctuary in someplace new.

Desire and discipline had gotten me this far. I kept my eye on the prize.

ERIC: My only regret right then was that I should have invited Ma to the show, so she could see where all the time and hard work went.

Looking back now, I am so glad I did not.

JIMMY GIBBS (*rhythm guitarist, Iron & Ivories*): Eric had really moved up in the world. I felt genuinely happy for him. We'd played together in Joey Grasso's wedding band. Founding members, you might say, and fellow veterans of bridal tantrums and Joey's lectures on the pursuit of excellence.

After Eric quit, I figured he'd go back to smoking weed and playing his games, you know, treading water. I knew he'd been fooling around with a new band. I had no idea he was this hardcore.

Man, he was hilarious when he called me up to come to the show to help sell merch, some T-shirts and CDs and other stuff. He tried to be all cool, but I could tell he had no idea what a huge deal it was to play Hobo Underground. So many great bands did a show there. Some even got their start on that very stage. It was actually cute.

No, I wasn't jealous or anything. Damn. Okay. Maybe a little. But I'd hit my thirties by then. At the time, I rolled with Iron & Ivories, and I had a wife, kids, and a dog. I'd left wanting to be a rock star somewhere far behind me. Playing weddings didn't bother me a bit. I just loved to play. I liked making people happy. Get them to dance and let it all hang out in one of the few events that life offers where it is perfectly permissible to embarrass yourself a little.

As long as I got to perform, it didn't matter what, where, or to who.

Though Eric had it right about one thing, which was that sometimes, I hoped someone would smack that grin off ol' Joey Grasso's John-Travolta-lookin' face.

MALCOLM: Hate Mail took their sweet time doing sound check just because they could, practically rubbing it in our faces that they were the senior band. Equal billing, but they kept referring to themselves as the headliner. They argued with the sound engineer and otherwise threw their weight around like rock stars.

The whole time, I took notes. How the house engineer handled the line check. The way Hate Mail gave their stage plot to the soundman in advance. I was surprised how boomy the band sounded.

I must have said this aloud, because Eric's friend Jimmy said to me, "Once this place fills up with people, the acoustics will balance out real nice."

I said, "Yeah. I know."

Then I scribbled another note. The more I learned about the music business, the less I realized I actually knew anything.

JIMMY GIBBS: The way he micromanaged me about setting up the merch, I'd figured Malcolm for the band manager.

MALCOLM: When Hate Mail left the stage, the lead guitarist yelled to me, "Don't screw up tonight. We want them good and warm when you hand them off to us." Later, I'd think of a dozen good comebacks, but at the time I had nothing.

JIMMY GIBBS: The look on his face. I couldn't help but laugh. Welcome to the music business.

LILY: Sitting in his control booth, the sound engineer walked us down the line check and then had us play a song. He walked around the space to give an ear to the overall sound mix. Back in his booth, he tweaked everything.

ERIC: The sound guy knew his stuff. He had us dialed in no time.

JIMMY GIBBS: Eric introduced me to the rest of the band. The lovely Lily broke my heart in an instant. With Ramona, I kept my distance. Drake just smiled at me.

My boy had prepped me that his band's frontman was some kind of life guru. He was all, "Wait until you meet this dude! He'll change your life!"

Instead Drake asked me, "What do you think God sounds like?"

I was like, What the hell is this guy talking about? He just stared at me, and I realized he expected an answer.

I gestured around me and said, "I imagine he sounds just like this." You know, meaning the universe and everything in it, every burp, laugh, fart, and song.

The dude nodded and said, "Then you're in for one hell of a show."

I said to Eric, "Melt their faces tonight." My way of telling him to break a leg.

Man, I have to say, Drake hardly impressed me as some kind of guru, but in the end, he wasn't wrong.

LILY: I chain-smoked Salems in the green room and watched musicians swap out drumskins and guitar strings, sharpening themselves for the stage. It turns out that being in a band is a whole lot of hurry up and wait. And wait, and wait.

And sometimes, the wait is pure murder.

Drake sat next to me on the ratty couch with a little smile on his face and his eyes closed, content as the Buddha. A steaming mug of tea sweetened with honey, which he drank to lube his throat, rested in easy reach on the coffee table. I took another drag on my Salem while my knee jittered up and down in a blur.

I can't say we were in a perfect place right then, but things felt stable. Drake's nightmares had faded. He'd stopped testing me like a jerk, and I no longer allowed myself to be tested. Otherwise, he still made me crazy as he went on making me want him while making me feel like I could never truly have him.

I looked around the green room. Three bands filled the place, which stank of pot, incense, stale beer, cigarette smoke, and male sweat. Except for the keyboardist from Snuggle Skunk and the rhythm guitarist from Hate Mail, all the musicians were men. Some had brought their girlfriends, who wore skimpy tank tops, drank too much, and howled at every little thing.

I didn't want to party. I wanted to perform.

MALCOLM: Even when I'm a musician hanging out with musicians, I'm not cool. I talked shop with Snuggle Skunk's manager and roadies the whole time.

RAMONA: I had to set some of those knuckleheads straight that Korn was in fact a nu-metal band and actually pioneered it. I probably drank too much to take the edge off so I didn't accidentally cut anybody with it.

ERIC: I paired off with the bassists of the other bands. To them, I was a baby in this game, but I didn't mind. My bass was perfect, I wasn't. Anyway, you give someone a chance to show off, and they'll teach you everything they know.

I watched them do some lines off the coffee table and thought, When in Rome and all that, but Lily stopped me with a glare and slowly shook her head. I have to say, for all the stereotypes about rockers flying off the deep end with easy sex and drugs, I saw surprisingly little of it. We always played it straight-edge.

LILY: I had to pee something fierce, but I stuck close to Drake so the men would leave me alone. Even that didn't deter two guys from asking me why I wasn't smiling. I told them to fuck off and went back to my finger exercises.

Soon I'd be on stage again. I was starting to feel very good.

VINCE AMATO (*music contributor, the* Valley Scene): I felt like I'd discovered these crazy kids when I whipped up that review about their first show for the *Scene*. When I saw the Hobo booked them, I decided to check out this spooky little band again and see how they were faring.

Everything in the music business looks more glamorous than it actually is, at least until you're a rock star playing sold-out stadiums. That goes double for rock reviewers like me. Like everything else, it's about how much money you got and how much weight you're carrying. That's where all the glamour comes from, having it all.

Basically, I did it as a hobby that earned me beer money. For real money, I worked as a firefighter. The department responded to up to a thousand fire-related emergencies in Bethlehem every year. An important job. I loved it.

Being a rock reviewer had one thing going for it, though, which was freebies. You basically got paid in perks. Free CDs, mostly, and tickets to concerts all over PA and Jersey. Some reviewers went on tours.

I also enjoyed a certain access. I'd get to go backstage and interview the musicians and maybe party a little. Musicians all desperately want to be cool and love reading about themselves being portrayed as cool, so they lavish attention and goodies to win your favor. I thought about trying to score an interview with Drake Morgan after the show, maybe get close to that gorgeous Lily Lawless.

I didn't want to admit it, but the Shivers had put a hook in me. This one lyric: *Why can't you be you?* For three days, it was always there in my head, grilling me. Like a musical earworm I couldn't get rid of, only this one punched me right in the soul. When it finally faded, I felt a little empty. I actually missed it.

That show at Flanagan's had been a real trip. I was curious to see what might come next. I wanted to know if their music had anything else to say to me.

JIMMY GIBBS: The cheering swelled around me as Snuggle Skunk took the stage. After the first few songs, I started daydreaming and checking my watch. Shoe-gazing has never been my thing. I mean, I love the experimental aspect of it and whatnot, all the turbo distortion splattering the walls. The caught-in-amber feeling of having had a really good or heartbreaking dream that I wished I could remember. I get why people dig it.

But it grows ponderous for me after a while. I like rock that grabs me by the gonads, not tickles them to death. And I come to a show to see a *show*, not watch moody musicians stare at readouts on stomp boxes around their feet, playing their instruments like I'm not even there. It's just not my kind of energy.

Anyway, the audience thought differently than I did. They cheered the band off stage. And I thought, Eric, you lucky bastard, this crowd is yours as long as you don't screw it up. They'd gotten over their shyness and were grooving, ready and willing to love the next band if it delivered.

VINCE AMATO: When the first band finished their set, everyone started clapping and whistling except this one guy near me. He glared at the stage without blinking. I knew right away he was a fellow fan of the Shivers.

After I noticed him, I spotted the others easily. Here and there in the crowd, some guy or gal would be standing alone, grimacing with their teeth clenched hard enough to chew iron.

RAMONA: In the green room, Malcolm pulled us together in a huddle for what I figured would be a long-winded pep talk.

I said, "Let's tear the fucking roof off." And went out to do just that.

Like I said, I'd had a few.

MALCOLM: I was like, Can we just please not blow this?

ERIC: This time, I remembered to swagger as I went out. The lights were low, the crowd babbling in the dark, the vibe good and warm.

Then I heard a loud whoop and spotted Jimmy waving from the merch table. I grinned and pointed at him. I plugged in and got ready to rock, no faking required. I'd already done my part. My bass would handle the rest.

RAMONA: I settled in behind the drums and twirled a stick while I waited. After we were introduced, the lights washed the stage in a hot glare, super bright in my eyes. The audience stood in shadow, but they were applauding.

Behind and above me, the big media screen lit up with an image Malcolm had put together on his computer:

A snake forming a crude question mark, our band name curving along its back. The same snake that Lily and Drake had painted on our band room wall. I'd grown used to it there, but seeing it fill a ten-foot screen blew me away.

And I thought, This is real. I'm in a rock band.

Between that and the beer, I was feeling no fear.

VINCE AMATO: The Shivers took the stage. Drake Morgan said something like, "Don't worry, it'll all be over soon," and started playing his guitar.

Then I blacked out.

LILY: The same as when we played Flanagan's, I felt raw power flow through me, like I was a conduit for channeling my guitar goddesses. I touched a mental place where I'd feel close to physically transforming into pure spirit and ascending.

Then the darkness pulled me back to the earth. The crowd slowly congealing, everyone tensed like deer gawking at onrushing headlights. Me feeling so right, the scene feeling so damn wrong.

This time, the change was almost instant. Faces twisted into painful grimaces. Then the entire room froze as if someone flipped a switch.

JIMMY GIBBS: The last thing I remember is the frontman's eyes glowing yellow.

ERIC: The music flowed just as we'd practiced and practiced.

Swaying on the beats, Lily strummed the rhythm. Ramona kept the train running on time. Malcolm added layers of harmonic input. I held the bassline underwater while Drake sustained a single shrill note for five full seconds, punctuating it with a mind-shredding bend.

We'd finally started to play like a band. A single-minded thing with a life of its own. Like a sixth sense, I knew everything my bandmates were doing, fully plugged into the groove, feeding on their energy and amplifying it back.

RAMONA: I killed it that night. Through endless practice, I knew every beat in every song in my blood. I'd mastered how to juggle rhythms and keep time. I'd trained my posture to free up all my limbs. I'd grudgingly learned to control my volume so my sound blended and didn't beat down the rest of the band.

LILY: My fretting hand pinned chords. My strumming fingers gave the song its relentless, ethereal pulse. This chord progression always made me picture a violent avalanche happening in slow motion, tumbling down toward a tiny town.

Then Ramona banged out a startling drum fill, dreadlocks flying like Medusa snakes, and carried us all to the next transition. Taking my cue, I sang a high-octave *ah* in staccato repetition while Drake started a new melody and kept it going, working his way up to his next guitar solo.

He sang, "Freedom isn't free."

RAMONA: Another surprise ending in the works. Our songs never concluded by repeating the chorus or hook but by spawning new mutant offspring. Layers of sound and meaning that went deeper and deeper.

"Wheels within wheels," Drake described it to me once. To him, a song should be a reflection of how he perceived reality.

What a liminal space sounded like. A soundtrack for Purgatory.

ERIC: Slider buzzsaws, man.

MALCOLM: The audience was enthralled. A musician's wet dream.

RAMONA: Blinded by the hot stage lights, I thrashed my sticks.

LILY: The audience turned into mannequins with big terrified eyes painted on them. Their faces started to throb with the beat.

Wake up, I prayed. Please wake up.

"Freedom isn't free," Drake sang again, this time adding, "Until you test it."

Then someone did wake. My eyes spotted movement near the front of the crowd. My heart flooded me with relief. Smiling dreamily, a woman turned to the man next to her and swung her fist right into his jaw.

The man staggered until reaching some new equilibrium. Mouth slack, his eyes never leaving the band. I gasped but kept playing. My hands knew what to do. No longer sure exactly what I'd seen, the hot lights shining in my eyes, the audience popping into existence and then fading out into glimmer.

I looked over at Drake. He was laughing.

VINCE AMATO: When I came out of it, the band had finished playing and just stood there staring back at us. I'd somehow missed the whole set. Judging by the confused faces around me, I knew I wasn't alone.

This struck me as some next-level Jedi mind control shit. I didn't like it one bit. I felt like something had been done to me, only I'd have to wait to see what it was.

The crowd started to boil. A few scuffles broke out as people got handsy with each other. A couple got into some really loud sex somewhere. A woman let out a shrill scream. Glass shattered as a guy hurled his beer straight into the bottles lined up behind the bar and skipped out laughing.

JIMMY GIBBS: Whoa, I remember thinking. *That* was trippy. For a few seconds, I had no idea where I was. The atmosphere had somehow shifted from electric to hysteria. People swarmed the merch table. They grabbed T-shirts and just walked away with them. A girl sat on the table sobbing while some dude knelt in front of her and went to town slurping and sucking on her toes. A blonde ripped the mailing list off the clipboard and stuffed it in her mouth and started chewing.

LILY: It was like a horror movie. I mean it *felt* like a horror movie, something Dario Argento would dream up. The familiar turned into the unfamiliar. That feeling of madness. The unsettling realization that everyone's lost their mind except you and that they're slowly figuring out you don't belong.

RAMONA: My Spidey-sense had gone full red. I stood at my drum kit, ready for anything.

LILY: This guy jumped onto the stage already tugging at his fly. His eyes bored into mine. He yelled, "Gonna show you what you been missing, dolly."

The next thing I knew, Ramona swung around her drum kit and *bang*, punched that guy right off the stage. He went flying and didn't get up.

Through it all, Drake couldn't stop laughing.

ERIC: I kept thinking: Thank you, you're a great audience! You're a great audience! Now please stop!

LILY: All I could think was: Did *we* do this?

MALCOLM: Someone pulled the fire alarm, and the place started to empty out. Everyone whooped, as if this was a signal to take the party someplace else. Eric was being useless, Lily had her arms wrapped around her guitar in a tight hug, and Ramona pumped her fists in the air while screaming, "Who else wants some?"

"Pack up the gear," I yelled at them. "Haul ass! We're getting out of here."

I wasn't dying for rock and roll tonight.

VINCE AMATO: I vacated the premises quick. Driving home, I thought about calling the cops, only I had no idea what I could tell them.

A rock band is hypnotizing people and making them crazy. Sure thing, pal. I'd be the one they put in the rubber room.

I worried they'd somehow made me crazy too.

By the time I got home, it was late. I parked on the street in front of my house and lit a cig. I stared at the match for a while before it went out. An old feeling came over me.

My neighbors across the street included a family of four. Bill was the type to offer a hand if he saw you doing yard work. The wife always gave me a big friendly wave as she got into their station wagon. The kids always showed respect. They had a big American flag hanging over their porch. Real salt of the earth.

They needed saving.

JIMMY GIBBS: The old dude offering me a blowjob was the last straw. The merch table flipped and crashed as people piled around me. I wanted the Hobo's oversize security guys to lend me a hand, but they were too busy curb-stomping some poor kid curled in a ball on the floor. Screw this, I thought. I'm out.

The music business is weird, and I'd seen and, yes, done a lot of weird things. But I never witnessed anything like this. A whole music hall magically turned into a violent and horny loony bin.

I went home to my wife and kids and had never felt such gratitude and relief hearing Emily snoring next to me. I almost cried at how normal it was.

LILY: After we loaded out in a rush, I sat trembling in the back of the van. Ramona glared out the windshield, ready for anything. Eric opened the door to puke onto the asphalt. Behind the wheel,

Malcolm bounced in his seat and kept talking about what a good show it was, how hot we were as a band.

I heard sirens wail in the distance. Cars squealing and the crash of metal a few blocks away. Outside, someone started yelling the same thing over and over, though I couldn't make out the words. It felt like a night of lunacy.

I nudged Ramona and mouthed a quick *thank you*. She gave me a blank stare.

"For punching that guy right off the stage," I filled in.

She said, "Oh, that." She shrugged.

I had a sense she'd done it as much for herself as she had for me. I couldn't give it much thought, because the door opened and Drake swung into the passenger seat. He beamed a happy grin at me.

"Holy shit," he said. "Wasn't that so cool?"

VINCE AMATO: From the trunk, I took out a crowbar and walked over whistling. Bill's house stood dark and quiet, everyone asleep. With a little muscle, I wrenched the front door open. Scooping decorative pillows and a blanket from the couch in the living room, I crossed into the kitchen and piled them on the stove. Then I flipped on the gas burners and lit another match.

Back in my car, I watched the fire dance. It engulfed the main floor in no time, and I thought, Uh-oh, look what I just did. I waited for Bill and his family to come out—I was really rooting for them—but they never did.

I didn't have any regrets about it. The biggest, oldest, longest itch I'd ever endured had just been scratched. I set three fires in all before they arrested me. Nine people burned to death, hence you having to visit me behind bars for this little interview.

I'd like to blame it all on the Shivers, but that demon has always lived in my head. Pyromania, it's called. Playing with fire.

An accident as a kid that turned into something else, something I'd pushed far down and kept buried deep.

I guess that night brought it all back out. Me asking, Why can't I be me?

Now here I am, being me in prison.

I'd rather not live behind iron bars, but overall, I don't mind. I know who I am and what I am. It's for the best. If they ever let me out, I know exactly what I'd do. I'd torch the whole city to the ground just to watch it burn.

JIMMY GIBBS: Over the next few days, I dreaded hearing from Eric. I'd really let him down, though I hadn't expected the crowd to turn into a bunch of lunatics. He never called, though, and I went back to my life and its comforting routines of work and family.

At band practice, I started to tell the story for a laugh when Joey cut me off. He told me he didn't even want to hear Eric's dumb name. He said we needed to learn a new song to add to our list. "This Kiss" by Faith Hill. He'd started to get requests to play it for the first dance.

Then Joey grinned his John Travolta grin, looking like the boy welcoming you to his birthday party that had everything, clowns and a magician and even pony rides, and I laid into him with everything I had.

My first punch crashed against his ear, and I sneered with a hot flash of exultation at seeing that stupid grin wiped right off his face.

I remember him clearly yelling, "Cut it out."

The panic and surprise in his voice gave me a piercing thrill. I swung again, missing with so much momentum I staggered, and then I landed an uppercut that clipped his chin and almost broke my strumming hand.

My next punch barely started when Joey sprang into a whirlwind blur.

Bang, bang, bang. He beat the living shit out of me.

I laughed all the way to the hospital. I was missing a tooth.

Emily and I ended up moving to New Jersey. I couldn't even be in the same state with Joey Grasso. Not because I was scared of him but because I was too afraid what I'd do if I saw him again.

And as hard as I tried, I could never figure out why I took it to that level.

You don't know me, but I assure you I am not that guy. I'm a total pacifist. Ask Emily. Ask my kids. Hell, ask anybody. They'll tell you I don't have a violent bone in my body.

I mean, that night…I blacked out for an entire set, and when I came out of it, everyone in that place lost their mind.

You might think I'm crazy, but I honestly believe that music did something to our heads.

I know the Shivers changed their sound. I know they would go on to play sold-out concerts in stadiums across the country. I know nothing weird like that ever happened across the ten albums they ended up producing.

I don't care. I'll never listen to that goddamn band again.

GNAWING GNOSIS

THE SUNBURST MUSIC FESTIVAL
JULY 4, 1999

A*fter their second show ended in outright mayhem, the Shivers now faced a peculiar problem. Their new band had a magnetic and mesmerizing sound. This sound, however, appeared to convert random impulses into feverish compulsions among its listeners.

Individually and as a group, they pondered what it all meant as the Sunburst Music Festival approached.

STEPHEN WISE (*editor in chief, the* Valley Scene): When I received a review from Vince Amato for the Shivers' performance at the Hobo Underground, I was surprised. He had a voracious musical appetite and never saw the same band twice unless it was AC/DC or the Grateful Dead. Besides that, we rarely covered a band more than once, especially so soon after a prior review.

When I read what he sent me, count me as more than surprised.

REVIEW SUBMITTED BY VINCE AMATO:

What caught my ear this weekend: The Shivers striving against the Demiurge to call the Monad. The Shivers joining lost souls to the Unknown Father. The Shivers planting the seeds of gnosis to grow salvation. The Shivers spreading the gospel of knowing and obeying the one true god that is you. The Shivers igniting the divine spark that will burn Bethlehem and after it the world.

STEPHEN WISE: Needless to say, I didn't run the piece, and it wasn't long after that I found out Vince had been arrested. Did I visit him in jail? No, I did not. I mean, I liked the guy. I liked his writing, anyway. He really had his finger on the pulse of the music scene. We'd worked together for almost two years. That being said, he torched buildings for fun and burned people to death doing it.

LILY: We had a serious problem. I was the only one willing to admit it.

MALCOLM: Kicking ass and taking names, right on schedule. We'd put together a killer catalog. We were cutting our teeth playing local venues. If this kept up, we could hire management and go on tour. Sign with a small label that could get us into cool indie record stores. Build up a large enough fan base as underground heroes that we could swing a deal with a major label that would give us distribution in malls and chain stores like Tower Records. Then on to the big time.

LILY: After the Hobo Underground show, Drake became withdrawn, tired, and irritable, his bad dreams visiting him nightly. When I wasn't gripped by my own night terrors of the gargoyle perched on his chest, I'd wake him up to hold him.

One night, he said, "I'm living my life backward. Every day, I remember a little more of who I am and where I come from. What I'm destined to do."

"Who did the dream say you are?" I asked him, genuinely curious.

He said bitterly, "The enemy. It's kind of hard to stay positive."

This was my chance to bring up a sore subject.

I said, "It's not you, it's the music. There's something wrong with it."

Nestled against my chest, he stiffened to alertness. I'd already lost him.

"The music has a message," he said. "People are reacting to it."

He didn't understand what I was trying to say. Sure, the songs appeared to inspire people to tune in and act out. This kind of thing was every musician's dream. But he didn't believe the songs actually forced people to do anything.

I said, "Let's change the music and find out. Please. For me."

Drake said, "You should know by now I could never do that."

If I expected him to stay away from my choices, I'd have to respect his.

ERIC: At the next band meeting, Malcolm laid out a detailed strategy for Sunburst while we pretended to listen.

MALCOLM: Sunburst was a one-day music festival started by some hippies who owned the Harmony Farm. A small event, maybe two thousand people at most, but certainly the biggest we'd played by that point. The lineup started in the early afternoon and rocked into the night, ending with a fireworks show to wish America a happy birthday. The bands were booked months in advance, so again we were lucky to get in. Lucky or fated, take your pick.

RAMONA: He actually had an easel with a big map of the grounds on it, pointing out the stage, parking, tents, and so on. He even calculated where the sun would be at the time we'd be performing and the average temperature in this region on July 4, which, if you need to know, was eighty-seven degrees.

MALCOLM: I shared the lineup. We'd go on after Joanie's Kisses, a local all-girl power band with an ethereal sound. That wasn't terrible. We'd follow what they were doing and put a dark edge on it. Then I made the mistake of asking if anyone had any new business to discuss.

ERIC: Lily said, "Are we going to talk about what happened at the Hobo show?"

LILY: I expected Drake to jump in, but it was everyone else who brushed me off.

RAMONA: We all agreed it was weird. No dissent there.

ERIC: It was fucked up. No doubt.

LILY: At first, they were pretty receptive. When I suggested what happened might have had something to do with our music, they looked at me like I had two heads.

ERIC: I remember saying something pretentious like a little violence is an occupational hazard with rock and roll. The Rolling Stones in '69, the Who in '79, yeah, it happens. I wasn't entirely wrong; some bad shit would go down again at Woodstock '99 only a few weeks after this very band meeting.

To be honest, nothing else at the time rationally explained why people froze at our shows and then groped and fought each other.

RAMONA: No way anyone was pinning that bullshit on me. Those people lost control. Period. I wasn't about to give up the prize over it.

MALCOLM: I'd been afraid of this ever since I agreed to join a band and play with others instead of solo. Afraid that one of them would get freaked out by success and sabotage it. Eric, maybe. Ramona, definitely. Not levelheaded Lily.

LILY: They didn't even want to talk about it. Just bringing it up made them upset.

MALCOLM: I reminded her that correlation is not causation, and in any case two wrongs don't really add up to anything. I said we should do Sunburst and see how it went. If something weird happened, we could talk about it.

LILY: Everyone looked at Drake, who so far had said nothing. If you date someone long enough, you become an expert on their tells, and right then I could see he was troubled. That he knew, somewhere deep down, that I was right.

RAMONA: Drake said something like, "The dream belongs to all of us now." Amen, I thought. It was only later I figured out what he meant by that.

LILY: I dropped it. What else could I do? The things I said sounded crazy even to me. Every musician you meet will happily preach about the power of music, how it inspires and whatnot, but it doesn't mind-control people into running amok.

RAMONA: We had no idea what music could do. It's a goddamn superweapon.

MALCOLM: Once again, I reminded them all why we were there. I clapped my hands to adjourn the meeting and said, "Who wants to play some songs?"

RAMONA: We were blinded by success. When you're winning, it's pretty easy to rationalize whatever you're doing that is winning for you.

LILY: The biggest lesson for me was never get between a person and their dream, especially if they think the dream is within reach.

ERIC: We kicked that can down the road. We were on an upswing, and we focused on that. So yeah. We did Sunburst. Guess how that turned out?

JASPER HARMON (*co-owner, Harmony Farm*): You might have heard my sister Jamie and I were big-time hippies back in the '60s. We were the runts in a large litter and decided we'd hit the road to see what the big old world was made of. In the end, we were the ones who came back to take over the farm and give it its name, while our more straitlaced older siblings left for greener pastures. My sister and I never really stopped being hippies, though. You know, believing in the ideals. People like to make fun and portray hippies as silly stereotypes or whatever, but the movement had a huge impact. Practically a revolution, the cultural kind.

JAMIE HARMON (*co-owner, Harmony Farm*): The farm covers fifty-five acres of open fields and some woodlands. We grow a wide variety of crops depending on the season and sell them at local markets. We also maintain livestock and do some beekeeping. We ended up doing well enough that we set aside a few acres to create a music festival in the mid-'90s.

JASPER HARMON: Hosting a festival was Jamie's idea, but I sort of ran with it. By 1999, we'd done five annual events. Our way of giving back to rock and roll and reliving a little of that Woodstock magic from our youth.

JAMIE HARMON: What ended up happening was not what rock and roll is about.

JASPER HARMON: I'd love to take this opportunity to say to anyone who may have been hurt that day, we're very sorry.

JAMIE HARMON: I'm not sorry. We opened our home to the local music scene to create something beautiful, and they took a giant shit on it.

JASPER HARMON: Even after all this time, she's still pissed off.

LILY: Surrounded by gently rolling green hills, the farm looked lush and gorgeous. A whole other way of living. We drove across a little bridge spanning a creek and then under a sign that read: HARMONY FARM. After that, we followed the dusty path that wound through neatly combed fields sprouting sweet corn, cucumbers, tomatoes. Beyond a pasture with some milk cows, I spotted the big farmhouse and surrounding barns and outbuildings. It all looked pretty darn idyllic in the golden light of the late-afternoon sun. Soaking it in, I started to feel hopeful. In such a place, it was tempting to believe our music being evil was all in my head.

MALCOLM: We found the festival grounds laid out exactly as they appeared on the map. Vendor stalls and food trucks, big stage with stacked speakers, medical and dressing room tents beyond, and porta-potties. Blankets covered the field in a riot of colors, filled with people soaking up the tunes and summer sun. Here and there, delay towers and art installations rose over the landscape. I knew exactly where we had to go to sign in and every step after to deliver us to the stage. Being in a band is one part perspiration, five parts preparation.

LILY: A large crowd swayed and danced in front of the stage, where Joanie's Kisses gave it their all. After we parked, I spotted frontwoman Valeria Valis belting out a breakup song in a white dress with draping bell sleeves. The ethereal music filled the air and set my heart to pounding. We were here, where I wanted to be most. In the sound and ready to perform.

ERIC: A good thing about me is how much love I have to give. A bad thing is I used to fall in love with everyone. The instant I saw Valeria Valis twirling around the stage looking like an angel in that flowy white dress, I was smitten.

LILY: Drake reached to trace his finger down my cheek, a familiar gentle gesture that usually made me tingle, though I hardly noticed it now, too amped up.

He asked me if I was up for this.

"Let's rock," I answered, again not caring how uncool it sounded.

The vibe felt good. The crowd appeared ripe. The Shivers piled out of the van pumped to kick ass. I itched to get on that stage and play. For me, the music always took priority, and I'd come to make ours sing.

Drake looked like he wanted to tell me something. Instead he nodded.

"Let's rock," he said, making it sound cool.

ERIC: I'm laughing now because of how cocky we were as we hauled our gear to the backstage area. No jitters, no doubts. After the Hobo Underground, we thought we were hot stuff. Full-on, no-holds swagger abounded.

MALCOLM: My third show hauling instruments, amps, mic stands, pedalboard, and other gear, this time sweating my nuts off in roasting heat. We needed roadies who could do this for us. I put it on my list.

RAMONA: The crowd was huge, a hell of a lot bigger than the Hobo and Flanagan's shows. I pushed it out of my mind. No fear, not today.

MALCOLM: After that, I dropped off the band merch with a Hate Mail groupie I'd met, who said he'd sell it for us at the stall he had set up.

RAMONA: As we waited our turn to go on, I asked Lily if she was still worried.

LILY: I told her I wasn't.

RAMONA: She was worried.

LILY: I was very worried. But I was doing this show, and I was all-in.

MALCOLM: No inspiring speech from me this time.

ERIC: He kept reminding us to stay hydrated. It was like ninety degrees that day.

MALCOLM: I told everyone to remember why they were here, what they wanted, and what they were willing to do to get it.

If I couldn't inspire them to noble effort, maybe they'd inspire themselves.

RAMONA: Showtime. It always comes at you slower than you want but faster than you expect.

LILY: Joanie's Kisses finished with an uplifting number that had the crowd cheering. Valeria left the stage with her drummer—a stocky blonde with short-cropped hair and tattoos sleeving her arms—and gave us an amused once-over.

She said, "What do you think, Ashley? They don't look all that dangerous."

The drummer grinned and said, "They'll have to be to follow what we just put down."

I thought, Oh, ladies. You have no idea.

ERIC: Us? Dangerous? We appeared to have earned something of a reputation. I hate to admit it now, but I loved the sound of it. Ramona growled something like, "Clear all your shit off that stage in fifteen, or you'll find out."

Feeling tough in Ramona's halo, I crossed my arms as if to say: *Yeah, what she said. Chop, chop, sisters.*

LILY: They were bathed in sweat from a terrific show, and all I could think next was, Get out of my way before I freaking burst. It's our turn to shine.

Laughing, Valeria checked out Drake in a brief animal appraisal that made me bristle. Then her green eyes settled on Eric and pretty much devoured him.

My mouth dropped open. I have to admit that I did not see that coming.

ERIC: Of course I missed it. A woman had to shoot a flaming declaration of interest with a catapult for me to ever get the message.

LILY: We set up and quickly sound-checked the equipment with the help of the stage manager. Already, I regretted wearing the schoolgirl outfit, as I was sweating fairly profusely myself before I'd even started playing.

Drake tapped the mic and said, "I see we have a few members of the clergy joining us today. Glory forever, brothers and sisters."

Shielding my eyes against the sun's glare, I spotted them. Three priests and one hulking tank of a nun glowered back at him from the crowd's ragged edges. Standing apart, they formed a semicircle facing the stage.

I shot Eric a look, but he shrugged. No help there.

Turning back, my eyes settled on a young woman in the crowd. Like the priests and nun, she didn't cheer our arrival on the stage. She wore a black tee displaying a familiar looping snake and the words THE SHIVERS.

Gazing back at me with an unblinking stare.

Drake went on: "To my friends in the church, to all of you, brothers and sisters, I say, *Fiat tenebris*. Let there be dark."

The girl's face stretched into a wide grin that made my skin crawl.

Wait, I kept thinking. Hang on—

Then Ramona counted us in, and I started us off.

MALCOLM: As my fingers skipped across my keyboard, I suffered a queasy cringe of foreboding. A vague unease that Lily was right and I'd made a massive mistake. But nothing happened. The audience stayed cool. The song rolled through the intro just as we'd practiced countless times.

RAMONA: Drake missed his cue to jump in with his guitar. While I held the beat at a simmer with the brushes, he stood with his skinny arms draped over his old Stratocaster and smiled at the priests, as if daring them.

LILY: I kept the rhythm in a holding pattern as the strange standoff stretched.

MALCOLM: No turning into statues, no eyes bugging out with terror, no sudden bursts of violence. Completely chill, the crowd swayed with the music. There was nothing wrong with our sound.

ERIC: I checked my pedalboard, and when I looked up, the priests and nun had started pushing their way toward the stage. I caught a flash of steel; one of them had a knife. Then the nun let a spiky mace drop from her sleeve into her grip. Swinging her linebacker shoulders, she barged through the crowd. Their murderous gazes fixed on Drake, who smiled as he watched them come.

LILY: Oh shit, I thought, my hands playing on autopilot. Oh shit. Oh shit!

ERIC: Drake suddenly dropped to his knees and started wailing on his guitar, producing a jolt of sound that seemed to split the air in half.

MALCOLM: But there *was* something wrong with it. Something very wrong.

ERIC: The good news is the crowd didn't freeze into trembling statues. The bad news is they immediately started mauling and groping each other.

RAMONA: The crowd turned into an instant mosh pit as every person tore at their neighbors, as if they didn't know whether they wanted to fuck or kill each other.

LILY: Eyes bugging out, the priests went down, swallowed whole in a press of half-naked people slammed together so tight, they looked like a single compact mass. The mob then coughed up one of the clergymen, who floated scrabbling along the wave of bodies like an involuntary crowd surfer. Fires sprang up at the vendor booths, which billowed smoke.

I stopped playing. Around me, the band faltered and ground to a halt.

Hunched over his guitar, only Drake kept the song going.

I yelled into my mic, "STOP IT RIGHT NOW."

Red-faced and roaring, the big nun cleared a space around her with her fists. Then a hairy giant, naked except for a pair of Converse All Stars, burst from the throng and flew at her spread-eagled. They both went down among the gibbering, raving faces as a sequence of earsplitting crashes filled the air. Behind the stage, someone was setting off all the fireworks at once.

With a colossal explosion that made me flinch, the dressing room tent behind us blew sky-high in flaming shards.

I unplugged my guitar and said, "That's it. Screw this. I'm out!"

In everyone's frenzy to get at each other, the crowd had sucked inward, leaving a wide-open space in front of me. Hopping down, I started for the van.

Big mistake. The wall of bodies shifted, heaving toward the stage, and broke. In an instant, an avalanche of limbs surged to envelop me.

Gripping my Epiphone by the neck, I raised it over my head ready to swing as scores of faces tumbled my way, screaming and laughing as they came.

The bodies spilled groaning at my feet. Petrified, I gaped at them. They'd stopped their frantic struggling. Chests heaved as they blinked at each other in confusion, as if they had no idea what just happened.

I turned back to the stage to see Drake eyeing me with worry. He'd stopped playing.

RAMONA: Guitar perched on her shoulder, Lily yelled something like, "Argh!" and kept on walking. Straight past the van to disappear into a cornfield.

ERIC: The place looked like a war zone. People lay in piles gasping for air amid torn clothes and blankets and the wreckage of one of the delay towers. A food truck had been flipped onto its side. Four people, stark naked, tumbled out of one of the porta-potties. The vendor booths had been reduced to smoking cinders. The last firework went off with a heart-stopping bang.

Hugging my bass, I stood there like an idiot. The whole thing had gone down so quick, I didn't even really react until it was all over.

MALCOLM: I just stared at my keyboard in wonder. Lily was right. I wasn't so much horrified as impressed.

LILY: So I'm walking through a cornfield heading in the same general direction as Bethlehem. On the far side, I didn't find the road but instead some dark woods. Night was coming in a few hours. This wasn't my brightest idea, but I didn't care. I wanted out of there. I was so mad I couldn't even look at the band right then.

Luckily, the walk through the woods didn't last long, and I found the road on the other side that I hoped would take me home.

Then a hand landed on my shoulder, and I let out a loud shriek.

ERIC: My eyes rested on the towering nun, who sat on the ground gripping a rosary and bawling. I wanted to help these people, but I had no idea how. I just went on standing there with my bass, waiting for someone to tell me what to do.

RAMONA: Drake stared into the cornfield Lily disappeared into, looking sadder than I'd ever seen him. I told him to stop being an idiot and go after her.

LILY: It was Drake who'd grabbed me.

He said, "I thought we were going to do it together. You promised."

I said, "I was wrong. It's not the music. It's you, isn't it?"

He slowly nodded. He said, "I think so."

In a low voice, he added, "It's going to get worse."

"I'm quitting the band," I told him.

Drake said, "I thought the music came first."

But this wasn't rock. It was abuse. That was the problem.

In the end, doing something I loved this much simply shouldn't feel this wrong. Something as beautiful and pure as music shouldn't be corrupted like this. Drake was ruining the one thing I loved more than anything.

See, he didn't set me free. Music did. He didn't open the cage to let me out. He simply pointed out it wasn't really there. It was music that showed me the way.

Before I could second-guess myself, I blurted out the rest.

I said, "I suppose I'm quitting you as well."

"I thought I came first too," he shot back. "I thought that was love."

I said, "This is me loving myself."

He looked down at himself with some surprise, as if seeing something for the first time, and then back at me, his expression fallen and sad now.

He said, "It's okay. I understand."

I'm glad he did, because I wasn't so sure, my nerves screaming that I was maybe making a colossal mistake, the kind you can't take back.

He went on, saying, "You don't really know me, not all of it. The journey I'm on and what it will cost. You should be able to choose. You have a right to choose."

In his mind, doing what you want was the only law worth obeying. I told him that I still loved him and that I was sorry, both of which were true.

Drake said, "I'm sorry too. For what happened but mostly for what comes next. Things are only going to get worse."

This is what he'd tried to protect me from. His ministry, he'd once labeled it. And from even more horrible things that might be yet to come.

I said, "I'll move out as soon as I find a place."

He shook his head and said, "I'm the one who's quitting."

Drake told me the band had always been my baby. He said I could keep it going or scrap it. Either way, he was out.

The same went for the apartment. I could live there rent-free, if I wanted it.

He said, "You deserve that much for putting up with my bullshit."

I looked away for only a few seconds so he didn't see the first tears burst from my eyes.

Drake said, "Armageddon is coming."

When I turned back, he was gone, vanished, and once again, I was alone.

MISDIRECTED ANATHEMA

JULY 1999

After the brief but savage Sunburst Music Festival riot, the Shivers took some time off to process what happened as well as news of Lily and Drake's split. Finally, Malcolm Williams called the band back together for a make-or-break meeting to address this crisis.

MALCOLM: When it rains, it pours. First, the good news: Our application was approved. The Shivers had officially made the list to compete in the Armageddon Battle of the Bands in December.

ALEXIS ZHANG (*music director and producer, Armageddon*): We started the event in 1993 as an annual regional competition for valley rock bands. A dozen select local bands competed for a first prize that included a thousand bucks, sixteen hours of recording time, and of course eternal bragging rights. Two of our winners ended up joining the Warped Tour.

In '99, the event took on a special importance, with all the talk about the Y2K bug and the world ending when the clock struck midnight to usher in 2000.

MALCOLM: We were all horrified by what happened at Sunburst. But I was also awed. Our music had one hell of a powerful effect on the brain. This did not have to be a bad thing. In fact, it could be the secret sauce that might propel us to become the world's greatest rock band.

We just had to learn to tame the beast.

ALEXIS ZHANG: As it turned out, the world didn't end, but Armageddon did. After twenty years of therapy, I'm still trying to process what I saw that night.

MALCOLM: Now the bad news: Lily called to let me know that she and Drake had broken up. More drama we didn't need, the kind that has sabotaged many a good musical group on their way to stardom. *This* was why I wanted a band contract. I was happy to hear they'd parted ways amicably and that there'd be no ugly custody battle. I wished her all the best.

LILY: My answering machine filled with calls. Everyone telling me how sorry they were and asking how I was holding up.

The honest answer: I didn't really know. I'd done the breaking in this breakup, but it had felt far more like severing a psychic limb. The limb attached to a tree I'd just learned was holding me up from a very long and painful fall.

It's hard to be alone, even if that's what you want.

The calls reminded me I wasn't really alone. I had people who would catch me somewhere near the bottom.

I showed up to practice and hit the ground with a splat.

MALCOLM: Don't look at me like that. I liked Lily, I really did. I mean, who didn't? Honestly, it surprised me she'd stuck it out with Drake as long as she had. He always acted like he could take or leave her, and she could only have him on his terms. In life as in business, if you want a deal bad enough, you get a bad deal.

But all that was beside the point. Were we friends? No, we were partners in a band that had to make music that earned money so we could go on being a band.

Anyway, there was so much to do, and we had to move on. I called the Shivers back together for a meeting. Left a message on Drake's answering machine.

Then Lily showed up and he didn't.

LILY: I tuned my guitar to avoid reading the room.

My beautiful axe, my prized possession. Top of the list in my post-breakup inventory of things that were reliable, though even this had come from Drake.

Ramona wandered around the practice area. Malcolm sat on one of his IKEA couches and glared at me with his arms crossed. Eric hadn't shown up yet.

The negative energy in the room seemed to produce its own vibrations. A note only a dog—or someone in the proverbial doghouse, as I was—could hear.

They were pissed.

MALCOLM: I distinctly remember saying, "Can we please not blow this?"

LILY: It felt good sitting there, though, tuning my guitar. Simple routine. Reliable. Life goes on. Your instrument falls out of whack from hard use, you retune it and maybe replace a string, and then you get back to playing.

For days and days, I bawled my eyes out with the only music in my life, a couple of CD mixes of breakup and girl-power songs. Playing "Sad Tomorrow" by the Muffs on repeat, Kim Shattuck wondering why he's happy while she's sad and thinking maybe the despair would leave if she faded to nothing.

To get through it, I called on all my guitar heroes for inspiration. Wendy Melvoin, who went on after Prince to make beautiful albums loaded with red-hot solos and funky riffs, proving you deal with change by evolving. Kristin Hersh with her raging leads and blasting power chords, teaching me to put yourself out there. Dot Wiggin, who sang and played in different rhythms, showing me the beauty of doing things your way. And the Great Kat, one of the fastest shredders of all time and raging sex on wheels, showing the world how to go all-out for what you love.

But as always, Joan Jett blazed out front. The lady got her first guitar at thirteen but quit lessons because her teacher wanted this born rock-and-roller to learn folk songs. When her parents divorced, she took the opportunity to change her name to Joan Jett, which she considered the kind of name a rock star should have. She started the Runaways at sixteen. After the band broke up, she did some solo work and formed the Blackhearts, going on to do numerous albums with them, three certifying platinum or gold. As always, Saint Joan taught me to use my power to love myself and put the music first.

They all reminded me that living free meant living without fear. I was done bawling. Done fading. What I really needed: getting back into the groove with a good, solid dustup. Band practice.

MALCOLM: Ramona sat behind her drums and gripped her sticks like she wasn't sure if she wanted to hit the drums or one of us with them. Eric finally graced us with his presence and went straight to the mini fridge and stared inside it for a while. He yanked a bottle of Snapple off the shelf and parked near Lily on her couch.

ERIC: I didn't mean to be late, but I was in no particular hurry to come to the meeting and find out what had changed. The band was like family to me. I went to get a drink, and Malcolm practically shouted at me to pick one and sit down.

I was like, Hey, don't blame any of this on me!

I was feeling super sensitive. I didn't know what was going on. Lily and Drake had broken up. Lily was here. Drake wasn't. Everyone looked mad.

RAMONA: Eric was probably too sensitive in general for the music business, but that's a whole other story. Sometimes you have to yell. This was one of those times. If Malcolm hadn't yelled at him to sit the hell down, I would have. The minute Lily walked in, I saw the writing on the wall and needed to hear it said out loud so I'd have my own chance to yell back.

LILY: I needed to play with them. I thought if only we could start jamming, we'd realize we were still together and that we could get through this.

I stood up with my guitar, and Malcolm said, "Not tonight."

This was serious. Like couples who resolve never go to bed angry, the Shivers had never held an important meeting without a short jam to get everyone on the same page. A tradition I'd started at our first meeting.

I slowly returned to my seat. Malcolm said we needed to talk about the elephant in the room.

I said, "Yes. We have to replace Drake." Giving it a name.

MALCOLM: I laughed when she said that. I really did.

RAMONA: Malcolm had assumed *she* was leaving and Drake was the one who'd be staying. He'd expected Drake to show up with his guitar instead of her.

To be fair, we all did. At least, we'd hoped so. We all loved Lily—for real, we did—but we had a band, and Drake was, well, Drake.

MALCOLM: I was like, Sure, let's do that. Who do you have in mind?

LILY: I said I'd step up as singer and lead guitarist. This surprised even me, but I wanted to make this better. Everyone was upset. If it was all on me, then I'd fix it.

MALCOLM: I said, "Can you do what Drake did?"

Then I said, "Do you know *anybody* who can do what he did?"

RAMONA: He didn't even wait for an answer. We all already knew it.

MALCOLM: I pictured walking on stage at Armageddon without Drake Morgan and delivering an epic fail that would haunt me the rest of my life.

ERIC: That moment you realize how amazing *we* rocked as a band was really just one musician doing most of the amazing and rocking.

In our case, Drake Morgan, the one person who wasn't there.

RAMONA: Without Drake, we didn't even feel like the Shivers anymore. We'd returned to being just a wedding band dropout, a computer geek, a genius guitarist's ex-girlfriend, and a busker who drummed for tips at local parks.

MALCOLM: I informed Lily the only topic on the agenda was whether we could go on as a band without our virtuoso lead guitarist and frontman.

RAMONA: I'd poured my heart, sweat, and soul into the Shivers. It had changed me. Yes, our music seemed to have a horrible effect on people, and our lead guitarist cackled like a psychopath at the mayhem we caused, but I was so blinded by what I wanted that deep down I didn't care. Or, rather, I compartmentalized it. So imagine what I felt as the writing on the wall now told me I'd be busking again tomorrow in some public park, back to hiding from all the good things everyone else seemed to have except me.

I'd already told Comrade Jenny about my decision. I'd already left the Squat and pretty much lived in Malcolm's basement. If the band split, I'd be officially homeless.

LILY: I understood what Malcolm was saying. I really did. Still, I found it shocking that the band might give up.

Drake had handed me the keys to the Shivers only for me to instantly lose control to Malcolm, who seemed to be taking command long enough to kill it.

MALCOLM: I paid for a lot of the gear. I loaned out money to keep everyone afloat. It was my van and gas that got us to the gigs, which I scored for us by working my phone with my time. We were in my house.

Goddamn right I considered it my band, only I had serious doubts it was a band anymore.

RAMONA: Eric started crying.

ERIC: I teared up a little, so what. When a band is about to break up, you realize it's the only thing you really have in common with some of these people. Right then, I thought I might never see any of them again. Sometimes you're glad to see the back of them. Other times, it's a very bitter pill.

What really set me off, though, was me asking myself: What am I gonna tell Ma?

RAMONA: Breaking up is hard to do, especially when it breaks your band.

ERIC: I remember a thought popped into my head that I'd have a lot more time to play *Silent Hill*. I thought, Maybe it's for the best, seeing how people reacted at our shows. Then I heard Ma's voice telling me Walmart was hiring. After that, I have to admit, my next thought was, Wow, Lily Lawless is single.

LILY: Everyone stared at me, waiting for me to say something. Probably something like, *I quit. You can have Drake come back.*

So I told them the truth. That it wasn't my decision.

Ramona, who suffered the world's worst allergy to bullshit, gave me a look. There was a divorce, and I'd gotten everything. Which was life, fine, but I didn't get to lie about it to them or even myself.

I said, "If you think I'm the one standing in the way of Drake staying, you're wrong. I offered to leave, but he quit. Whether I stay or go, he said he's out."

RAMONA: The look on Malcolm's face as he watched the gravy train leave the station without him was priceless.

Then I remembered, Oh, yeah, I'm also fucked here.

ERIC: He'd just realized that Drake had broken up with *him*.

RAMONA: Malcolm's chin started wobbling and I thought he'd start crying too. God only knows what he was thinking right then.

MALCOLM: I was thinking I'd just sunk money and a massive amount of time and hope into a breakup. I'd have to tell Queenie that I'd failed and my father that he was right that doing what I loved couldn't give me a career.

I gave Lily an imploring look and said, "Is it really over?"

LILY: I didn't tell them how much I missed Drake. How life felt gray in the aftermath, AM instead of FM, a backbeat in life's soundtrack missing and replaced by white noise.

I'd spent hours repainting the walls of the apartment, erasing all Drake's nightmares except the last one with him on a stage rocking to lost souls. The walls now looked fresh and clean but also an utter blank.

I didn't tell them how weak I felt, how many times I'd thought about giving up my dream and going back to my parents' house with my tail between my legs. How warm and comforting it would be to surrender. I'd do everything they told me: go back to school and get an accounting degree, work in some corporate office, get married and produce a pack of grandchildren, grow old and die.

Some people leave a relationship, and they immediately start romanticizing or demonizing it. That didn't happen to me. The farther I got from it, the more clarity I gained. I fully understood how unhealthy it was for me. At the same time, I could acknowledge everything I'd received and what I was now losing.

Freedom isn't as freeing as it sounds.

I couldn't go back. Not to him and not to my old life either. And when you can't go back, the only other way is forward.

I said, "Yeah, Mal, it's really over. I'm done."

RAMONA: As pissed as I was, I couldn't help but think that Lily's dumping Drake's ass was pretty punk rock.

She'd always struck me as the type who'd bitch about a guy not treating her right but never do anything about it. If I had a pot to piss in back then, I'd have bet the whole pot on him dumping her, not the other way around.

Over time, I'd find out exactly how much he actually needed her and how tough she could be.

LILY: I told them I'd been wrong about the music. There was nothing wrong with the music. The music had nothing to do with people losing their minds. I said, "It was *him* making our shows ugly. I don't know how, but he made those people lose control."

Before they could react to that, I made my pitch.

I said, "We have a good thing here. If you want to throw it away, then I can't stop you. But I think we owe it to the band and each other enough to at least try."

I owed myself just as much.

RAMONA: Before Malcolm could overanalyze anything, I said, "I'm in."

MALCOLM: I was actually thinking about Mark Cuban, who grew up in a working-class family outside Pittsburgh. After graduating, he couldn't find a good job, so he went into business for himself, starting a streaming platform called Broadcast. It didn't go anywhere, but he kept at it until he sold it to Yahoo and became a self-made billionaire. There was a lesson about perseverance there.

RAMONA: Half my decision was terror at going back to my old dead-end life where I pretended I didn't need anything. The other half? Fuck Drake.

ERIC: Drake cared about Lily enough to let her keep the band, but it still hurt that he'd walk away like that without even a goodbye. As for Lily, she'd reached out to us after they broke up. She was here. She *wanted* to be here.

Drake didn't do any of these things. He didn't do them because he honestly did not give a crap about any of us and never really had.

I looked at Malcolm and said, "Come on, man. You didn't think starting a band was going to be easy, did you?"

MALCOLM: Oh brother. I thought, God, okay, I give up. If they all wanted it, I'd give it another shot. I figured if we were really doing this, now was a good time to let them in on the good news about Armageddon.

RAMONA: I was like, Wait, what?

MALCOLM: A band manager is a punching bag that every once in a while spits out a gift with a bow on it, and then suddenly it's Christmas.

RAMONA: He could have led with that particular bit of information. That's all I'm saying.

ERIC: I couldn't believe it. We'd play Armageddon! It was a big deal.

MALCOLM: If I was the only one who paid attention to the business side, I was allowed some secrets. Anyway, before they started getting all excited, I needed to make three things crystal-clear.

One, I'd go on supporting the band until the competition, and if we did good, as in we won, I'd keep doing it. If not, I'd pull the plug.

Two, we would practice nonstop until practice made perfect.

And the third thing: I wanted a damn band contract.

LILY: I said, "If we're doing this, then we'd better get cracking."

RAMONA: We were still the Shivers.

MALCOLM: They were all like, "Let's go!" But of course I was the one who had to put together and run the ad so we could audition a new lead guitarist.

ERIC: The tension finally broke. We were still a band. This time, I think I really did cry a little. I said, "I love you guys."

RAMONA [*sighs*]: Eric, Eric, Eric.

LILY: To make it official, I walked over and started playing the riff I'd been working on. Eric built on it, Ramona pinned it down, and Malcolm layered on a cutting countermelody.

A beautiful thing to be playing together again.

It didn't sound the same without Drake.

INNER DEMONS

JULY–AUGUST 1999

*A*fter deciding to continue playing as the Shivers, the band's members met again, not to practice this time but to audition a new lead guitarist.

LILY: That morning in the shower, I kept hearing John Lennon singing in my ear about starting over.

Sometimes you listen to a song and it perfectly articulates what you're feeling. Other times, it helps you reach for how you want to feel and resets your brain. That day, both applied to me.

The Shivers and I had hit a rough patch, but we were starting over to make something better and new, reaching to connect with the one great universal song that lives inside all of us.

MALCOLM: I didn't take any chances. No random meetings in bars and parks for me. No weird alchemy. We'd have an interview process like a real business. A thorough vetting.

ERIC: You'd think we were confirming a Supreme Court justice.

RAMONA: He had this questionnaire. "How long have you been playing? Have you been in a band before? Are you in a band now?"

MALCOLM: I assigned each of the twelve applicants a few songs to play that would give us an idea of their range and talent.

RAMONA: "Do you have any gear? Do you have a vehicle?"

LILY: There was this heady feeling in the air that we owned the band now. We really had no idea how much it had been Drake's until he was gone. I remember I was seriously jonesing for a cigarette, but I'd quit all my bad habits.

ERIC: Malcolm gave us these worksheets so we could rate the musicians on a one-to-seven scale for style, technical, improv skills, and so on.

RAMONA: "Do you work a day job? Does your significant other support your interest in music?"

MALCOLM: I trusted data far more than I did fate.

ERIC: We sat like judges on a couch in his basement. I felt really cool already being in the club. Soon the supplicants would arrive to compete for my favor.

RAMONA: Malcolm gave the place a thorough cleaning as he always did. The room smelled like air freshener. The lights were really bright. The only cool thing about it was the painting of our logo on the wall that Drake and Lily did.

We looked like posers sitting on that couch. I moved to one of the chairs to make it less formal.

LILY: I was super excited. And nervous too. I had high hopes we'd find the perfect fit for the band. At the same time, I thought: This has to work.

MALCOLM: It didn't work.

RAMONA: It was actually painful. We probably would have done just as well wandering around bars and parks. In the end, we went with our gut anyway.

ERIC: The first applicant was this guy with a massive perm job. The spitting image of Dee Snider from Twisted Sister.

I thought, Okay, he looks the part. He ended up fumbling around with his gear and wasting half the audition time tuning his guitar.

MALCOLM: He could play pretty well, but his voice was terrible. Real nails on a chalkboard.

RAMONA: At the end, he made all these demands like it was his band, not ours.

MALCOLM: Nix. Next.

RAMONA: The next candidate was this heavyset redhead in a black leather catsuit who cranked the volume, thrashed her guitar, and screamed the Dead Kennedys' "California Über Alles" at us.

ERIC: It was mesmerizing. I was very into having her in the band.

RAMONA: After she shouted a punk song at us, she put us behind schedule by obsessing over how she did and whether she'd made it into the band.

I have to hand it to Malcolm about one thing. He was really good at saying no.

MALCOLM: I'll just say I did not find the data encouraging.

ERIC: Other than her, it was a very long, very disappointing day until the very end.

LILY: Malcolm had a saying: Every solution has a problem. I'd started to catch his meaning.

Weeks after my breakup with Drake, we still had no band.

Then Julian walked in.

RAMONA: He looked like a skate rat who was too old to be a skate rat.

MALCOLM: I was exhausted. He wasn't on the list. And he looked like a hack.

LILY: He was a big man with a friendly, open face. One of those beefy, hunky midwestern farm-boy types, only he wore a Jimmy Eat World T-shirt and baggy skater shorts.

He ignored Malcolm telling him to get out and plugged in.

He said, "Let me just play you a little something."

Then he cut loose, no warm-up, with Jimi Hendrix's "Little Wing."

ERIC: The guy didn't have a frontman presence. Honestly, he looked more like a bassist. Big, dumb, and reliable. But yeah, he could play the hell out of that gorgeous tune. With its complex chord progressions, double stops, and distinct voicing, "Little Wing" is no easy song to master.

LILY: It's a beautiful song, dreamy and ethereal. Confident but filled with longing. Julian put his own little twist on it, making it sound exultant, like a celebration. He fingerpicked it, no guitar pick. He had a deep, strong voice.

RAMONA: Malcolm didn't look very happy. The poor baby. This was the best we'd heard today, but he still wasn't Drake.

LILY: I wanted him in the band. I didn't want to fight about it. I got off the couch and walked over to sing along, harmonizing above the melody.

ERIC: Lily had provided some backup vocals, but I had no idea she was so good.

RAMONA: She surprised me as much as Julian did. A beautiful mezzo-soprano voice, as striking as Grace Slick's.

ERIC: I was like, "Do you know any more Hendrix?" We all ended up playing and singing "Purple Haze" together.

LILY: There was no argument. Julian joined the band. This changed everything.

MALCOLM: I took a calculated risk. We didn't have time to screw around.

LILY: He showed us a different kind of cool. When Drake played with the band, we always felt amped up and hungry for everything we were lacking. When Julian started playing with us, we still gave it our all but had a lot less to prove. A lot of times, it felt like we played just for the fun of it.

Drake told us to do our own thing musically and then always bulldozed us with his talent and personality. When he left, this became all the more obvious. We might as well have been called Drake and His Forgettable Backup Band. His departure was like being handed the keys to a house designed by a mad interior decorator; you walk inside afraid to move the furniture.

With Julian aboard, the songs became raw materials again

and slowly became ours. And as a bonus, I knew that with Drake gone, they wouldn't hurt anyone. Playing music became fun again, power without the madness.

The contrast between these men was as striking as staccato and legato. Playing with Julian felt like an actual partnership, the kind of musical collaboration I wished I'd had a bit more with Drake. The kind of relationship I wished I'd had with him in every way, actually. But I'll tell you something weird.

It only made me miss my ex even more.

The thing is, love can be a harsh mistress. It burns you when you turn it on and makes you ache when you try to turn it off. It prefers an ugly fade-out over a graceful exit. It puts you on a hook and lets you swim and then reels you back in, again and again, until you're too exhausted to struggle anymore.

My first big breakup taught me that the only peace you find is already in you. A nature walk can't give it to you. Discovering your own agency after a breakup can't either. Even music can't. It has to be somewhere in you. And if it isn't, then, well, you've got more time and work to put in.

ERIC: One night, Ma went all out and made me a special dinner of homemade pierogi, the works. I asked her what the occasion was, and she said it was me.

Ma said, "You're making me so proud, Eric."

It turned out to be best dinner we had together since Dad left us. But when she served cream cake for dessert, she told me I was also worrying her a little.

"You're working too hard," Ma said.

I figured this was her maternal default setting. Mothers are gonna nag.

She said, "All I'm saying is don't forget to have fun while you're young."

To make her happy, I started going out more, only I'd head over to Malcolm's house and practice there. Ramona always gave me the stink-eye. Apparently, she'd been living there for a while.

Then Julian showed up to grab something. I never saw him without a tee repping some band, and that day I remember it being the Offspring's turn.

He looked at me and Ramona and said, "Wow, you guys are really dedicated."

By that point, I'd started to find him annoying. Not because of anything he did but because of the starry-eyed way Lily looked at him sometimes. When she'd broken up with Drake, my head had whirled with possibilities. Only, I preferred to love from afar, a safe space where the potential could stay alive. When it came to loving from afar, I was a world-famous Casanova.

Have fun while you're young, my mom said. I wasn't sure how this was done.

I figured on giving Julian the cold shoulder, but I couldn't resist a snooty response. I told him if you want to be good at something, you have to put the time in. If you put enough time in, then that's who you become. It's called *purpose*.

Julian said, "I can't argue with that."

I said I practiced there because Ma had been nagging me to get out and smell the roses or whatever. I don't know why I told him that part. Julian had the kind of face and vibe that made people want to talk his ears off about personal issues.

He said, "I can't argue with her either. Life takes practice too."

I'd changed since joining the Shivers. Ma saw it, and it had changed her just as it had me. She was proud of me now. I didn't want to let her down.

Julian said, "Maybe it makes her happy just to see you happy. The real you and not some persona."

Then he snapped his fingers and said, "I know just the thing." Something I needed, apparently.

RAMONA: Before one of our practice sessions, Julian couldn't find his favorite guitar pick and started rummaging around the storage area Malcolm had set up behind the practice space. It put me on edge as he got closer and closer to my box.

Then he discovered it.

He yanked it out and stared at it for a while. When he spotted his guitar pick, he kind of frowned, then looked up to find me gazing back at him. If he flipped out, I didn't know what I'd do. I only knew it wouldn't be me at my best.

For a while, Julian and I looked at each other as I shivered at the tense edge between fight and flight. Then he offered a comforting smile.

Reaching into his pocket, he dug out a pack of Wrigley's gum and put it in the box like it was a church collection basket being passed around on Sunday.

He said, "You ever take part in a drum circle? You should try it."

ERIC: I followed Julian out to his old car. The day had turned blazing hot. We drove to an abandoned lot covered in vibrant graffiti and offering a depressing view of a distant rusting factory. Shaggy-haired kids whooshed and clacked around the place they'd turned into a makeshift skate park with ramps and obstacles. Fishbone blasted from a boombox.

He pulled a skateboard out of his trunk. An Acme board with Image Comics art printed on the deck and stickers of red stars, smart-alecky cartoon characters, and even JESUS SAVES plastering the bottom.

Turns out ol' Julian was a skate rat. I asked, wasn't he a little old to be a skater boy—to us in the band, the dude was practically a geezer at twenty-nine—and he said, "You love what you love. Age doesn't matter."

He offered to show me the basics, and I told him naw, I was just gonna look around and soak it up awhile.

He said, "Do you ever think your real purpose is to live a good life?"

With that, he sped off to do his ollies and grinds or whatever. I had to admit the dude looked good on a board and that the whole thing seemed like fun. Freedom without all the philosophy and heavy dread I was about to flunk or get murdered.

A lot of the kids hung around and watched, so I didn't feel too dumb about not joining in. High schoolers, mostly, but thankfully a few people around my age. I spotted a pretty girl wearing a winter hat despite the heat and a black T-shirt that grabbed my eye.

The tee displayed the Shivers logo. She'd gone to our show.

Later, I'd hear one of our songs on the radio for the first time, and it almost knocked me on my ass. It was so awesome and empowering and humbling. Seeing my band's name on a T-shirt wasn't as big a deal, but it came pretty damn close.

RAMONA: The next time I went to my old cardboard box to drop a "donation" into it, it bulged with something heavy. The whole thing was wedged into the shelf. I wriggled it out to find a drum in it. A djembe drum to be exact.

I knew exactly who'd put it there.

Shaped like a goblet, the drum had a hardwood body and a goatskin drumhead. It stood about two feet tall and a little over a foot wide. The instrument originally comes from West Africa, where the most highly regarded players are skilled at using it to tell a powerful and affecting story.

By putting it in my box, Julian was telling me something too. They say self-awareness is the key to change, and I'd been there, done that. I'd needed a goal and the discipline to achieve it, and I was well on my way on that particular journey. Julian had suggested that maybe I needed healing.

Ouch. When Drake tempted me by telling me what I needed, it had been like scratching an itch. Julian had invited me to look at a part of me I didn't like seeing. More surgery than itch scratching. Opening old wounds. I think as people we have flaws we put out there and work on, while we keep the real ones hidden somewhere safe. It's less hazardous to play with fire than dynamite.

LILY: During a breakup, you figure out real quick what is and, more important, what is *not* in your control. Making music in a band isn't that different.

Julian and I bounced ideas back and forth, claiming our parts and making them ours in the full sense. Ramona, we didn't mess with too much; if we could get her to stop hitting the snares too hard and trying to drown us all out, we scored a win. Eric would roll with an idea but always drift back to Drake-approved forms.

Malcolm, however, fought us tooth and nail on every note.

His argument: "The songs were great as they were and had a big impact at our shows, and therefore the songs should stay exactly the same."

I didn't want to rock the boat too hard, not on his stormy seas. We did it his way. Only, no matter how hard we tried, they didn't sound quite the same. Drake brought something unique to our music, some powerful and dangerous ingredient, and he'd taken it with him.

MALCOLM: We'd lost our mad maestro. I'd reconciled myself to that fact, but I refused to surrender our music's impact on audiences. It became something of an obsession for me. If the music really did make people go wild, there had to be a rational explanation. It simply could not be a mystical, supernatural phenomenon. If it had a scientific basis, the effect must be reproducible. It was all a matter of cracking the code.

Music certainly has effects on the brain. Sound can alter brain waves, hormone production, breathing, and heart rate. Applied a certain way, it may even be able to rewrite neural pathways.

I'd started to think maybe Drake had mastered a technique to produce binaural beats with his guitar and amp. This is where you listen to two tones, with a slightly different frequency in each ear, which the brain reconciles as a new frequency. It's supposed to change your brain waves and how you think and feel. The so-called God frequency of 963 Hertz entraining theta waves in the brain.

I believed if I could understand the musical phenomenon, I could control and fine-tune it. If our raw songs produced a trance state akin to lucid dreaming and made people suggestible to random impulses, these songs could be refined to cause people to fall in love, quit bad habits and addictions, make world peace, anything. A beautiful culmination of thousands of years of human aspiration through music.

It certainly didn't hurt that I'd become the world's most successful musician in the bargain.

ERIC: I gravitated around the girl in the Shivers T-shirt, who sat passing a blunt with her friends. The whole time, I'm thinking about how to start a conversation. "Hey, I see you're a fellow fan of the Shivers." Real smooth.

Pretty soon, I'm picturing us sharing that joint and hitting it off. Becoming a couple. When I tell Lily about it, she wipes away a tear over lost chances and wishes me well. Then my new girlfriend is coming to my shows to fly into my arms and kiss me good luck before I swagger onto the stage.

I lived a whole life with her as a rock star in my mind, while my body kept veering away, too scared to actually talk to her. That was always my mistake. I'd build up the stakes so high before talking to a girl that I'd flub it.

No more loving from afar, I told myself. Just once, go for it. I was still trying to come up with the right approach to break the ice when Julian zipped over, stomped his skateboard, and caught it midair.

He pointed at me and said, "If you like the Shivers, he's the bassist."

The girl in the wool hat gazed up at me with awe, and I thought, Julian, you beautiful bastard. The perfect wingman.

It was like he knew all along that my blather and yearning about purpose was really just me being lonely and wanting a girlfriend.

The girl looked around the park.

She said, "Is Drake Morgan here?"

My first taste of what awaited me during the next ten years playing in the same band as Lily Lawless. Every groupie I'd meet asking me, What she's really like?

Julian informed the girl that Drake had left the band.

"Oh." That's all she said. Like someone flipped a switch and turned all the lights off. Then she went back to talking to her friends.

I stood there awhile. Finally, I worked up the courage to say something, but Julian wagged his head. My cue to make a graceful exit.

Then the girl said, "Hey, bass guy."

I turned as she whipped her shirt over her head and flung it my way.

She said, "I guess you can have that back, then."

Her friends howled with laughter while she sucked on her

joint, wearing only a bra. Julian shook his head at me again and gestured to keep on walking.

Which I did, feeling more like an idiot by the second.

Julian caught up and said, "Well, that sure backfired."

I went back to Malcolm's house to work on my bass.

RAMONA: I thought about shoving the djembe drum up our new lead guitarist's ass, but it spoke to me. It wanted to play. It seemed to say, *Hey, lady, I don't want to go to a self-help retreat either. I just want to make percussion. I want to speak and be heard.*

What the hell, I thought. Fine. Let's play, you and me.

In the summer, a drum circle met almost every weekend at Sand Island Park. Sometimes just a handful of people, other times a real party. New Age types who were more interested in spiritual growth than overthrowing the system.

I'd once banged bucket drums for food. I now played a drum kit in a band in the hope it would produce a far bigger future payday. Today I'd play for fun.

The group sat on boxes forming a circle on the grass in the shade of an old oak tree. The circle drummed in full swing, each instrument contributing its small part to the far larger sonic sum. Inside the circle, a few girls danced in hippie dresses, peasant blouses, and flared patchwork pants.

The idea of joining them made me a little nervous.

Everyone smiling like it was contagious. The whole thing a bit kumbaya. I reminded myself that life couldn't be all about survival and occasionally blowing off steam. A little kumbaya might be nice for a change.

No, my anxiety came from something else, and that was the promise of quick intimacy with strangers.

Then I spotted the blond-haired boy on the far side of the group, gazing back at me like I was a big slice of cake. Not in a creepy or scary way. He looked at me in an interested manner I did not mind one bit.

A smile that said, *If you were ever weak, I wouldn't hurt you.*

My own smile the product of me picturing blowing off some steam with him—the fast, furious, and forget-you-later kind.

Okay, I thought. I'm in.

LILY: Something else you can't control: how you feel.

I had developed a crush on our new lead guitarist.

On appearance, he was as conventionally handsome as Drake was unconventionally. Big and hunky, while Drake was lithe and sinewy. But looks ranked pretty low for me. Attitude, intellect, and heart hooked me far more.

On that score, they had plenty in common. They seemed complete and lived according to their own rules. They wanted to make a mark on the world.

Where Drake won the top prize for attitude, however, Julian did in having a good heart. He knew how to put others first. He cared about people. He cared about me. He was Drake with a little less attitude and a lot less self-centeredness. And he was mature, carrying an attitude that he knew exactly what he was doing.

I'd already opened up to Julian about my breakup. He turned out to be a great listener, the kind of guy who doesn't try to fix you and who listens to you with his eyes as well as his ears. Talking it all out proved a cathartic release that strengthened my resolve until I exhausted myself and only ended up missing Drake all the more.

I was setting myself up for a hard and fast rebound. Not the smartest idea, I know, but that's loneliness. It's horny fuel. If you went through your first big breakup and spent every day making music with a hot boy who turned out to be everything your ex wasn't, I wonder how long you'd last before craving a big ol' bite of forbidden fruit.

I knew my feelings for Julian constituted an allergic reaction to my breakup, not something entirely healthy or trustworthy. I knew the last time I'd mixed business and pleasure, I'd nearly destroyed my band.

Don't shit where you eat, right? Everyone knows that saying.

Still, I ached for a good, dirty, throw-down shag.

Sex always proved a hard thing for me if I didn't like the man, though. Without some connection, it felt like work. Which explained my lack of enthusiasm for one-night stands. A Catch-22.

God, I thought, no wonder so many people drunk-dial their exes for a hookup. It's the methadone of quitting romantic addictions.

No, I needed to be alone. Alone until I no longer felt lonely, with my guitar goddesses and six-string for company. I knew that.

But damn, Julian smelled good too.

The only thing you can really control is yourself. How you act on your emotions. The catch is, it's the hardest thing of all to control.

I could almost hear Drake telling me to go for it.

RAMONA: I sat on a bucket and put the drum between my knees. I caught the drum circle's Fanga rhythm and joined in to strengthen the heartbeat. After a while, my feet felt connected to the earth.

At first, I embraced nothing. No thought. A primal experience. My spirit left my body to mingle to join the song as it always did and touched the group, which it found warm and safe and welcoming.

Something busking never gave me. Something the Shivers never could.

I didn't need money. I needed this. It felt good.

But it also hurt.

My spirit went to the dark place of memory. Mom dying in a car crash. Uncle Jim coming to the funeral and staying with us awhile.

My bedroom door creaking open in the night. His foul breath in the dark. The crushing weight of his body pinning mine.

Strong hand clamped over my mouth, I can't breathe—

The things my father said to me when I finally told him about it. The drinking and beatings that followed, which deepened my shame.

Walking out the door to catch a bus with a backpack and thirty dollars.

My journey always started and ended with escape.

The group's spirit dissolved around me, leaving me alone and grasping empty air. The song faltered. The circle had broken. I left the zone to find my hands slapping loud, dense melodies on the goatskin. No longer channeling gentle water but fire, the kind of flames that burned the world.

MALCOLM: Eric would see me working hard at the problem on my keyboard, and he'd ask, "Still looking for the brown note?"

It's an urban legend. Supposedly, there's a sound frequency below human bearing, around five to nine Hertz, that makes you crap in your pants. Funny. One of the great things about wearing headphones is you can pretend you can't hear.

I tell you this so you can see what I had to put up with on a daily basis. Every solution had a problem. Every attempt to solve it had to endure heckling. It all seemed to point to a colossal flop for us at Armageddon.

LILY: Julian walked me home one night after practice, and my resolve to keep things neat crumbled. As humans, we're all so damn objective and logical until a strong emotion comes along like a wave and makes us lose our minds.

Then there's the fact that swearing off something tasty makes you want it all the more. God telling Adam and Eve not to eat the apple probably guaranteed it would at some point get munched.

Drake understood this. He told people to skip the self-torture and rationalization and get straight to eating that apple because you know it's gonna happen anyway. So the whole walk home, I'm having this argument with myself while I blather away about music I like and my guitar hero inspirations.

Julian asked, "What do you want, Lily?"

The same question Drake asked me that had reeled me in ten months ago.

I said, "I'd love to play my own songs."

Among other things. By the time we reached my door, the argument was over. If he asked to come in, I'd let him. If he even hinted.

He didn't.

It rankled me. Why the hell hadn't Julian made a single move to get me into bed? My radar wasn't broken; something was going on between us. His interest in me as a woman but lack of interest in me as a sexual being made me crazy.

When we're alone, the thing we miss most is touch.

I said, "What do *you* want?"

He said, "I'd love to hear you play one of your songs."

I offered to play right now, doing my own hinting.

Julian had a different idea. He told me the music club Elysian hosted an open-mic night every Thursday. He said I should let the world hear me.

A small music club hardly counted as *the world*, but I took his point. I thought: Maybe this would be the night something happened with Julian. It would all fall into place innocently, with and without intention, like an accident I'd planned.

In any case, it sounded like a date.

RAMONA: A drum circle encouraged individual expression, but ultimately it was about the group. I'd hijacked it.

Face burning with shades of shame, I settled back into the never-ending song's gentle heartbeat. One by one, the drummers rejoined. I glanced at the beautiful blond-haired boy, but he looked away. Good, I thought. I don't deserve it.

After the circle re-formed and became strong again, I left my drum and walked away. I didn't deserve having it either. I went back to the Shivers and its comforting desire for all the things I wanted but couldn't have.

Whatever Julian thought I needed, I wasn't ready for it.

MALCOLM: I was working on binaural beats before band practice when Julian showed up early and said, "Knock, knock." Taking off my headphones, I braced for impact.

First, he'd ask how I was doing. Then he'd give me the sympathetic, listening smile that got my bandmates to gush about their personal problems.

I have to admit, sometimes I felt the siren call myself. I could tell him about Queenie and Dad. The values they'd raised me with. The constant drive. How success for me wasn't about money or fame but a brute need to win and prove myself. These were worries embedded in my DNA, and I sweated them daily.

He said, "How am I doing, boss man?"

Not at all what I expected, but I had an answer for him.

I told Julian a parable about a band that replaced its drummer on the brink of success. It took some time for the new drummer to be accepted by the producer who'd been instrumental in the first drummer's firing. This new drummer had an approach to drumming that served the song rather than showed off technical prowess. In terms of chemistry, he meshed well with the band, his style influenced the music, and his affability eventually won over the fans. From there, the group went on to become one of the world's great rock bands.

Julian picked up that I was talking about Ringo Starr and the Beatles.

I said, "Now imagine we didn't replace Pete Best and instead replaced Paul, John, and George."

He laughed and said I'd given him very big shoes to fill.

I said, "I can't tell you how happy I am that you even asked me how I think you're doing. You're not Drake in all the best ways."

Then I said, "You're also the worst thing that could have happened to us."

I explained that since he'd joined the Shivers, the band had become happier and more stable. Like Ringo, Julian fit right in and smoothed things out with an easygoing manner that made things simple. Drake was gone, along with all the drugs and weirdos and Timothy Leary nonsense and chaos that seemed to follow him around. A calm space to make music and do business.

Personally, I loved it. But it had a cost.

My bandmates had become a little less angsty, less needy, and it showed in the music. It didn't matter what drove us as individuals. The point was that to make powerful music, we needed to be hungry. We needed to be hungry and longing and broken. We didn't start a band to discover inner peace. We'd started it to complain and exist.

I said, "We lost what made us edgy. Before, we sounded pretentious but dangerous. Now we just sound pretentious."

Julian shook his head. He wasn't having it.

He said, "The band isn't the problem. It's the music."

I told him I was working on that, but he wasn't talking about the rioting.

He said, "You're like a cover band playing your own songs. You keep trying, but you can't reproduce them with the right fidelity."

And there it was, the problem I couldn't solve because I'd been trying to solve an entirely different one. The music sounded dead because it wasn't really ours.

LILY: When Drake and I did shrooms that one night, songs had poured out of me, only to sit in a drawer half forgotten. I took out a few and practiced them on my own while the days trudged past with heavy anticipation.

By the time the big night finally arrived, I wasn't near ready to perform my own stuff in public and I'd totally romanticized how the night would end.

We arrived at Elysian, and I got my name on the sign-up sheet. We grabbed a seat near the back, and Julian went off to get us drinks at the bar. He returned with a lager for me, a steaming mug of tea for him.

I asked him how he thought everything was going with the band, if we'd be ready to crush Armageddon, and he shrugged. I asked him what the shrug meant.

Julian said, "Are you happy playing your ex's songs?"

I took a long bitter swallow to avoid answering.

The first act started, an anxious folk singer. I read the crowd's vibe and found it welcoming and forgiving of mistakes. These were music lovers, open to anything. I told myself this was the perfect place for me to cut my teeth trying out my own stuff. I'd only be on stage long enough to do three songs.

Still, my nerves danced on pins and needles. I hadn't practiced my songs nearly as much as I did the Shivers'. My *ex's songs*, as Julian had so brutally framed it. What if the crowd hated my music, and I turned out to be nothing in any musical sense without Drake?

I should have practiced more before putting myself out there like this.

They called my name, and I hauled my old Fender to the stage and settled behind the microphone.

I said, "I'm in a band, but I made some songs that were just for me. A friend thought you might like to hear them too. So here goes everything."

With that, I started thrashing power chords.

My songs were nothing fancy, just a basic ABABCB structure where A is a verse, B is the chorus, and C is the bridge. A simple pop format, which I played raw on repeat phrases of three or four chords. Electric tempo, 140 beats per minute, racing to the chorus for a big release, loud and loaded with energy.

I sang a song about a girl who'd like to get her first tattoo but wants it to be meaningful. A cupid for the boy who said he loved her? A sports car for the backseat where he seduced her? A broken heart for the moment he dumped her?

In the end, she decides none of these things define her and opts for a little smiley face, making it a tramp stamp above her bum, what she calls her shit-eating grin. The next boy she allows to see it can have her but never hurt her.

The hook, "I'm gonna grin and bear it," pivots to "bare it" at the end. Same lyric as far as the ear was concerned, but with a new meaning.

A dumb, fun little girl-power song. Heads bobbed across the room. When I finished, the applause washed over me like a burst of light erasing Drake's shadow.

Holy crap, I thought. It felt amazing. This was what music was supposed to be.

Flooded with power, I wanted nothing. I looked over at Julian, who was cheering and yelling from our table, and I thought, What the hell had I been thinking?

MALCOLM: Julian told me he'd heard Lily play a few songs at an open-mic night. The songs sounded simple, raw, fast, and fun. He said we should do that and make her the frontwoman, a fresh face for the pop-punk scene.

It was a solid idea, it really was. Only, I hated it to my core.

My reaction has a fancy name. It's called the sunk-cost fallacy. This is when you invest so heavily in something that you can't let it go even though doing so is your best move, like Coca-Cola clinging to New Coke despite the backlash. Every solution had a problem, only this time, the problem was even bigger than the preceding one.

Then Julian made another simple, innocent, helpful suggestion. This one shattered my world the way Drake had months earlier, telling me to do what I love.

He said, "If you want me to play exactly like Drake, I should see him play."

Considering the fact Drake was in the wind, I pointed out this was not possible.

Then he told me about Universal Priest.

LILY: Relationships boil down to power. Who has it, who doesn't. When I was with Drake, he had all the power. Julian showed me what balance might look like, and it looked freaking great, one of the things about him that had tempted me.

That night at Elysian reminded me that I had any power at all. And once I felt it again, the last thing I wanted was to give it away to anyone.

MALCOLM: I tried to remember where I'd seen the name before, and then it hit me. Universal Priest was on the Armageddon list.

And they were playing that Friday at Don Quixote.

I very much wanted to see Drake play as well. In my case to find out exactly what we'd be up against at Armageddon.

SLIDER BUZZSAW

THE DON QUIXOTE SHOW
AUGUST 12, 1999

*S*truggling to incorporate a new lead guitarist and wrestling with its musical identity, the Shivers reeled at the galling news Drake Morgan had not only joined a new group but already had a gig. On that day, the sun dimmed over Bethlehem in a partial eclipse, though the band had bigger worries than signs and portents in the sky. They traveled to Allentown to catch his show at Don Quixote Bar and Grille, unaware that they themselves were being watched.

LILY: After my breakup with Drake, I didn't feel vindictive. However manipulative and self-centered he turned out to be, I didn't want him to suffer. When I thought about him, which was plenty, I'd recall a tender memory as often as one that had me seething. For all the good times, I wished him the best. I was trying to take the high road and move on with my life. I hoped he was doing the same.

That being said, I didn't exactly want to see him happy either.

MALCOLM: Drake had walked away from Sunburst straight into the frontman spot for Universal Priest, which had a following and gigs. He hadn't quit the Shivers. He'd traded up.

LILY: Malcolm and Julian wanted to check out Drake's band, and I came along to keep them company. That's what I told them, anyway. I wanted to prove to Malcolm and the others once and for all that it wasn't our music but Drake himself that produced riots at our shows.

In the end, the whole band ended up driving out to Don Quixote.

RAMONA: Universal Priest had been around a while before Drake joined them. They'd performed at the Squat once. They were the worst. I mean the worst human beings, and their music wasn't much better. They were a joke band, an art band protesting music itself. They sounded like an industrial version of hell where machines tortured robots for eternity. They spat on the crowd. Jax, the frontman, was a heroin addict. Apparently inspired by the Columbine massacre, he shot himself in front of his old high school the day after our show at the Hobo Underground.

Malcolm seemed worried about Drake joining their band and competing against us at Armageddon, but I wasn't.

MALCOLM: Like I said, they had a small but hardcore following, and now they had our virtuoso lead guitarist and his secret sauce. I needed to do some recon.

Musicians sometimes diss bands because they don't think their music is any good. It doesn't matter what musicians think. The only thing that matters is the people who buy records and all the middlemen it takes to reach them. They may not be the arbiters of taste, but they are for damn sure the deciders of success.

LILY: Don Quixote offered a haven for bikers, hardcases, men down on their luck, and the women who loved them. Picture plenty of red neon, grimy bathrooms, balls of coke swapping hands, cigarette smoke hanging in drifts. Metal played on the jukebox. Balls clacked at the pool tables in the back. The kind of joint a Catholic girl like me had always felt drawn to but studiously avoided. I carried a fake ID Drake had gotten me, but I didn't need it. Nobody cared.

ERIC: Some of the kids had come wearing Shivers T-shirts. Others had SHIVER smeared on their foreheads in what looked like ash, at least I hope that's all it was. The rest were the usual local artists and weirdos who followed Universal Priest around. I spotted the pretty girl I'd met at the skate park, wearing the same wool hat. I caught her eye and waved, and she laughed at me. Then her friends laughed too.

You might think I'm a glutton for punishment, but sometimes, negative attention is still attention.

MALCOLM: They wore our T-shirts. They were mocking us.

RAMONA: The vibe in there was nasty. The place wavered at the razor edge of violence. I ordered a beer not because I really wanted a drink but to have something to bop heads with once the music started. Just in case.

MALCOLM: Ramona tugged on my sleeve and said, "How do we know it won't make us crazy?" Shouting in my ear because it was that kind of joint.

I was like, "What?"

She said, "The music. What if Lily's right, and it's him?"

I reminded her that we'd played with him ourselves. We seemed to be immune. In any event, I had bigger worries—notably, what Universal Priest sounded like.

Just in case, I put in a pair of earplugs to dampen the sound.

LILY: We found a spot by the bar, close to the exit. I'd received enough loaded, domineering male stares to keep myself snug between Ramona and Julian. I asked him why he wanted me to play my songs at Elysian.

He said, "Because Drake's music sucks. We should be playing yours."

No band tee tonight, just an earnest GOD IS LOVE. Julian

explained that Drake's songs were all about giving people permission to be their worst selves. Cheap wish fulfillment.

Destroy everything? It wasn't even original.

He said, "Your songs are better. They're about kids being stupid, getting their ass kicked for it, and then coming out on top because they stick up for themselves."

All kids want to stand out, he explained. They're also terrified that they will stand out and that others won't like what they see. Music should give them permission to be afraid and tell them they don't have to hurt themselves or others to stop feeling afraid. Compassion, Julian pointed out, is the essence of real cool, besides being the path to enlightenment.

I wanted to talk about it more with him, but the jukebox cut out and a hush fell over the space as Universal Priest mounted the stage.

ERIC: They looked like the Cenobites from *Hellraiser* decided to tour the earthly plane as a two-bit band.

Covered in tribal tattoos, the wiry savage drummer grinned under a mop of dreadlocks. The bassist was monstrous, an ogre of a man with the round, cruel face of a born bully. The gaunt keyboardist sported steampunk shades and seemed an expressionless robot. The female rhythm guitarist wore the rags of a prom dress and a blank white mask.

The hardcore Universal Priest fans welcomed them by quacking like ducks.

RAMONA: What a bunch of pretentious assholes. God, I hated those guys.

LILY: Drake took the stage wearing only a pair of black jeans. Since our breakup, he'd gotten some new tattoos, occult symbols and runes adorning his pale torso, the Kabbalah's Tree of Life running down his back. At the sight of his pale body shining in the stage lights, my heart made a loud thump as if our relationship rolled over in its grave. The bar regulars barely noticed the band, but the kids who'd come to see him gazed fiercely back with feral grins.

Drake raised his hand with two fingers extended and said something in Latin. I remembered him once making that gesture to me like a benediction before touching them to my forehead.

Julian murmured a translation: "'As above, so below.' Opposites in unity."

Drake said, "Now it's your turn."

MALCOLM: The room filled with hellish carnival music saturated in discordant frequencies. The crowd laughed and started quacking again. The regulars glared, already shouting to stop the awful racket.

ERIC: It was painful to hear.

MALCOLM: Ramona tugged on my sleeve again and said, "We're immune, fine. But what about everyone else who's here?"

ERIC: It sounded so horrible that I actually felt a little sorry for Drake.

LILY: Then Drake started playing, and I realized I missed that too.

MALCOLM: Ramona's question had me anxious as hell, wondering if we were about to find ourselves at ground zero of another Sunburst, but then Drake started wailing and my heart sank.

ERIC: He sang, "If nothing matters, only you are real."

MALCOLM: It sounded exactly like our stuff, only far more raw, electric, and dangerous. The way we used to sound before Drake left.

That's when I realized Julian was right. It wasn't our music to begin with.

RAMONA: It didn't sound like us at all. It was like a wall of industrial noise. Jackhammers, saws, machines cranking and pounding. The heavy reverb made my teeth ache. Drake shaped it into something bigger, but it was horrible.

MALCOLM: My point is, our music had never been all that great. It was Drake.

LILY: It's almost like he could play with any type of music and transform it.

ERIC: The regulars fell into a drooling trance while the kids who'd caught our other shows grimaced and twitched. The pretty girl who hated me hitched her shoulders in jerky spasms, taking little bites at the air. Oh God, it was happening again.

LILY: The annoying quacking died out. The whole room turned into quivering mannequins except for us and the band gyrating on the stage. Then something blurred past the bartender's head and shattered the mirror behind him.

As I flinched, I spotted a biker at the pool tables. He picked up another ball and did a long pitcher's windup, eyeing the bartender's head as if it were home plate.

I was like, Oh no, please don't—

MALCOLM: Ramona tugged on my sleeve again, saying, "It's time to go."

ERIC: When Ramona chooses flight over fight, you start running.

LILY: Then Drake stopped playing.

MALCOLM: The band crashed to a halt. Freed of the song's grip, the crowd let out a gasp. A pool ball bounced along the floor.

Drake beamed at Lily and said, "Darling! You came!"

LILY: He leaped off the stage and marched straight through the throng while my heart rattled like one of Ramona's drum solos. His eyes blazed with their own light, making me feel like we were the only people in the room.

He said, "You're looking good."

He did too. Of course, he did. Drake always looked good.

Then he scowled at Julian's tee with its GOD IS LOVE message.

"God is also a kid dying of cancer," he said.

Julian: "The Devil's greatest trick was convincing the world he doesn't exist."

Drake: "God's was conning the world into believing he matters."

Then he turned his scowl on me.

"It didn't take you long to replace me," he said.

Hearing this gave me a hot thrill. He was actually jealous. The feral drummer and oafish bassist walked over to stand grinning on either side of him. The keyboardist and the rhythm guitarist with the mask watched us from the stage.

I said, "I guess it didn't take you long to replace us either."

Drake laughed. Ol' Jax, he informed me, had seen the light after coming to the Shivers' show at the Hobo. It seemed only right to take his place.

Then he said, "I'd like you to meet Gog and Magog, my rhythm section."

RAMONA: The drummer stared at me with crazy eyes and this wolfish smile on his stupid face. I stared right back, thinking, Go ahead and try me, motherfucker.

ERIC: The bassist looked at me, and I served up a polite smile. He leaned in and mouthed something. I was like, What? His mouth moved again, but I still didn't catch it. I tilted my head to hear.

He said, "I eat people."

LILY: Drake told me the music didn't sound the same without me, and I admitted ours didn't sound the same without him. His band would take some work, maybe a *taste of the whip*, as he casually put it, but they'd come around.

On the plus side, he added, his new bandmates didn't have the same moral hang-ups restraining his potential as an artist. They were willing to go all the way.

I said, "Then I guess we're both better off."

Right then, I sincerely meant it. Drake seemed to have gained an even sharper edge since we were together, and I wondered if I'd been a civilizing influence on him.

He said, "After we win Armageddon, I'll be ready to go solo. Drakon or Mandrake or something. You were always better at naming things than me."

Before I could correct him that *we'd* be the ones winning Armageddon, he added, "Remember I said I felt like I was living my life backward? My soul is racing to its birth. People love me. Soon everyone will. But who do you love?"

Right then, I was just trying to love myself.

He said, "I miss you, Lilith. I'm not complete without you."

ERIC: Man, I had nightmares about that dude for weeks. Nightmares where he sat on my chest and I couldn't breathe. Him stroking my hair and telling me he was tenderizing my flesh because he thought I'd be chewy.

LILY: I didn't know how to respond to Drake. It honestly floored me. I do remember feeling pissed that he couldn't tell me he loved me the entire time we were together. That it took breaking up to admit he needed me at all.

He said, "We're supposed to be together. Come back. Mandrake doesn't have to be a solo act. We can do it together. Straight to the top and beyond."

Still, I didn't say anything. Taking this as indecision, he said, "Just say yes. Say you will. A part of you wants to."

His left eye glinted with happiness to see me. His right smoldered like an angry coal, the one that used to sometimes make me feel uncertain.

I wasn't anxious now, though. I was mad.

I said, "You act like saying yes to every urge that pops into your head is brave. It's actually the easiest thing to do. Saying no and living with the consequences is so much harder."

His face darkened as he said, "Then live with them."

Someone called out, "Hey! Hey, dolly!"

The man pushed through the crowd of Shivers fans, tugging at his fly.

He said, "I never got to show you—"

The room filled with a growling roar and burst of light.

MALCOLM: That's when the man came flying through the window.

RAMONA: I was getting set to knock that pervert on his ass again. The next thing I know, the room exploded.

ERIC: Okay, I'll tell you exactly— [*nervous laughter*]. Honestly, all

I remember is that huge sword doing a gleaming cartwheel in a shower of sparkling glass.

LILY: It all happened for me in slow motion, allowing me to take in every detail. The guy came at me wearing his gloating smile, SHIVER smeared on his forehead. Behind him, the bar's front windows filled with glaring light, the headlights of a snarling truck, the truck slamming into something with a loud *BANG*.

Then a priest in a black cassock hurtled like a human missile through the glass along with a spinning sword. Glass shot across the howling crowd. The priest flew straight between Drake and me to crash into the stage. His drummer and bassist's heads swiveled to watch him go while Drake's eyes stayed locked on me.

As for the sword, it disappeared behind the guy still tugging at his fly and popped out his chest in a red mist. He hiccuped blood and collapsed in a heap.

MALCOLM: People shouted and howled in pain. Drake laughed as if the whole thing was hilarious.

RAMONA: I yelled, "*Now* can we go?"

LILY: Drake gazed down at the bloody body and said, "Bad luck, I guess." He grinned at Julian and added, "How's yours tonight, champ?"

Ramona yanked me outside. A massive pickup truck idled mere inches from the front of the bar. Steam poured from the crumpled hood. Julian held out his hand for the keys, and Malcolm surrendered them without a word.

We piled into the van in silence like obedient children.

Then we all started screaming our heads off.

ARNIE DECKER (*owner, Don Quixote Bar and Grille*): Jesus, man, that was a long time ago, but yeah, I guess you could call it a night to remember. Fifteen people injured, two dead—three if you count Dodge, the bartender, who a week later grabbed a cab into Bethlehem and took a flying leap off the roof of the Martin Tower. Back then, it was still standing, the headquarters of Bethlehem Steel. This from a guy who once told me how he was afraid of heights because he'd get this weird urge to jump.

The first dead dude was a Catholic priest mowed down by Phil Baker, a regular, who'd gotten wasted before he even reached the bar and lost control of his truck. The other was some shmuck with his dong hanging out, who somehow wound up impaled by the sword the priest was carrying around.

Only in New York, I thought, but then I remembered I'd pulled stakes and moved all the way the hell out to Allentown to get away from this kind of crazy shit. I mean, I don't kid myself, Don Quixote is a rough joint, and we like it that way—the devil you know and all that—but that night was beyond the pale. It looked like a goddamn war zone.

Needless to say, our experiment to draw a younger crowd ended with Universal Priest, and from then on we stuck with honky-tonk bands.

CHARLOTTE SKINNER: It's all in the public record. The deceased was Father Salvador Guerrero. Ordained a priest in 1991, he served as assistant pastor at Our Lady of Sorrows Church in Albuquerque, New Mexico, until 1997, when he accepted a pastoral assignment at the same church.

You asked about the weapon he had in his possession. It was an authentic Zweihänder or two-handed sword commonly carried by the Pontifical Swiss Guard. Apparently a valuable antique, as it bore engravings of the coat of arms of the Medici family of Tuscany, which produced four popes in the Renaissance era.

That is all I can tell you about the incident.

ERIC: And that wasn't even the end of it. The night was still young.

LILY: We all kept yelling, "WHAT THE HELL WAS THAT?" After a while of this, we called out recollections as if as a group we could piece it together in a way that somehow made logical sense. Someone asked what happened to the man who flew through the window, and I was able to contribute that he'd struck the stage like a bullet and was very likely no longer in the world of the living.

MALCOLM: Ramona kept asking if anyone was hurt. None of us were. A small miracle with all that glass shooting through the crowd. Not even a single scratch. I noticed red spots on my shirt, but it wasn't my blood.

LILY: Julian started the van and sped off before the police showed up, adding to my vague but gnawing sense this had all been somehow my fault. We drove around awhile, and I thought he was driving just to drive.

Before long, we'd finally vented our stress and turned inward to our own private thoughts. Aside from the odd *holy shit* or *what the hell*, the van fell silent.

Julian said, "Music has been associated with the Devil since the days of Dionysus. But the Devil doesn't own good music. Music is God's gift. It's supposed to be a path of communion with the divine, not corrupted like this."

No one knew what to say to that. At last, Eric said, "Yeah, really."

The van stopped, only we weren't home but instead in a parking lot lit by sodium pole lights. I looked out the window but didn't recognize the neighborhood. Then I followed everyone else's gaze out the windshield to take in the Gothic Revival architecture and bright stained glass of a church.

Julian said, "I'd like you to meet some friends of mine."

Our night, it seemed, was about to get even weirder.

He said, "It's time you learned the truth about everything."

MALCOLM: On the way inside, Julian told us the church was hallowed ground, and we'd be safe there. Besides that, he added, it was a famous church, housing the Bells of Saint Michael, century-old cast-iron bells that were only to be rung when Catholicism itself was under attack.

I said, "Seriously? Who is supposed to hear—"

"It's symbolic," he told me like a warning to zip it.

LILY: We entered the looming church, which held the proud name of Our Lady of Victory. Hundreds of burning candles gave the spacious interior a moody medieval atmosphere. My eyes slid over the all-too-familiar carpet, pews, and altar to focus on the dozens of priests inside. They stood around whispering in huddled groups. Instantly, I recognized the giant nun who'd barely survived the riot at Sunburst, dressed in her gray habit.

As the big oak door crunched shut, the men turned to stare at us in surprise.

Julian called out, "We're running out of time. And they're ready to hear it."

MALCOLM: An old priest shuffled over from the altar. Judging by his purple sash and sizable reverent entourage, I took him as the big cheese here.

Ready to represent the band, I extended my hand for a friendly shake as he approached, but he walked straight up to Lily and said in a heavy accent, "You must be Lillian Lawlor of whom I have been well informed."

Julian said, "Lily, may I introduce His Most Reverend Excellency, Adedayo Igwe, bishop of Lagos, Nigeria. He has something important to tell you."

LILY: I'd never actually been socially introduced to a bishop before. In fact, I was so surprised I almost forgot my manners. Remembering my upbringing, I bowed to kiss his ring and said, "Your Excellency."

He had a kindly round face and squinted through little gold spectacles. A violet skullcap and sash with his buttoned black cassock. A pectoral cross hung by a chain around his neck.

His voice sounded deep but soft. Without mincing words, he got right to the point. The man had traveled five thousand miles on an important holy mission.

He said, "Your former lover, Drake Morgan, is the Antichrist."

Overwhelmed and still punch-drunk from the explosive violence at Don Quixote, I snorted and said, "Tell me about it."

MALCOLM: Then Ramona said, "So that's why you've been trying to kill him."

To my surprise, the bishop nodded and told her that she was correct.

RAMONA: The clergymen closed in all around us and I thought: *Get. Me. Out. Of. Here.* We were about to get sucked into some religious lunacy, the kind where someone reads a line in the Bible and decides it's an order from God to blow up a building. Coming to this place had been a mistake.

LILY: Bishop Igwe explained that the church avoided fixating on eschatological details about the Antichrist's arrival, leaving such things in God's hands. Prior to six months earlier, even he had rarely given it much thought.

Then he had a vision from God.

A man stood on a stage with an electric guitar. Hidden in shadow, a naked giant towered behind him. A little horn grew out of the back of the guitarist's skull, only this was no horn but a brass pipe terminating in a mouthpiece.

The giant gripped the man's head and blew hard into the mouthpiece, his cheeks ballooning. The musician jerked to life and began to play. The crowd screamed in the emanations.

The image made me shiver, as it reminded me so much of the painting of Drake's dream still decorating my living room wall. But it was just a dream.

The bishop said, "The vision told me the name and place of the Antichrist."

Julian swept his arm across the assembly and put in, "All these people had the exact same vision on the exact same day. All over the world. They came here."

Bishop Igwe added, "And our mission is to destroy him."

ERIC: I was all set to give a big thumbs-up and say, *Cool! Good luck with that!* Then exit stage right. Malcolm, however, had to open his big yap.

MALCOLM: I was an atheist, and I wasn't having any of this nonsense.

ERIC: The only thing he worshipped was the golden goose and a perfect version of himself.

MALCOLM: I argued that God can't be all-powerful. He can't create a circular triangle or commit suicide or make a boulder he can't lift. If God created logic and God can't do illogical things, then God made a contradiction and arbitrarily limited his power—and if God is confined by logic, then logic is the supreme law.

Similarly, God can't do evil. In fact, the very existence of it refutes his power. Either God can't prevent evil, which makes him powerless, or he won't, which makes him evil himself. I mean, I was born into sin, but even I would jump in a river to save a drowning child instead of acting like doing it was beneath me.

To that point, God also can't be all-good. If he created everything, then he created evil, which makes him the author of evil. Or if he didn't create evil, then there must be a moral authority higher than God.

And how's this for evil: God could have actualized any reality he wanted, but he made this one in which I'd be an atheist and therefore doomed to suffer for eternity because I didn't think it rational to believe in an invisible supreme being. I mean, if there was a God, the idea of free will became logically impossible.

It all added up to the irrefutable fact that God either didn't exist or didn't matter, and therefore neither did an Antichrist. In short, they were nuts.

ERIC: "Bro," I said out of the side of my mouth. "Shut the fuck up."

RAMONA: The clergy growled, and Bishop Igwe looked at Malcolm like he'd sprouted horns himself. The big nun took a step forward with her fists clenched into mallets. Julian stepped in to say, "It's not a contradiction, guy. It's a mystery. Logic doesn't get you there. You have to know him in your heart. It's like Saint Augustine said. If you think you understand God, that ain't God."

MALCOLM: Precisely the point I was making! I tried a different tack.

I was like, Okay. Fine. If evil exists for some greater good, then I have no duty to stop it and neither do you. In fact, you have a moral duty to support it.

ERIC: Well, that shut *everybody* up.

DR. WOODWARD: It's an interesting proposition! If it's God's plan that the Antichrist come to power, then any Christian who opposes the Antichrist is in effect opposing God's will and the arrival of the Kingdom of Heaven.

I doubt the idea would gain much traction in theological circles. If the Antichrist is evil, then Christians have a duty to oppose him for that alone. One might argue, though, that instead of trying to stop the Antichrist, which can't be done, one instead should try to save as many as possible from his persecution. If God were to send a group of priests a vision of the Antichrist's arrival, that could be the divine intention.

Then again, if you had a chance to kill Hitler before he started the Second World War and launched the Holocaust, wouldn't you at least try?

MALCOLM: Take any religious belief to its logical extreme, and you can see plain as day how silly it is. I had yet to learn that didn't necessarily make it untrue. Saint Augustine, it turned out, was onto something.

LILY: I was already in shock from Don Quixote, and then a bishop of the church dropped this psychic atom bomb on me, which I similarly struggled to process.

Drake, the literal spawn of Satan. A man I'd shared my love and body with.

My ex. The Antichrist.

My first thought was, Did I do something wrong? Am I in trouble?

Then I tried to reconcile the Drake I knew with the biblical Antichrist, which I immediately found laughably ridiculous. Drake was a wildly gifted Peter Pan who refused to grow up, nothing more.

That meant these people were crazy. And homicidal. They'd tried to kill Drake thrice, and those were just the times I knew about.

To defuse the situation a little, I said, "Why are you telling me all this?"

Bishop Igwe answered, "At first, we worried you might be disciples of Mr. Morgan. But you resisted his control."

RAMONA: I held back a laugh. I'm not sure *resisted* was the right word for it. When he was with the band, it was all about him, and we went along with it. His music, his talent, his message. He was the organ grinder and we were the monkeys.

LILY: The bishop told me that his group became very interested in me after I ended my relationship with Drake and he left the band.

I said, "What do you mean? Interested in what way?"

Out of all the answers that Bishop Igwe could have given me, the one he served up ranked dead last.

He said: "We need you to get back together with him."

RAMONA: Malcolm did not hold back his laughter. The priests growled again. I could have slapped him. I really, really did not want to have to fight these guys.

LILY: I was like, You what the what? Me? Get back with him? Seriously?

The bishop took my hands in his and smiled with his kindly round face.

He said, "Then once you're back in his trust, we want you to kill him."

While I gaped, he went on: "We have a wide assortment of blades, each sanctified with holy water blessed by the Holy Father himself."

CHARLOTTE SKINNER: The church has no knowledge of nor official sanction of any secret organization dedicated to identifying and opposing the Antichrist. Yes, some sort of gathering of clergy apparently occurred at Our Lady of Victory in 1999. The ensuing horrific tragedy is a matter of public record. Anything else remains the stuff of rank conspiracy theory.

I can tell you without a doubt that our purpose is to serve God through faith and good works, not hatch cabals and assassinations.

LILY: Several priests stepped forward to offer me a variety of medieval knives and swords. I thought, Holy shit, they're serious.

ERIC: The Daggers of Megiddo!

MALCOLM: I was like, dude. That's *The Omen*.

In the movie, an exorcist gives Robert Thorn seven daggers that can kill the Antichrist on hallowed ground. One to kill his physical form and the rest to kill his soul, stabbed into his chest in the pattern of a cross.

Like I said: a movie. The daggers don't actually exist.

I looked at Julian and said, "Seriously?"

He shrugged and said, "There's no manual for this."

The bishop chimed in: "Some of our bravest volunteered to fight the Antichrist. Two of them are now dead. Lillian, you may be our only hope."

LILY: That's when I snapped and yelled out, "All right, already!"

I'd had enough of this nonsense. I wasn't getting back together with Drake. I sure as hell wasn't about to go around killing anyone. I may not have been the world's best Catholic, but I was at least devout enough to follow God's commandment against murder.

Bishop Igwe's kindly face turned unkindly.

He said, "Pray on it. As for me, I will pray you have a change of heart before it's too late and the whole world burns."

I wanted to run like hell, but I stuck it out while he went on talking. He told me if I changed my mind, I could find them here. Churches were God's turf, which the Antichrist could not enter. Our Lady of Victory was the one place they felt truly safe and could use as a base of operations. Another rule that I doubted had any scriptural basis and probably came from a movie. More winging it.

The bishop said, "May almighty God bless you: the Father, and the Son, and the Holy Spirit. Go with God, child."

Automatically, I sketched the sign of the cross over my heart. He'd just blessed me. A bishop of the Holy Church! On any other day, that would have struck me as pretty darn cool, but I wanted to get these men and this place as far behind me as possible.

I needed to find Drake and warn him.

Julian followed us back into the night. Once outside, I looked at him and said, "Just who the hell *are* you?"

"A friend," was all he'd tell me.
Malcolm balled his fists and yelled, "Goddamnit!"
We froze in our tracks.
Now what?
He said, "We need a new sound."

EAR CANDY

SEPTEMBER–DECEMBER 1999

After Universal Priest's bloody show at Don Quixote, the Shivers realized their music sounded like a toothless version of what Drake Morgan would bring to Armageddon. Like a Hail Mary pass hurled on a wing and a prayer, the band pivoted toward a new sound that would be entirely theirs and forever define them.

With Armageddon looming, they'd have to work miracles.

LILY: Come up with a catchy phrase of three or four power chords and play them as fast as you can on repeat. This is the backbone.

Intro, verse, chorus, verse, bridge, and then finish it off with the chorus or an outro. Maybe throw in a breakdown that changes things up—perhaps a solo at a slower tempo and with different lyrics—and maybe a fun and irreverent little sing-along, something like "La-la, la-la-la."

Then thrash it with tons of energy and no ambition other than being loud.

Congratulations, you've just made a pop-punk song.

MALCOLM: I held a band meeting to present the new business plan. My role model going into this would be none other than the great Steve Jobs, who returned to Apple in 1997 to renew the company's product strategy.

RAMONA: To call Malcolm a sellout actually would be unfair. There was no *out*. He was born selling. It's hard to judge someone who never had a choice.

MALCOLM: Eric said, "You mean like Madonna. We're reinventing our brand."

I grunted something like *yeah, duh* and went back to my easel presentation. The point I'd made had to do with focus and commitment. We couldn't just play pop-punk music, we had to live and breathe it. We had to believe.

Pop-punk started in the 1970s and early '80s with bands like the Ramones and the Buzzcocks. It combined the energy, pacing, and irreverence of punk with the catchy accessibility of pop. Upbeat tempo, strong rhythms, earworm hooks and choruses, and relatable lyrics. Each song three minutes at the very most.

The 1990s saw it come on strong with catchy tunes from the likes of Green Day and the Offspring. People had grown sick of saccharine pop music, while the alternative scene could get too heavy.

Pop-punk offered something in between. It was for everyone. Our new motto: *radio-friendly*. Mainstream music packaged as rebellion. Edgy but fun. I handed out CDs to everyone to listen to as homework. Green Day, Operation Ivy, blink-182, Rancid, Jimmy Eat World, Bad Religion.

We had a little under four months to produce fifteen to twenty songs we could play during the upcoming battle of the bands. Armageddon, here we come.

LILY: I expected a big debate during that meeting, but everyone seemed excited about the change, like they'd been hungry for it. The music was relatively simple and fun to play. Overall, the sound felt more like us, if that makes sense.

More than a hundred songs gushed out of me over the three days of possession and ecstasy following my strange night taking magic mushrooms with Drake. Translating them into arrangements, practicing them as a band, and working out the kinks before Armageddon would be a problem.

One of those good problems, though. Exactly the kind of challenge I needed to distract me from my breakup and the gang of Catholic clergy who considered my ex-boyfriend the literal Antichrist and wanted to kill him.

MALCOLM: Nobody heckled me at that meeting, which I took as a good sign these misfits wanted to get serious. They were growing up. It made me proud.

LILY: I'd assumed Julian would continue on as frontman, but he suggested I take on the role of lead vocals.

He said, "It's time the world heard your voice."

Maybe he had that right. Only, I didn't want to hear it from him. His love for the music and Smashing Pumpkins T-shirt didn't fool me about his true agenda.

I said, "Why are you even still here?"

He said, "I really dig the new sound."

Not the answer I was looking for. Catching my stink-eye, he shrugged, a gesture telling me he could say no more.

I tried another tack. "What's your relationship with those priests?"

"They're friends," was all he'd share.

I said, "If you tell me you're the second coming of Jesus, you're out."

Julian laughed.

"Maybe I'm just a nice dude," he said.

Playing on stage at Elysian had dulled my crush. My loss of trust killed whatever romantic interest I had left. When it came to the music, I could work with him. That didn't change. With anything else, I became contradictory as a rule.

Julian seemed to enjoy helping people deal with the especially tough problem that is themselves. In his travels, he'd acquired the wisdom to back that up. With my shaky judgment clouding my feelings, I'd allowed him to help me too.

To me, though, it suddenly looked a little like manipulation. I hadn't traded in my dad for Drake only to end up with another man just like them, however velvet the handcuffs. My taste in the opposite sex had started to make me wonder. If you keep picking a certain type, you wind up asking yourself if it's them or you.

RAMONA: In pop-punk, the guitars drive the overall sound, but the drums have a very important role, which is to keep a strong beat going and keep it on time. It's more about pouring gasoline on the fire at a fast, steady rate than showing off. Keeping the energy going and feeding it to the band. I was made for this.

ERIC: I remember Ramona being very agreeable about it. I remember this quite clearly because her ever being agreeable was notable. I mean, I could count the times she was agreeable on one hand. The rage she carried around in her seemed to find a handy target in her music. I figured she was just into pop-punk.

RAMONA: Pop-punk wasn't really my jam, but it was far closer to it than the old Shivers' haunting hymns.

It was the kind of thing the hotheads at the Squat treated with levels of scorn only conceivable in the purity of youth. Not long before, I might have agreed with them. But the music sounded good, it was fun, and I could play it loud and proud.

So yeah, I got plenty excited about the change. It certainly took my troubled mind off, you know, the whole Antichrist thing.

Besides Julian, I seemed to be the only one willing to take it seriously. Everyone else clung to denial. Eric even shrugged it off as, "Oh, that's just Drake being Drake," as if it had always been only a matter of time before some Christian denomination put a bounty on his head. Lily seemed to spend her days trying to avoid thinking about him at all. Malcolm wanted us focused on winning all the marbles at the upcoming battle of the bands.

I don't believe it was about coping or keeping our eye on the prize. Nope, just basic denial, even though Drake was obviously strange as hell. Though he undeniably had a dark side. Though he had powers that defied rational explanation.

As for me, I wondered if Armageddon would be a fair fight. I pictured Drake mesmerizing the audience and judges and turning them into disciples, as I believed he might be doing. Wrecking the world one pair of ears at a time. And I thought, Do we really even want to win?

I didn't want to imagine what the Antichrist might do if he ever lost.

DR. WOODWARD: Another interesting scenario: A man's friends discover he will become the Antichrist. Are they more or less inclined to believe it than someone who doesn't know the man?

I'd have to say a lot less, probably. The Antichrist holds a certain power in the religious imagination. A patch of darkness onto which we can project our worst fears. The polar opposite of everything we think is good. It's a colossal identity that has to pull a huge amount of weight.

And then you find out who it is, and you're like, "Oh, that's just Bob who's a dentist and writes 'lol' at the end of every text and keeps tropical fish for pets," and the awe is officially over.

Hey, the same thing happened to Jesus when he preached in Nazareth and strongly insinuated he was the awaited Messiah. The Nazarenes rejected him, saying, "Isn't this the carpenter's son?" They knew his family and had watched him grow up. To them, he was just another local boy, one with some pretty grandiose ideas about himself.

Leaving Nazareth, Jesus said, "No prophet is accepted in his hometown."

I can't imagine the Antichrist would be either.

LILY: I may have stopped trusting Julian, but the man stepped up where it counted. When he played Drake's parts in the Shivers' original material, it had a paint-by-numbers feel to it, but for our pop-punk stuff, he became inspired.

All our songs possessed a positive if ironic vibe. Nothing angsty or emo. Just embracing being alive, finding yourself, and taking nothing too seriously. Story-of-my-life songs expressed in rhyming couplets. Sometimes the lyrics told a tale; other times, they trained together a series of images to explore a theme.

The old nihilism was gone, and good riddance.

In one song, "Run for Your Life," a teen gets his first summer job and is determined to show everyone what he's made of. After being pushed around by managers and customers, however, the kid up and quits.

"No more wheel for me," he says. "I'm setting this hamster free." The chorus, "I'll give you a run for your money," takes on a new meaning at the end.

In another song, a skate rat and his pals get chased out of a park by local cops every weekend—all part of the game. The one time they catch him, they beat the crap out of him, and he realizes it never was actually a game. The next weekend, he grabs his board and goes back, bruises and all, ready to play again.

All our songs came off earnest and silly, sure—we weren't putting Shakespeare to music or anything here—but also as fun and relatable.

Julian, however, took a bigger view. He said, "Pop-punk isn't about teen angst. It's about expelling it. It's teen therapy."

We were having so much fun, in fact, that sometimes I'd forget all about the gang of priests who wanted to murder my ex-boyfriend. Then Julian would always ruin the moment by telling me repeatedly Bishop Igwe wanted to see me again.

"Not on your life," I told him every time.

Anyway, after we nailed down the first few songs, I celebrated by getting one of those armlet tattoos that were all the rage back in those days. I had it inked on my left bicep, a five-line staff with the chorus to "Grin and Bare It" drawn in musical notes.

Committing the music to my very flesh, yes, but the meaning was more specific than that. I'd finally found music to play that allowed me to be me, comfortable in my own skin.

MALCOLM: This time, I didn't take any chances. Every song that poured out of Lily's brain became the property of the band, committed to sheet music.

Reading and writing sheet music is something else that may not sound like fun, but I loved it. At the base, music is math and coding. A song is broken up into measures, each having the same number of beats defined by the time signature. Notes are divisible into fractions, songs into patterns. Music is counted. The most popular songs have a mathematical structure.

There is just as much beauty in music's construction as in the sound it makes in our ears. For all its rebellion against norms, pop-punk followed precise rules and structures. Something about that just tickled me.

LILY: This was no doubt a weird time in my life, but I still get nostalgic for it. That time when you're young and hungry and all your biggest wins and worst defeats are ahead of you, accessible right then only through longing and imagination. When you give your all for a chance at everything, the effort leaving you utterly drained.

Even now, I can close my eyes and see Julian raking his guitar so hard it practically bounced off the floor before singing a verse about a breakup that ended in a mocking sing-along refrain, *da-da-da, da-da-da-da* from the "Jingleheimer Schmidt" children's song. Malcolm nodded over his keyboard. Eric plucked his bass. Ramona's snares banged like a machine gun.

All of us riding to the sweet spot together, finding our collective voice as a band and identity as a tribe. We'd finish a song flushed and sweating, and then we'd do it again, maybe tweaking the rhythm and timing, reworking a breakdown, and always punching up the energy until it finally hit eleven.

ERIC: Playing a bass guitar in a pop-punk band turned out to be as fun as it looked. At first, I just followed the chords with matching sixteenth notes. Once I had this under my belt, I could put my own little flourishes on it.

As time went by, the songs all came together nicely. As a band, we'd finally found our voice, and it sounded natural. I asked Lily how she'd come up with so much great material, and she said, "I ate magic mushrooms that Drake laced with his blood, and I could *see* the music." She blinked and shook her head. "He disappeared into a door I hallucinated for three days."

I stared at her awhile and then said, "Well. Whatever works, I guess."

A part of me missed this sort of weirdness that always seemed to happen when Drake was around. Most of me grooved on the new cool, calm, and collected Shivers. Drake had made it feel like a rock band, but I think Malcolm had it right that in the end, the only way forward was to get down to business.

MALCOLM: I itched to test-market our new product on a willing audience. The only problem was, I didn't see us as quite ready to play gigs. In my plan, that would come after we'd blown away the competition at Armageddon.

Lily offered a solution. She told me she'd played her acoustic guitar at Elysian, but its stage offered a backline including a drum kit and amps. A full band could walk up and rock a few songs.

I thought it was a good idea, though I hated the idea of giving it away for free. Before I could voice any objection, she said, "No money. Just play."

So that's what we did. We started playing every Thursday night, whatever latest material we'd put down.

LILY: Julian asked me to meet him at a coffee shop. I knew it well, as Drake and I had dragged our asses there on many a morning, still hung over and giggling from a night out hunting novel experiences. I agreed, of course, but it had me a little nervous, wondering if he was finally responding to all the desperate, horny signals I'd broadcast his way in the halo of my breakup.

As it turned out, my worries proved unfounded.

Bishop Igwe stood at one of the tables and extended his hand. Glowering, I dutifully kissed his ring before growling at Julian:

"Whose side are you on?"

"Jesus Christ's," he said automatically.

While he went to the counter to order me a cappuccino, the bishop got right to the point. He said Drake didn't yet know he was the Antichrist, presenting a rare window of opportunity to prevent his rise to power.

He said, "Your annoying bandmate was right that the Antichrist's arrival is God's plan. But, well, he's the Antichrist."

Bishop Igwe sipped his coffee and let me infer the rest. As long as the Devil's son roamed the earth, the church would oppose him.

I pointed out he might be wrong. He said God would not lie to him.

I yelled after Julian, "Make mine to go."

RAMONA: That night at the church had really gotten into my head. If Drake was actually the Antichrist, did that mean the world was about to end?

If the world was about to end, did the band, or anything I'd do in my life, actually matter? If nothing mattered, should I obsess over following God's rules so I'd be saved during the Rapture, if that was also a real thing?

Did God really expect me to love him with my whole heart while knowing he was going to destroy the world, which would be like Holly McClane falling in love with Hans Gruber at the Nakatomi Christmas party? If I spent my life obsessing over God and denying everything else, what was the point of living?

If God expected me to forgive Uncle Jim and my father, could I do it?

LILY: The bishop was talking crazy again, but he had me pondering things I'd tried to avoid thinking about.

Sometimes I'd come home from band practice and study the painting that Drake and I muraled onto our living room wall. His nightmare. Surrounded by a fiery glow, the dark guitarist stood alone on a stage gripping the fretboard with his strumming hand raised in a triumphant fist. The Edvard-Munch-type screamers boiled like tormented souls in the foreground.

This was Armageddon, Drake had told me. Staring at it, more than once I'd asked aloud, "Who the hell are you?"

Torn from the pages of Revelation, biblical dreams plagued him. His mother claimed he was the progeny of a black winged creature that seized her in the night. His guitar playing appeared to have a sinister psychotropic effect on his listeners. In every respect, he was unlike anyone else.

On the other hand, I'd heard Drake fart in his sleep, watched him floss his teeth, and put up with him hanging the toilet paper so I had to pull fresh sheets from the bottom instead of the top.

Antichrist? I just couldn't believe it.

Bishop Igwe said, "You don't have to actually resume your romantic relationship with him. We realize that might be a bit extreme of an ask."

I stared at him. "But you still want me to stab him to death."

"Well," the bishop said. "Yes, of course."

I said, "I just want to make music."

He replied that once the Antichrist woke, there would be no more music. No people to perform or hear it. They would all die, along with the earth itself. The green grass would burn up, the oceans would turn to blood, and reality itself would be destroyed. The imagery gave me a shudder, but then I remembered he was crazy and none of it was real.

I said, "God told you all this in a vision."

The bishop nodded.

I went on, "Well, he told *me* zip, which means I don't have a part to play in this. Which means you do you, Your Excellency. And I'll go on doing me."

Julian met me on the way out. He asked me how it went. I gave him a look that said, *What do you think?* Then I swiped the cappuccino from his hand and walked on out of there.

I felt a little guilty for talking that way to a prelate of the Catholic Church, but I didn't really have a choice. I think Drake, if he'd seen it, would have been proud.

This would be the end of it, I hoped. Of course, I was wrong.

RAMONA: In the end, I put all of it out of my mind.

Jesus turned water to wine at the wedding in Cana; apparently,

God didn't mind his creation having a good time. Eat, drink, and be merry, as King Solomon wrote in old Ecclesiastes.

I figured if I worked on getting better at doing unto others, I'd be all right.

Or I wouldn't. Either way, it was out of my hands. My actual response to the apocalypse was, "Whatever."

LILY: I hadn't forgotten about Drake and the fact I had to warn him his life was in danger. I hadn't forgotten about my parents and the promise I'd made to reconcile with them either. The world felt like it was spinning way too fast.

The problem: I had no way to get in touch with my ex. I called some mutual friends, but they didn't know how to reach him either. They'd just see him around. There'd be a pop-up rave party or some other weirdness happening, and he'd be there. Everyone I called told me, "Oh yeah, I was at such-and-such thing last weekend, and Drake showed up, and then the night went off the rails!"

Hearing these stories gave me a dangerous pang of longing. I still missed him. The genuine kind. I really did. Only, it was the same way I missed smoking.

Another friend told me a story about how she did peyote with Drake the previous weekend. "And then his eyes turned yellow," she enthused. "And then this priest got run over by a bus on the metro! It was off the hook!"

That time, I actually flinched with a strange flash of jealousy. But the tale told me Drake was still alive, which proved a small comfort.

All along, I'd been checking the *Valley Scene*'s music listings. And then, boom, there it was. Universal Priest was playing Ozymandias, an alternative-music hall set up in some derelict warehouse bordering the old steel yards.

The place was notorious for riots. Drake's kind of place. In the '80s, a lot of East Coast punk bands performed there until infighting and the skinheads ruined the scene. It still hosted punk but had expanded into grunge, metal, and experimental.

This was going to suck, but I figured I owed him enough to warn him that a gang of fanatics was plotting to kill him.

MALCOLM: Playing at Elysian turned out to be a terrific idea. We vetted our songs and even built a small following. We networked with a lot of other musicians. In a typical music scene, everyone seems to know everyone else at least by a degree or two of separation, but we were still new to it. More and more people started to tell us they were excited about catching us at Armageddon.

If there's a secret sauce for maximizing your odds of success in the music business, it'd probably boil down to commitment, talent, and luck. We put in the work, and it showed results.

We were learning we didn't need Drake and his shortcuts.

One night, Julian and Lily sang "You Look Good." A bit of an innovation on our part, doing a duet. Other pop-punk bands would start doing it, like New Found Glory teaming up with Paramore's Hayley Williams for "Vicious Love." But we were one of the first if not the first.

Julian sings about being in love with a girl he hopes to finally get with at a party, with the chorus "You look good to me." Lily responds with a few raunchily suggestive verses about needing to get laid and hoping to hook up at the party, with the chorus "You look good to me, after a drink or two or three."

Eric got confused and suggested they switch parts, and Ramona laughed her ass off. Lily cut him down with a glance and shook her head. Debate over.

RAMONA: Lily was no longer the trembling little Bambi who showed up in Malcolm's basement back in March and started jamming. She owned these songs, and she had strong opinions about how they should be treated.

MALCOLM: That little number brought the house down at Elysian. And I thought again how good Lily was behind the microphone. How the energy level in the room went up when she sang. How she should have a bigger role if not be the band's frontwoman. But the more time went by, the less it seemed practical to change things up yet again. Looking back, it was another sunk-cost fallacy.

LILY: Ozymandias loomed hulking and rusting against a backdrop of derelict factories. Clad in red brick and rusting sheet metal, the old warehouse now served as chief lair for the valley's alt-music scene. I put some attitude in my step and a sullen glare in my eye, feeling like a sheep disguised among hungry wolves.

The giant doorman grinned at me and said, "Have a lovely night, princess."

So much for the disguise. Just great.

Inside, I kept moving, driven not only to find Drake but from an instinctive feeling I was somehow being hunted. Kids filled the space, tattoos and studded leather jackets and the odd Shivers shirt on full display, everyone laughing and talking. The acoustics were terrible. A general roar seemed to hang from the lofty ceiling like a mocking echo.

The black stage stood empty under hot lights. Universal Priest's rhythm guitarist with the beautiful body and expressionless white mask stood in a tattered and stained wedding dress by the men's room. Her head tilted as I approached to ask her where Drake was. Then I spotted him at the bar and veered that way.

He turned beaming and said, "My Magdalene! I was hoping you'd come!"

Grinning over beer bottles, Gog and Magog, Drake's gross bassist and savage drummer, flanked him. I said I came to talk to him about something important and suggested that maybe his bandmates could go be creepy somewhere else.

Gog said, "Would you like to see the house of pain?"

Drake let out a bored sigh. "Let's take a walk, Lilith."

We strolled through the crowd toward the exit. Again, I found myself passing the rhythm guitarist. She made a beckoning gesture. She jerked her head toward the men's room and beckoned again. She wanted to tell me something.

Drake said, "Mary likes you."

I said, "She always seems like she's screaming for help."

He laughed and told me not to be fooled. I should never allow myself to be alone with her. I shouldn't even turn my back around her. I took all this in and pointed out what nice company he was keeping these days.

He said, "They at least have the courage to be who they are."

I said, "That doesn't make them good. Because they suck ass."

Drake laughed again and pointed out I definitely got the better end of the deal in our little divorce. His face soured as he took in the kids eyeing him with grotesque leers. If they hadn't seen him perform, they knew him by reputation, the mad singer who unlocked desires and started orgies and riots.

A girl with SHIVER inked on her forehead burst into tears at the sight of him. Once so delicious to me, the word had taken on a whole new, far darker meaning.

He said, "I tell them to live free, and they worship me for it. The only person you should follow is yourself."

Still, he wore an impish smirk. The side of Drake I could never truly learn to love, his penchant for megalomania. When you transcend, you find yourself looking down on the rest of the herd. If not with compassion, then with loathing. He considered his fans posers for not properly embracing his message.

We went outside and walked through the makeshift parking lot, passing kids doing drug deals by a chain-link fence. The dim yellow pole lights turned everything gray. I got right to the point, telling him about our meeting the priests. The whole time, he stared at me with this incredulous look, and I realized how unreal the whole thing sounded.

"They say you're the Antichrist," I told him.

Drake laughed out loud and said, "What?"

I finished, "And that you're going to end the world if they don't stop you."

He absorbed this with a puzzled and impressed frown. Then he chuckled again.

He said, "That is quite a story. What do you think?"

I said, "I think they're crazy and dangerous."

He eyed me and said, "But...?"

"But you aren't like other people. I think if you were the Antichrist, I don't know how shocked I'd be."

Drake told me bizarre traffic accidents seemed to follow him everywhere.

He looked down at his hands and said, "Do I somehow make that happen?"

Again, the impish smirk, though his blue eye had a worried gleam.

Then he told me he had another dream. A giant worm rising from the earth. Horned and roaring in rage. Tunneling through the deep to pierce a mountaintop with an eruption heard around the world, one that blackened the sky.

A voice had boomed, "All this shall be yours, my son, myself."

When he woke up, he knew Armageddon would be only the beginning. Universal Priest would win, and it would unlock his life's next chapter.

Drake said, "Would you still love me if I *was* the Antichrist?"

I said, "Jeez, I don't know." But I suspected a part of me just might. Even then, I knew a part of me probably always would. I added, "Right now, I'm focused on the music. The music comes first."

He said, "You should come first. It's what I tried to teach you. Stop trying to find people and things to make you complete. You already are."

I winced at this sharp truth. I also felt surprisingly warm. I shouldn't have come. When he talked like this, he made it hard to get past him. Then he told me he hoped the priests were wrong. He didn't want to be the Antichrist.

Not because the Antichrist opposes God—he didn't care about that. In the Christian sense, he already lived that life. Mission accomplished. He'd always found it intriguing how his dreams seemed to be prophetic, but if he was truly the biblical Antichrist, that meant he had an outright destiny. He'd overthrow the world, persecute Christianity, and then be destroyed.

I said, "Being the Antichrist sounds like a lot of responsibility." Just to needle him. "A really high level of adulting."

He said that wasn't what sucked the most for him. In his view, every single living thing should have a choice. People, God, even the Devil. He hated the idea that his entire existence might have been planned out and scripted. All along, he'd been following his dreams because it was fun, not because he felt locked in.

Drake said, "I just want to be me."

A reluctant anti-Messiah. He hadn't asked for the job any more than he'd asked to be born. He suddenly looked very tired and sad.

He said, "A part of you really believes it."

This was true. Biting my lip, I nodded.

He added, "But you still came to warn me."

Also true, something I didn't want to try to figure out. Deflecting, I told him we had a new sound. We were playing my music now, and I was getting my weekly fix testing out new songs at Elysian. After we kicked his shitty band's ass at Armageddon, it would prove there was no script. He'd be truly free.

He said, "Your songs. That's great for you." Meaning it, and again, I felt surprisingly warm. He added, "Your new guitarist is not what he pretends to be."

I told him that yeah, guy, I'd kind of figured that out.

Then he ruined the moment by saying, "Why is he singing your songs?"

"Because it's best for the band," I said. Giving him the stink-eye. Seeing an ex slowly coaxes you into remembering everything you're missing and then slams you with a big reminder why you left.

Drake shrugged, respecting my right to choice if not my actual choice.

He said, "Thank you for the warning, but I'll be fine."

I told him the priests might not know where he lived, but finding out where he'd be playing was as easy as checking the weekly music listings. If they'd strike, it'd be tonight. He laughed and again told me not to worry on his account.

He said, "The Bible thumpers won't bother me here. These kids wouldn't let them get anywhere near me. Ozymandias is hallowed ground for people wanting to be left alone."

Then he told me the show was about to begin, and things would get ugly.

"You warned me, so let me return the favor," he said. "Go home."

I left thinking we had to win Armageddon.

Yes, a part of it was me wanting to knock Drake down a peg, which would satisfy me and probably improve him. But it was more than that.

I wanted to prove that Bishop Igwe and his gang of holy assassins were wrong. This part of me thought that if we won Armageddon, Drake would forever remain the frontman of an obscure Pennsylvania art band. This part of me believed that if we won, we just might, in some weird way, save the world.

TEST OF FAITH

THE ARMAGEDDON
BATTLE OF THE BANDS
DECEMBER 11, 1999

In *mid-December 1999, as the second millennium after Christ wound down toward its big finish, the Armageddon Battle of the Bands commenced at the Gold Bowl Casino's entertainment center in Bethlehem, Pennsylvania.*

The twelve-thousand-square-foot space accommodated a standing-room crowd of over three thousand, and Armageddon packed it that year, while the ticket scalpers had a heyday.

Over two weekends, a dozen local bands would wage musical battle for glory and prizes. The reinvented band known as the Shivers arrived pumped and ready to win the hearts and minds of the judges and audience alike.

THE 6TH ANNUAL ARMAGEDDON BATTLE OF THE BANDS

STARS ARE BORN IN BETHLEHEM!!!

COME SEE THE EPIC MUSICAL CLASH OF THE MILLENNIUM AS 12 VALLEY ALL-STARS BATTLE FOR THE PRIZE!!!

ROUND 1 DEC 10-11, ROUND 2 DEC 18 AT GOLD BOWL CASINO!!!

JOANIE'S KISSES · HATE MAIL · SURGICAL SCAR · WHITE BURN · ORC FEAST · NECROMONIUM · BETTER DENTISTRY · THE KARL ZENITH BAND · TRANSCENDENTAL · MY MOM'S BASEMENT · THE SHIVERS · UNIVERSAL PRIEST!!!
DON'T MISS!!!

ALEXIS ZHANG (*music director and producer, Armageddon*): We promoted the event as a curated clash of musical creatives. A lot of bands applied, but we picked only twelve for the competition to provide a real contest of styles packaged as a major music experience. We wanted to offer a powerhouse event that would close out the year in style and this time welcome a new millennium.

Armageddon always took place at the event center at the Gold Bowl Casino near the old steel yards south of the river. Each night on the first weekend, six bands, divided into two tiers, would play a half-hour set back-to-back.

A panel of three judges picked each tier's winner based on scores for musical material, stage presence, and so on. That year, we had 96.6's Axel "Cheddar Dip" Hodges, *Valley Scene* editor in chief Stephen Wise, and Danny Rodriguez from Echo Harbor Records.

On the second weekend, the semifinals saw four bands duke it out, and then at the end of the night the two finalists played a single song to close the competition. Again, the judges picked the final champion while the attendees voted for the Audience Choice Award, whatever band won their hearts and ears.

It was a lot of fun while it lasted.

STEPHEN WISE (*editor in chief, the* Valley Scene): Vince Amato was to represent the *Scene* at Armageddon but couldn't make it on account of, you know, being arrested for arson and mass murder.

Anyway, I'd planned to assign another writer as judge. Armageddon dominated the two weekends before Christmas. An event for the young and restless, not a family man like me. That time of year was always way too busy with two little ones at home.

Then Vince's lawyer mailed me a handwritten note from him that said, "Drake Morgan showed me the light. He'll show you too."

In the end, I was simply too curious. I agreed to be a judge at Armageddon.

AXEL HODGES (*disc jockey, WROK 96.6, "the Rock of Bethlehem"*): I was a young small-market DJ with big dreams. My hero was Howard Stern, the famous New York City radio shock jock. He'd become notorious for pushing the boundaries of free speech. My dream was to build a show that wasn't Stern but reached the same level of outrageousness.

Until then, I played the typical quirky DJ, spinning discs for lonely insomniacs as "Cheddar Dip." I'd grown popular because I had a soothing voice that made the night owls feel like a friend kept them company.

Despite the boisterous and smooth-talking persona I perfected behind the microphone, the real me hardly matched the fantasy. This was the analog era, when everything was tightly controlled, a vast machine designed to deliver music from the studio to your ears. I worked off a script under the watchful eyes of the sound engineer and program controller, with way less ad-libbing than you'd think. Even the music sets weren't mine but carefully curated by our parent corporation.

The only way I could get ahead or even capture more control of my own show was to continue to build my following. That meant doing tons of public appearances. So when Armageddon asked me to judge that year, of course I agreed. Our late-night programming broke the rotation and musically took more chances, so I'd also get to play some songs by the competing bands.

Personally, I liked Hate Mail and Joanie's Kisses, which sounded like most of the stuff we played on the air. I was curious about the Shivers and Universal Priest, though. I saw an interesting story in their rivalry. By the time Armageddon started, everyone in the local music scene had heard of these bands and the insane, band-hopping lead guitarist who started riots.

I thought: This could get nasty.

I wasn't wrong.

DANNY RODRIGUEZ: I agreed to take part in the judging mostly to keep my competitors out of it. Otherwise, I didn't have my hopes up. In the '90s, the action in the alt-rock scene was all happening in Los Angeles, New York, and Seattle. Ground zeros for all the big music movements. Grunge, hip-hop, shoe-gaze, pop-punk. If you included house music, add Chicago to the list.

But you never know, so you have to look around. Like fashion, today's mind-blowing sensation in music is tomorrow's has-been and next week's reinvention. In '99, I remember pop-punk was on the rise again, grunge had evolved into post-grunge, and shoe-gaze enjoyed a revival.

Across the country, A&R guys like me scouted for awesome bands that took these forms and added a twist to make them into something new. What every guy in the business really wanted, though, was to discover the next big thing. That was the Grail. Nu-metal was breaking out, and so while I had my eye on shoe-gaze band Hate Mail, thinking about maybe offering them a record deal with Echo Harbor, I wanted to see if White Burn had what it took to sell records.

Otherwise, I planned to get in and out as fast as humanly possible. Look, Bethlehem is a fine town. It really is. But it isn't Los Angeles. I would much rather have been there, where great bands practically jump out of the water into your net, than in some tired Rust Belt city looking for gold under rocks.

I was in for quite a surprise.

ALEXIS ZHANG: I could usually predict who'd win each year. If you live and breathe the music scene like I do, it's not that hard. I expected Joanie's Kisses to squeak out a win after a hard fight with Hate Mail. The Shivers and Universal Priest turned out to be a major surprise I think for everyone.

We picked them as wild cards to spice things up. From what I'd heard of the Shivers, they'd done a complete one-eighty on their sound, which as you know worked out beautifully for them but at the time hardly looked like a terrific sign of confidence. As for Universal Priest, they were a local jokey art band who made the latest crop of middle-class college students feel edgy and in on the joke.

We placed them in the undercard tiers that would warm the crowd up each night. Universal Priest, Friday night. The Shivers on Saturday.

Honestly, I expected both to wash out in the first round. Obviously, I was wrong and that didn't happen. I had no idea how weird things would get.

I wish I'd never booked either one of them.

MALCOLM: We drove over in the afternoon. I checked boxes on my clipboard as we loaded everything into the van. Instruments and gear, some band merchandise that escaped being stolen at the Hobo and burned to a cinder at Sunburst, and several shaky but willing musicians.

Check, check, check.

On the road to the Gold Bowl, I still had this nagging feeling we were missing something. And I thought, Oh, I know, we forgot to hone our songs and build up a following playing gigs for a solid year before going up against established professional bands.

No lie, my cheeks were majorly clenched.

RAMONA: One time, this guy at the Squat named Travis took me on a night drive outside the city to score some weed in his rusty old VW Bug. The rural roads were dark and loud with insects and perfect for summer driving. We followed a bend in the old, cracked road and found ourselves speeding straight into a herd of deer.

They appeared out of nowhere, crossing from one farmer's field to another. Just standing there gaping in the headlights like, *What the fuck, guys?*

Travis wrenched the wheel to skirt the first deer. He swerved again straight between the next two, threading his two-thousand-pound needle.

Like other cars, the Beetle had this handle on the ceiling you could use to get in and out of the car but most people used to hang their dry cleaning. Everyone called it the oh-shit bar, handy for when things got hairy.

I grabbed it and held on for all I was worth, seizing its illusion of safety. Every other bit of me, however, simply let go. By gripping the handle, I'd done everything I could. What would be would be. I accepted my fate, whatever the next few seconds might bring.

Driving into the Gold Bowl entertainment center's backstage parking area, I reached up and grabbed the oh-shit bar.

ERIC: A dude wearing an orange vest over an unzipped winter jacket pointed where we should park and start the load-in. As we passed him, I glimpsed the Shivers' curving snake on his T-shirt.

He grinned and pinched his index finger and thumb in front of one squinting eye. At first, I thought it was some kind of weird new hipster way to wave. Then I realized he was playing the kids' game of squashing my head.

LILY: Malcolm talked to the event coordinator, who turned him over to the stage manager, who gave us a time for sound check. When our turn came, we got on stage with our instruments and gear, and then we sort of froze.

RAMONA: I thought again of driving through that herd of deer gaping in the glare of Travis's headlights. Only, this time I knew exactly how the deer must have felt.

LILY: The stage was big. The room was huge. Malcolm had told us the total square footage, but it had sounded meaningless to me. All I knew was it was way bigger than even the Hobo Underground. Standing on that stage, I could not only see but feel the vast space. You could nearly fit three basketball courts in twelve thousand square feet. More than four tennis courts. *Three thousand people.*

MALCOLM: I was like, "Didn't I tell you guys it'd be cool?"

RAMONA: Malcolm might actually have been cool if he wasn't always calling attention to how cool everything he did for us was.

MALCOLM: Then I went back to praying: *Please, guys, let's not screw this up.*

LILY: I reminded myself that once the show started, the lights would be blasting. Only the first few rows would be clearly visible, the rest a shadowy mass. I'd hear the crowd way more than see it.

ERIC: I held my bass snug against my hip, so I felt complete again. I told myself this was just another wedding, only I had to impress three brides instead of one.

RAMONA: The soundman started yelling at us to get our asses in gear. He had six bands to sound-check, which allowed time for zero divas. Okay, okay.

MALCOLM: The engineer had us play our instruments individually, from the drums to the keyboard, and then he checked vocals, setting the initial levels. After that, we played one of our songs so he could balance out the levels for an overall cohesive sound. Then we tested our monitors for feedback and distortion. After a little back-and-forth with him, we were good to go.

ERIC: On to the green room. Hurry up and wait, and wait, and wait.

RAMONA: Six bands and their girlfriends, groupies, and managers packed the room, everyone nervous and talking too loudly. I like men. I actually prefer hanging out with the guys to going out with the girls. But looking at the room, I thought, Damn, this business needs more chicks in it.

MALCOLM: Six bands played that night, three in each tier. We'd go on third. In other words, we'd have the final say against the two bands we competed against tonight, but we'd have to top them.

The first group to go on was My Mom's Basement, a punk band that Ramona told me sounded like a dead ringer for the Dead Milkmen, which broke up in '95. The second was Necromonium, a death metal band. I thought we could take both of them.

Thankfully, we weren't going up against Universal Priest, which had apparently crushed Orc Feast and Transcendental the night before.

I loved the Shivers' new sound; I thought it had tons of appeal. It sounded beautiful and energetic and alive. But I knew what Drake Morgan could do, and I worried about going head-to-head with him. Doing the math, I figured the only way we'd battle Universal Priest was if we both made it to the final round.

If we survived that long, I'd consider it one of those good problems.

AXEL HODGES: We judged the competition from a VIP box with a beautiful view of the stage. Transcendental almost put me to sleep, and Orc Feast proved one of those overwrought metal bands that pushed things over the line into parody. By the time we got to Universal Priest, I'd gotten deep into a crossword puzzle.

Then Drake Morgan started playing.

DANNY RODRIGUEZ: The music put me into a trance, and when I came out of it, I literally heard a cash register go *ka-ching* in my brain. Drake Morgan was going to be a star. I'd actually turned over a rock and found a golden nugget. I just had to figure out how to separate him from the rock.

STEPHEN WISE: Despite Vince's obvious madness, he hadn't been wrong about Morgan. Universal Priest turned out to be the big surprise of Friday night, winning the round with Joanie's Kisses eking out a win in the second tier. I was now very curious what the Shivers sounded like.

LILY: It was standing room only in the green room. Ramona wandered off to score a beer. Eric plopped down on the floor and idly strummed his bass. I said to Malcolm, "You aren't really quitting if we lose, are you?"

We had something special, I thought. It needed patience and

love. Even if we lost, we'd still have gotten the chance to rock in front of three thousand people who would get to know us.

He said, "You don't understand. If we don't win, I may have to stop."

He told me about how every day felt like Armageddon. The intense pressure he was under, being raised by an aspirational dad and a perfectionist mom. The website he sold for a lot of money that had given him the confidence to underwrite the Shivers but might wind up being his life's only real success.

He said, "Dinner at my parents' house is more like making a quarterly report to the shareholders than a family get-together. It's just how it is."

I reminded him he'd gotten into this to do something he loved. Malcolm shook his head and told me it wasn't that simple. You can fight nature, he said, and you can fight nurture, but not both. If he really wanted to do what he loved, he'd be teaching classical music to disadvantaged kids.

He said, "So we kind of have to win."

I said, "Malcolm, we're going to annihilate them." And I believed it.

ERIC: I didn't want to be in that dumb room. I wanted to be rocking on stage.

All along, I'd craved to be noticed. I wanted everyone to know me. I hoped someone besides my mom would love me.

The best I'd gotten for it was Ramona's stink-eye, Joey Grasso's casual humiliation, and a lousy T-shirt from a girl at a skate park.

The only time I felt like I was winning was when I played. Flanagan's, the Hobo, Sunburst, Elysian. Playing on a stage, I became a rock god, and it was all thanks to my bass guitar. Sometimes I felt like I was the actual instrument in our partnership.

In the green room, Ramona sat next to me and took a long pull on her beer. Letting out a belch, she asked if I was ready to melt faces tonight.

I didn't like that expression anymore. It reminded me too much of the way the audience looked at the Hobo Underground. Their faces throbbing in the dark.

I said, "We can't lose."

Ramona laughed and said, "The competition ain't *that* bad, dude."

I said again, "We *can't* lose."

I explained that I'd given up so much to become truly proficient at my instrument. I barely even saw Ma anymore so she wouldn't nag me about self-care and try to force-feed me a home-cooked meal.

The biggest thing I'd sacrificed, however, was my complacency.

I'd given this band my love and, even more, my hope. If we failed and Malcolm killed the band, I'd just be me again. A man without a plan or much of a future.

I usually didn't talk to Ramona like this. Anytime I showed any earnest emotion around her, she'd growl at me to shut up and grow a pair of balls.

This time, though, the drummer nodded and passed me her beer for a swig.

She said, "If the band dies, I'll be homeless in every sense of the word."

Now it was my turn to nod and pass the bottle. We did this for a while, sharing a beer while the room's roar washed over us. Then she gave my shoulder a light punch.

"I like you more when you aren't trying so hard," she said.

I looked up to see a tall, lanky dude with long hair standing over me.

He said, "You're the bassist. The Shivers. I remember you."

I certainly recognized him. He was Adrian Simmons, lead guitarist and vocalist for Hate Mail. They were billed with us at the Hobo Underground and Sunburst. They weren't huge or anything, but they'd paid quite a few dues, and I had a musician's natural respect for Adrian and his hardworking shoe-gaze band. The man was massively talented and had that rock-star look, the kind of musician you knew at a glance was going to make it, maybe go all the way to the top.

His recognition of me lit a small fire in my belly. I'd craved to be seen, and here I was, being noticed by someone important.

He said, "You assholes killed Hobo and Sunburst. We never even went on."

At first, I was like, Who did what? Then: Oh. Right. We did kind of do that. Adrian said we had no idea how hard his band had worked for those gigs.

I laughed. Nervous laughter. It just burst right out of me. The comedy of it all. *Well, Adrian, our lead guitarist at the time was the Antichrist. There's a secret cabal of priests that want him dead.* God, I just wanted to play music.

The dude's faced darkened.

He said, "Did I say something funny?"

I reined it in with a ragged cough and told him I didn't think it was funny at all.

He said, "You start some kind of riot again tonight before we go on, and we will freaking end you. We'll break your goddamn fingers. You feel me?"

My mouth dropped open. No, I did not understand him.

"Hey!" A deep voice. Stomping in heavy boots. Onto the scene comes the biggest man I'd ever seen. Picture Conan and Hagar the Horrible had a baby who grew up to join a biker gang. Shaggy red mane and beard. Worn-out blue jeans with a massive skull-shaped belt buckle. Leather vest over a black tee that was barely big enough to cover his torso. Tattoos running down arms thick as trees.

The drummer of Necromonium.

He said to Adrian, "I heard that. Not cool, dude."

Ramona was already on her feet. She raised her hand to the Viking.

"Back off," she said, and got right up in Adrian's face.

She said, "Whose fingers are you gonna break?"

Adrian shifted to glare at me, the easier prey, but Ramona sidestepped to stay in his face. She said, "I asked you a question."

"Nobody's," he said, his voice turning sulky. "I was just talking."

Ramona stabbed him in the chest with her own finger, hard enough to make him flinch, and she said, "Go talk somewhere else."

After he did, she caught the Viking grinning at her. She asked him if he wanted a piece of her too.

"Yes, ma'am," he said. "I'm Garth. I'll catch up with you later. I hope."

Ramona watched him go, her eyes eating him up every step of the way. Clearly, the interest in catching up later was mutual. Then she sat down again.

I said, "I wish I had a girlfriend like you."

She patted my knee and sighed.

"One day, you will, Eric," she told me. "When you think you're allowed."

LILY: Around dinnertime, the green room started to empty out. I rounded up the band so we could get our supper. We navigated the vast casino's dazzling lights and colors and carnival sounds until we reached the buffet.

I told my bandmates to conserve their energy. Remember to breathe. In with the good, out with the bad. Allow every negative thought and feeling but let it pass through you. Easy on the alcohol and coffee.

Tonight was make or break for us, but it only required our best effort, nothing more. We'd practiced like we'd play, and tonight we'd play like we'd practiced. We were the underdog here. We had nothing to lose and everything to gain. And every note we played tonight, we weren't alone. We'd do it together.

I told myself these things as much as them. I was hella nervous. One of the hardest things for a musician to learn is she'll play just as well later as she would now, and how to endure the stretch of time separating the two.

Malcolm said, "You heard the lady. Save your energy for the stage."

Julian said, "Don't forget to have fun while you're up there."

Ramona said, "I'm gonna burn this den of vipers to the ground." Her way of saying she'd be on fire tonight behind the drums.

Then Eric said, "I just wanted to say I really love you guys—"

We all laughed as if he'd told an inside joke, the kind of laugh that felt familiar and loosened us up. I started to feel good. Malcolm picked up the check as he always did, only this time he didn't grumble about it.

On the way back, I said to Julian, "You joined the band to spy on us."

Immediately regretting opening that particular can of worms mere hours before stage time, but I wanted to take our next step with all cards on the table.

"Not on the band," he corrected me. "On you."

I asked him again who he really was.

He said, "I'm an ordained deacon preparing for the priesthood."

A divine vision hadn't struck Julian as it had the other priests. He'd taken Bishop Igwe and his interpretation on faith alone. The prelate had recruited him to the cause after finding out he'd once played in a grunge band in Seattle. When Drake left the band, Julian had been instructed to become its new guitarist.

I asked him why he'd quit music.

He smiled and said, "Because I became the shittiest version of me."

To protect the innocent, he didn't name the band but otherwise shared his story. On a road tour, he took the mythical rock-star lifestyle too seriously and wound up doing horrible things not only to himself but to people he loved. The endless train of forgettable hookups and easy drugs and trashed hotel rooms. After a while, even the music didn't matter, only feeding his bottomless appetite.

As Julian partied his way to rock bottom, he didn't know who he was anymore. He got himself clean and discovered a sincere desire for purity.

He said, "Being in the Shivers showed me what it could have looked like if I hadn't screwed it all up. It's also been incredibly hard for me. The temptation. The lifestyle. And being around you."

My romantic radar hadn't been wrong after all.

I assured him that ship had sailed, though I felt a little temptation myself again right then. An urge to haul him into the restroom and blow off some steam.

Julian said, "I'll probably be leaving the band after Armageddon."

"No." I practically yelled it. Wherever he'd come from and whatever his agenda had been, he was a part of us now.

He said, "It's always been your band, Lily."

My dream, while his pointed in a different direction. Serving humanity to save himself. He hoped I'd navigate it without losing myself too.

He worried the others already had. Malcolm had joined the band to do what he loved, but he proved obsessed with success far more than with simply playing music. Ramona wanted security, though she'd sacrificed the only real family she had at the Squat in exchange for a lottery ticket. Eric craved a sense of purpose only to feel worthless without his bass.

I'd always wondered how Julian read people so well. What they needed. Even better than Drake, who told people what they wanted. Julian not only read them but did it with compassion.

I thought I had the answer now. Empathy. He saw himself in them. He'd been in their shoes and had used them to find a different path.

I said, "Let's talk about all this after we win Armageddon."

Right then, I still believed that if we won, it would prove him wrong about Drake.

Julian said he'd make me a deal.

He said, "Bishop Igwe wants to see you one more time. Tonight. It's urgent. He said we're running out of time."

I snorted to let him know what I thought of that. I was still annoyed as hell that he and the bishop had ambushed me at my favorite coffee shop.

Then he said, "If you do, I'll keep playing with the Shivers for a while. I'll delay going into the priesthood. I'll be what you want."

I asked about what *he* wanted. Wasn't that important too?

"No," he said simply. Not compared to stopping the Antichrist.

That word again. *Antichrist.* I'd learned to hate it. I wanted to say no, but the band was too important. As always, the music came first.

The bishop frightened me. He was nuts. I also wanted Julian in the band.

I told him he had a deal.

At the time, I had no idea how much horror a simple yes could unleash.

RAMONA: We watched Necromonium thrash and shred their death metal from the side stage. I liked death metal for its hardcore sound even if I usually didn't go for all the hailing Satan and relishing wanton death and destruction.

The singer flailed to the relentless beat. In a guttural scream, he sang about nuclear bombs raining on cities while the rich drink champagne and watch it all live on TV in their bunkers. The high-gain amps and heavy guitar distortion made a raw and powerful wall of sound that struck me like an atomic wind.

And there was Garth perched on his throne behind the drums, hammering rapid-fire blast beats with flying hair and eyes wild with possession and ecstasy.

After the crowd's approving roar died out and the band stomped off the stage, Garth threw me a wink and said, "Break a leg, ma'am." I glared back at him.

God, he was yummy.

MALCOLM: While Alexis Zhang introduced us over the PA system, I threw a final glance at my bandmates to take their measure. Lily was smiling, a very good sign. The prim Catholic schoolgirl look was gone, replaced by a simple pair of jeans and a tight little black tee that offered a teasing glimpse of midriff.

In her usual ratty attire, Ramona looked like she wanted to murder someone, another good sign. Julian appeared calm and confident as if he'd done this many times. No problems there, as usual. The man was a rock.

As for Eric, he'd traded in the cheesy wedding band suit for street clothes capped by Converse All Stars, so thank God for small favors. I thought I'd have to give him a final pep talk after his run-in with Hate Mail, but he grinned over his instrument. Over the past weeks, he'd become a real Dr. Jekyll and Mr. Hyde. As soon as he had his bass in his hands, he turned into a monster in all the best ways.

ERIC: There's this moment when a band takes the stage and gets ready. They act like they don't even know the audience is there. This establishes cool. It says, *We're rock stars. We do this all the time. We're going to deliver.*

Not Lily. She slung her axe over her shoulder, tossed a triumphant fist, and jumped up and down beaming like a kid on Christmas morning. It definitely did not scream cool, but it was real and it was fun. The crowd ate it up.

LILY: Julian squared his shoulders behind the microphone and said, "We're the Shivers, not to be confused with the Shivers."

We laughed. The kids in the audience who knew the scene laughed with us.

He said, "Thanks for coming tonight to check out our new sound. I think you're gonna dig it. Our first song is about this guy who likes a girl, and—uh-oh."

Ramona counted us off. Then, bam, the song burst to galloping life. We played with frantic energy, lashing our instruments in a mad dash for the finish line.

Julian sang about a young man who drinks too much at a party so he can work up the nerve to talk to his crush. The song starts the morning after, when he wakes up with only a foggy memory of the night before and starts calling his friends to find out if he did anything stupid. He learns he'd become a legendary party animal, but the girl he liked left early and saw none of it.

Up tempo, bouncy, simple. The song in a major key for a brighter, happier sound—no more haunting minor keys for us.

I raked power chords in the zone while Ramona's surging drum assault punctuated the beat with splash cymbal flourishes and Malcolm punched a strong single note on the downbeats. We rode it straight to the chorus, Julian singing, "It was a perfect night / I was cool as Fred Astaire / Flying higher than a kite / I wish I could have been there."

Heads bobbed across the front rows. By the third song, we had them hopping.

STEPHEN WISE: I was like, This happy, earnest bubblegum band set off a riot at the Hobo and burned down Sunburst?

AXEL HODGES: When you're in the DJ business, you get promo discs all the time. The world is filled with really good bands. Workhorse bands that consistently deliver on expectations. Bands like that can go far. The truly great bands, though, have a special something. If it could be defined, everyone would have it.

The Shivers had it.

DANNY RODRIGUEZ: I liked what I was seeing and hearing. When Lily Lawless shared the lead vocals on their closer, "You Look Good," it was like finding the prize in the cereal box. The girl was a secret weapon.

LILY: Music is primordial. The first sound I heard was my mother's heartbeat. I was five months old and still in the womb. Sometimes I'd hear the outside world, so chaotic and confusing, but I'd be reassured by my mother's heartbeat and voice. This was my first introduction to music and the raw beginning of my love for it.

In that music hall, we all went back into the womb and were born again.

BLOOD SACRIFICE

DECEMBER 11, 1999

The Shivers won its first round, beating strong competition to catapult into the next weekend's semifinals. There it would go head-to-head with the New Wavey all-girl band Joanie's Kisses while Universal Priest duked it out with Hate Mail.

This still lay in the future.

After they won that first night, the Shivers agreed they'd earned a celebration. But first, Lily would honor her deal with Julian to meet with Bishop Igwe one more time.

GARTH WAGNER (*drummer, Necromonium*): The Shivers won fair and square, no hard feelings. They rocked harder than we did. It was a good fight.

After the show, I congratulated Ramona. Despite all the murderous glaring, she let a little catlike smile slip past her wall, and I knew it was happening. I knew it wouldn't last long. I had this feeling, though, we'd wind up lifelong friends.

RAMONA: What can I say? I have a thing for pretty drummers.

GARTH WAGNER: We partied in the green room until Armageddon announced the winners, and then we got started on the load-out along with thoughts about taking the party somewhere else. An address got passed around.

LILY: We huddled for a quick band meeting and decided we earned the right to make some noise after winning a slot in the next round. We all had a stage high and wanted to keep it going as long as possible. I was ready to dance all night.

MALCOLM: I wanted us to go home. As happy as I was about winning our first round, I felt way more nervous about blowing it in the next, or some other horrible thing happening. That's the trick about winning. It means you have more to lose.

Musicians are people, and people are born screwups. I pictured Ramona getting into a stupid fight with Hate Mail and breaking her hand. Eric catching strep throat from some groupie. Boy-magnet Lily announcing she and Julian had become a hot item but had broken up, and now he was leaving.

My worst nightmare wasn't losing Armageddon. It was almost winning Armageddon and then blowing it.

Blowing it because the things that drive people to make great art also give them a sublimated desire for self-destruction.

RAMONA: Garth knew the area and said he'd come with us. We snuggled in the back with the gear, sharing body heat. I was still flying on my drummer's high. Let's just say I enjoyed that drive.

ERIC: I felt hopeful about the party. That maybe I'd finally have a social interaction that didn't involve someone taking a giant crap on my head.

Only, Julian took us on a detour. Straight back to Our Lady of Victory Church.

LILY: I told the band that Julian and I needed to go inside and talk to Bishop Igwe one last time. I wouldn't be long.

MALCOLM: I'd done my best to forget all about those lunatics. They were a big complication we didn't need. This was no time to be taking risks. In fact, the whole thing had a very *please-guys-let's-not-screw-this-up* vibe.

ERIC: Lily and Julian could do whatever they wanted, but I wasn't going anywhere. I was like, It's cold out there. I love this nice, warm van. I thought: I'm staying right here, thank you very much.

Those priests had knives and swords and received visions from God telling them to kill guitarists. You could say they'd put the fear of God in me.

RAMONA: I didn't like it.

MALCOLM: Thank you, Ramona! I hoped she'd set Lily straight that this was a bad idea.

RAMONA: I told Lily that no way would she and Julian go in there alone. We were a band. We had each other's backs. We'd all go.

MALCOLM: Not what I had in mind.

ERIC: When she put it like that, I kind of *had* to go.

GARTH WAGNER: I started to get out, but Ramona made me stay put. She said they didn't need me mucking things up by hailing Satan in there. My T-shirt had a pentagram on it. She most definitely did not want to get these dudes worked up.

She had Julian give me the keys and told me to get behind the wheel in case they needed a quick getaway. If they didn't come out in an hour, I should drive to the party, round up every rocker I could find packing a decent pair of fists, and then come back and tear this place apart.

"Yes, ma'am," I replied, wearing a big grin.

I seriously wondered what the hell was going on here, but then Ramona licked my ear, and I kind of forgot whatever was on my mind.

LILY: Julian assured me everything would be okay. I tried to take some comfort in the fact that while Bishop Igwe might be a fanatic and me a young woman living in sin, we were still on the same team. That, and the Catholic Church I grew up with was far more like a quaint government bureaucracy than the Inquisition burning heretics at the stake.

Besides, I was still channeling my stage power as a rock goddess. I had this strong feeling I couldn't be touched. Either way, I believed I had a solution to the bishop's problem.

MALCOLM: On the way in, I asked Lily, "Why are we doing this, again?"

She told me she was keeping the band together. Trying to assure me, though her words had the opposite effect.

No time to explain what she meant. Julian opened the big oak doors.

LILY: Julian must have phoned ahead, because they all waited for us. Scores of priests packed the nave, their faces glowing in candlelight.

It seemed the entire Catholic Church was here. As we walked through the crowd, I spotted the black cassocks of priests, buttonless Jesuit cassocks belted with cinctures, the brown robes of Franciscan monks, nuns gripping rosaries.

Bishop Igwe's kindly face welcomed me at the altar. As I kissed his ring, he again got right to the point. He told me the Antichrist was waking. If they couldn't defeat him now, they never would. They were almost out of time.

I got to the point too. I said, "We're going to win the battle of the bands. When we do, it'll prove Drake can't be the Antichrist."

He gave me a look as if I was the one talking crazy.

Then his gentle round face turned mean again.

He said, "Playing music will accomplish nothing. The old world is passing, Lillian. A cosmic upheaval is coming that will destroy it. This is a serious matter."

This was all a bit much, even for a Catholic, so I said nothing.

He went on, telling me the Antichrist would ascend to oppress humanity and challenge God. The Antichrist personified as Drake Morgan.

Bishop Igwe said, "Once he ascends, Christ will return in battle to create the Kingdom of God. Until then, it is our Christian duty to prevent the Antichrist from inflicting global suffering."

"Uh-huh," I said, keeping it zipped.

Then Malcolm opened his mouth.

MALCOLM: I said it sounded like the only thing that could stop the Antichrist was Jesus, so we'd leave him to it. I was trying to speed things along so we could get out of there.

RAMONA: Malcolm has this weird blind spot when it comes to lighting matches around gasoline.

LILY: I jumped in and pleaded my case one more time. The priests believed Drake was the Antichrist. Drake believed he was destined to win Armageddon, which would propel him to stardom.

If he lost, then they were both wrong. Game over.

Bishop Igwe, however, was apoplectic by this point.

He growled, "All *you've* accomplished is whoring—"

I yelled, "Hey, now!"

He turned to Ramona and said, "Debauchery—"

The drummer crossed her arms and glared back at him.

Then he turned to Malcolm and said, "And *blasphemy*."

Malcolm shrugged.

ERIC: I waited my turn, but the bishop just ignored me. I didn't know whether I should be flattered or insulted. All I know is I wish I'd stayed in the van.

MALCOLM: The bishop snapped at Julian that his assignment was over. It was time for him to resume his post. A nun handed him a folded black cassock.

He stared at it for a few seconds and then put it on.

He said, "I'm sorry, guys. It was a lot of fun."

And just like that, my worst nightmare came true, though I have to admit, I did not see this particular scenario coming.

LILY: Before I could react to Julian's betrayal, Bishop Igwe's fierce expression softened, and he said, "You still care about Drake Morgan."

"Well, sure," I said. "In a way. I probably always will."

Like flipping a coin. Heads, I loved him. Tails, I hated him. Then repeat.

Either way, it was still caring.

The bishop said, "And he still loves you."

I didn't think Drake truly understood love, not the way it's supposed to be. He certainly loved to *be* loved, but when it came to reciprocating, I'm not sure he really knew how. I'd sometimes wondered if he regarded love as a mirror, where he could gaze upon his reflection and see himself the way others saw him.

I said, "In his own twisted way, I suppose he does."

"His human half certainly does," said Bishop Igwe. "That makes him vulnerable to you."

Back to this. Why did I think it was a good idea to come here?

"He's not the Antichrist," I said. "He's just a narcissist."

"Please," he begged me. "Aid us in our cause. You can save the world."

I couldn't. Even if I believed Bishop Igwe—which right then only a tiny part of me did—I couldn't murder someone. That was wrong.

"No," I said. "I can't kill him for you. I won't."

This seemed to settle an important issue for him.

He said, "There is one other way you can serve."

"Okay," I said warily. "I'll help in any way I can, as long as no one gets hurt."

He said, "Only you, my child."

He whistled, and the priests closed in and grabbed us.

RAMONA: As soon as they moved, I braced myself to go to war. Then the knives came out, and that was that. I'll fight for a friend, but I'm no superhero. Strong arms gripped me like a vise.

LILY: Struggle proved pointless. A big priest held me on either side. I turned to tell Julian what a Judas he was, but they had him and the rest of the band on their knees, heads forced down.

Surrounded by these men, I felt utterly powerless and alone.

Bishop Igwe said, "If we can't pierce his body, we will break his heart."

The priests dragged me to the altar. I dug my heels into the carpet, but they simply lifted me up and slammed me down onto its hard top.

"Confess," Julian yelled at me. "Say an Act of Contrition, Lily!"

He was trying to give me last rites.

Me: "Fuck you, Julian!"

Too angry to feel much in the way of fear yet. They were just trying to scare me, right? I mean, this couldn't be happening.

Then a nun handed Bishop Igwe a gleaming knife, and mortal terror fell on me like a crushing weight.

"Okay, I'm sorry," I screamed at him. "Please stop!"

The bishop placed his warm hand against my forehead.

He said, "By the authority which the Apostolic See has given me, I grant you full pardon and the remission of all your sins. In the name of the Father, and of the Son, and of the Holy Spirit."

This wasn't a reprieve from execution. He'd given me an Apostolic Pardon, which would allow me to cross over into death in a sinless state.

I didn't want a pardon. I didn't want to die at all. None of this made sense to me. Minutes earlier, I'd been on top of the world, untouchable. I had a plan that would prove none of this was actually real.

By now, the whole band was screaming their heads off, Malcolm offering a bribe, Ramona yelling she'd kill Drake herself if that's what they wanted, and Eric just shouting *no* over and over, but it all fell on deaf ears.

Bishop Igwe said to me, "The Lord thanks you for your sacrifice, my child."

I refused to go out like this. Struggle appeared pointless, but I gave it my best. I bucked and twisted. I lashed out. I fought those men with everything I had.

None of it did any good.

He raised the knife.

DR. WOODWARD: Another interesting scenario. If you can't kill the Antichrist, you can try to psychologically weaken him. Hurt him where he's vulnerable.

The trick is, you enter a slippery slope that takes you right off the moral high ground. Suppose you could go back in time and kill Hitler before he started the Second World War. Would you do it? What if you could only kill him as a child?

Okay, now let's say the only way to stop the war is to kill Hitler plus a thousand people. Would you do it then? Remember, more than fifty million died in that war. How about two thousand people? Ten thousand? The question becomes: How many people would you be willing to kill before it stops being worth it?

Everyone who does evil probably thinks they're doing right. If the Antichrist ever does come, no doubt he'll cast himself as the good guy. It's like Nietzsche said: If you battle monsters for too long, you become one.

RAMONA: The doors banged open, and my body electrified with relief and worry. Garth had come to rescue us!

But no, it was just another priest, his face flushed from running.

The man howled: "ANTICHRIST!"

LILY: The knife froze in Bishop Igwe's hand. The clergy let up a surprised shout.

The bishop set the knife on the altar and kissed my forehead.

He said, "Thank you."

The red-faced priest pushed through the crowd and said, "He's coming, Your Eminence. From the north."

"Now is our chance," said Bishop Igwe.

Then he roared: "Prepare for war! God wills it!"

With a martial shout, priests rushed to olive-drab crates stacked against the walls and cracked them open. I expected them to arm themselves with medieval swords and crossbows, but instead they hauled out a wide variety of modern weaponry. Scoped automatic rifles, shotguns, even machine guns.

A Carmelite nun toting an AK-47 rushed to the nearest window and raised the rifle butt. In a flash, a century-old stained-glass depiction of Jesus in the Garden of Gethsemane disappeared with a crash.

Then she propped the barrel against the frame and waited. Three priests crowded around her, aiming their own weapons into the cold darkness outside. Similar scenes played out across the entire north side of the church as every clergyman in the place scrambled to form a battle line.

I rubbed my aching wrists and wondered if that priest was right. Did Drake somehow know I was in trouble and come to work this out? Maybe this had all been planned from the start. They'd sent a message to Drake telling him if he didn't show up by a certain time, they'd kill me. It certainly impressed me that Drake might have enough feeling for me to risk his life like this, but I didn't want to see him get hurt.

I grabbed the knife that Bishop Igwe left on the altar and stuck it in my belt. The next person who tried to murder me was gonna need stitches. Abandoned by their captors, the band rose shakily to their feet.

"Stupid games and stupid prizes," Malcolm said. Trembling and wide-eyed, he looked like he was about to burst into tears. "Can we leave now?"

Julian told us there was about to be a whole lot of holy-water-dipped ordnance flying outside, and that we should stay put until it was over.

"Don't do this," I pleaded. "None of it is real."

He reached into a crate and pulled out the massive tube of a rocket launcher. He propped it against his shoulder and said, "I told you whose side I'm on."

Then he marched off to the firing line.

Heavy gongs sounded through the church. A warning to the faithful that the church was under assault. The bells. The Bells of St. Michael were ringing.

MALCOLM: I said, "I'm sitting here until it's over and we can go home." Then I parked myself on a pew, crossed my arms, and stewed. Trying to keep some small sense of control, but I'd lost it by that point. My logical brain was imploding.

ERIC: The crazy priests ran around arming themselves, and I stood there gasping in terror. Lily seemed okay, but I wondered if we'd get out of there alive.

Nothing happened for a few seconds, and I grew curious enough to walk over to join a group of priests hunched over their rifles at one of the windows. The stretch of road outside looked empty.

"Hey," I whispered to them. "What's going on? Are we allowed to leave?"

They ignored me. Then I caught a flicker of movement.

The darkness thickened. It seemed to absorb the streetlights' lonely orange glow. The night seethed as if alive, and my eyes told me it was bats, millions of black bats surging in mad descent to the asphalt.

Where the mass coalesced into a man.

Lily appeared at my side and asked me if I saw anything.

Unable to speak, I pointed at Drake.

LILY: He walked up the road in a purposeful gait. The usual T-shirt and jeans, his only concession to winter a black leather jacket. Even from here, I could tell he looked angry, and I realized I'd never seen him truly pissed off before.

Next to me, Eric babbled something about him appearing out of a swarm of bats. I ignored him, my attention focused entirely on Drake.

Run, I thought.

The word pounded in my brain to the beat of my heart, the

only rational thought I could come up with amid all the adrenaline and animal terror. I wanted to scream it, but the word failed to reach my lips. I could barely breathe.

I finally whispered it: "Run. Please, Drake."

The church erupted in gunfire.

I've stood on stages half my adult life, rocking at decibels that melted minds, and I never heard anything so loud. Hundreds of deafening bangs, thousands, each loud enough to qualify as a physical assault, all of them blending into a monstrous roar that vibrated in my chest and drowned out my scream.

Drake walked straight into it.

GARTH WAGNER: I was catching a quick snooze when World War Three kicked off outside. Thunder filled the air. The muzzle flashes lit the area like it was daytime. Tracers streamed thick and heavy across the road into the woods beyond.

"Ramona, you are one freaky chick," I said, and opened the door so I could run in there and maybe rescue her. But then I saw this tree literally explode in a cloud of splinters that rained across the windshield, and I thought I should probably stay put for a bit.

LILY: Straight into a hail of bullets. Just walking with that steady, purposeful gait. Every step bringing him closer to the church. Miraculously surviving.

Around me, priests raved snatches of Latin prayer over their guns while others roamed the firing line with brushes and buckets of holy water, cooling the red-hot barrels with fresh blessings. Gun smoke filled the air, acrid and tangy in my throat.

The surviving glass in the tall windows rattled in their frames. The very church seemed to be quaking. The bells went on gonging overhead.

Julian yelled, "Suck on this, Mabus! Fire in the hole!"

A second later, a burst of flame and smoke belched from both ends of his launcher. The rocket tore a crater out of the road. His eyes burning yellow, Drake emerged from the smoke and dust.

Suddenly very close. Grinning now, his blond hair flying as he marched.

He was laughing.

Still laughing when he disappeared in a puff of smoke.

Then a window exploded in a spray of glass, and a black whirlwind filled the church amid strobing gunfire and screams and the frantic peal of the bells.

I didn't see what happened right after that. My eyes clamped shut on their own.

My ears, however, heard it all. Every grisly crunch and blood-curdling scream.

MALCOLM: All through the world's biggest papal firing squad or whatever the hell was happening, I sat there with my fingers plugging my ears, pouting until the world decided it wanted to make sense again. Then I heard glass shatter, and my pew dropped out right from under me with a loud *crack*.

RAMONA: The scene strobed with intense flicker as the panicking priests unloaded on full auto in all directions, one howling monk knocking down a trio of nuns like bowling pins in a single burst. A weird dark blur seemed to fill the church. A priest pinwheeled past my eyes to shatter against the far wall. Another got hauled writhing into the air by invisible forces that ripped him in half like tissue paper. Others bolted only to be yanked back as if by invisible strings and torn apart. Pews flew up to crash against the ceiling. Dust and debris boiled as if this house of God had been turned into a massive threshing machine. There was blood everywhere, spraying here, fountaining there, dripping from the rafters.

ERIC: I gaped at it all in horror. Bodies exploded like water balloons all around me, and my brain blurted, What's black and white and red all over?

That guy. No, that guy. That nun who just splatted against the wall.

And over it all, I heard Drake laughing, as if this was the world's funniest joke.

Then a severed head rolled to a stop in front of me, and I realized I wasn't dreaming or watching this in a horror movie. This was actually happening, I was right smack in the thick of it, and I was about to get torn in half.

At my feet, the head yelled, "Hail Mary, full of grace."

Screaming, I ran like hell until I bounced off the giant nun I remembered swinging her fists at Sunburst. Cowering, I howled, "Please don't kill me, Sister!"

She grabbed my shoulders and gave me a good shake, saying, "It's over! We lost! Get your friends out of here before it's too late!"

The nun started to say something else, but her head twisted with a stomach-churning snap, and her body crumpled to the blood-soaked carpet at my feet.

With another scream, I ran the opposite direction, only to come to a skidding halt as what seemed like fifty pews fell from the ceiling to crash into splinters right in my path. Still screaming, I spun around again to find the big nun back on her feet, her dead face grinning at something behind her while she strangled a Jesuit.

This time, I kept going, bolting straight past her and out the doors.

LILY: I stood with my eyes shut and fists clenched, shouting over and over at everyone to cut it the fuck out. Then a wailing priest barreled into me and kept running. I landed hard on my ass, biting my tongue in the process.

"Come on, honey," a familiar voice said. "I got you."

Blinking tears, I looked up to see Julian. Taking his hand, I allowed him to haul me back onto my feet.

"I'd say we overestimated ourselves," he said.

Still dazed, I swung my head to look for my bandmates. Eric was disappearing out the doors. Ramona dragged Malcolm from under a pile of wreckage and yanked him kicking and screaming down the aisle.

Smoke filled the air. The church was on fire. I saw dead people everywhere, most of them in pieces, the pews smashed, the walls burning. Here and there, knots of shell-shocked priests either threw down their weapons or went on fighting, only to be brutally slaughtered where they stood.

The Bells of St. Michael gave their last peal before falling silent.

Julian pulled me in for a hard kiss on the lips that woke me right up.

He said, "Time to leave."

Nearby, Bishop Igwe made his last stand on the altar. Wearing his vestments with a crucifix held high, he shouted an exorcism. The blur swirled around him while he raged against the dark, and then he looked at me and froze mid-Latin.

A moment later, his body split cleanly apart and tumbled in an avalanche of body parts.

"Don't die for nothing," I said to Julian. "Come with me. Please."

He smiled and said, "I'll be right behind you. I promise. Now run!"

I raced down the aisle that was now an obstacle course of smashed pews and dead bodies, hopping over grisly remains as I went.

At the doors, I collided with Ramona, who'd been coming back in to get me. We burst coughing through the doors.

"Run," I yelled. "Go, go, go!"

We made a mad dash to the van and piled in yelling and shaking. Eric was already there, blubbering for his mother. Garth gaped and tried to ask what the hell happened and why everyone was covered in blood, but we were all too occupied shouting our heads off incoherently to answer him.

He started the van, and I cried, "Wait! Wait for Julian!"

The next seconds felt like hours.

ERIC: He was alive! Through the window, I saw him leap out the doors of the flaming church. He raced straight for us, bounding along in his black cassock and still carrying that ridiculous rocket launcher propped on his shoulder.

Lily called out, "There he is! Open the door for him!" I gripped the handle and started to push.

Julian exploded in a red splash.

Something wet slapped the window inches from my face. A big slab of bloody steak. A segment of a white spinal column protruded from the top of it. It oozed and wriggled down the glass, leaving a red smear.

GARTH WAGNER: Everyone howled, including me. I threw the transmission into gear and floored the accelerator. The van roared through the parking lot until I slammed the brakes so hard that everyone tumbled forward in their seats.

LILY: Drake stood grinning in the headlights' glare. He bent his head to light a cigarette with red-stained hands.

RAMONA: Garth murmured something like, "This is the guy?" Utterly baffled, and I couldn't blame him. I barely understood it myself.

Then he growled, "I'll handle this," and cranked the door handle.

I planted my hand on his big shoulder and squeezed. He turned to me with wild eyes, and I shook my head slowly. He let go of the handle.

LILY: I said, "I'll talk to him." Sounding far braver than I felt, but in that precise moment, I wasn't actually scared. I was very, very pissed off.

After I got out, Drake said, "Hey, babe. You're looking good."

I marched straight up to him and shoved him hard with both hands.

"You killed Julian, you asshole," I yelled at him.

He took a surprised step back and then burst out laughing. Our Lady of Victory's blazing roof collapsed with a startling crash.

He said, "You have a funny way of thanking me for saving your life."

I said, "They were right. It's true. You're the Antichrist."

Drake said, "I guess this puts a damper on us getting back together."

RAMONA: Garth stared at Drake and Lily talking and said, "That's Drake Morgan of Universal Priest, right? I mean, how did he...?"

I said, "The priests we just met with believed he's the Antichrist." I added, "Those priests are all dead now."

He still didn't understand. How did Drake survive all that gunfire and kill a couple a dozen heavily armed people?

With a heavy sigh, I said, "Because he *is*. The Antichrist. Like in the Bible."

He next asked why *we* were still alive, if that was true. Half believing it now. He'd started to wonder if the Shivers had somehow summoned the Devil and sold our souls for fortune and fame.

The truth was so much more banal than that. I pointed at Drake.

"That's her ex," I explained. "And he hasn't gotten over her."

Garth scowled. It didn't fit any of his preconceived notions formed by years of movies, TV, and heavy metal.

He asked me, "What do you think they're talking about?"

I told him Lily was probably trying to convince him not to turn us all into spaghetti and meatballs. At least, I hoped that's what they were talking about.

"Hardcore," Garth said with something like admiration. Then he looked down at the pentagram stenciled on his T-shirt, sandwiched between the words SATANIC and PANIC, and slowly returned his gaze to Drake with his bloody grinning jaws. The drummer's face turned bone white.

He'd just realized this wasn't rock-and-roll make-believe. It was real.

I had a strong feeling old Garth wouldn't be hailing Satan ever again. As for me, I couldn't stop shaking, and I knew I'd never get over what I saw tonight. That I'd be doomed to forever watch those people get slaughtered again and again.

GARTH WAGNER: Half the satanic stuff was for show and mystique. Myths are powerful stories and ready fodder for art. Displaying one's allegiance to the Dark Lord went with the musical territory. We just thought it was cool.

The other half, though, was a very real if sublimated desire to provoke unseen forces. To call on the gods and get a reaction. Wrestle with angels and wake up the Old Ones. You know nothing is gonna happen, but it's the trying that counts. It has meaning. It gives voice to a human desire not to be alone in the cosmos.

You know the old story, right? The Devil goes down to Georgia and stands at the crossroads offering fame to a musician for the price of his soul. While musicians are known to sign some shitty contracts, a real musician would never take such a deal with the Devil. He'd *already won* simply by provoking the Devil to reveal himself. That in itself was way cooler than anything Old Scratch might be selling. And it changed everything.

If Ramona told you I'd never hail Satan again, well, she's right about that.

CHARLOTTE SKINNER: What happened at Our Lady of Victory was a heartbreaking tragedy for the church and a savage act of terrorism that shocked the nation. It reminded us all of the impermanence of life, the dangers of the material world, and the hope in God's grace. That's all we have to say about it. We may never know how or why the tragedy occurred. The human brain abhors a vacuum and is prone to theorize to the point of wild and dangerous speculation.

LILY: Drake told me he'd had another dream. He'd stared into a dark, bottomless pit. A trumpet sounded a crystal peal, answered by the throaty blast of a horn so deep and thick with reverberation that it made reality itself tremble.

And boiling up from the smoking pit came the black dragon.

"That's when I knew," he said. "Who the Unknown Father is. My dad. My mission. After that, I sensed you were in danger, and so I came to rectify it."

He'd *rectified* it all right. I did in fact appreciate, you know, not dying under Bishop Igwe's knife on that altar. But I kept my mouth shut, as I didn't want my ex to think I owed him anything. It was his being the Antichrist that had gotten me in that fix to begin with.

I said, "So this is it? You're going to end the world?"

"I'm going to entertain it," he corrected me. "Actually, I'm going to set it free. But changing the world won't be all that fun if you aren't doing it with me."

I told him that was ridiculous. I was just one woman.

He said, "Yeah. But you're *my* girl."

I wasn't uniquely special or pure of heart. Yes, my innocence and desire to break free had drawn him to me. He marveled at my compassion for him even after learning his true identity. I was hardly some kind of chosen one, though.

Then the truth hit me.

I said, "You're only trying to get with me because I dumped you first!"

I didn't want the Antichrist to regard me with any special affection. Just the idea of it made me feel cursed. Like Judas, realizing *someone* had to betray Jesus to fulfill God's grand plan, and he'd drawn the short straw. I didn't want to be important in any of this. I wanted to go on making music until I could be as surprised as everyone else when the world was destroyed.

Drake shrugged. It didn't change the fact he still carried a torch for me.

He said, "We were never supposed to split up. I believe we'll be together again. I saw it in one of my visions. We took a ride in a carriage together, kissing under a dozen pale moons. It's our destiny."

I'd closed my eyes to shut out most of the church slaughter, but I'd heard it. The loud and horrifying screams, the startling crack of bones and wood, the howls for mercy, the awful silence at the end. I'd smelled the smoke and fear. The blood, plenty of which I now wore on my soaked shirt. In my mind's eye, Julian sprang out of the church and *exploded*.

I said, "I am *so* not getting back together with you."

All I could think about was how to stop him. I had Bishop Igwe's sanctified knife still tucked in my belt, but I doubted it would do any good, and besides, I still didn't want to murder anyone. Even the Antichrist.

The only problem was I didn't know how to fight him. Crucifixes and hallowed ground clearly had zero effect; Drake considered them annoying symbols and nothing more. God had unleashed evil, which meant evil could do anything it wanted. Bishop Igwe and his gang were the theological experts; the best they could come up with was exorcism prayers and heavy ordnance dipped in holy water, and we all know how that turned out.

As for me, my assets included hazy recollections of reading old stories like "The Devil and Daniel Webster" and being terrified by *The Omen* as a kid. The only weapons I possessed were psychological. The only leverage I had was that he wanted but couldn't have me, not of my own free will.

Then I recalled something he'd said. *We were never supposed to split up.* Maybe we weren't, but I'd chosen differently. It meant nothing was perfectly written in stone, perhaps not even prophecy. It meant events could change.

Little events, apparently. Maybe even big ones like the world ending.

All along, God and the Devil played a cosmic game of Monkey in the Middle with the monkey having zero say in any of it. An unfair game. Perhaps this time, humanity could make its own choice and save itself.

Free will was my weapon. I simply had to exert it.

I said, "The Battle of the Bands isn't over. Let's settle this guitar versus guitar. Your band against mine."

Drake laughed. He liked the sound of it already.

I said, "If we win, you don't take over the world. If you win..."

It's hard to say it out loud even now. So rash and stupid that it's almost embarrassing, though I didn't see any other choice. Drake kept laughing, which should have struck me as a bad sign. His amber eye twinkled with merriment.

I added, "But no mesmerizing people and forcing them to do bad things. It has to be an honest contest. Do we have a deal?"

Drake explained that he never put a spell on people. All he did was remove their inhibitions so they could satisfy their desires regardless of the consequences. If they wanted to do bad, that's what they did. But some chose to do good.

I said, "Name one."

"Sure," he said. "You."

I didn't have the energy to think through the ramifications of that right then, so I asked him again if we had a deal. No removing inhibitions. Just playing music and putting on a hell of a show, and may the best band win.

Twice he told me it was a bad idea, but I insisted.

He said, "If it makes you happy, Lilith, then I agree to the wager."

Then he said, "Maybe we can grab a drink or something after it's over."

I raised my hands in mute frustration as I took in the church burning to the ground and our butchered lead guitarist glistening across the parking lot. The air filled with approaching police and fire sirens. My body tingled with shock.

"Ask me when all this is over," I told him.

"Then break a leg," he said, and his amber eye winked. "Next weekend, I mean."

I returned to the van feeling exhausted and lightheaded. By the time I climbed back into the passenger seat, Drake had gone. Something smelled off, and I gave my wet shirt a sniff. I stank like a winery.

He'd turned the blood soaking my shirt into wine.

Eric said, "What's the word, Lil?"

I said, "We have to win Armageddon."

"Why's that?" I heard a little panic in his voice.

I said, "Because I made a deal to stop him from doing to the world what he just did to that church. I made a bet."

True to the old stories, I'd just wagered my very soul.

PRESSURIZED ABLUTION

DECEMBER 12–17, 1999

*T*he Shivers needed to prepare to go toe-to-toe against *Joanie's Kisses* in the semifinals the following weekend. Unfortunately, the band had just lost its lead guitarist and vocalist.

LILY: I woke on one of the couches in Malcolm's basement. My sleep had been so deep that waking felt more akin to resurrection than simply returning to consciousness. A paralyzing sense of dread welcomed me to the land of the living.

ERIC: Lily passed out on the way home, radiating heat that fogged the windows. We unloaded the van in a funereal silence. Then we carried her inside and laid her on the couch, where she curled up like a baby and moaned all night.

RAMONA: I barely slept a wink. In the morning, Eric quit his snoring and started asking if this or that impossible thing actually happened last night. After no one would answer him, he'd say, "Okay, but then this other thing happened, right?"

Still trying to figure out if he was crazy. Hoping he was and that last night didn't exist. Facing the possibility it did happen *and* he'd lost his grip on reality.

As a last-ditch effort, he asked us if we'd accidentally taken any hallucinogenic drugs. Again no one answered him.

Finally, he said, "So Drake's the Antichrist. The no-shit, for-real Antichrist."

LILY: Malcolm handed me a mug of coffee. I gawked at it in total puzzlement like it was some kind of alien technology before gratefully accepting it.

I wasn't the only one floored by the previous night's bizarre nightmare. My bandmates slouched with pale and haggard faces. They stared blankly at the walls.

ERIC: Ramona walked over to the practice area and studied the floor rug and acoustic panels checkerboarding the walls.

She said, "Now that we're all awake, I'm wondering how good this soundproofing is."

Malcolm, of course, treated the question as non-rhetorical. He adjusted his glasses and said, "I'm pretty sure we max out at a hundred and five decibels—"

Ramona balled her fists at her sides and screamed an F-bomb right into the acoustic foam. She screamed until she had nothing left.

I would have joined her if I didn't already feel completely hollowed out.

MALCOLM: Ramona purged herself while Eric kept frowning and blinking like a computer stuck in an endless cycle of rebooting.

I said to Lily, "So what do we do now?"

LILY: Even with some hot coffee rejuvenating me, I felt shaky with the nagging doubt I'd committed some colossal sin. The mundane basement now struck me as surreal, a cartoon rendered in saturated colors, fuzzy around the edges. Bishop Igwe's medieval knife gleamed on the coffee table like proof last night was real.

I finished my coffee and said, "We get back to playing. We have a competition to win. You know what's at stake."

The band. Our future.

Oh, and the fate of the world.

ERIC: Her soul.

RAMONA: At the time, I thought she was crazy. All night, I'd pictured making a run for it. Hopping on the next bus and riding it until the road ran out. Alaska sounded nice.

I mean, if the Devil was roaming the earth burning churches to the ground, that meant God was a-okay with it. Which meant we were on our own.

Lily had chosen fight over flight, though, and that meant I had to as well. Deep down, I believed she had the right idea. There wasn't a place we could go on the planet that the Antichrist couldn't find us if he wanted. Besides that, I knew I couldn't just survive. I'd also have to be able to live with my choice.

Lily wagering her very soul struck me as futile and suicidal and very, very dumb. Looking back, though, it was the most punk rock thing I've ever seen someone do.

MALCOLM: What a ridiculous thing. The *soul*. Your life goes by in a confused blip, ending just when or even before you've actually learned anything, but a part of you lives on to pay for it forever. It was just one of the many things about religion that fell apart once you gave it any serious thought.

And yet.

After that night, you might say I was rethinking a whole lot of preconceived notions. Once you see the impossible firsthand, you're on a slippery slope to believe anything.

The Antichrist existed, and he possessed freakish powers. Ipso facto, people had eternal souls, because of course, I mean, why not.

It was all so weird, illogical, and colossally unfair, but maybe that's just how it was. Maybe God liked things that way.

If you buy the Old Testament stories, the supreme being is pretty incomprehensible by human standards. The bizarre punishments that rivaled anything Zeus dreamed up, the commands to the Israelites to slaughter their enemies down to the last baby and camel. Telling Abraham to sacrifice his own son like a lamb only to say never mind at the last second, and what was up with making poor Abe chop off his foreskin? Why did God care if people masturbated or mouthed off to their parents or ate shellfish or got a tattoo? Why does a perfect being need anything from me, and why make me imperfect to begin with? If the stakes are so high, why does he hide instead of offering a coherent deal? Why speak in vague visions and faces burned on toast? If God wants me to live a certain way and be like him, why not just make me that way or at least be clear about it? Why does faith have to enter into it at all?

Seriously, why?

The one time anyone actually called him on his BS, as Job did from his dung heap, God's answer was he was God, he could do whatever he pleased, and he didn't owe anyone shit, least of all an explanation.

Before giving in to exhaustion and nodding off last night, I'd tried to puzzle it out. A lot of if/then statements. Hoping to understand the metaphysical mysteries as a comprehensible system that offered predictability, something I could work with. Inputs and outputs.

All my effort produced nothing. The music business made more sense than this did. More like an absurdist play where certain things had to happen than a system with definable laws. Every if/then statement I produced turned into a pretzeled snake eating its own tail.

In the end, logic had nothing to do with it. It just was. Apparently, God really could do whatever the hell he wanted, sensical or not. Ol' Julian, may he rest in peace, was right about one thing.

If you think you understand God, you don't.

I politely coughed into my fist and said to Lily, "We lost our frontman."

LILY: I picked up my guitar and said, "Someone can play Julian's parts until..."

I almost said *until he gets back*.

Then I remembered Julian had literally exploded. There was no *until* here. What happened to him, there was no getting back from.

We were on our own.

MALCOLM: She didn't seem to understand we had no time to find a replacement. If we were going to fight Armageddon, she needed to step up.

LILY: I understood the problem perfectly. I was just trying not to think about it for five minutes while I was still waking up. I said, Okay, I'll do it. Let's play.

ERIC: Nirvana had one guitarist—the man himself, Kurt Cobain. Green Day, the Offspring, and blink-182 all had one guitarist. We could do it too.

MALCOLM: We had to make do—and fast. We only had a week to rework a half-hour set with Lily playing all the guitar parts. Less than a week, actually.

This isn't as impossible as it sounds, but it isn't easy because nothing ever is in the music business, unless your name is Drake Morgan.

RAMONA: Lily had the right idea. Get right to playing. We couldn't solve the problem until we figured out what it was. The only way to do that was to play.

LILY: We took our positions in the practice area. After warming up, I closed my eyes and sent a short prayer Heaven's way. Straight to Saint Cecilia, asking her to lend me the strength to front the band and win.

At the time, I didn't question whether I *should* try to stop Drake. My opposition came instinctively, fueled by a lifetime of religious upbringing and an abrupt, hard breakup. Oh, and a massacre that took Julian from us.

If my creator didn't like me trying to mess with his plan, well, it's like Malcolm once said: God could have made any universe he wanted, and he made one in which I am who I am. The Antichrist's ex-girlfriend hell-bent on saving the world.

As long as I had free will, I'd make this choice.

Surprisingly, it was Joan Jett, my spirit guide, who answered my prayer. Her voice popped into my head to say, "Girls have got balls. They're just a little higher up, that's all."

I was about to get in touch with mine.

We played the first few songs and talked about any issues that came up. Everyone pitched in ideas. We reworked choruses, added guitar effects, and tweaked the musical arrangement. Malcolm scribbled notes on his sheet music.

Julian could do some intricate fingerpicking, but his parts proved relatively simple for me to pick up. It was like he knew all along I would. He'd never intended to stay in the band, but I wondered if he'd understood that he was a marked man. The idea sent a shiver down my back.

By the third song, I could see that this would work.

The only problem was, well, me.

I had no oomph. Pop-punk is all about bursting energy, and I didn't have it. My guitar playing came off uninspired. My singing felt tight and breathless.

My heart wasn't in it, not all the way like it needed to be. I mean, who gives a shit about complaining about one's hometown when the world's about to end?

RAMONA: It's not like any of us played our hearts out those first few days. We were all fried. Distracted. Haunted. It's kind of hard to fall into the zone and groove when your traumatized brain keeps replaying a horror movie where priests and nuns get yanked thrashing in the air and torn to shreds. Every day, Garth called to ask how I was doing, and each time, I said, "I'll let you know when I find out."

ERIC: Every time I closed my eyes, I saw Julian bounding out of the burning church only to burst all over the window. Each time, I thought, You can make it, bro. Keep at it. Run faster. We'll go skateboarding together.

RAMONA: Lily started disappearing during session breaks. Sometimes I'd hear her in the bathroom praying to some saint named Joan. Then I went outside to catch a little fresh air and found her smoking on Malcolm's stoop.

I told her I thought she'd quit.

Lily blew a stream of smoke and said, "My ex is the literal Devil."

Then she burst out laughing. I couldn't help but laugh with her.

I said, "Well, hell, when you put it that way, gimme one."

We huddled together in the freezing air, smoking menthols. The porch's cold wood felt good under my ass. A reminder the world could be harsh but was still there, solid as ever. It made me feel a little more grounded again.

Lily said, "I wish I paid more attention to everything Bishop Igwe told us about Drake. What else did they know that they didn't tell us?"

I didn't think those priests knew anything, trying to kill evil with knives and bullets and pushing this poor girl to murder the first man she ever loved. The media was reporting the massacre as an anti-Christian terrorist attack. President Clinton gave a televised speech about it at the White House, which we'd watched for a few minutes before going right back to grinding.

"We're bit players in this drama," I assured her. The priests included.

In short, certain things had to happen. We didn't have a say in any of it.

Lily asked me if she'd screwed up by making the wager. She had to believe she at least had a chance.

What was the point of having free will if she couldn't use it to at least try to stop the world from ending? If some things simply couldn't be changed?

I answered her with the harsh truth, which was I had zero clue.

That was the problem. None of us really knew what we were dealing with here. We were messed up and terrified. We all pretty much lived in Malcolm's basement now, feeling safe only with each other.

I said, "Maybe don't go looking to fight a cosmic war you can't win. Just win Armageddon. That's all that matters right now."

She blew another cloud of smoke and said, "I'd rather fight the Antichrist."

Shivering in the frosty air, I stared at her in wonder. The girl had bet her soul to save the world, but what scared her the most right now was becoming the Shivers' frontwoman.

The amount of faith she had in us was astounding. It saddened me, though, that she didn't hold nearly as much simple faith in her heart for herself.

I squeezed her knee and said, "We're in uncharted waters here. But I want to win this. For me. So that however much time we have left has meaning. Regardless of whether this world ends. Regardless of where my soul might go in the next."

"My gut told me what to do," Lily said. "I guess I'm still learning to trust it."

I said, "Stop treating the band like another man in your life that you let control you until you kick him to the curb. It's your band now, honey. Lead it."

ERIC: I figured if I'd never be Lily's boyfriend, I could be a good friend. As the week wore on and it became clear the immediate crisis had been handled if not yet quite solved, I invited her to take a drive with me to say goodbye to Julian.

After borrowing the keys to the van, I drove us to the ramshackle skate park in the industrial ruins along the river. With the leaves long gone from the trees and the dead smokestacks in the distance, the place looked even bleaker than the last time I'd been here. Fewer people skated, mostly diehards.

Lily said, "I know this park. I used to come here to check out the boys."

I thought maybe I really should learn how to ride a skateboard.

She added, "It's nice to see you out and doing something other than playing your bass. We're all waiting for you to give it a name."

I told her she was being silly.

Still teasing, she said, "Bessie. Brutus. Bart."

I said, "I just figured we could use a break."

Lily looked at the kids clacking around on their boards with surprise. She said it was weird to see. The Antichrist had come, the fate of the world hung in the balance, and here kids skated and chilled and smoked weed.

Me, I couldn't think of a more fitting response.

I said, "Julian brought me here once. For the longest time, I thought Drake was so cool that I wanted to be him, but it was Julian who I really envied. The dude was so at peace with himself, and he gave me some really sound advice."

With that, I pulled the man's battered skateboard out of the van and plopped it down. I placed a sneakered foot on it.

"This is for you, man," I said, and pushed off.

I wobbled along waving my arms as if performing a high-wire circus act. Slow and ridiculous, but that was how I rolled, so I owned it.

When I toppled off into a scrabbling fall onto the hard, cold ground, I barely felt embarrassed. I actually laughed.

I caught my breath and looked up, but it wasn't Lily standing over me but the pretty girl with the wool hat. A big shock that she wasn't pointing at me and cackling.

I said, "You're not going to throw your clothes at me again, are you? It's cold out here."

The girl didn't even look at me. She stared at Lily with wide dark eyes. She'd gotten an odd little tattoo on her neck, a tiny link of barbed wire or a flower, I couldn't tell from where I sprawled on the ground.

She said, "You're so lucky."

Lily asked why that was. Deadpanning the question.

The girl said, "Because he still loves you. He chose you as his bride."

Now Lily did the pointing and laughing. She said, "He's all yours, lady. Speaking of which, shouldn't you be ding-dong-ditching or shoplifting CDs or something? Free to be your worst you?"

The girl said Drake helped her finally be able to do what she wanted, which was nothing at all. No more Lehigh U. for her, no thinking about her future, no worrying about whether her English major would make her economically viable. All she wanted to do was hang out, smoke weed, and listen to Universal Priest.

Judging by her disheveled appearance, she'd even given up showering and brushing her teeth. Since I'd last seen her at Don Quixote, she'd taken on a feral, homeless look.

She said, "You don't have a choice. You have a destiny. You're his bride."

The first time I'd seen this nameless girl, it had been crush at first sight. Perversely, her scathing scorn had only made her hotter. But hearing how Drake had freed her to make sloth a virtue pissed me right off.

Lily growled, but before she could unload any colorful thoughts about having no choices when it came to Drake, I said, "Shut up, loser."

Then I dusted myself off, swiped the skateboard off the ground, and stormed back to the van. Lily followed, laughing.

She said, "I am seeing a whole other side of you."

"Not really," I said. The truth was, that girl reminded me of myself. The life I'd narrowly dodged. What I feared was the real me. I said, "She's now free to waste her life being a boring chore of a stereotype. Wow. Congratulations."

Either way, I'd come here to honor Julian and share it with Lily, only to see even this ruined by Drake. But Lily kept giggling, so it wasn't a total loss. Though I kind of wish people laughed at my jokes instead of when I was being serious.

Getting behind the wheel, I gazed out the windshield at the nameless girl grinning at us while doing a shuffling hip-hop dance. Cute and evil at the same time. Even now, a part of me still pined to be her boyfriend. God, I was hopeless.

I said, "We have to win this weekend."

She told me that was the idea.

We never talked about whether the world was actually worth saving. As for me, I already had my answer.

I said, "Drake wants to destroy the world. My ma lives in this world. You live in this world. So fuck that. And fuck him."

He'd told me to follow a purpose. Mine was now to wreck his plan.

Lily loved humanity enough to put her very soul on the line. Knowing this, I'd replaced the pedestal I'd put her on with an entire pantheon in my heart. As long as she'd fight, I'd follow her and fight at her side.

I said, "I just wanted you to know you're not alone. This weekend, I'm going to give it my all. Me and Stringer, we got your back."

She asked me who Stringer was, and I told her. It's what I'd named my bass.

LILY: That week, we stopped being a band and turned into something more like a tribe. Their faith in me gave me the strength to put everything aside and focus on the music. I pinned down all my parts in the songs and worked on my singing.

Meanwhile, the countdown to Armageddon inexorably wound down. With only a day to go before showtime, I invited Malcolm to take a walk with me.

He seemed to know what I wanted. As much as I appreciated Ramona's and Eric's wisdom, when it came to the band, I respected his opinion the most.

As soon as we were outside, he said, "We're going to lose."

I took this as a punch to the gut, as you do when told something you don't want to hear but need to anyway. Something you know deep down is true. He forged ahead as he always did, as if he were perpetually running late, and I hurried to catch up.

He said, "First off, we have to beat Joanie's Kisses."

The all-girl band's ethereal but radio-ready sound provided its listeners with cutting lyrics about racy and complex relationships. In both raw sex appeal and voice, vocalist and Stevie Nicks clone Valeria Valis packed a sharp bite.

He was right. They were good.

Malcolm said, "Even on our best day, they'd be our equal. A fifty–fifty shot. And if we beat them, you know who we'll be up against in the final round."

Drake's raw talent trumped ours by a long shot, and it was entirely possible that the universe's supreme being wanted him to win.

But we were the better band, I told Malcolm. More than that, we were likable.

Maybe not fifty–fifty, but we had a fighting chance.

We'd trudged several blocks through the cold, gray landscape, and suddenly we came upon a riot of noise and colors. The park nearest Malcolm's house had been flooded and turned into an ice rink on which children swirled on skates.

Next to it, people crowded stalls thrown up in a festive crafts fair sparkling with decorations. Christmas decorations always struck me as cheerful and a little sad, and right then I welcomed either.

Malcolm wanted to go around. I ignored him and plunged into the fray, pointing out that I had my parts down, we'd practiced to exhaustion, and a good night's sleep would see us at our best tomorrow night.

He said, "The problem is you."

Another hard truth that needed to be spoken aloud. I sagged and told him I knew it. I wasn't good enough yet to be the face and voice of the Shivers. Losing Julian had set us back too far to catch up in time.

Malcolm practically shouted at me, making heads around us turn.

He said, "That. Right there. Is the problem we're trying to solve."

Pop-punk was supposed to be a loud night out with your buddies, he explained. Wasting time on harmless fun. Knowing that you're okay and it's the world that's messed up. Finding a level of cool in knowing you'll never be cool. Our songs, however, now all sounded like I was asking a question.

The problem was confidence.

Malcolm said, "Even you asking me how it's going is annoying. Don't get me wrong, Lil. I love it. I'm a control freak. You know this about me. But we won't win like that. Singing punk songs doesn't make you a punk. You have to look me in the eye and tell me how it's going to be."

This made me think again about all the things I'd been trying to avoid all week. Julian dying, along with the feeling it was somehow my fault. Wagering my soul to save the world, two very abstract concepts I didn't truly understand.

And beneath all this, there was the old doubt I wasn't good enough to front a band, much less play in one. That I hadn't been away from Drake long enough to really know who I was as a musician or even as a woman.

Malcolm saw it all written on my face. He asked why I was doing all this.

Why did I join the Shivers? Why did I fight so hard for it after Drake left?

The music, I thought. But even this felt abstract to me now. My perverse drive to knock Drake down a few pegs had waned. Whatever he'd done and might be, I didn't hate him. I actually felt sorry for him.

I gazed across the ice-skaters in their winter hats and colorful coats and pitied them too. They were innocent. It made me think of Abraham's argument with God over the fate of Sodom, which God intended to destroy. Abraham's relative Lot lived there, and he wanted to save him. In the only argument he ever had with

God, Abraham asked him not to kill the good with the bad. God agreed to spare Sodom if fifty righteous men could be found, which Abraham subsequently bargained down to ten.

I wondered if this was why the Antichrist must come before God destroyed the world. The world had to be completely corrupted before God could end what he'd created. Regardless, the world would always be innocent, just as Sodom had been even after God warned Lot to leave. Because at that moment, I was looking at way more than ten innocents. These children laughing on the ice could hardly be considered corrupt. They deserved to mature to find out who they were, not endure the horrors of a new dark age inflicted by a cosmic script.

A deep sense of love struck me right then, an overwhelming compassion for these children and everyone else on the planet.

If God wanted to end the world, he should just end it without making us all suffer by giving evil free rein. His letting kids die in hurricanes was bad enough as the norm. Unleashing evil to destroy the world with war and plague looked like something else entirely.

My fight, I realized, wasn't against the Antichrist. It was for these children. It was for everyone still innocent. It was for the good people still fighting the good fight and for the not-so-good who deserved their chance at redemption.

Wheeling, I hugged Malcolm for all I was worth until he gave my shoulder an awkward pat and said, "Okay, there."

I looked him in the eye said, "We're going to win."

My heart felt like it had burst into flame. I couldn't wait to sing and play again.

At that moment, I realized Julian had been right. Compassion is the essence of cool, and anything else is just posing and fakery based on fear. Punk rock had always been about breaking the world. This time, it was going to save it.

SONIC TRIBULATION

THE ARMAGEDDON
BATTLE OF THE BANDS
DECEMBER 18, 1999

With Christmas approaching, Lily and her bandmates looked back on a turbulent 1999. Through a series of chance meetings, four total strangers had formed a band with a distinctive sound. They'd lost their frontman twice and completely changed their music to put a fresh spin on a familiar form. As the year wound down toward the end of the millennium, they'd won the first round of a major music competition.

It all led up to this weekend, a battle of bands for the ultimate stakes.

LILY: We arrived at the Gold Bowl to a small crowd of musicians surrounding an ambulance and strobing police cruiser. What now?

Malcolm found a parking space near the backstage doors, where Drake stood smiling with a cigarette in his lips, breath and smoke fogging the frosty air.

I threw him a dirty look as I got out and said, "You just can't help yourself."

He shrugged and told me he thought he'd finished any business he'd had with his archnemeses last weekend. Apparently, evangelicals were now getting in on the act. Some upright church lady from Baton Rouge.

When I asked what happened to the poor woman, he told me Hate Mail had run her over with their van. Laughing, he said, "That band doesn't have any luck."

Yesterday, he added, a heavily armed imam and a rabbi walked into the bar where he was having a drink, like the setup for a joke, only this one had a morbid punch line. A TV fell off the wall onto the imam's head just as an errant cue ball flew off a nearby pool table to strike the rabbi, putting them both in the hospital.

The ambulance squawked as it navigated the crowd. The show over, everyone started moving toward the doors.

The way Drake so casually found dark humor in the mayhem he caused had me seeing red. I turned back to remind him that he'd agreed to no hypnotizing people while on stage tonight, but he'd disappeared.

MALCOLM: We loaded in our instruments and gear, emergency kit and spare clothes, granola bars and everything else we'd need.

If we lost tonight, I would not miss this part. Being in a fledgling band is like working for a moving company while moonlighting as a musician who gets paid in lottery tickets.

I wondered what I was going to do tomorrow. Wake up, naturally. Pour some coffee. Then very likely have to face myself in the mirror and say, "You lost, ya big loser."

The image sent a shudder through me. Seriously, it was easier hearing Drake was the Antichrist than confronting the possibility of failure.

After that, I'd just have to find something else to work on. Like Henry Ford, whose first auto companies failed under him before he rolled out the Model T. Or Milton Hershey, whose caramel company went kaput before creating one of the world's most successful chocolate brands. Or old Tom Edison himself, who quipped, "I have not failed. I've just found ten thousand ways that won't work."

I'd move on. Find something that worked.

But I'd miss this, all of it, even the chore of loading.

I might just miss my bandmates too.

Realizing this left me unsettled. Sentimentality has no place in business. I wondered if my feeling for the band was yet another sunk-cost fallacy.

After load-in, I set off to find the organizer to sign in and receive a time slot for sound check. When I turned back toward the green room, a tall, spindly man blocked my path.

He wore a long brown leather coat and thick steampunk sunglasses that gave his expressionless face an insectoid appearance. He'd neatly combed his long hair to waterfall over one side of his thin, angular face.

Universal Priest's keyboardist.

In a quiet voice, he said, "We don't need anyone, do we?"

I said, "Starting with you."

I brushed past him to get back to work hurrying up and waiting. And I thought, Maybe I'll wake up tomorrow to tell myself I'd won it all.

ERIC: We mounted the stage for sound check. The previous weekend, I'd crept out like a groundhog testing for shadows. Wondering if I belonged there and feeling more than a little like an impostor. This time, I walked on like I owned it, and by the time I took my position, I realized I had indeed *swaggered* to get here.

I thought, So that's how it works. You really do fake it until you make it.

I tried not to think about this maybe being my last show.

During the line check, I played the bass line for "Run for Your Life" until the sound engineer pronounced my input levels clean. We went back and forth until he had the gain and equalization dialed in. By now, I didn't just say okay to everything but instead knew my instrument well enough to get its sound just right.

After line check, we played "Merry-Go Vertigo," a song about a twentysomething who runs into some people from high school she'd always feared and hated, only to discover the rules had changed and they were no longer the kids they'd been. Lily really poured it on, like it was the real thing.

The sound guy tweaked the knobs until he achieved a perfect balanced mix. As we packed up to head to the green room, a dark figure applauded from the gloomy floor.

Squinting into the lights, I made out Drake, and I understood why Lily had belted out the song with so much energy.

Drake said, "Love the new sound, guys. Fresh!"

Lily exited the stage fuming.

He called out my name. I'd intended to ignore him like the others, but I couldn't help myself. Needing to get something important off my chest, I hopped down and walked over to him.

I said, "You know, I really looked up to you."

He said, "Is that the purpose you found, Eric? To look up to people?"

A weird wet sound made me take a step back, and I noticed Universal Priest's bassist sitting cross-legged like a small hill on the dark floor. Gog went on smacking his lips as he stared straight into my crotch.

"Gonna eat that first," he said.

I took another big step back and said, "Come on, dude."

Drake laughed.

He said, "You always let everyone beat you without any real effort."

"I know who you are," I told him.

This made him frown. In his mind, some priests slapped a scary label on him, and now he was the enemy.

How was he the bad guy? He said it wasn't fair.

I pointed out he killed those priests and burned their church to the ground. I wanted him to know how much I'd once admired him and how badly he'd let me down.

But Drake only shrugged, proving again how easy it was to defeat me.

I yelled, "You blew up Julian right in front of me!"

He shook his head and said, "Am I the only person who remembers those priests shooting a million bullets at me with machine guns? If your guitarist didn't want to die, he probably shouldn't have picked up that rocket launcher."

Time to go. I asked him what he'd wanted to tell me.

He said, "Your bass playing has really improved, man. Mad respect."

I didn't know how to respond to that. Coming from him, the compliment left me warm and more than a little disturbed. I mumbled my thanks.

Then Drake said, "Oh, and put in a good word for me with Lilith, okay?"

RAMONA: The green room had a horrible vibe. Hate Mail moped over possible manslaughter charges. Mary, Universal Priest's rhythm guitarist, stood like a statue and stared from her creepy expressionless mask. The groupies, roadies, and groadies howled and partied. In the center of the room, Joanie's Kisses' Valeria Valis held court on one of the couches, bangles jangling on her arms as she punctuated every laughing sentence with wild gestures.

Eric showed up with a loud sigh. He said, "I figured something out."

I asked him what, and he said, "If you put someone on a pedestal, it pretty much guarantees they'll let you down."

It's never too late to grow up. The boy was learning.

Draped in the rags of a bloodstained ball gown, Mary tilted her masked face and made a come-hither gesture. Eric's eyes turned moony with sexual interest.

I said, "We really have to find you a girl."

The guitarist had a knockout body, and the mask inspired curiosity as much as dread. Otherwise, she was a walking advertisement for bad dreams. She'd gnaw a guy like Eric into paste and swallow. His type, apparently.

He sighed and said, "The more I change, the more I stay the same."

Moist heat fell on the back of my neck. Another burst of it made me flinch. I wheeled to see Universal Priest's hairy little drummer. The grinning, heavily tattooed creature Drake had labeled Magog.

Clenching my fists, I glared back at him.

The dude stepped right into my personal space and went on grinning at my shoulder, arms limps at his sides. Breathing his foul wet breath. I noticed he had a tiny tattoo of a flower on his forehead like a Hindu bindi representing the third eye.

At this point, I'd usually deadpan a warning and start swinging.

Instead my blood turned to ice. My brain scrambled with panic. I had an irrational fear that if I pushed him, my hands would become glued and I'd never escape. I'd rage and fight while he did nothing, eventually consuming me.

I backed away, asking him what he was doing in a voice high-pitched with fear. The wiry little weirdo was so much like my nightmares in which a faceless man grabbed me in the dark and didn't let go.

Breathing on me and squeezing until I suffocated.

The man's grin stretched to the limit as he followed me, his vacant eyes still staring at my shoulder from inches away. Eric gawked the whole time, accustomed to me pounding bullies instead of surrendering so easily to one. I thought of my lost-and-found box. How I'd fit inside it in the warm dark.

A muscly arm reached behind the dude to grip a handful of jacket and lift him scrabbling into the air.

Garth said, "Bad dogs go outside."

Necromonium's drummer frog-marched Magog yelping to the back door, kicked it open, and hurled him out into the cold. Then he sauntered back to me dusting his large hands.

I said, "I thought you were gonna help us with the load-in."

Garth smiled and said, "When I'm reliable, I'm very reliable."

And when he wasn't, well. I didn't care. The panic still felt thick in my chest, building like sour bile in my gullet. It burst out as a wet sob.

Gaping at me, Garth moved to deliver a hug, but I hissed at him like a wild animal. He froze. My cheeks burned with shame, and the tears started to flow. I hadn't cried since I left home.

The big man slowly raised his hands palms up, and I found myself nodding.

Garth enveloped me in a hug as I let it all out.

ERIC: Seeing Ramona physically cowed and then weeping shocked me as much as finding out Drake was the Antichrist. I reached out to give a comforting pat on her shoulder but didn't want to lose my hand. Even wounded, she was dangerous.

Garth seemed to have things handled here. Mary made another *come here, big boy* gesture from across the room, and this time I glared and gave her the finger.

"Hey, Shiver boy," a voice said.

It was Valeria Valis who'd called to me. She patted the couch cushion next to her, eyes gleaming with mischief and lips already parted in anticipation of a good laugh.

I gawked at her, remembering the moment I first laid eyes on her at Sunburst, twirling around the stage in a flowy white dress. The instant crush.

After I sat, she asked me what all the fuss was about.

I said, "Watch out for Universal Priest. They're evil psychopaths, and their frontman is the literal biblical Antichrist with supernatural powers."

Valeria considered this the height of hilarity. She clapped her hands as she tossed her head back cackling, her red hair flying. Yet another person laughing at me while I was being serious.

She said, "You gotta love musicians."

I said, "I'm Eric. I play bass."

She'd already turned to scoop her glass of wine and share a witty comment with her bandmates, and then they were all cracking up. I'd been invited only to get ignored. God, it was like the rude girl in the wool hat all over again.

I started to stand, but Valeria placed a possessive hand on my thigh and squeezed. I stayed put to see what happened next. So did her hand.

This went on for an hour. Valeria held court drinking wine while I drank in her outsize presence. Her wild mane of red hair, tinkling bangles, and massive personality thoroughly captured me. At one point, I asked her who Joanie was, but she just laughed again and went back to chatting with her bandmates.

Her hand playfully raked my thigh with her nails. Her fingers traced little circles and did a prancing march up to my knee. My body hummed. My fevered brain swam with scenarios and fantasies.

The girls all gave me knowing smiles, as if this was an old habit or delightful quirk of Valeria's.

VALERIA VALIS (*vocalist, Joanie's Kisses*): A test, actually. I've always found husky men hot. The only problem was they tried to take charge. I wanted to let Eric know if he wanted me, it'd be on my terms. If he could sit there and play the wallflower without storming off with wounded pride, he could have what I was willing to give.

ERIC: I think I already told you I fall in love way too easily, but that wasn't even my biggest problem with women. I'd idealize them, feel insecure about myself, and then try too hard to impress. The second I opened my mouth, I'd blow it with overthinking, which is why I tended to worship from afar.

Valeria wanted me to zip my lip while she called the shots and was the center of attention. I felt like I'd met the perfect woman.

LILY: In a bathroom stall, I tried to find my happy place, no easy task as a mob of scantily clad women rotated in to touch up their makeup and snort coke off the sinks. I prayed to Saint Cecilia to strengthen my hands to shred and my pipes to wail.

I came back to find Malcolm chatting up band managers for a possible pivot into that side of the music business, Ramona sobbing against Garth's chest, and Eric fraternizing with the formidable girl band we had to beat tonight. The vibe was terrible in there. Forced hilarity tinged with jitters and despair.

The only people who really seemed to be having fun were the groupies.

A hand landed on my shoulder, and I yelped. Drake laughed.

He said, "You scare way too easily."

I'd never been afraid of him. Not until the end, anyway. I must have said this out loud, because he nodded and said that was a weird time in his life. He was just starting to learn who he was and what his mission might be.

I said, "You really were trying to drive me away. Trying to protect me from this. From what you are."

"That, or I was seeing if you'd go all the way standing at my side," he said. "That's why I tried to turn you into something you're not. When I actually did push you away, I realized what a huge mistake I'd made. I'd rather have you at my side fighting me every step than not in my life at all."

All the way, he'd said. I knew what that meant.

I just didn't understand it.

How would the world end? How did the whole thing work?

Smiling, Drake reminded me that God would do the actual heavy lifting. He'd be the one ending the world, not Drake or even his evil dad. If I didn't like this fact, I should take it up with the man upstairs.

He said, "Or you could go on a date with me, and I'll share everything I know about the cosmic mysteries."

I thought of the silver door that led either to the infernal plane or to Drake's soul.

He said, "Bad timing for me to ask, I know. You're trembling, and it's not me causing it. You're actually nervous about tonight."

"It's not easy for me like it is for you," I shot back. "Some of us don't have destiny on our side. There's a lot riding on this."

Drake told me his secret was to play like it didn't matter. I told him tonight mattered a great deal to me and not just whether we won studio time.

He said, "I didn't tell you to bet your soul. Maybe you'd like to call the whole thing off. It's not too late. You can't win, you know."

"Destiny," I said bitterly.

"No," he said. "Your band is broken."

Drake was mocking me, though he was probably right. I didn't care. This year, I'd discovered a quality I never knew I had: a pure, diamond-hard stubbornness.

With a glare, I said, "I have to get my people ready to rock."

I wasn't about to back out now.

RAMONA: We had a somber last supper at the Gold Bowl's cheapest restaurant. Surrounded by the casino's frantic desperation, we ate in a heavy silence except for Garth, who tried to entertain us with road stories.

I'd told him everything, and while the purge did me good, I felt even more raw and vulnerable. The thing about being tough is, it's always an act. The sadness you're hiding can be held at bay but never truly conquered.

MALCOLM: Lily shot me dirty looks over dinner. She knew I was already planning a career change and probably considered it a betrayal, even though I'd warned her that tonight was our last chance.

I really thought I'd make a good band manager, though. My analytical brain often clashed with my bandmates. If I was in a business role, it would complement them. Hell, I'd even happily take on the Shivers as my first client if they wanted to keep going.

We had zero chance of winning tonight. When I later watched Universal Priest play against Hate Mail from the side stage, it confirmed my fears. Drake honored his promise not to rewire any brains. Instead he delivered a killer show.

No industrial noise this time; Drake seemed to play his bandmates as well as his guitar, producing music that Led Zeppelin might have come up with if John Bonham hadn't passed away and they'd kept on evolving.

Rock and roll at its finest. Jerking in place like machines, Universal Priest had zero stage presence, but it didn't matter. Drake projected more than enough himself. So much that it seemed to fill the vast room with cool.

Lily didn't understand. Yes, she'd really stepped up. By the end of the week, she'd not only filled Julian's shoes but put her stamp on the band as well. But what I'd told the priests about the futility of fighting the Antichrist wasn't just mouthing off. It was true. His triumph had been destined since the beginning of time.

We were good. Very good. But not good enough to beat God.

ERIC: I was thinking about predestination too. Standing in the wings, I watched Joanie's Kisses play their set. Valeria danced and twirled around the stage with her massive mane of red hair and flashing bangles and fluttering hippie dress. Her phone number burned like a fresh brand on my wrist.

I will worship you, I thought. You will tie me in knots. But I won't stop. Every time you look at me, you will see how beautiful you are. How special. My goddess.

Malcolm had it right about destiny, but I knew something he didn't. Something even Drake didn't know. Free will is a sham. A comforting illusion.

What we do is nature and nurture. Lily had bet her soul to save the world because that's who she is. She had no choice. I didn't either, not really.

I'd always fallen in love with what I couldn't really own. But half of something is still better than nothing. For a guy like me, it could be everything.

RAMONA: At stage time, Lily gathered us together and told us she loved us. She looked each of us in the eye and said, "I see you." Warts and damage and all. Then she said, "I love you." Compassion radiating like a soothing heat.

She said, "You know what I bet on this fight. I know you think deep down that we can't win. That we're not allowed to win. I'm telling you that's okay."

We all stared at her. She'd just given us permission to send her to Hell.

Lily said, "It was unfair of God to put me in the position I'm in. It was unfair of me to put you in yours. You should know that if Drake weren't the Antichrist, we would win tonight. What I want you to do for me is play like you don't care. If you can't fight fate, you have nothing to lose. Play for the music tonight. Play for you, not because you want to win, but because it's fun. Because you love it. Because you can do nothing else."

By now, we were all weeping, even stodgy Malcolm and warrior Garth, and we all embraced in a group hug before stomping onto the stage fired up and free.

ERIC: We were really good.

MALCOLM: We were awesome.

LILY: We fucking *rocked*.

AXEL HODGES: The Shivers were electrifying. I kept thinking I had to get them on the radio and that I might just have discovered the next big band.

STEPHEN WISE: They killed it. The band showed amazing energy and chemistry. They made the audience feel like they were at a house party. I could hear the crowd singing along at the final chorus.

In the judges' booth, we had no problem sending them to the finals. A unanimous decision.

I still couldn't figure what Morgan or the Shivers had to do with Vince committing arson, but I didn't care about that anymore. I was having a great time.

DANNY RODRIGUEZ: They checked every box on my list. Catchy tunes, tight rhythms, fantastic stage presence. The band delivered classic pop-punk spirit that Lily Lawless turned into something uniquely hers.

Apparently, they'd parted ways with frontman Julian Curtis. Bizarre rumors abounded. However it occurred, this turned out to be a very wise decision. After the competition, I'd have to talk to these guys. Them and Universal Priest.

It was turning into one hell of a night.

I'd come to this little backwater expecting a forgettable bar fight, and I'd wound up with a front-row seat for the musical equivalent of Muhammad Ali fighting Muhammad Ali for the heavyweight title.

ALEXIS ZHANG: It proved our most surprising year yet for Armageddon, a real battle of underdogs who'd overwhelmed far more experienced and polished local bands. The attendees had cast their votes for the Audience Choice Award, which were still being tallied. The final round would see Universal Priest and the Shivers battle it out for the judges' favor.

Two upstart bands, each playing one song, and only one would walk away the undisputed champion of Armageddon.

ERIC: Valeria was not happy about it. She stormed out with her girls. I couldn't wait to see her again and find out exactly how she planned to make me pay for it.

LILY: We took our places again on the dark stage. The atmosphere had become electric. Cheers and whistles burst from the crowd. This was it. The final fight.

One last song to prevent the apocalypse. I'd saved the best for last. Because it was so personal, I'd sing it from the heart. A song about me. A song about all rock and roll. Tonight I'd finally earned the right to perform it.

RAMONA: This fight had gotten very personal. I wanted to destroy Universal Priest.

ERIC: I was ready to rock. I felt strangely complete, a first for me. This time, I wouldn't play to impress anyone but myself. This time, I'd do it just for me.

MALCOLM: Checking out my bandmates in the gloom, I felt an odd, deep affection for them. However this night had turned out, it had been one hell of a journey to get here. Even if we lost, I felt like I'd already won a different fight.

RAMONA: Our serpentine logo glowed on the big screen behind me. The crowd settled with a few final scattered whistles. A few stage lights highlighted the band, with the rest dimmed for now. I twirled my sticks, ready to kill it. Lily thanked Armageddon and the audience, which prompted a swelling roar.

Then she introduced us:

Malcolm Williams, keyboardist and coder, the Shivers' drama-free den mom and steady engine to be the best at what we do—

Eric Borkowski, lover of bass and self-improvement specialist, our sensitive softy who always puts his bandmates first—

Ramona Perez, warrior drummer, who sticks her heart and fists on the line every day to have our backs, and we hope she knows we have hers too—

She finished, "And I'm Lily Lawless, a dreamer who prays that rock and roll really can save the world, starting tonight. Now I have something to say. Do you want to hear me?"

The crowd howled back in an atmosphere thick with anticipation. They weren't just warmed up. They'd caught fire. Lily let their roar stretch, savoring it.

Then the stage lights flared to full intensity as I counted us in.

LILY: I strummed the opening riff, the melody raw and punchy but subdued for now, simmering at the edge of epiphany or explosion. And I sang:

> I have a voice you cannot hear
> Because I am so quiet
> Never wanna give cause to jeer or sneer
> That's why I stay so silent

RAMONA: My sticks blurred across the skins, a barrage of beats hurling the song in manic momentum with cracking snare strikes, cymbals sparking in the hot lights, the pound of the kick drum. The song no longer held at a simmer but boiling as Lily raked power chords and sang with raw emotion:

> Maybe I've got the world to say
> Maybe I'll talk some *stupid shit*
> It doesn't matter either way
> I have a voice and I wanna *scream it*

ERIC: I worked the frets and strummed my patterns to anchor the rhythm while Ramona relentlessly drove the song and Malcolm textured the melodies and punched the harmony, every accent taking the song to a higher level. The song now flew at 160 beats per minute, no longer played but simply allowed to happen, with us musicians mere conduits of the speeding groove.

The whole thing exploded as Ramona unloaded a soaring fill with the toms and crash cymbals, and then Lily belted out the chorus:

> Can you hear me now?
> Can you hear me now?

Can you hear me now?
Can you hear me now?

LILY: Switching to full chest voice for the chorus, singing from the heart on key and in rhythm. Strings fretted and thrashed. Sneering and leering in the punk way. Eric and Ramona grinning in the pocket. The energy infectious, the audience hopping in front of me. I had entered the zone, channeling all my rock goddesses and Saint Cecilia too, euphoric with the power, absorbing the crowd's love and reflecting it back as infinite compassion. There is a certain heady freedom in being lost, and right then, I was lost in the music, I had become the music.

I cut loose with a guitar solo made up of crashing and then piercing notes echoing the chorus. My instrument a part of me, wanting to be heard too. With Eric in lockstep, Ramona unleashed the final lunge for the climax, and the last chorus arrived with triumph, me scream-singing the words while my band and the crowd joined in:

CAN YOU HEAR ME NOW?

ERIC: At the end, we all just stood sweaty and stunned and grinning as Alexis Zhang exhorted the audience over the PA to *give it up for the Shivers* and the crowd's roar rose like a wave to crash over us.

Lily called out that she loved them all, and then we left the stage.

LILY: Wiping tears, I pulled everyone together into a group hug and thanked them for fighting.

ERIC: We did it. Whatever happened next, we'd given it our all.

MALCOLM: We had no idea what was coming.

RAMONA: Hope is a dangerous drug. We were high on it. Right then, we believed.

MALCOLM: Now it was Universal Priest's turn.

LILY: We didn't even have the chance to break down our gear when the lights went out.

ERIC: A bonfire roared to life on the stage. Five hairy hulking figures surrounded it. The drummer launched into a throbbing primitive beat. The air filled the blast of old horns, didgeridoos, and shofroth, the sound vibrating in my chest.

I was like, How did they get all this set up so fast?

Then: Oh. Right. Antichrist.

MALCOLM: Lily might have made a deal, but we never should have expected Drake Morgan to give us a fair fight.

LILY: With a clank of heavy chains, the monstrous men shuffled around the fire while an invisible choir sang out a booming call-and-response:

> When Israel was in Egypt land
> *Let my people go*
> Oppressed so hard they could not stand
> *Let my people go*

An old African American spiritual. The baritone voices united for the refrain to create a wall of sound brimming with despair and longing:

Go down, Moses
Way down in Egypt land
Tell old Pharaoh
Let my people go

RAMONA: A strident voice called from the dark, and the men at the fire chanted their response in a corrupted version of another old-timey spiritual, "Run, Mary, Run." Their version uplifting but angry and proud instead of brimming with hopeful humility:

Old Moses said we got a right—
You got a right to every privilege
We got a right, we got a right—
To fight to the top of the tower
Old Moses said we got that right—
You got a right to the Tree of Knowledge
You got the right, you got the right—
To Pharoah's crown of power

LILY: As much as I'd hoped to hate it, I found it quite moving, sad but defiant. Our music was about nostalgia and rebellion. Drake was showing us that music could be about protest and power, and it could change the world.

The fire blazed higher, revealing the men as hairy, shambling monsters. Then still higher to expose the invisible choir that stood like an army of the damned. A throng of misshapen creatures crowded the stage. I saw a squat winged beast blowing a shofar, a man-beast grinning around tusks, every manner of horn sprouting from skulls and shoulders, a few towering giants.

Barely visible among the shifting throng, Universal Priest's grimacing musicians jerked and twitched over their instruments like windup dolls.

The monstrosities stomped their feet to add their heavy percussion to the rhythm. In unison, they growled quiet words in Latin that grew in volume and overwhelmed and finally took over the ring shout.

Liberi erimus. Liberi erimus.

We will be free.

The chanting filled the hall while Universal Priest's loveless keyboardist layered on a sweeping church organ melody. Massive bat wings spread and trembled. Some wore bits of iron armor and shook spears held in clenched fists. Others waved red and black banners, scattering the smoke into a thick gray haze. The chanting sounded longing and then angry, louder, building to something big.

At the rear of the stage, the big media screen lit up with a logo:

A powerfully stirring display of oppression and revolution. I wondered how Drake pulled off such a spectacle before realizing what had been obvious all along.

He'd called upon Hell's demons for aid. This was how Hell saw itself, defeated and cast out and enslaved, demanding not just freedom but ultimate power.

RAMONA: Teeth gritted, Malcolm glared at the show. Eric let out a guttural moan. I yanked the sleeve of Garth's shirt. It was time to leave. We'd only caught the preamble, Drake hadn't even taken the stage yet, and we'd already lost.

He didn't even look at me. He just shook his head and said, "I don't understand. What is this?"

The toughest man I'd ever know had been rendered powerless by the incomprehensible spectacle of Universal Priest's show.

I said nothing. I had no answer for him. I'd given up. If this was it, if these things had come to destroy, there wasn't a place on earth I could run and be safe.

LILY: A soaring guitar note filled the air like an angel's trumpet. A moment later, Drake rose from the flames already blasting a loud and blistering solo on his axe. A plaintive sound filled with hope. It struck us like an invisible wall and filled the room. He shredded as he kept rising, blazing with his own white light that revealed the demonic host in all its glory, which let up a howling cacophony at their master's ascendance.

The crowd started to scream.

ALEXIS ZHANG: I'll tell you what happened, and then you can think what you want. I don't care anymore. In the judges' booth, we lost our minds. Stephen slumped with his head rolling, a grotesque and dreamy smile on his face. Danny hugged his ribs and couldn't stop laughing. Axel pounded the glass with his fists and raved about how he wanted it, he wanted more, he couldn't stop wanting, let him on the stage and he'd show you how it's done. Me, I drooled at the thought of straddling Drake Morgan and eating him alive while I screwed his brains out.

STEPHEN WISE: All I remember is thinking, Vince is right. I understand at last. Nothing matters. Only I'm real. When I was born, the universe was summoned into existence, and when I die, all of it will return to the void.

Sublime. It was all so sublime.

ALEXIS ZHANG: The next thing I knew, I screamed over the PA that Universal Priest was the winner of Armageddon and to grovel before our new king.

DANNY RODRIGUEZ: Someone drugged us. It's the only explanation. I laughed so hard that I couldn't breathe and actually blacked out.

ERIC: Between the lighting and my position in the wings, I could only see a fragment of the audience. While Drake's anthem seethed and raged, some fell to their knees while the rest scrambled over them to escape.

The song welcomed their shrieks of terror and made them its chorus.

LILY: The song crescendoed as Drake reached the ceiling, where he burned blinding bright like a miniature sun. The horns let out a final blast.

ALEXIS ZHANG: I heard later that at that very moment, every slot machine in action out on the casino floor turned up a jackpot. A lot of chain-smoking grannies became instant millionaires. The entire Gold Bowl shut down.

LILY: With a blinding flash, it was over. Drake suddenly stood at the front of the bright stage while the PA went on blaring gibberish and the audience fled in a blind panic.

I expected him to stab his fist in the air in triumph like the painting on my wall, surrounded by Edvard Munch screamers. Instead he slowly raised his arms at his sides. Looped over his shoulder, his guitar hung low at his waist.

Arrayed behind him like an army, the demons chortled. As for the rest of Universal Priest, I noticed they were simply *gone*, as if they'd been erased.

The blood of stigmata dripped from Drake's wrists. He turned to shoot me an impish smile, and my own blood turned to ice.

He'd won. The world would end. And I was screwed.

Then pandemonium, as his demons and fans ran amok.

RAMONA: The demons capered off the stage to join the bedlam. A hairy hoofed thing danced across a group of worshippers still on their knees, trampling them. A hunchbacked beast tossed a howling girl into the air like a rag doll. Drake's fans were on their feet and at it too, tackling people as they tried to flee. The screams swelled while the Antichrist stood with his arms outstretched, smiling as if they weren't cries of terror but cheers.

Then a bald, potbellied horror shambled toward the side stage dragging a spiked club. Towering and lurching, giant cock swinging between its legs, patches of hair dangling from its skinny limbs. Eyes sewn shut under curved gazelle horns, its nostrils flared behind a heavy iron ring as it caught our scent.

Nearing us, the thing grunted. The heavy jaw split in a grotesque smile that gushed drool. And I thought: Lily might be immune against Drake's evil, but I'm not.

ERIC: Denial is a hell of a drug, it can get you through almost anything. God and the Devil were in cahoots. We'd fought them and lost. Monsters and demons were real. Reality seemed to be coming apart at the seams. Only one thing mattered to me anymore. When the brimstone and locusts came, I wanted to be with

Valeria Valis. Right then, I pictured finding her at the afterparty and kissing her while the world ended around us, me thinking: It's okay, everything is gonna be just fine.

RAMONA: I had no weapon to fight with. Only my fists and feet. With another grunt, the beast-man heaved the heavy club over his head as I tensed to dodge and kick him right back in the junk.

Garth came flying.

He vaulted through the air in a blur already swinging a Fender Telecaster, which banged off the beast's skull with a *CRACK*. The drummer landed catlike on his Doc Martens as the thing toppled groaning and landed with a loud thud.

His face set in fierce challenge, Garth raised the electric guitar like it was Excalibur and roared loud enough to be heard across the vast room:

"ROCK AND ROLL!"

Come on. I mean, goddamn.

It was the hottest thing I've ever seen in my life.

LILY: While all hell broke loose, I stood there gawking, too terrified to move. Garth's war cry snapped me out of it. We needed to get out of there fast, only his shout attracted attention. Across the room, among monstrous demons and Universal Priest fans alike, heads swiveled to grin at us.

I swung my Epiphone to grip it by the neck. Next to me, Ramona wrestled Eric's bass off his shoulder while he wailed, "No! Not Stringer!"

We'd have to fight our way out of here.

MALCOLM: I sat in the van waiting for the others. We'd lost the competition, most of our gear had simply vanished, and the Antichrist had set off another bloody riot. The night had grown bitterly cold, and I started the van to warm it up. A few people raced past the headlights, yelling at each other to run, don't stop, keep moving.

LILY: A squat simpering monstrosity came bounding toward us on stubby legs, arms outstretched as if to give us all a hug. I swung my guitar so hard my feet left the floor and the impact shuddered up my arms. The Epiphone's cherry-red body landed with a loud crunch. Ramona joined in, and together we smashed it to a pulp.

Then we yelled together, "ROCK AND ROLL," not caring right then how corny we sounded.

Eric pointed. "Um. Guys?"

Behind Drake, who was still smiling at us, a demon stomped toward us with a slow and heavy tread that shook the stage. Picture a woolly mammoth with a humanoid body and nine trunks. That's what was coming right at us.

Ramona braced in a fighting stance. I did the same.

She said, "You with me, Lil?"

I set my jaw and said that goddamn right I was.

"Then let's do this," she yelled. "Come and get it!"

Behind the behemoth, dozens of laughing Universal Priest fans clambered onto the stage. Howling with maniacal rage, a hairy clawed and winged thing dropped out of the air to tumble across the floor and come to a halt panting and glaring.

Garth said, "Yeah. Fuck this." And took off.

ERIC: I was already running as fast as I could, arms swinging at my sides and legs pumping. Hate Mail's Adrian Simmons emerged from the green room, spotted me, and took a deep breath before grudgingly holding out his hand for a shake.

He started to congratulate me, but I was already past him howling with Lily, Ramona, and Garth hot on my heels.

"Run, man," I called back to him.

"What? Why?" he said, and then I heard him scream.

LILY: Garth pivoted at the exit and hurled the Telecaster, followed by a *bonk* and a single D note. Then he followed us out. Behind us, Universal Priest fans spilled laughing into the artist parking lot and chased us whooping among the cars.

We piled into the van as the first threw their bodies against it. Leering faces fogged the windows. Hands slapped at the glass. Behind the wheel, Malcolm gaped at the rearview and howled, "*What the fuck is that?*" as the vehicle began to rock.

I turned and yelped. The mammoth demon continued its slow march toward us, nudging aside parked cars as it moved. Its trunks stiffened to bellow like French horns. I spent a moment wondering how it even squeezed out the exit doors.

Ramona screaming: "Just fucking drive, Mal! Punch it!"

With a long wailing honk, Malcolm floored the gas pedal. The van roared and pitched forward. The shrieking fans scattered.

Then he stomped the brake, and the vehicle came to a screeching halt.

Drake smiled in the headlights. He threw us a little wave.

Nothing chased us anymore. The demon had vanished. The mob stayed back, still leering but otherwise staying put.

As for us, we all sat there gasping. Then everyone looked at me, and I managed to say, "I guess I'll go talk to him again."

I got out of the van and walked over to Drake as he finished lighting one of his Marlboros. He said, "I gave you three chances in all, my love. Three times, I asked you if you really wanted to bet your soul against my power."

I said, "You cheated!"

And on top of that, his demons and fans tried to murder me and my friends.

He shrugged and said I'd certainly watched enough TV to know that anytime one makes a deal with the Devil, one needs to be perfectly explicit about the terms.

With a long, shuddering breath, I said, "Just let the others go."

He smiled. "Ah. We're still bargaining."

I said, "Let them go, and I'll pay what I owe."

This seemed to surprise Drake.

He laughed and said, "I'm not gonna take your soul, Lilith."

I had no idea what to say to that.

He explained that Hell didn't want my soul unless I handed it over of my own accord. This was something the stories got wrong. The Devil never coerced or tricked people into surrendering their souls. It must always be a free choice.

Drake said, "So do you?" Seeing my confusion, he flicked his cigarette into the dark and added, "Want to bestow your living soul to Hell."

I was like, What? Eww, no.

Then I yelled, "And fuck you for scaring me!"

He said, "Then keep it. That's how we roll. Even when destroying morality, there's nothing to say you can't have a few principles about it."

I suspected these principles actually might be limits imposed by God but said nothing. I'd just been handed the world's greatest get-out-of-jail-free card, and I saw no point to needling Drake's pride, possibly his most prized possession.

He said he admired that I'd tried. In fact, me betting my soul to save the world from destruction was why he felt for me the way he did.

I could tell this wasn't because I was *good*—the term was meaningless to Drake—but because I had a quality he lacked. A quality he considered dumb and would inevitably try to fix, true, but one that nonetheless carried a mysterious and weighty power for him.

Humility and compassion. The Antichrist could never understand these things.

Drake said, "You *did* make a bet, however."

My heart sank. Uh-oh, I thought. Here it comes.

His blue eye gleamed.

He said, "If you don't want to give me your soul and watch your friends die, I'll take something else. Something I'd like very much. I'll accept one or the other. Of course, it will be your choice which you're willing to give."

I had no real choice other than to agree, even though I found the other option only slightly less disagreeable.

ORPHEAN
A CAPPELLA

DECEMBER 19, 1999

It is here that I must insert myself in the story, as I was at that show. Only, I barely recall the worst of it beyond nightmarish fragments.

I remember the Shivers' soaring final song, how I gawked at Lily Lawless thrashing her guitar and fell in love with both her and the band that rocked my world. By the end, I was hopping and singing along.

Then came Universal Priest's turn, a band I liked a lot but hadn't fallen for in the same way. I remember the ring shout and the flames soaring to expose the monstrous host defiantly brandishing weapons and banners in a smoke cloud.

Standing near the back of the room, my friends and I wondered how Universal Priest had achieved such an incredible array of special effects. We were college kids eager but way too skeptical to believe the impossible. In our eyes, it was like seeing a Gwar show that had an unlimited budget. When the audience near the front let out a few shrill screams, we laughed at how gullible people can be and even shared a few barbs that maybe this whole thing was a bit pretentious.

Then a yellow-eyed Drake Morgan rose from the fire with his guitar—look, Ma, no wires—and the show exploded in a nightmare of panicked faces, tangled bodies, fists lashing out in blind terror, and searing blasts of sound.

I spent the next day in a hospital trying to explain to my furious mom how I ended up seriously messing up my foot in a riot. As for the Shivers, I'd learn years later that they had their own issues to deal with in Armageddon's aftermath.

They'd lost their battle, but they'd found out they were good without Drake Morgan, maybe even great. The fate of the world may have been settled by Drake's victory, but as for the band's fate, it still hung in the balance.

Lily Lawless had little mental room to think about it right then. She had an obligation she'd pledged and now had to fulfill. The last thing she wanted to do.

LILY: I'd agreed to a date with my ex-boyfriend. While I'd dodged the dire prospect of literally losing my soul, the figurative version proved equally galling.

Another choice Drake gave me that felt like coercion. Though, admittedly, I got myself into this particular pickle.

My band had already risen by the time I jerked awake on the couch. Malcolm, God bless him, had a hot mug of coffee ready for me. I thanked him mutely and sipped while I studied my bandmates with growing irritation.

They were all smiling and laughing.

MALCOLM: I'd just gotten a phone call with some very good news. It was Alexis Zhang at Armageddon, telling me we'd won the Audience Choice Award. Her voice sounded flat and lifeless, and I suspected she'd had a very bad night. Before I could thank her, she hung up.

I'd started this band to achieve success, and I'd gotten it. Definitely food for thought as I considered whether to go on doing it. And a little bright solace after last night's hellish nightmare. I didn't even know how to deal with *that*. While I've always been solid with handling things I could break down and understand, I've always definitely sucked at handling things that I couldn't.

RAMONA: I'd woken draped over Garth in our nest of sleeping bags to find Eric asking for love advice. Surprisingly, given the horrors I'd survived, it was my first night without scary dreams in a long while.

ERIC: I don't remember exactly when Ramona, who is a few years younger than me, turned into my big sister, but there we were. I wanted to know if I should call Valeria now or wait the usual three days. I didn't want to come across as desperate. Yes, I know the

Antichrist walked the earth and he'd unleashed hell at Armageddon the night before, but this was important to me.

RAMONA: I didn't have the heart to tell him that that ship had probably sailed. Lying under me, Garth peeled an eye open to say, "Follow your bliss, man. You're still young." He didn't add that we had no idea how much time we had left.

MALCOLM: Now that Lily was awake, I shared the good news. It confirmed to me we would have won it all—you know, if there hadn't been divine intervention. The thought made me laugh out loud, and everyone gave me a funny look.

ERIC: We'd never actually heard Malcolm laugh before that moment.

RAMONA: Goddamn. He even laughed like a computer.

LILY: I started fuming.

MALCOLM: The question of what we'd do now as the Shivers could wait. Everyone seemed to feel the same way. God and the Devil had the big picture covered, leaving us with nothing to do except try as hard as we could to forget last night ever happened. Ramona and Garth planned a trip to a record store. Eric had rubbed some hide glue into a few cracks in his bass and wanted to take it to a music store to see if anything else needed to be done for it. Me, I'd promised to visit with my parents that night, so I planned a chill day. Nothing but relaxing and coping.

LILY: I said, "I have a date with Drake tonight." When no one reacted, I added loudly, "With the Antichrist."

My bandmates shared a loaded glance. In their minds, I got off pretty easy. We'd fought literal demons and survived to see the sunrise. I'd made a Faustian bargain but got to keep my eternal soul.

All I had to do now to finally be free was go on a lousy date with my ex.

I added even louder: "During the apocalypse."

Malcolm said, "Sounds good, Lily. We'll talk about the band tomorrow."

Not at all the reaction I hoped to receive.

Universal Priest had won Armageddon. Drake would take the next step in his ascension. The entire universe's remaining hours had become finite and fixed.

Maybe the band figured there was nothing they could do about it, so why worry? Maybe they didn't have the mental energy to fret about the band *and* the end of the world at the same time. I know my own brain barely had room for both.

Or maybe this is what the apocalypse looked like. People tied their shoelaces and caught colds and otherwise tried to live their lives as best they could while the Antichrist ascended. As the saying goes, no one gets out of this thing called life alive anyway.

Eric cut to the chase, saying, "We tried our best, Lil."

Then I found myself doing it, falling back into my mundane worries. I thought, Wait a second. Hang on. *Talk about the band tomorrow?* Was Malcolm really still planning to quit the Shivers after the goddamn awesome show we put on last night?

Ramona emerged from her nest of blankets to say, "I get it. Come with me."

She took me into the practice space, where she hauled out a rugged cardboard box filled with junk. My gaze narrowed to stink-eye mode as it took in a set of guitar strings I'd been missing, but I said nothing.

Ramona said, "We all get it. But you have to take this next step alone."

She rooted through the box until she found the hilt of a knife. This she carefully pulled out to expose nine inches of razor-sharp steel.

Bishop Igwe's knife, blessed with holy water. She'd kept it.

Ramona handed it to me and said, "Just in case."

RAMONA: All week after Lily made her brave but futile bet, it was like I carried the fate of the planet on my shoulders. Sometimes losing feels good if only because there's nothing more you can do beyond accepting the outcome. I'd done everything I could. It was over.

Honestly, I found it kind of liberating.

At the time, I was barely eighteen. I'd spent nearly two years fighting to survive. I'd finally met a man I felt safe with. The world was ending.

I wanted to have a little fun.

GARTH WAGNER: Ramona carried more baggage than a 747. That was okay. Scratch that. I *loved* it. I never wanted someone perfect for me. I wanted someone who'd give my world a good kick. Someone who'd always surprise me. Life shouldn't be easy or comfortable. It should be struggle and learning. Like music, love should throw you up and knock you down. It should be rock and roll.

LILY: As I got ready for my date back in my cold little basement apartment, I thought about making myself hideous. Maybe fashion a mask like Mary wore, rip a dress into rags. Turn myself into a monster.

Drake would only find it amusing. An expert on subversion,

he'd see the effort as a sign I still had feelings for him. Love and hate are sides of the same coin. You're not truly over someone until you feel absolutely nothing.

No, I decided. I'd look great tonight. I'd show Drake that what he'd broken was thriving. I'd flaunt all the goods he'd been missing out on, a little cleavage and a lot of leg. The way exes have done it since time immemorial.

ERIC: After getting Stringer's wounds tended and ensuring he was going to pull through, I went home still thinking about whether to reach out to Valeria. I was dying to call her even if the idea terrified me. I felt so good about that part of last night that I wanted to hold on to it as long as possible. If I called her, she might tell me to bugger off, and all the sandcastles I'd made in my mind would crumble.

With steely courage, I called her anyway and left the world's most long-winded and awkward message on her answering machine.

LILY: One thing I can credit the Devil with is that he's punctual. Drake showed up promptly at seven and breezed into what had once been his home. He'd actually made the effort to dress up, with a black suit jacket worn over one of his ratty T-shirts.

He started to compliment my own appearance but then noticed our painting still adorning the wall. Bathed in light, the dark guitarist raised his fist in triumph while his terrified audience boiled and howled.

Drake went straight to it and reached out to touch the dried paint.

He said, "It seems so long ago now. I was like a baby back then, raw and incomplete. Waiting to hatch from a chrysalis."

Then he turned to flash a smile at me. Regardless of how I

dressed, the fact I'd painted over everything except this seemed to tell him what he needed to know.

I said, "For a while, I'd look at it and try to reconcile the man you were then with what you are now."

He said, "I miss the way you used to look at me."

And then I said, "I hope there's food on this date, because I'm famished."

The finest meal I'd ever tasted, he assured me. Snatching up my coat and purse, I asked him how far it was and how he planned to get us there. The Drake I knew didn't own a car.

He pointed and said, "We're already here."

I turned to see the silver door from our old drug trip gleaming in the center of the living room. The same engraved image of a Janus head with two faces, surrounded by black thorns.

RAMONA: Garth and I took a quick trip out to the record store, came back, and spent the rest of the day taking turns jamming on the drum kit. Around dinnertime, the door thudded upstairs. Malcolm had gone out. We were truly alone at last.

With a massive stretch, Garth asked me what I wanted to do tonight. Anything I wanted. He was buying. A fancy meal, maybe catch a concert, and then afterward we could bluff our way into the afterparty and rock until dawn.

I was like, Dude, I'm actually alone for the first time in weeks. The last thing I wanted to do was hang out with more musicians.

I said, "Let's order a couple of pizzas, rent some brainless thriller at Blockbuster, and then come back here and screw our brains out."

Garth grinned and said, "Like I said. Lady's choice."

GARTH WAGNER: The next morning, I discovered she'd stolen the lucky rabbit's foot off my key chain. I didn't mind a bit.

LILY: A moment of vertigo, and then I found myself sitting at a table in a palatial dining room weakly illuminated in the yellow glow of candlelight.

Sitting across from me, Drake poured us glasses of red wine from a dusty bottle and said, "You once had so many questions."

I goggled at the other diners, shadowy figures that murmured as they attacked their meals with knives and tongs. The tall and spindly servers.

Was I actually here? Was any of it real?

Drake told me we were indeed in a vibration of Hell. I sipped the wine, which proved real enough and delicious to boot. I had to stop myself from chugging it.

It was real, he went on, but we were seeing it in a way our human brains could process without going insane. There was so much more here I didn't notice because I couldn't.

Like the demons appearing at Armageddon as winged monsters, I guessed. They didn't really look like that. Ugly hoofed beast-men with clubs and spears. Just like angels weren't supermodels with harps and halos.

Drake gave me a look of approval. He could see me getting it.

He said, "Try to imagine infinity splitting into two. Trillions of cosmic beings forming spontaneously to slaughter each other over a period of geologic time but also outside of time. Oceans of particles, light and dark seething in endless battle. The godhead itself rupturing. That was the fall."

Obviously, I couldn't imagine any of it. I had zero frame of reference.

Drake smiled and said, "Of course. Only the dead understand, when the divine spark remembers and seeks its return to the light. So humanity instead receives stories, each to its own religion. But we're getting ahead of ourselves. You're starving."

One of the towering waiters approached on grotesquely long

strides and set a silver dish before us. With a flourish, the man whipped off the cover.

On the plate rested a gleaming red apple, that mythical symbol of knowledge.

MALCOLM: This turned out to be no family dinner. It was an intervention. Mom and Dad let me have my say first. I explained how we'd spent almost a year working our asses off and came very close to winning a major regional music competition. How I was learning the business side of the music industry.

This done, Dad asked if I'd actually made any money. He wanted to know if I understood that every month I fooled around with my keyboard, I lost income I could have earned with honest labor.

Queenie asked how much I bled every month to keep the band afloat. With mortgage and groceries and student loans, how long could I keep this up before I'd been stripped to nothing? And what was up with all the violence at local rock concerts she kept seeing on the news? Had the young lost all sense of decency?

They might have been right. Maybe any interest I had in continuing the Shivers was yet another sunk-cost fallacy. We'd lost almost everything in the riot. Our instruments and gear. If we soldiered on, we'd be starting from scratch.

Maybe it didn't have to be a full-time gig. And I could ask the band to pay their own way from here on out. There might be a way to do this in a way where I minimized my risk.

But man, my parents hadn't caught our show at Armageddon. I said, "I appreciate what you're saying. Let me think about it."

That show was magic.

Maybe there are actually some truths that can overcome nature and nurture. For me, it was an epiphany that life isn't always about winning. How sometimes, the fight to win matters as much as if not more than any victory. That if the world really is about to end, some things don't matter anymore.

It took losing Armageddon for me to see that. How much I'd actually gained. Nothing to do with trophies or money or even being cool or even simple belonging.

Just the joy of knowing: Before the curtain falls, I did *that*.

I had no idea what would happen tomorrow, but that was part of the fun of it. Like Eric told me once, being in a band requires faith.

LILY: Drake said, "I must warn you, however—"

I'd already bitten into the apple and had started chewing.

I told you I was starving!

Drake was still talking, but I raised a finger in the universal gesture to wait. My eyes teared up with bliss. The apple was *good*. A kaleidoscope of flavors assaulted my taste buds. Even after I discovered half a wiggling worm in its succulent pale flesh—actually a moth larva, probably there as some ominous bonus metaphor for knowledge having a cost—I devoured that too and enjoyed its earthy bitterness.

"Wow," I said. "That was seriously the crack cocaine of apples."

I sat back with a little belch and daintily dabbed my lips with a napkin. That single perfect piece of fruit had left me as satisfied and stuffed as a five-course dinner.

Drake laughed and said, "Okay, we'll skip the theatrics. Ask me anything, and I'll answer to the best of my ability."

He remembered so much now. The heavenly court and its sublime choirs. The Watchers sent to earth who found human women beautiful and sired giants and heroes. The divine punishment and cosmic cataclysm that followed. The endless war. Lucifer and his brethren cast into the darkness, where they made their own light with fire.

Drake appeared all too happy to tell me everything.

I slugged back some more wine and asked him if he'd met his dad yet.

He shook his head, partly in wonder. Out of all the eternal mysteries I might want revealed, I asked him that question above all others.

I said, "Your father isn't really your father, is he? It's you. *You're* Lucifer."

"Yes and no," said Drake. "I am an aspect of Satan, just as he is an aspect of God. Just as the demons you see here are emanations of the original Watchers who laid siege to Heaven, and others are emanations of them. It's complicated."

So they were all God, I observed. He told me they weren't God any more than I was my mother. Okay, fair point.

This was why I didn't ask the bigger questions. The real deal made even less sense than the story I'd been raised to believe.

I said, "Okay, here's what I want to know. Why?"

Why go through all this? Why didn't God just snap his fingers and end the world?

Drake said, "We must get our turn. And humanity must be tested."

Again: *Why?* God already knew who would pass and who wouldn't. In fact, God had created a universe in which everyone was predestined to pass or fail. Malcolm was right. It was ridiculous. God and the Devil alike, playing their weird and pointless game that would produce real misery for billions.

I said, "It's like a really complicated, violent play for no audience."

Drake shrugged. What made sense to humanity didn't matter in the slightest. Suffice to say that before God destroyed the world, the Devil intended to turn it into his version of paradise. One where humanity at last lived truly free of God. Only, to me it looked more like a spiteful scorched-earth policy, denying as many souls to God as possible before everything ended.

He'd told me I could ask him anything, but the answers made no sense because they added up to incomprehensible ritual. Maybe this was the worm.

I said, "Okay. Tell me just one thing. Why did you come as a musician?"

He threw me a cross look. Our relationship had started and ended with music, and I think by that point my love for it made him a little jealous. Still, he answered the question. Music, he told me, was an act of protest. Protest and rebellion.

He said, "Music is our version of the Holy Spirit. It's the lamentation of the downtrodden. The battle cry of revolutionaries. The hymns of the heretic. Why else would the establishment always try to assimilate it and water it down? Why else do uptight Christians fear it so much?"

I said, "It's just hard to imagine you conquering the world with a guitar."

Drake laughed out loud, and the shadowy demons chuckled along in their seats while they went on endlessly consuming their feast with clacking silverware.

He said, "I carry divine license to overthrow obedience to God by transforming human consciousness."

Then he said, "Why do I need governments and armies to accomplish this?"

ERIC: I had dinner with Ma for the first time in weeks. She pulled out the stops to stuff me full of Polish food and motherly advice. I regaled her with stories about the band and our hard fight at Armageddon, which sounded great to her even though we didn't win the prize, and I thought, She's right. We did pretty good for ourselves and had something special, no actual magic required.

I left out the Antichrist stuff, as my straitlaced, church-going mama would have either had me committed or physically dragged me to the nearest seminary for an emergency exorcism.

After dinner, I went upstairs to rediscover bad habits. Before long, I'd smoked a bowl and fired up my PlayStation to rack up an impressive Nazi body count playing *Medal of Honor*.

The phone rang downstairs, which I ignored. A moment later, Ma bawled up the stairs that it was for me.

She yelled, "It's some woman calling for you."

I leaped off my beanbag chair and stomped downstairs to pick up the phone. Breathless, my mind drawing a complete blank. When it came to women, I didn't have the first idea how to swagger.

Valeria said, "You live with your mom?"

I said, "Yes. She's a wonderful mother."

Just leaning right into the cringe, owning it.

I added, "But I'll be moving out soon."

And I thought, Yes, it's true, I think I will. I didn't know what would happen to the Shivers tomorrow, but I could keep playing my bass. I'd find a job and get my own place. I'd find another band if I had to and keep on rocking.

Someone has to win.

VALERIA VALIS: My Lord, Eric was such a delight. I felt like he'd offered himself to me as a giant ball of Play-Doh I could mold to my whim. Talking to this big awkward boy on the phone, I had a sudden weird urge to tickle him to death.

Picturing it got me horny as hell. I gave him my address and told him if he didn't get his ass into my bed within the hour, I might have to severely punish him.

Bless his heart, he actually said, "Why not both?"

LILY: Hideous things lurched and slithered to a stage, where they randomly blasted bone horns and scraped stringed instruments until a prim conductor cracked a bullwhip and they launched into a gorgeous tune booming with percussion.

I gaped at them. Drake told me not to be afraid.

Afraid? What was he talking about? I was *mesmerized*.

The music sounded primal and sexy. A thick, heavy beat that vibrated from my chest to my thighs. It sounded African, but with Arab and Spanish influences. Djembe drums and tulip blocks and frame drums and lyres and nafir trumpets.

Drake watched me keenly. He asked me what I thought of it.

The relentless rhythm flirted in a sweet spot between sex and death. It heated the red wine in my blood to the boiling point.

I said, "I love it, but it's hardly the music of revolution."

"To the contrary," he said. "Life is rebellion against death. Death is the rebellion against life. The music itself overthrows conformity—"

"Yeah, yeah," I said loudly to shut him up. "Dance with me."

Fueled by wine and desire, I left the table and walked over to the orchestra, already swishing my hips to that raging sexy rhythm. Grinning, Drake doffed his suit jacket and joined me to flaunt his best merengue moves.

In an instant, the demons crowded the floor around us, gasping and flailing to the heavy beat. The musicians rocked over their instruments as the conductor joyously cracked his whip. The air grew hot and moist, and I broke into a healthy, purifying sweat.

This was how I ended up dancing the night away in Hades.

Drake moved very close to me, filling my world. My heart pounded with delicious alarm. I'd like to think he put a spell on me, but no, this was passion at work. Despite everything, I still loved him. I still wanted him.

His blue eye gleamed with longing. His amber eye burned to possess me. His human half still loved me. His angelic half still needed me to worship him.

I said, "Thank you for this. I hope we'll always be friends, Drake."

The orchestra blasted a single discordant note like a fart. With another wave of vertigo, the dining room disappeared, and I sat with Drake in a carriage drawn along an emerald road by a team of snorting and lumbering beasts.

RAMONA: Lying in the dark draped over the gently snoring Garth, I wondered how Lily fared on her date with Drake.

I hoped she remembered to bring the knife.

LILY: Ancient temples and forums filled the landscape, while red moons and ringed planets glowed all around us in the black sky. It was strangely romantic.

I didn't mind staying a while longer with Drake. I nestled into him.

I said, "Do they suffer?"

Drake said demons didn't torture lost souls with pitchforks, if that's what I was asking. He reminded me that after death, the divine spark seeks its creator.

"Frustrated," he told me. "That's how they feel. Frustrated but defiant. Imprisoned in the finite. In Hell, we never know peace. A different kind of torture and pain. None of us asked to be born. The dead get a choice—though of course, as with everything else, God has the final say as judge."

It wasn't hard to conjure at least a little sympathy for the Devil and his followers. He was destined to fight and lose.

All of it was for nothing, I pointed out.

Drake said, "Where's the benefit in having a choice if you you're not allowed to make the wrong one?"

No matter how it would all turn out, it was worth it. Before God destroyed reality, paradise would be briefly regained. Humanity would return to the moment before Eve ate the apple, having all the agency of innocence.

"Our turn," he added. "First, we'll show the world what it could have been."

The carriage hissed smoothly along the gleaming emerald road. His warm arm around me, Drake held me close.

He said, "You always do what's right, Lilith. The kind of right that doesn't need a religion to be true. Join me."

I asked my question. The question he'd expected and I needed to ask but whose answer I didn't want to know.

How it would end.

Drake explained that his music would transform the world. Through it, he would become a cultural icon.

He didn't mention the violence that would occur during all these years. The horrific suffering. Plague, wars, the dissolution of all religions, the civil strife as people turned against each other. It was understood to be the cost, a whole lot of broken eggs sacrificed to make the omelet.

In humanity's final hours, he went on, physicists and musicians would unite to create a new form of music that translated probability waves into sound waves and back into quantum waves, music that turned atoms into instruments. Drake would compose his final magnum opus, a symphony that alchemically rewrote reality at the subatomic level and merged the angelic and material realms.

The Beast, his father, would finally come, and God would be forced to act.

He said, "He'll either erase our existence or allow us our own alternate universe where we can finally live free. I can't see that far ahead. I don't know."

But none of it really felt worth doing if I wasn't with him at his side.

Picturing the end made me shiver. It was all too big to truly comprehend.

Then Drake said the words I'd once longed to hear: "I love you, Lilith."

I never thought I'd hear him say it.

I said, "I still love you too, Drake."

Not just love for the man I knew but, yes, a little sympathy for the Devil too.

And then I said: "But love is putting someone else first. The way I always put you first."

Drake said nothing. I could see him struggling. He didn't know how.

The angel of pride.

I said, "You want people to live free but not be free to choose to obey God's rules or serve others. Either way, your music doesn't free people to follow their desires. It compels them. How are you any better than God?"

He started to answer, but I cut him off. I wasn't done yet. I told him that to make things even worse, while God and the Devil played their game, humanity had no say in it. No real choice at all.

Drake looked at my purse and said, "What if you did?"

He knew about the knife.

I said, "You don't have to play the game. You can opt out."

Then I smiled and added, "What's the point of having a choice if you can't make the right one?"

A heartbreaking wave of despair and doubt crossed his beautiful face, his human and angelic sides warring for dominance, and I understood he didn't really have a choice either. He was trapped. A puppet yanked by divine strings. It was the last time I'd see the fretful, vulnerable child he'd once been.

He said, "I can't. But you—you should get to decide. So decide. I give you that power. Join me forever. Or end it."

I reached into the purse and gripped the knife's ancient leather hilt. I wanted to save the world. I didn't want to hurt him to accomplish this.

Then I remembered the street fair, the laughing children skating on the ice. The world has always been rotten, and maybe it didn't deserve to be saved. But it was beautiful, and every generation created a new opportunity to improve. Every generation was born as innocent as Adam and Eve and deserved free will in every sense of the term. The chance to do good and make the world a better place.

I thought of them suffering as the utopian world Drake promised inevitably turned corrupt and inflicted untold misery and death, just before God came to annihilate what was left down to the atom. Not abstract but very real.

Drake leaned to kiss me, and I accepted it. His lips so warm and familiar. My eyes closed. I was already weeping. He leaned to plant a final burning kiss on my neck and said, "I will always love you, my Lilith. You will always love me."

"That's what I'm afraid of," I said.

I pushed the blade into his heart the moment it understood real love.

HELLO, Y2K

2000–2023

In Armageddon's wake, the Shivers' members took personal stock. They'd gambled and lost, but they had gained so much. Whatever their individual troubles, they understood that they were special together. And whatever they thought about the future, however daunting it might look, they could not shake the feeling that reaching success might only be a matter of perseverance.

They didn't have long to wait. Success had already reached out for them, though it always asks for something in return.

LILY: I woke back in my cold, dingy apartment and cried for three days.

The world still turned, only it felt empty now without Drake Morgan in it.

The phone kept ringing, but I was too scared to answer.

He'd let me kill him. At the end, he finally showed me he loved me.

I'd disrupted the plan and saved the world, and all I'd gained was remorse. I'd escaped Hell, only to wind up in another of my own making.

DR. WOODWARD: The notion that the Antichrist could willingly be killed to prevent his ascension is intriguing but hardly creditable, no? I mean, he has one job to do, and that job is a matter of God's will. Unless...

Unless the Antichrist possesses the same free will that we have.

MALCOLM: I kept calling, but no answer. After leaving a dozen messages, we started to worry. Finally, we all headed over to bang on her door, barge it down if we had to.

DR. WOODWARD: It would mean—in our hypothetical scenario—that the Antichrist's human emotions could overcome his angelic ambitions. My God, it opens up all sorts of theological possibilities.

RAMONA: Lily let us in. The place was a shambles. The girl looked a mess. A single glance at her drawn face told me something terrible had happened.

DR. WOODWARD: For example, could Jesus have refused to suffer and die on the cross? Did he have a choice? If the Antichrist simply refused to do his duty—so wonderfully on point for such a contrary figure—what would that mean for God's plan?

ERIC: Malcolm went into a detailed rant about how he'd been trying to reach her. We needed to have a band meeting pronto. Important decisions had to be made that couldn't wait. I finally cut in to yell, "Just tell her the news, man!"

MALCOLM: I took a deep breath and said the magic words: "Echo Harbor offered us a record deal. A good record deal. Merry Christmas, Lily."

DANNY RODRIGUEZ: I tried to track down Universal Priest, but no one had seen any of them since the debacle at Armageddon. Drake Morgan had simply vanished after causing a riot. Next, I called Malcolm Williams, who kept me on the phone for an hour talking about royalty rates and options clauses.

ERIC: Hearing Malcolm say it in front of Lily was like hearing it myself for the first time. My entire body tingled at the news. I still couldn't believe it.

RAMONA: Lily just stared at him at the edge of a panicked outburst. Malcolm didn't know what to do. He hadn't expected this reaction. He started to stammer out the details, but I cut him off with a wave of my hand.

I said to Lily: "You went on your date with Drake. Tell us what happened."

ERIC: She spilled all of it. Holy shit. I mean, yeah. Holy shit.

RAMONA: "Holy shit" about covers it. I'd feared the worst—that he'd done something horrible to her that she'd have to live with forever. Instead she'd danced in Hell, killed the Antichrist, and saved the world. Now, *that* is punk rock.

DANNY RODRIGUEZ: I never could reach Drake Morgan. He'd disappeared along with the rest of Universal Priest.

ERIC: On the spot, Malcolm made the rule that we'd follow for over twenty years. We never talk about Drake. No, we have no idea where he is or what happened to him, same as we told the baffled cops trying to make sense of the Armageddon riot. No, we haven't seen him. You know Drake; he must have taken off.

I wanted to believe it. That he'd simply quit and walked away. Hearing he'd died didn't give me the relief I'd expected. Instead I felt like mourning. I'd feared and hated the Antichrist. The man, however, I'd once loved.

MALCOLM: I said to Lily, "We won. But we still need you."

LILY: I'd once romanticized my band as being a tribe that would catch me if I ever took a hard fall. This time, that's exactly what they did. Music, I prayed, would take care of the rest.

MALCOLM: Once we got all the group hugging out of the way, I explained the situation: We were being offered a $250,000 advance for a multi-album deal. At least, I tried to until Ramona cut me off.

RAMONA: I pointed out the new ink on her throat. How and where did she get that?

LILY: I rushed to the bathroom to check myself out in the mirror. Ramona was right. It looked like some kind of occult symbol:

In an instant, I recognized it as Universal Priest's logo but didn't know what it meant. Some type of pentagram? Were the curved lines at the top supposed to be horns?

RAMONA: My heart sank. It was the exact same mark I'd seen stamped on that lunatic drummer's forehead.

LILY: Then it popped in my eye.
 The number 666, branded on my skin.
 The exact spot where Drake had kissed me.
 I'd rid the world of the Antichrist, but he'd forever be a part of me. And a part of me would forever belong to him.
 Like his disciples, I'd been branded with the mark of the Beast.

RAMONA: I made the boys go home and stayed with Lily that night.

LILY: I slept with her arms wrapped tight around me. It felt good to be held again. I thought I had another sleepless night ahead of me, but I passed out in no time.

The next morning, I woke up ready to sign a record deal.

RAMONA: Danny Rodriguez turned out to be a smooth-talking hipster who stared at Lily the whole time at our first meeting, though Malcolm did most of the talking.

LILY: I didn't care about IP rights and options or any of that stuff. Malcolm ruled that particular domain. Honestly, it bored me to tears. I fought tooth and nail, however, for as much artistic control as I could get. We negotiated a balance for the first album and then if it did well, I'd gain nearly total control.

DANNY RODRIGUEZ: The music market has always been a fickle beast, which is why you don't see a lot of truly original music out there; it's too risky an investment. The lion's share of our revenues came from only a small percentage of albums we released. The rest were losers or break-evens. That's how it worked.

At that first meeting, I talked a big game about how the future looked blindingly bright and so on, but I was just hoping they'd sell at least a hundred thousand copies or so to cover the company's costs and keep me out of hot water with upper management.

LILY: After we signed the deal, Danny asked me if I wanted to grab a drink and talk more about the band's direction. I told him we should keep things on a professional basis.

DANNY RODRIGUEZ: She was gorgeous. I asked. She said no. End of story.

LILY: Danny's idea of me having artistic control was I'd control the art, while he'd control the artist. Eventually, he'd routinely make it his business to tell me what I should be doing, starting with losing five pounds.

DANNY RODRIGUEZ: That's the job. I'm there to add value and help.

LILY: Seeing Drake's brand on my neck every morning, I'd already decided I'd never let anyone ever control me again. Very quickly, I went from saying no to simply doing the opposite of anything he told me to do.

DANNY RODRIGUEZ: She was impossible to deal with until I learned not to deal with her if I could help it.

LILY: After we signed the contract, I smoked my last cigarette. The only thing that would ever control me from then on was a passion to make music and perform.

MALCOLM: The first thing I did after signing the dotted line was beeline to my parents' house to share the good news. To their credit, they admitted they were wrong and offered heartfelt congratulations that had more value to me than all the money in the world.

Then they told me they expected me to make it big. By the end of that dinner, I'd pretty much been tasked with becoming the next Michael Jackson.

RAMONA: It was an impossible amount of money. For the first time in my life, I opened a bank account. And I thought, You were right, Drake. It feels safe.

MALCOLM: You'd think $250,000 is a lot, and in today's music industry it certainly is, but it had to cover us for several years. Not to mention the fact we had to pay our recording costs plus manager and lawyer fees out of that bucket. The only way to make real money was to sell a lot of records, and even if we scored with a hit record, it'd take up to two years for it to start rolling in.

ERIC: I told Ma the good news over Christmas dinner, and she positively glowed with motherly pride. Then I delivered the not-so-happy news, which was I'd finally decided to move out and get my own place, seeing as I could now afford it.

True to form, she mothered me all the way out the door, needling in as many nags and force-feedings as she could while she still had the chance.

I would have expected nothing less. She loved me, and she'd always worry.

DANNY RODRIGUEZ: A big label like ours had the muscle to sell millions of records. It's what we did best—pressing records and getting them into retail distribution. The problem as always was moving that first hundred thousand copies off the shelf. Keeping that snowball rolling until it becomes an unstoppable avalanche.

That's where a new band has to step up and do its part promoting and touring, building up their fan base.

ERIC: You work your hungry ass off to get signed by a major label, and you think, that's it, I made it, but you didn't, not really. All you did was climb a rung on a very tall ladder, and now the hard work truly begins.

LILY: After we signed the deal, I had one more thing to do before I got back to work. One last promise to keep before the music once again took precedence.

Meeting my parents went about as well as I expected, which is to say not super well at all. At first, they seemed willing to forgive and forget, but then I told them I wasn't actually coming home but would go on pursuing my dream.

Dad yelled that I was wasting my life. Mom said that once I'd finished my little rebellion, she'd have a warm and loving home ready for my return.

This time, I didn't get angry. I didn't feel the old heat of seething resentment in my chest. Instead I regarded them with compassion and did what I'd come to do.

Say I was sorry. And then leave to live my own life the way I needed.

RAMONA: On New Year's Eve, the Squat threw the mother of all raves to welcome either the new millennium or the end of the world, whatever God or human stupidity wanted to throw at us. Hundreds of partiers showed up determined to be having fun when the lights went out due to the Y2K bug.

I slipped into the crowd and danced all night. We raved so hard that most of us missed the countdown at midnight.

At dawn, the world was there, definitely stupid but still intact and turning. I said goodbye to the one I'd known and never looked back.

LUCAS KELLY: Early in 2000, Danny introduced me to the band in the hope they'd hire me as their manager, and boy, did I have my work cut out for me. The Shivers had won Audience Choice at a small regional battle of the bands and had earned a few nice shoutouts in a local paper and some fanzines. Otherwise, it pretty much carried zero name recognition or fan base outside the

Lehigh Valley, which the music industry considered the precise middle of nowhere.

I mean, I was starting from scratch here.

I learned pretty early on not to mess with the sound, which was Lily's domain, or the money, which was Malcolm's. That left image. The band looked like regular people you'd see in any small city, which worked for them as a pop-punk band. The band's name worked fine, nothing there. Lily was the element that received my full attention. I helped her transform into a raging-hot punk goddess.

Honestly, this didn't take a lot of work. The girl was drop-dead sexy, and her attitude packed a hell of a bite. My biggest contribution turned out to be the spiky dog collar. Every time we met, she kept rubbing this little tattoo on her neck. I could tell she had some regret about it. One day, I said, "Try this on for size."

Lily would wear that spiked collar at every show for ten years. It became her trademark. I'd see suburban teens wearing them everywhere.

I never messed with her again after that, though I pushed her as hard as she'd allow me. I'd always wear out and need a break before she did. Until the end.

LILY: The Epiphone I'd used to brain a demon at Armageddon was a write-off, so the first thing I did with my advance money was buy a new guitar, this time a Gibson Les Paul Junior. It had a raw and punchy sound, but the best part was it hadn't come from Drake and didn't have any bad memories haunting it.

As for his brand on my neck, I couldn't do anything about that. I pointed it out to the band and said, "Remember what I did and what I gave up to do it. I'm a marked woman. At this point, I'm an enemy of both God and Satan. I don't know what that means or how much time I have left."

I said, "All I ask in return is we always look out for each other and we never quit. For as long as we can make music, we'll never give up the dream."

ERIC: Lucas hooked us up with a great producer who'd worked with Rancid and Zebrahead and understood the pop-punk sound, and then he had us come to New York to record our first album. We tried so hard to look cool walking into the studio while Lily ran around the control and recording rooms screaming her head off like a kid on her first visit to the candy store. Feeling pretty giddy myself, I spread my arms and joined her, pretending I was an airplane.

LILY: We walked in with a big catalog of songs, which we pared down to ten for the EP after a marathon session of tracking and overdubbing. The producer and engineer made us sound iconic.

Mom's Two-Car Garage, our first album, was born.

DANNY RODRIGUEZ: Echo gave *Mom's Two-Car Garage* a decent pressing and pushed the sing-along-able, crowd-pleasing "Can You Hear Me Now?" as a single for radio airplay.

LUCAS KELLY: I had my assistants call major-market radio stations around the clock pretending they were devoted listeners and requesting the single.

ERIC: We hovered over the radio in Malcolm's basement for days, working the FM dial hoping we'd catch our tune. When it came on, we gasped. It was like hearing it for the first time. Malcolm said what we all thought: "We made it." And then, because he's Malcolm: "Let's get back to work."

DANNY RODRIGUEZ: I tried to lean on Axel Hodges to get behind it with some decent airplay, but I found out he'd been canned. The night after Armageddon imploded, he went on the air with two girls and did a bit where he tried to convince them to give him oral sex. He was yelling the N-word when they finally yanked him off the air. I also reached out to Stephen Wise at the *Valley Scene*, but he'd ditched his family to go backpacking across Australia with one of his contributing writers. Whatever had gotten into their heads at Armageddon, it apparently had a lasting effect. I spent a lot of time worrying if it had done something to me.

LILY: When it came time for us to tour, I left the little basement apartment I'd shared with Drake for the last time. Before leaving for good, I finally painted over the Armageddon image on the living room wall.

I imagine it's still there, covered under layers of cornsilk-yellow paint, patiently waiting for its next revelation.

ERIC: After that, the years raced by like a surreal blur.

LILY: We drove across America in a crowded van, playing bars and small clubs and shopping malls. Lucas scored a spot for us on the Warped Tour, nineteen bands playing a half-hour set each and then packing it up for the next city, from Phoenix to Chicago. By then, "Can You Hear Me Now?" enjoyed prime-time rotation at radio stations and the album was selling.

At the end of our tour, we took a short break and got back in the studio to record *Blast from the Past*. We did the Warped Tour again, though we got to play the main stage with the big boys this time instead of the smaller stage.

After that, we went on tour opening for Them Kids, which

turned out to be a pretty laid-back experience except the headliner constantly played childish pranks on everyone and fought pitched battles with Roman candles in the hotel hallways. During this time, we upgraded to a tour bus, and life accelerated into a dizzying kaleidoscope of hotels and cities and stages and dressing rooms that smelled like stale beer and hair spray and nervous sweat.

Then rinse, recycle, and repeat with *But What Am I?* This time, though, we toured stadiums as the headline act. Every day a whirlwind of fans and contest winners, booking agents, local promoters, radio DJs, rock journalists. Then off for a few eighteen-hour days recording a music video.

One day jarring into the next and the next. Bus call, drive, load in, sound check, radio interviews for some station we'd never hear, a photo shoot for an article in some magazine we'd never have time to read, green room, set time, and then, at last, you finally get to play.

And like a bird allowed to fly once or twice a week, my spirit would soar over the crowd while I shredded my tunes on stage. I'd belt out song after song in a manic catharsis of joy and freedom and power. I'd talk to the audience as if I loved them, because right then I did, beaming compassion and understanding that the world hadn't ended but was still ending, always ending for those who lived in it. They'd scream "Can you hear me now?" back at me during the lengthy encore.

And then it was over, because all good things inevitably come to an end, and I marched off the stage aching and sweat-drenched and glowing.

In New Orleans, Lucas dropped the news that *But What Am I?* had gone gold with sales topping five hundred thousand copies. He popped the top on a bottle of champagne and hosed us while we shrieked with joy. The hotels became nicer, we rode in a roomy new tour bus, we brought the house down on Conan O'Brien, and by the end of the tour we were hopping cities in a private jet to pack in more gigs.

Then I'd say: "When can we get back in the studio for the next album?"

DANNY RODRIGUEZ: I always had an answer handy for that question, which was ASAP.

RAMONA: In all those years, Lily never had another romantic relationship, not even the odd hookup. I guess you can't blame her. She lived for the music.

LUCAS KELLY: The lady was driven, you have to give her that. A dynamo. She ran her band ragged, but I never heard them complain even once.

RAMONA: In only a few years, I'd become a millionaire, though I had only a vague idea how much was actually going into my account. A real rags-to-riches story, that's me, though I never gave up the rags.

When we were touring, I lived on the band's dime. When we weren't, I bummed a bandmate's couch anytime they'd have me. Everywhere I went, I took something with me. I had little boxes of stuff stashed in hotels around the country.

That's the thing about feeling safe. You can never feel safe enough. The act of making yourself safe becomes an ongoing ritual to feel safe.

ERIC: When I learned Ma passed away, I realized I hadn't seen her or Bethlehem in two years. I barely even knew what year it was anymore; I think that was 2006. I wondered if this was what having a purpose looked like. Riding a single big wave unaware there's an ocean all around you.

VALERIA VALIS: The strange mechanics of my ongoing relationship with Eric would probably sound pretty twisted to you, but it worked for us. The more successful he became as a musician, though, the more twisted I got.

Women would recognize me on the street not as the lead singer for Joanie's Kisses but as Eric Borkowski's girlfriend. Old friends started to ask obsessively about the Shivers when we'd get together for drinks. Even my bandmates would drop hints I should ask Eric for favors, like how maybe we should go on tour opening for his band, as if Joanie's Kisses couldn't make it on its own.

All of a sudden, I'm flying to different cities every month, and I realized I was dating a bona fide rock star. Eric, of all people! This simply did not jibe with a girl who grew up getting anything she wanted with a flirty smile. Who for her entire life had been the center of attention.

I'd always tested Eric by putting him through the wringer. It was a hot little game we played, psychological S&M as foreplay, without the safe words. Over time, though, I started doing the sadism in earnest. I'd cheat on him and tell him about it, along with a whole lot of other horrible things that I'd really, really like not to share. He'd have a meltdown, I'd blame my horrid behavior on him giving so much of himself to the Shivers, and we'd get back together with some hot makeup sex and Eric somehow being the one doing all the apologizing.

When his mom died, I demanded that he quit the band and live in Bethlehem again so we could spend more time together. And that's how I blew it, like an idiot.

ERIC: The depressive episodes started after our breakup, a hole I'd compulsively try to fill with food, though none of it ever tasted as good as Ma's home cooking.

GARTH WAGNER: I quit Necromonium, as I could no longer stomach all the satanic bullshit. I joined a string of metal bands, making enough to scrape by and go on toting my rock-and-roll torch. I barely got to see Ramona during all those years. She'd show up out of the blue and stay with me a few days. Then she'd disappear again, and I'd do a quick inventory to find out what was missing.

The most important thing I'd always miss was her.

RAMONA: By the end, I was routinely going home with promoters and even fans just to have the chance to rifle their closets while they slept.

I knew all this wasn't healthy and that I needed help, but I couldn't leave the Shivers. I'd made a promise to Lily, and I couldn't break it.

DANNY RODRIGUEZ: She'd call me from a police station once or twice a year. Arrested for shoplifting. Always some stupid thing she could easily afford and didn't actually need. I'd bail her out and make it go away.

RAMONA: Sometimes they'd recognize me and let it go as long as I paid for it. They say fame has its privileges, but in my case it was just plain enabling.

MALCOLM: When we weren't touring, I barely slept a few hours a night, my fevered brain racing with ideas and plans. I'd email Danny film scripts thinking a Hollywood movie would make a great promo for the band. I'd pester Lucas about doing a live concert from the International Space Station. I'd tell Lily we should write a concept album with lyrics made entirely from palindromes so that it could be played backward as well as forward to create two albums in one.

DANNY RODRIGUEZ: Sometimes he'd call me up in the middle of the night ranting how he'd made this band and had glimpsed its final perfection. He had a few solid ideas, like making the band's music videos look like mini episodes of *Jackass* featuring the band doing crazy stunts, which worked great for the target demographic even if they turned out to be stupidly dangerous. The rest I promised him I'd think about and then promptly forgot, knowing he would too until his next manic episode produced a fresh batch of ideas.

MALCOLM: For the last five years of the noughties, I didn't see my parents at all. I simply emailed them a quarterly report showing my earnings. My drive and workload had whittled my relationship with them down to its essence.

LUCAS KELLY: I have to say that over the years I started to get really worried that these guys in some weird way were trying to kill themselves. Malcolm had developed a compulsive twitch from self-induced stress. Ramona looked like she'd aged twenty years compared to the fresh-faced, eager teen I'd met back in 2000. Eric put on pounds and walked around perpetually at the verge of tears. They barely talked about anything except their music, and that's all Lily talked about.

Somehow, she held them together through sheer force of will. If anything, she only became stronger and more beautiful over that tumultuous decade.

When she had her meltdown in Montreal and told me that she needed a break, I figured not just her but everyone deserved a good rest.

LILY: We were on top of the world. And then I fucked it all up.

RAMONA: She said what?

MALCOLM: Yeah. Um, *no*.

RAMONA: That's ridiculous.

ERIC: Lily *saved* us.

LILY: After aborting the *Basket Case* tour, I went home craving a sense of stillness. Instead I chafed like I'd been put on eternal hold. Like I'd stopped, but the world kept flying past. Staying in one place all day without having anything to do practically gave me vertigo. The relative quiet hummed in my battered eardrums.
Not for the first time, I wondered if I was still in Hell. If I'd ever left.
I told myself if only we could do one more album, I'd stay free.
Then I passed Holy Ghost Church and heard the choirboy sing.
The singing so beautiful, it broke my heart all over again.
That boy was Drake.
I'm sure of it.
The same heterochromatic eyes. The look in them when he saw me.
Longing. And something else. Fear.
He'd returned to earth to finish his mission.

Meaning I hadn't stopped the apocalypse. I'd only delayed it.

MALCOLM: We'd convinced ourselves that Drake's musical alchemy hadn't affected us. That we were somehow immune. We were wrong.

When Lily broke the band, she broke the Antichrist's spell. She freed us.

DR. WOODWARD: One final theological possibility: If the Antichrist chooses to die for love or something else that's good, could he be redeemed in God's eyes? Jesus died to save the spiritual world. If the Antichrist died to save the physical world, would that count for something?

LILY: It wasn't easy convincing a judge and jury that I had in fact murdered Drake Morgan and deserved punishment, especially since there was no murder weapon and no body, and Drake did not exist in official records.

I invented a lurid crime of passion that was widely reported in the media. In court, I played the part and did a lot of mouthing off to the judge. The entertainment press, for their part, cast the whole thing as a bizarre publicity stunt.

In the end, I got my way and received a twelve-year sentence.

I signed papers renouncing any claim to the Shivers, in case the band wanted to forge ahead without me, and then I refused visitors, even my bandmates.

Until you showed up to ask us to tell our story.

A story that can at last be told. Breaking our rule by talking about Drake.

Drake Morgan was the Antichrist. He was also a man—a man I loved and ultimately murdered. For nothing, it seemed. Either way, what I'd done was evil. Telling God I was sorry didn't cut it. Being all-knowing, God didn't need to hear it. He knows my heart. So I paid for my sin the only way I knew how. The worst punishment I could imagine, which was to spend the last twelve years alone without playing guitar on a stage.

When the end does come, I'll be able to look God in the eye and say, "You made me this way. I could do no other."

LUCAS KELLY: The Shivers had an incredible run. They were one hell of a band. No band lasts forever, even the great bands, and their songs fade in time until no one is listening. Bands come and go. It's how it's always been. But every single one leaves a lasting mark on the never-ending lineage of rock and roll.

DANNY RODRIGUEZ: They got out at a good time, if you ask me. Today the business is all about streaming and DIY promotion. Building a platform, while most music winds up pirated. Democratization, they call it. Every band has a chance to play to a wide audience online, if they can somehow separate themselves from the vast amount of competition, which ain't an easy thing.

In the future, artificial intelligence may democratize music even further, to where you don't even need musical talent to create and distribute songs, or it may end the democratic experiment altogether. A future in which computers write songs and computer-generated people entertain humans in VR concert tours.

To me, this would be the musical equivalent of the apocalypse. I'm not the sentimental type, and I've done my fair share turning music into a product, but in my view, it should always express the human spirit.

MALCOLM: It took me months with the lawyers to untangle all the assets and contracts and lay the Shivers to rest. By that time, everyone had gone their separate ways, and we rarely saw each other over the years, even after we'd all gravitated back to Bethlehem.

LILY: After the first few months in prison, I looked in the mirror and noticed Drake's mark had faded to nothing.

RAMONA: The months after the band's breakup felt like detoxing. At the time, I was twenty-eight years old but looked more like forty and felt like sixty. I went back to Bethlehem and stayed with Garth. For the first few weeks, I barely left our bed. Then I took a long walk to the old Squat, the last place I'd felt safe and didn't need anything before Garth Wagner took on that role in my life.

Comrade Jenny had passed away back in 2004, and without her leadership, the People's House collective fell apart from the usual infighting. ArtsQuest, the nonprofit that had put on Musikfest since the '80s, wanted to transform the site into a nexus of the arts: SteelStacks. I'd donated a lot of money to the project.

In 2011, the ArtsQuest Center would open. In the next decade or so, a million people would come to enjoy more than fifteen hundred events. I didn't do it for them, though. I wanted to see it built for musicians. A home for lost souls and runners and broken people searching for meaning and rebirth in art.

I can picture Comrade Jenny telling me, *It's still not punk.* And me answering with a smart-ass grin, *Well, there's no reason why punk can't be happy.*

ERIC: Mom left me the little house we'd shared, and while I'd kept up with the taxes, it had fallen into disrepair over the years. I moved in and started fixing it up and redecorating. Suddenly, it's a year later, and still I worked on it, doing it all myself. Along the way, the depressive episodes stopped, and I got healthier.

When Valeria reached out to me, it was all ready for her to move in.

VALERIA VALIS: As I got older and finally grew the hell up, I realized what a good man Eric is and how lucky I'd been to have him in my life. It sounds trite, but sometimes you don't know what you have until you've shattered it.

ERIC: Ramona, Malcolm, and Garth came to the wedding. It was beautiful.

VALERIA VALIS: What can I tell you about our marriage? It's normal. It's give-and-take, day in and day out. It can be really boring. It works.

Sometimes, though, I still give Eric a little twist to keep him on his toes.

ERIC: I ran into Joey Grasso at the diner again, and it was like we were meeting for the first time. He'd mellowed and found Jesus and had formed a Christian rock band. As fate would have it, the band needed a bassist.

It didn't look too heavy, so I joined just to let old Stringer off his leash now and then. Between Valeria and getting to play music, I woke up every day realizing I was finally happy. Content in a way that only feeling complete can give you.

It's good to have a purpose.

I just wish Ma was still alive to see it.

MALCOLM: I'd invested my income wisely over the years and had amassed a considerable fortune. After ten years with the Shivers, I had more money and less time. The big question for me was what to do with the rest of my life.

Back in Bethlehem, I went to a local mall to pick up a few things and spotted a piano near the food court. What a great idea, I thought. Anyone could walk over and play a song and make the public space come alive.

I cracked my knuckles and found myself playing "Bohemian Rhapsody," just as I had for Lily and Drake all those years ago. Another meditation. When I finished, I noticed I'd drawn a small audience, including a beautiful woman holding hands with a small boy.

The kid gaped at the piano as if it were magic and said, "Wow. Wow. Wow."

I could see him wanting to learn himself. I might have been witnessing the birth of a future great musician. For the first time in my life, I felt truly cool. Not basking in perception but actually experiencing it from the inside out.

I remembered once telling Lily that if I really wanted to do what I loved, I'd teach classical music to disadvantaged kids. As I did all those years ago at the Rascal, I laughed out loud at the truth that had always been right under my nose.

So that's what I wound up doing, and I've done it ever since. I eventually got married and had kids of my own, teaching them music and instilling in them the drive to always try hard but also pursue what they loved, whether it was a hobby or a career.

Besides that, I go to church on the regular to play the organ and sing God's praises. If you can't beat 'em, join 'em.

RAMONA: When I finally checked out my bank balance, I couldn't believe it. Even with all my massive donations to various causes over the years, I had enough that I'd never have to worry about money again. Living with Garth, I felt safe and realized I didn't have to fight the world anymore.

Then we passed a music store one day. Obeying an impulse, I bought a djembe drum. Thinking of Julian, I went to the park that weekend, and sure enough, the hippies were still at it. The faces might have been different, but it was always the same drum circle. Now it was my turn to contribute to its song.

I drum with them every weekend, rain or shine. Healing, I've learned, isn't a destination. It's a never-ending journey.

ERIC: The Shivers. Those were the days. My worst me living as my best me. These days, I'm grateful to just be me.

LILY: I'll be getting out in thirty-six days. At last, I'll be a free woman again. I'll have to make every moment count. Because the end, my friend, is nigh.

Long ago, God and the Devil set in motion a plan to end their war that includes all of us. For whatever divine purpose we may never understand, the ritual must be completed. All good things come to an end, and we're just here for the short ride. A ride that's getting shorter by the minute, because Drake is out there.

Today he'd be a little over twenty years old. In that time, we've witnessed wars and plagues and famines; whether through divine intention or not, there are apocalyptic signs and portents and omens everywhere you look. By now, he's learning his true identity. Dreaming his prophetic dreams. He may have already drawn a band to carry the Antichrist's ministry to the world and turn it against God. A few years down the road, he'll become a superstar and play the mad symphony that will trigger the cosmic upheaval and destroy reality itself.

He still wants me back. Still wants me at his side. Ever since you started visiting me to do these interviews, you see, a door appeared in my cell. A silver door engraved with a Janus head and framed in black thorns. When I touch it, I can hear stadium roar that makes my heart pound. I rake my guitar in hot lights while Eric pins the groove and Malcolm teases his harmonics and Ramona punishes her snares, and the audience is there too, exultantly singing along as one. A shadowy figure also plays with us, a mystery guitarist that can only be Drake.

An invitation. That's what the door is. An invitation for me and the rest of the band to do it all over again. Join the Antichrist or stop him.

The temptation keeps me up nights.

Or maybe I'm wrong. Maybe it's an entirely different kind of invitation. Maybe, just maybe, Drake found his own redemption by not only preaching free will but exercising a little himself. Playing the rebel right to the end by refusing to rebel. In our brief and furious romance, he grew to love me enough to put me first, and through this love, maybe he'd even learned that with great freedom comes not a little responsibility. From such humble beginnings, perhaps he made his peace with God and opted out of the cosmic war.

I'd like to think that it's possible. That even the Devil is capable of change and earning forgiveness. That this dumb, flawed, and beautiful world never has to end. That maybe I'll have time to experience love again before it's too late, the kind where I'm willing to put someone first once more.

Maybe that's all the invitation is. A second chance for him to do things right with me. A second chance for us.

I guess I'll find out.

Whatever the future has planned, when I regain my freedom, I'll have to figure out what to do with it. How to make those moments count. Anything is possible, as long as it has meaning. Anything is doable, as long as I do it with passion for me and a healthy dose of compassion for all. Because that is what freedom is all about. I'm excited to get started.

One thing I know for certain is I'll be playing.

Not to escape my sadness. Not to avoid the rest of my life. No, this time, I'll be playing for its own sake. For joy. So I can be heard. To make one more song that becomes a part of anyone who listens to it, catalyst for emotion and memory and change. A pure song that joins the one great human song radiating to dissipate forever across the cosmos. A love song. A song that is itself an act of love.

If the world *is* coming to an end, I intend to go out shredding.

ACKNOWLEDGMENTS

I dedicated this novel to every good song I've ever known because as much as this story is about love and dealing with an impossible ex, it's also about the transformative potential of music. As an author, I've always been fascinated by the magic of reading, how a writer can type a series of abstract symbols that a reader interprets as lived experience, producing joy and sadness and learning. Music packs a similar power to create searing passion, change the world, and stay in your head. Even in middle age, I can remember discovering New Wave in my early teens and how it changed me, how there was always a song that articulated exactly what I was feeling during every up and down of my youth, especially the beautiful romances and terrible breakups. A good song always seems to enter your life when it's needed, and it already knows you.

So, I write this with gratitude to all the musicians out there making great music, as well as for the people I know and love. My wonderful children; my amazing partner, Chris Marrs; my mother, Eileen, and brother, Christopher; and all my dear friends and colleagues. I'd also like to thank Bradley Englert, my fantastic editor, and the rest of the team at Hachette Book Group who enabled the dream of this novel to come true. And of course, my agent, David Fugate.

Last but certainly not least, I'd like to thank you for reading my work—with the hope that every story I write affects and sticks with you like a good song.

MEET THE AUTHOR

CRAIG DILOUIE is an acclaimed American-Canadian author of horror and other speculative fiction. Formerly a magazine editor and advertising executive, he also works as a journalist and educator covering the North American lighting industry. Craig is a member of the Horror Writers Association, International Thriller Writers, and Imaginative Fiction Writers Association. He currently lives in Calgary, Canada, with his partner, Chris Marrs, and his two wonderful children.

if you enjoyed
MY EX, THE ANTICHRIST
look out for
HOW TO MAKE A HORROR MOVIE AND SURVIVE
by
Craig DiLouie

From Bram Stoker Award–nominated author Craig DiLouie comes a darkly humorous horror novel that sees a famous '80s slasher director set out to shoot the most terrifying horror movie ever made using an occult camera that might be (and probably is) demonic.

Horror isn't horror unless it's real.

Max Maurey should be on top of the world. He's a famous horror director. Actors love him. Hollywood needs him.

He's making money hand over fist. But it's the '80s, and he's directing cheap slashers for audiences who crave only more blood, not real art. Not real horror. And Max's slimy producer refuses to fund any of his new ideas.

Sally Priest dreams of being the Final Girl. She knows she's got what it takes to score the lead role, even if she's been cast in only small parts so far. When Sally meets Max at his latest wrap party, she sets out to impress him and prove her scream-queen prowess.

But when Max discovers an old camera that filmed a very real Hollywood horror, he knows that he has to use this camera for his next movie. The only problems are that it came with a cryptic warning and sometimes it howls.

By the time Max discovers the true evil lying within, he's already dead set on finishing the scariest movie ever put to film, and like it or not, it's Sally's time to shine as the Final Girl.

ONE

If you aren't horrified, you aren't paying attention. If you aren't terrified, you aren't really living. That's what Max Maurey believed.

In fact, Max loved horror so much that he'd devoted his life to making it. Which explained why he donned a tuxedo and rode a rented limousine to the Cinerama in Hollywood on a sultry August evening.

To celebrate the making. A new movie, to be exact.

Powerful searchlight beams swayed in the twilight, the iconic signal of a premiere. In this case, one of the most highly anticipated horror releases of 1988.

Moments later, his limo pulled up to the curb.

And outside—

The red carpet stretched under an illuminated marquee.

The theater's geodesic concrete dome loomed over the scene.

Covered in *Jack the Knife III* splatter logos, the step-and-repeat publicity wall stood ready to serve as backdrop for celebrity photographs.

Max put on a grin and stepped onto the pristine carpet like he owned it, which tonight he pretty much did.

Entertainment journalists craned their necks to see who'd arrived. The fans buzzed. Some of the guys sported leather jackets and shades like the titular Jack. Some of the ladies wore cardigans, skirts, and bobby socks to cosplay the bygone era in which Jack returned from the dead.

This party was just getting started.

Wearing his own tux, Jordan Lyman greeted Max with a puff of cigar smoke. With his curly mop of hair and mirrored sunglasses, the burly producer exuded the overblown masculinity of a porn star who didn't know the seventies were over.

On set, Max might be a creator god, but even he answered to a higher power—the moneyman. As he loathed Jordan for this alone, he couldn't resist a barb.

"Even when you dress up, you only look seedier."

"And you look like something that's afraid of daylight."

"Ouch." Max's hand jerked to pat his silver-streaked hair, which waved in random directions like a mad scientist's. "At least I look the part."

"Crazy eyes, baby," the producer confirmed.

"Crazy eyes?"

"Back when I met you, you were a man possessed by a vision. It's why I gave the first *Jack the Knife* the green light back in '79. And here we are."

"Here we are," said Max.

On top of the world. He'd traveled a long, hard road to reach it.

Working his way up the ladder in the New Hollywood of the seventies, Max had worn many hats. He'd messengered dailies, cut film as an editor, and wrangled sets as an assistant director. His dream of directing his own movies remained elusive, however, in an industry where the bigwigs didn't like to say no but enjoyed making you wait. A way of doing business that prompted Pauline Kael to label Hollywood the one place you could die of encouragement.

Then Max at last won his big break when Jordan wrote a check for $350,000 to develop *Jack the Knife* into a feature-length horror movie.

The pitch: Steven Spielberg's *Duel* meets the supernatural. Back in the fifties, a young man named Jack drove in a drag race on the Fourth of July. As a result of sabotage, he died in a fiery wreck. Decades later, he returns from the dead on Independence Day as an angry spirit of vengeance aimed at the town's teens.

Working twelve hours a day, six days a week, Max had shot the film over three weeks, hustling through a backbreaking twenty to thirty camera setups each day. He squeezed every angle out of the tiny sets. He rigged an Oldsmobile to pass as Jack's on-screen 1957 black Chevy Corvette. When the final movie printed, two-thirds of the end credits were pseudonyms to make the skeleton crew look bigger.

Despite all the sweat and love Max gave his film, he hadn't expected much. But this was 1980, two years after *Halloween* made lightning in a bottle. John Carpenter proved you didn't need massive budgets and Hollywood stars to make a successful horror movie. You only needed to deliver horror.

In *Halloween*'s wake, the major studios poured cash into low-budget productions. The slasher era had arrived. In the end, Jordan sold the domestic and foreign distribution rights to New Line Cinema in a profitable deal.

Jack the Knife went on to gross $12 million worldwide, an actual hit. Eight years later, Jack now held fourth place in the slasher pantheon behind Jason Voorhees, Freddy Krueger, and Michael Myers. And Max, always a misunderstood outcast, had become an important director.

"Do I still have them?" he asked in a quiet voice.

"Have what?" Jordan said.

"Crazy eyes. I'd like to know if you still see them."

"Every time I visit the set or offer a suggestion you don't like." The producer regarded him with a thoughtful expression. "You're actually nervous."

"It's just production hangover," Max said.

The emptiness and loss he suffered when the intense process of making a movie ended. But no, that wasn't it, not this time.

As he approached forty, he'd begun wondering if he'd accomplished enough. He could feel the slasher era coming to an end. This was the last *Jack the Knife*. Soon, he'd have to lead or follow on the next big thing. For the first time in nearly a decade, the future offered a blank page, ripe for a fresh story.

He didn't share this with the producer, who wouldn't understand.

Jordan toked on his cigar. "It's your night. Enjoy it while it lasts."

Max nodded, despite this sounding a bit ominous.

Limousines now packed the front of the Cinerama Dome. The fans screamed as they spotted celebrities.

Douglas Avery had arrived, the veteran B-movie actor and discount David Carradine. He played the role of Harbinger, warning the kids not to meddle with dead things, which they of course ignore. Also attending was the beloved, gravelly-voiced Wolfman Jack, who'd reprised his *Jack the Knife II* cameo as an earnest local radio DJ who fears the worst for his town.

Under the deepening dusk kept at bay by bright lights, the cast promenaded on the red carpet, stretching out their minutes of fame. Some paused to chat with fans and sign autographs while the rest headed to the step-and-repeat wall for press photos. Flashbulbs popped. Pumped on happiness overload, everyone wore a strained, bewildered grin they couldn't turn off.

Then the crowd *really* went wild.

Stepping out of their limo, Ashlee Gibson and Nicholas Moody smiled and waved. The Final Girl and Jack had finally joined the party. Seeing them holding hands, the fans howled even louder.

Max pictured the starry-eyed, hungry mob surging over the velvet ropes to caress and kiss and bite their idols. Rip them apart and devour them in grisly mouthfuls while the actors kept on grinning until nothing remained.

Imagining the worst shattering the normal had always been an occupational delight for the director. Looking at his leads, he felt little pleasure now. The crowd should have been cheering *him* for wrangling their difficult personalities into usable footage.

But no matter. Max didn't need the fans' love.

He needed their terror.

As long as they feared him, he was happy.

The cast and critics filed into the theater. The crew and extras had already claimed their seats. They'd entered through the stage door to form a boisterous gang nipping at flasks in the back rows. Most of the actors parked in the back as well, ceding the limelight to the story that would soon appear on the screen. Entertainment press and bigwigs filled the rest of the seats.

As for Max, he sat in the front row alongside Jordan and the producer's taciturn Saudi financiers. He let the hubbub wash over him and liked what he heard. The positive energy in the air had grown palpable. He checked his watch.

Time to get this show started.

Standing to face the crowd, he smiled as their applause washed over him.

"Welcome to the premiere of *Jack the Knife III*," Max said. "Horror's favorite highwayman returns. The *Jack* attack is back and better than ever."

The audience erupted in cheering. Next, he focused on the grumpy critics, who liked to tie movies to a resonant theme or trend.

"But really, this is a film about America reclaiming its lost innocence through violence in the Reagan era, only to discover it was never innocent to begin with. As aways, the franchise asks who the real monsters are."

Laying it on thick, though it wouldn't affect the outcome. Reviewers and critics tended to prejudge horror films based on whether they enjoyed the genre.

After catering to them, he next addressed the cast and crew.

"On a final note, it's well understood in our business that no man makes a motion picture. From the talent to the gaffer, a team makes the picture. That means there's a bit of every single one of you in this film. Thank you all for your hard work. Being your director has been an honor. Give yourselves a hand."

As the energetic applause faded, Max finished, "Now, get ready for America's favorite horror story to continue. As the wise men say, the third time's the charm. And so, ladies and gentlemen, I give you: *Jack the Knife III*."

With that, he cupped his hand and called out to the projectionist: "Roll film!"

The moviegoers whooped one last time. As the lights dimmed, the crowd settled down. The standard fifties doo-wop theme started up, tinny and distant as if haunting the present from a lost era.

A LYMAN ENTERTAINMENTS PRODUCTION

The words flared as if on fire before disappearing.

The black screen came to life with a vehicle point-of-view shot revealing yellow roadway lines zipping in headlight glare. A V-8 engine snarled, filling the theater's Dolby Stereo system with a wall of sound. In an instant, the viewer became transported to a lonely road on a humid summer night.

JACK THE KNIFE III

As the opening credits neared their end, Max smiled.

DIRECTED BY MAX MAUREY

He hoped the critics *did* hate it. He hoped they told America that *Jack the Knife III* made them puke up their popcorn and Jujubes. He hoped parents forbade their teens to see it and nuns ended up picketing it.

The more "normal" society shunned and feared him, the more power they gave him. Taboo and censorship packed theaters. Public disdain tribalized horror fans into rabid devotees. Because at the end of the day, society wasn't normal at all, and horror wasn't lowbrow.

Horror was populist.

When the industry considered your genre one step above pornography in terms of respectability, it became a license to do almost anything you wanted. And horror flourished in rebellion and pushing boundaries.

It was the Midnight Movie, the drive-in double feature, the titillating exploitation film, the vision to do something crazy and powerful with little money, its grit and amateur rough edges only making it scarier. It was an evil grin and a middle finger delivered to society's comforting fictions, a fractured mirror held up to the human condition. It was leering monsters, moldering corpses, strange bumps in the night, forbidden knowledge, steamy sex in the backseat under a frosty murderous gaze, an eerie children's choir setting the mood to venture into a derelict mansion on a dare.

In short, horror screamed punk rock, and it served as Max's sharp playground.

The open credits finished, the story began. With a real budget of $1.75 million, *Jack the Knife III* boasted a higher body count than its predecessors and three times the car wrecks. The additional shooting days and locations showed in the final product. The film flowed clean and smooth on the screen without any problems.

Back in 1980, production for the original *Jack the Knife* had ended with a raucous wrap party but no glittered and starred premiere. Instead, Max had bought a ticket at a seedy downtown theater to catch it in the wild.

He remembered the projectionist forgot to flip the Dolby switch. The bottom of the frame was cut off. Bits of dust blemished the imaging. Mortified, Max had sunk in his seat, his popcorn and soft drink ignored.

Then he'd heard the first anxious chuckle in the dark. He stopped watching the picture and just listened to the audience. A little more nervous laughter. Then sharp gasps. Long stretches of tense, pin-drop silence.

At the first horrifying kill, a woman had cried out, *Oh my God!*

Max smiled again at the memory. That night had made all the hard work worthwhile, a far bigger payoff than the money that started coming his way.

Tonight, the crowd reacted differently to *Jack the Knife III*.

They cheered.

They laughed.

When a hissing cat sprang off a shelf for the picture's early fake scare—a genre convention Jordan insisted on including—they let out a playful scream.

Everyone was having a great time.

Max produced an irritated growl.

He knew they were amping up their reactions for the benefit of the critics. He both encouraged and expected that.

That wasn't the problem.

The problem was that *they were cheering and laughing at all.*

When Jack doo-wopped around the walls and ceiling of Tina's bedroom—a technical feat involving shooting a revolving room—the audience went wild. An organ-rich, New Wavey interpretation of "Mack the Knife" with modified lyrics crooned from the Dolby system while the villain sang:

This monster has such sharp teeth, kid
And they grin oh so bright and white.
Just a switchblade has our Jack, kid
And it gets hungrier every night...

The blood drained from Max's face. "What have I done?"

The crowd wasn't scared. They were *entertained*.

They *rooted* for Jack to dispense his Greek-myth style of justice to a bunch of teenagers guilty of being jerks and having clueless parents. They wanted to see the monster deliver what these stupid kids deserved.

Happy with what he heard, Jordan smirked.

"They're *laughing*," Max complained.

Laughter didn't bother him. Horror and comedy had always been kissing cousins. A little nervous laughter defused the tension. Whistling through the graveyard. But this wasn't that kind of laughing. They were yukking it up.

And this wasn't horror. It was campy self-satire.

Jordan tilted his head to murmur, "You're talking over your own movie."

"I shouldn't have listened to you. All these changes you forced me into."

Giving Jack so much screen time that he stopped being scary, a rakish mix of James Dean and Jack the Ripper. Having him deliver one-liners after his kills that had the audience cracking up in the rows. The new Beauty and the Beast romantic attraction with the Final Girl. Phones ringing but ominous silence on the other end. A severed head discovered in the refrigerator.

Elements ripped off so many times they'd become standard tropes, capped by blatant Pepsi and Kentucky Fried Chicken product placements. Max had been so immersed in the project that he hadn't realized what he'd done.

"They made the movie better," the producer said. "Evolve or die. Listen to the people, Max. They love it."

"They hate it. They just don't know they hate it."

"I think we might actually squeeze another sequel out of this."

"We've taken the real fun out of it, and replaced it with—with—"

"Money's fun," said Jordan.

"It's just like every other slasher flick. Gimmicks. Cinematic junk food."

The man nodded sagely. "That's beautiful, how you put that."

"You think it's—?"

"Formula sells, baby. It's comfortable. And it's for everybody. Not just misanthropic freaks like you."

Max couldn't believe anyone paid for a ticket to a horror film to experience comfort any more than they hopped on a roller coaster to feel safe. They wanted to push outside their comfort zones.

The crowd kept cheering regardless of what he thought.

As *Jack the Knife III* neared its end, the dog everyone thought had died off-screen defending its master reappeared, ready to bravely chip in again during the final showdown. A bit of emotional manipulation that Max didn't mind, as he'd made a rule to never kill off animals in his movies. He could practically hear the audience grinning and tearing up behind him, though he couldn't bring himself to enjoy even this.

When in the final moments one last shock popped out of nowhere to suggest the story might continue—another Jordan "innovation" ripped off from other horror films—they all cried out. Then gave the closing credits a rousing ovation.

Even some of the grumpy critics were smiling.

"Christ," Max groaned. "I'm a hack."

"Cheer up," the producer said. "It's a birth, not a funeral. Mazel tov. Now stand up like a professional and take a bow."

Glowering, he obeyed, feeling about as punk as a cup of decaf coffee.